MW00328729

EVEREST

S.L. SCOTT

Copyright © 2017 by S.L. SCOTT

All rights reserved.

No part of this book may be reproduced in any form or by any electronic or mechanical means, including information storage and retrieval systems, without written permission from the author, except for the use of brief quotations in a book review.

Design: RBA Designs

Photography by Scott Hoover Photography

Cover Model: Lance Parker

Editing:

Marion Archer, Making Manuscripts

Karen Lawson, The Proof Is in the Reading

Marla Esposito, Proofing Style

Kristen Johnson, Proofreader

ISBN: 978-1-940071-59-6

Reach For The Stars While Holding Kindness In Your Heart.
May All Your Dreams Come True.

ALSO BY S.L. SCOTT

To keep up to date with her writing and more, her website is
www.slscottauthor.com to receive her newsletter with all of her
publishing adventures and giveaways, sign up for her newsletter:
http://bit.ly/1TheScoop

Join S.L.'s Facebook group here: http://bit.ly/1TheScoop

The Kingwood Duet

SAVAGE

SAVIOR

SACRED

SOLACE

Hard to Resist Series

The Resistance

The Reckoning

The Redemption

The Revolution

The Rebellion

Talk to Me Duet

Sweet Talk

Dirty Talk

Welcome to Paradise Series

Good Vibrations

Good Intentions

Good Sensations

Happy Endings

Welcome to Paradise Series Set

From the Inside Out Series

Scorned

Jealousy

Dylan

Austin

From the Inside Out Compilation

Stand Alone Books

Everest

Missing Grace

Until I Met You

Drunk on Love

Naturally, Charlie

A Prior Engagement

Lost in Translation

Sleeping with Mr. Sexy

Morning Glory

EVEREST

Six foot three. Dynamic green eyes. Utterly irresistible.

Ethan Everest stole my breath the first time I saw him. He romanced me with skill, dazzled me with his charisma, and proceeded to steal my heart right after.

I might have fallen for his easy-going smile the first time we met, but I fell for *him* the second time.

Honey-colored hair. Cherry-kissed lips. Captivatingly gorgeous.

Singer Davis was the first, and only, woman to ever intimidate me. She spoke to my heart with her wit, seduced me with her eyes, and became the only thing that made sense in a world that made none.

I let her slip through my fingers once. I won't make that mistake twice.

Secrets broke us apart. Can a second chance bring us back together?

From *New York Times* Bestselling Author, S.L. Scott, comes a ROMANTIC SUSPENSE STANDALONE that will have you on the edge of your seat and swooning over this new ALPHA BILLIONAIRE.

1

Singer Davis

THE FIRST TIME I heard the name Ethan Everest I was at a party in the Bronx. I was sitting on a futon sandwiched between a blonde model from Romania and some girl who kept sighing out of boredom. The model exhaled and said, "One day I'm going to climb Everest."

I thought she was referring to the mountain.

She wasn't.

She was referring to the man.

Almost a year later, he's sitting just three barstools down from mine. This is not the first time we've seen each other since that party. It's just the first time he makes his way over since then.

The memory of the first time I saw him comes back so readily.

At six three with a presence to match, Ethan Everest is impossible to ignore. Wearing an Astros cap in the middle of Yankees country, a white smile livens full lips, and dynamic green eyes manage to instantly brighten the dingy Bronx apartment.

Our eyes catch twice across the crowded living room and my palms begin to sweat. Ethan Everest doesn't fit in with this crowd. He's too happy, too content in his life, too much personality and has drawn the center of attention from both males and females. Yep. Impossible to ignore. *No matter how much I try.*

I turn away abruptly, not sure if I'm ready to talk to him.

We almost kissed last year. His lips were almost pressed to mine . . . and then they weren't and he was gone. A sharp elbow to the ribs causes me to flinch. "Ouch." After fifteen years of friendship, my best friend and I still haven't perfected our non-verbal skills, so I ask, "What are you doing?"

Her lips twist to the side and she rolls her eyes. "Behind you."

For a brief moment I convince myself he's going to walk by and go to the restroom or order a drink. He doesn't. I turn, and there he is in all his majestic glory—*Ethan Everest.*

The Man.

The Myth.

The Mountain.

He bites his lip as shyness shadows his light eyes. Then he smiles. "It's good to see you again, Singer."

The hum, the electricity, all that I felt on that fire escape, returns as my name rolls off his tongue in a purr, reminding me of what almost was.

His body folds to ease out the window, and he sits on the small staircase several steps down from mine. His presence consumes the small space high above an alley. It doesn't feel like an invasion of my personal space, but more like a coup, considering the many women inside vying for his attention.

With a charming smile aimed at me, he casually says, "Avoid the discussion inside." *Enticing enough to let down my guard, his tone is easygoing, his voice deep and soothing.* "They're arguing that freedom is the illusion of the American consumer." *The small southern cadence to his words is something I could listen to all day.*

What he said isn't funny, but I laugh anyway, a nervous reaction to the hot-blooded masculinity rolling off him in waves. With movie star good looks, I can't turn away. "What do you think?"

He chuckles. "I think I prefer being out here with you."

I don't remember blushing in a while, but with the weight of his gaze heavy on me, my cheeks are hot even if the weather isn't.

Ethan Everest is rugged with his unshaven jaw and casual clothes, yet refined in his mannerisms as he offers me a beer. "I brought you a beer if you'd like it."

"I would. Thank you." I reach for it and our hands wrap around the can, the tips of our fingers weaving together. I hold on just long enough to look up and see the intensity of his eyes. On me. Sitting on the fire escape, I'm suddenly a girl who's stumbled onto an Adonis and knows what she's discovered—a male masterpiece made up of muscles and a hard body.

Add in that boy-next-door charm, and I'm caught in his gravitational pull. The female population of New York doesn't stand a chance against the allure of this man, much less me when he cracks a smile.

When he releases the beer, he opens one for himself. "Cheers." He taps his can against mine and my whole body awakens.

"Cheers."

His eyes remain on mine as he tips the beer back and the lager flows into his mouth. My gaze dips to his throat where I become mesmerized by his Adam's apple as he swallows.

Good Lord.

Watching him swallow has to be one of the most erotic sights I've ever seen.

My chin is lifted, and my eyes meet his. "Hey," he says with a deep chuckle. "Up here."

Holy mother of all things humiliating. Was I staring at his throat? I glance back down. Yep, I was. He interrupts my fantasy involving the five o'clock scruff shadowing the hard lines of his jaw and his throat. I squeeze my eyes closed and then look at his eyes that are fully amused it seems at my expense.

Licking his lips he says, "I was thinking we could hang out sometime."

The suggestion comes as a surprise. "Really?" It's been a lot of this cat and mouse, flirting not flirting, have we met or are we strangers keeping our distance game. I'm confused why he crossed enemy lines tonight.

"Really," he replies easily.

When my words don't come quick enough, Melanie steps in. "She'd love to. When did you have in mind?" Ethan and I both look at Melanie sitting next to me in her eagerness to make this happen, whatever *this* is.

I'm just about to respond, but she presses on, "Singer's free all weekend."

Wow. Did that just happen? It did. No, I don't feel pathetic at all . . . Nope, I feel totally humiliated. I may not have any plans, but she could have lightened the blow to my ego. "Geez, thanks," I mutter under my breath.

Ethan glances to me but responds to Melanie. "Let her know I'll see her at MacDougall's on Sunday. The game starts at three."

"Football?" she asks.

Even I know the answer this time. I've made sure to pay more attention to the seasons. "Baseball," I whisper to her and sit back, letting them continue to set up this date . . . friend get together . . . hangout they're planning like I'm not sitting right here.

"How do you know she likes baseball?" Melanie asks, crossing her arms and challenging him.

"I don't, but I figured I'd find out pretty fast at the sports bar." He relaxes in his stance. There's a twinkle to his eyes and a curve to his lips that reveals amusement.

Melanie finally eases up, sitting back proud as a peacock with her smug grin. "She'll be there, and she likes lagers. Just in case you were wondering."

"I *was* wondering," he replies, sending me a quick wink. "It's good to know we have that in common. See you Sunday, Singer." He rejoins his friends, and I die a slow death of incomparable mortification.

I drop my head in my hands. "Oh God. What just happened?"

"I just got you a date on Sunday."

"You got me a date? I'm fairly certain he was already going to ask when he came over."

"Pshaw. I *set up* a date for you with the hottest guy in this place."

Maybe it's just starting to sink in, but holy wow. I whisper, "Ethan Everest."

When I look up, she's grinning widely. "You're welcome. Now don't mind me. I'll just be here drowning my jealousy in booze." The slurp of her straw grates on my nerves, which she knows, and I'm pretty sure she's doing it on purpose, but her pity party makes me laugh.

"Jealousy? *Pfft*. It's nothing. It's a sports bar at three on a Sunday afternoon, not dinner and a movie on a Saturday night."

"Damn it. I should have insisted on Saturday night, but I didn't know if you had a date."

"Nope, no date. Anyway, Sunday is what he'd prefer for hanging out, I'm sure."

"You don't know that."

"He's just been worn down from seeing me around so much. He probably figures we should be friends at this point. I mean it is kind of silly to keep running into each other like we have and not make the effort to get to know one another better."

"No guy asks a girl to hang out who he's not interested in —*sexually*."

"Ethan Everest just did."

"Want to bet?"

"I'll bet dinner on it."

"I'll take that bet," she says confidently. "And prepare yourself. When I win, I'm going to skip lunch and be extra hungry for dinner. It will be awesome to eat on your dime."

There's no point in arguing with her. She's the queen of the need-to-be-right, so I order another round of drinks, and try not to freak out that I'm meeting up with Ethan Everest in less than forty-eight hours.

We didn't kiss the last time we spoke, though we were so close. Our time on the fire escape was real, a connection made, one I feel deep inside even today. It's a feeling I've held on to, an unfair expectation placed on my dates since that party. No guy has made my body hum or buzz with excitement since him.

Since that night, we've seen each other on occasion. Melanie's coworker dates his friend, so we end up at the same party or in the same bar every so often.

Before tonight, we hadn't spoken since then, but I always felt that hum between us, hanging on at the back edges of hope. The buzz remains as I peek over at him a few barstools down from mine. He winks and I look away quickly, smiling.

The bar gets more crowded as the night carries on. I've had three drinks when I promised myself I'd only have two. "Two more, please."

We mingle with our friends and laugh with a guy who can't seem to notice I exist because he's so attentive to Mel. When it comes to my love life, she's all over it. When it comes to her own, she fails to notice the obvious. Mike, who's in finance we find out, is sweet. His flirting is not heavy-handed, but he's not let another guy within an inch of Mel in the last hour.

I eventually work my way out of the conversation as sparks begin to fly between them.

When I turn, the right side of Ethan's mouth goes up in such an inviting way that I'm not sure if I'm supposed to smile and wave, go over and talk, or stand here like I am and debate myself out of doing anything.

I want to turn away from him, but I don't. I can't. I like his eyes on me. I like the way he looks at me like we have some unfinished business to tend to. I take three gulps of my drink because I'm pretty sure that will make me forget about this embarrassing heat settling inside my cheeks.

It doesn't. The warmth causes me to put my glass to my skin in hopes of finding relief just before I'm spun around, coming face-to-face with Melanie. "Let's go," she demands.

"Now?"

"Yes, I need to go."

"Okay." When she's ready she is really ready, and pushing it might mean a stint in the bathroom holding her hair back. I set my nearly empty glass on the bar, but when I turn, my gaze finds Ethan once more. I watch him and those lips that almost kissed mine. I watch even though he might think I'm self-indulgent or shameless. But at this point, I've drunk enough to not care.

"Come on. I'm ready." I take Melanie's hand and we make our way outside. When it comes to Ethan, there's something that I'm missing, a piece of the puzzle I keep hoping to find, answers to unasked questions. Maybe the full picture will never come into focus, or maybe I just need to ask what I want to know when I see him on Sunday.

2

Singer

The air outside is warming up. There's a slight chill remaining, but that might be my insecurities. With our arms looped through each other's, Mel and I walk a block to the nearest train station. I never feel safe riding the train at night, but I can't afford to pay for a cab to take us home and Melanie sure can't either. Just as I hear the clicking of the clock above our heads, the announcement is made of the arriving train and we step forward to the line.

Our hold on each other has tightened and the laughs have stopped. We settle in like all the other poor, partying saps traveling home. "I hate the train at night," she says, scrutinizing the train car.

"We'll be fine." I'm sober enough, and strong enough, for the both of us.

I find comfort once we're seated. Other women are traveling by themselves, men who drank too much look harmless as they slouch in chairs. I keep my eyes open while Melanie relaxes next to me, staring out the window. She goes through different stages when she drinks, and the high she had at the bar with Mike is now a low I get to handle. It's easy to be depressed when things don't go your way. I choose a different tactic, a positive outlook on life that keeps me moving forward, even when it's easier to give up. "Two stops to survive." I'm pretending to tease even though it feels more like the truth. "We need better paying jobs. I'd take a cab home every time."

"Or better paying men."

I laugh, but it's not funny. I get where she's coming from, but it sucks to put your hopes on meeting a man so you can take a cab home after a night of partying. This city is tough for single women. The ratio is out of proportion with men having their pick from any type of woman they want, and we're expected to settle for anyone that gives us the time of day. "I'd rather focus on my career."

"And what are you doing toward that?" she snaps abrasively. "Reading alone in your room at night? Have you applied for a job in publishing recently?"

There's that low I've become too familiar with. She wasn't always a mean drunk, but the city gets to everyone eventually. "I've sent out more résumés. It's a small industry. I have to keep trying until there's an opening."

"Trying. Trying. Trying. My degree in journalism didn't prepare me for legal assistant. If we stay, I'm starting to think I need to become a paralegal. That's a needed profession in New York City." Leaning her head on my shoulder, she adds, "I'm lonely, Sing."

"Mike seems nice."

"He does." A dreamy smile is in place when she closes her eyes momentarily. "We're going out tomorrow night."

"On a Saturday night? That right there is the difference between what happened in our nights."

"Stop it. Maybe Ethan is shy."

"Is it even possible for someone that looks like Ethan Everest to be shy with all the attention he gets?"

"Not really, but I've seen the way he looks at you. He likes you, or at least likes the way you look." She laughs. "You never see yourself the way others do." She yawns then says, "He'd be lucky to date you. But if he's not the lucky one, someone else will come along and see what I've known all along."

"What's that?"

"That your beauty is more than skin-deep. If someone doesn't see that, screw 'em."

"Literally?" I tease.

She shrugs with a laugh. "If they're cute."

The train stops, but we stay seated. "Why'd we go out again?" I ask, teasing her. She always gives the same pie in the sky answer, and it usually brightens her mood.

We're moving again when she looks at me and says, "To meet our soul mates."

"Oh that's right. How'd we do?"

Hope returns to her eyes, and she laughs. "I'd say better than average, considering we both scored dates." The train announces our stop and she stands, wobbling a bit on her heels.

Maybe it's more for her than me, but I stand and take her by the elbow to steady her. "Come on, let's get home."

The area of the city we live in isn't the greatest, but it's safe enough. Even in heels and a little tipsy, we cover the three blocks back to our apartment quickly.

The familiar figure of our resident homeless man is perched against the brick wall next to the stoop. Resident and homeless always did feel like an oxymoron, but I've come to appreciate him being there. I feel protected with him around. Frank looks to be asleep when we approach, but it seems he sleeps with one eye open. "Evening."

"Evening, Frank. Sorry, if we woke you."

"Nope, just catnapping. Have fun?"

"Too much," I reply. "Gotta get Mel to bed."

"What did I warn you about, Melanie?"

Melanie's giggle echoes down the empty street. "I know, but one led to another and then bam, I was drunk."

Laughing while taking her wrist, I encourage her up the steps while rolling my eyes. "Night, Frank."

"Night, Singer."

Once inside, I stand at the counter with a knife in one hand, a day-old baguette in the other, and a tub of butter in front of me. I butter the bread while Mel sits at the stool on the other side of the kitchen bar. Three pieces are devoured before calling it a night. The bread will help to soak up some of the liquor, and hopefully we won't wake up with hangovers.

Our place is so small the tiny bedrooms barely have enough room to walk around the full-sized beds. The wall that separates the rooms is paper-thin, and we often lie in our own beds talking until we fall asleep. I start tonight's conversation, though it's one we've had many times before. "I gave myself three years to make it to the West Side."

"Time's almost up." That comment earns her a roll of my eyes even though she can't see it. She says, "I'm tired of living in shitty apartments, working a shitty low-paying job like somehow paying my dues makes it more respectable." She sounds sleepy. "I'm too tired to even maintain my blog. I'm tired of working fifty hours a week for that asshole lawyer. How will a magazine hire me if I can't even update my blog with stories? I'm tired of paying my dues. They're not even dues for what I want to do. And I'm really tired of coming home to an empty apartment, or rather bed. I miss having a man's arms around me at night."

I feel her pain. I do, but I can't fix it. "We're doing our best. What do you want me to do?"

"Come snuggle with me, Sing."

"No."

"Come on. Please."

"No, you hog the bed and kick."

"But I need you."

"You think you'll feel less lonely, but you don't need me, Mel."

"I do," she says, her voice reflecting her drifting asleep.

I get it. I have nights when I'm lonely, too. "Love you."

"Love you."

AFTER DOWNING a glass of Melanie's hangover cure—orange juice, ginger ale, and a dash of hot sauce—I flop onto the couch. The drink doesn't cure hangovers, but I do get a kick of energy after drinking it, so I humor her and insist it's a cure-all.

She's on her laptop at the bar and picking up our conversation from last night like eight hours didn't interrupt it. "We're not failures if we move away from the city. There are other cities and other places that are way more affordable and, and"—I hear the exasperation in her voice—"there's always home."

The suggestion surprises me, and I look up. Boulder was never big enough to contain Melanie's ambitions. She talked about leaving from middle school on. Graduation always seemed like the far-off future until it was upon us. Too scared to make a big move, we ended up going to the local university. For four years we talked about following her dreams. Where Melanie went, I went. That's what best friends do. So we packed two suitcases and moved to New York the Monday after we accepted our bachelor degrees. Her determination might have carried us to the East Coast, but somewhere along the way, I discovered my own dream and intended to pursue it. "I'm not ready to give up."

"I want the dream, Sing, but I don't think my dreams are going to come true here." Her voice is clear and there's a serious tone to her words. With her shoulders slumped she leans against the counter.

Trying a new angle, I go low. "What if Mike's the one? What if he's your destiny and you leave before giving that relationship a chance?"

"Wishful thinking, but I'll know within five minutes tonight."

I raise my chin in smug naïveté. "I'll hold out hope then."

She flops down next to me dramatically with her arm over her eyes, all those acting lessons paying off. "You always were the dreamer."

"Funny. I thought you were." Bumping her with my knee, I lean my head on her shoulder. "One day we'll run this city."

"I'd settle for walking it."

Laughing, I add, "Fine, we'll walk it together, in style."

"Until then?"

"Until then we'll live in our shoebox apartment, keep applying for our dream jobs, and continue working for assholes."

She pauses and says, "I want to feel everlasting love. Love so powerful you ache inside. Love that feels so good it lessens the pain of being disappointed in my life."

Even with her eyes closed, I only see the woman who inspires me daily. When she sits up, I reach over, and we hug. "Don't give up. Not yet, Mel." I eye the magnet on our fridge and recite the quote, "You're pure potential."

"I love when you lie to me."

"That's why you keep me around, though I still maintain that I only speak the truth."

"Because you're the best." After standing, she says, "Never stop dreaming, Singer. I'm going to the store. Need anything?" Heading toward her door, she looks back.

"I would love some wine for later."

"Cheap stuff okay?"

"I can't tell the difference."

With a smile on her face, she taps the front door with her fingers and opens the door. "Good because it's all we can afford."

The door closes, and as I slide down on the cushions, I kick my feet up on the coffee table.

Sitting in the living room of our tiny apartment, I stare out the window. Sirens sound in the distance, a noise I've become accustomed to. It makes me realize that I never expected that to be the sound I found comfort in. It's so a part of this city, of this little life I'm living. It's become a song played on repeat from the soundtrack of my city life.

I've been thinking about dues being paid, and although I'm not necessarily living the life I always dreamed, I'm living a pretty damn good life.

So I'll take sirens lulling me to sleep and eating ramen noodles for dinner. I'll take nights out with my best friend and cheap wine and movies in. If dues are to be paid, it could be a steeper price than the one I'm paying.

Grabbing my book, I open it up to where I left off and start reading and continue to dream.

3

Singer

People-watching is an Olympic sport in Central Park, and I'm a gold medalist. I can usually make it to the final qualifiers like a pro, but today my thoughts are elsewhere. I wish I could say they're on the opened book on my stomach. That's not it. It's on tomorrow and a certain man of intrigue.

I'm not sure what to think about the invitation to "hang out." Should I guard my heart and restrain my hope? Should I look at the invite as merely an opportunity to make a new friend? Or is Melanie right? He's hot, but way out of my league hot, almost godly. Makes me wonder whose league he's in. No woman's I've ever seen. Not even the ones who fill his time.

Could there be more behind the afternoon invitation? Or is it as simple as hanging out at sports bar drinking beer . . . *with Ethan Everest*?

Sitting up slowly, the book drops to my lap, and even though I lose my place, I don't care. I'm suddenly hot, and definitely bothered, so I fan myself with my hand. When that doesn't work, I take off my sweater. The thin straps of my tank top fall to the side, and the breeze feels good against my bare skin. I lie back on the grass still frustrated that I'm letting him affect me like this. Closing my eyes, I try to enjoy the sunshine instead.

Friends.

Hanging out.

That's all he wants. I need to set my expectations, so I don't get hurt.

Suddenly shadowed in darkness, I open my eyes to find the sun blocked. With my hand hooding my sight, I look up, and up, stopping on Mr. Sinful himself. His face is hidden by the bright sun, but I know that body outlined in light. I also know the voice when he says, "Singer."

That honeyed tone.

Deep timbre.

An R that lingers at the end of my name.

"Say it again," I plead silently.

Ethan tilts his head and the sunlight hits my eyes, blinding me until he readjusts, securing me in his darkness once again. I see the phone, hear the click of a camera, and complain, "Hey, no fair. I wasn't ready."

"That's the point." With ease, he lowers himself to sit next to me with a grin full of good fortune. "Hope I'm not bothering you."

I should be nervous like every other time I see him, but I'm not for some reason. Catching me off guard is working to his advantage. "You're not at all."

"Good. You looked content alone."

"That sounds sad."

"I think it's beautiful. Most people jump from one relationship to the next, desperate to avoid being alone, to avoid getting to know themselves. That sounds sadder to me."

Stealing a glance his way, I ask, "Do you know yourself?"

"No. Not yet, but I'm finding my way."

I smile and lean back on my elbows. "Aren't we all?"

"Are you lost, Singer?" There's a lilt of hope in his voice that draws my eyes back to him.

"Finding my way," I repeat his words, while tossing a few blades of grass into the wind. My answer makes him smile. Seeing him again apparently makes me smile. "Is this a coincidence or are you stalking me?"

"Stalking. Definitely stalking you."

I start to laugh, but stop when he doesn't laugh with me. My eyebrows shoot up. "Really?"

"No, not really." He chuckles then adds, "I was walking in the park and saw you." Tapping the book on the grass, he bends his neck to the side to read the spine. "What are you reading?"

"Tales of unsettled hearts, otherwise known as a romance novel."

"Sounds heavy." Chuckling again, he picks up the book and opens it. I watch as he scans the page, and then to my embarrassment he begins to read. "'Her eyes. Her eyes drew me in and held me captive in the blue depths. Her lips. Her lips kissed mine, branding them with her signature red. Her heart.' Wait, I thought romance novels were told from the female point of view? This is the male's perspective and what the female looks like to him."

Shrugging, I confess, "Women like to know what goes on in a man's head."

"And this book will give you that?"

"No, this book will tell me what's going on in *that* hero's head."

"Fascinating," he replies, turning the book over to look at the cover. Ethan reading to me has to be one of the sexiest things I've ever heard, so when he sets it down, disappointment settles in.

I'm quick to recover though, more curious about him than worried about my book. "Do you always go around taking photos of strangers?"

"We're not strangers, Singer."

"The photo you took is probably awful. My face was scrunched." I shake my head, trying to blow off the embarrassment and enjoy the fleeting minutes.

"I don't think you could take a bad photo if you tried." Staring at the screen, he holds his phone up. "See?"

"Ugh." My eyes roll automatically after seeing it. "Are you going to keep that?"

"Would you like me to delete it?"

Our gazes hang a second or two longer, before I break the connection and watch a couple in the distance chasing their loose dog. I don't know what I'm thinking, my mind mushy around him. "You can keep it if you like."

"I would like that." The simple confession brings my eyes back to his as he lies down on the grass.

His hand slides over his stomach, the tips of his fingers resting on the bared skin where the hem of his shirt has risen up. The waistband of his jeans exposes the top of his underwear and he makes no move to pull down the traitorous fabric. He says, "Nice view."

Glancing to his eyes again, my mouth falls open when I realize he caught me staring at his body. Signaling around us, he says, "This spot gives you a nice view of the park."

I laugh. We both know I was busted, but he's polite enough not to call me out on it. Closing his eyes, he leaves a lingering smile on his lips.

The movement of his hand draws my gaze again as it dips to the waistband again, piquing the age-old question:

boxers or briefs? What does a man like Ethan Everest wear? The sun shines new light on taut skin over defined abs, and this time I appreciate the view.

It's been a few weeks since my last disaster of a date and more than a year since I indulged in anything more erotic than that little sliver of exposed skin. My mind is turning dirty, and by how relaxed he appears to be, I hope he intends to stay awhile.

The green in his eyes is brighter today, vibrant like the grass. He looks happy. It's a good look on him. "Why do you want to know what goes on in a man's head?" He opens his eyes and looks at me, a look I remember from before.

His gaze fixates on my mouth and I can't stop myself from licking my lips. His confidence is sexy. He wagers, "If I were to guess the taste of those red lips, I'd go with cherry."

Holding my own, I touch the tip of my tongue to my upper lip then reply, "Strawberry, actually."

The half-smile, half-smirk that appears is intoxicating, and his close proximity makes me lightheaded. As hints of his cologne —ocean and musk—fill the air, we look into each other's eyes, and a connection is made. He doesn't look at me like I'm a girl, but instead like a woman, a woman he would make love to and then hold all night. Ethan makes me feel everything in those few seconds.

With his eyes moving between my eyes and my mouth, he sighs. "God, I love strawberry." My breath comes short when he leans in, his lips drawing closer to mine. He closes his eyes, and my heart begins to race. He gets so close I can almost taste him.

"Oh um . . ." Thinking back on the book, I reply, "Women, speaking generally, of course, like to know a man's deepest thoughts. In the case of romance novels, we like to know that love affects men like it does women. We get that through the male point of view."

"You make it sound a whole lot better than it is. Trust me, Singer. Our thoughts aren't that deep. They're simple. We think about food, work, money, and sex. *See?* Simple."

"I think you underestimate the power of love." I laugh, mainly at myself, feeling foolish for saying that out loud. "And try to forget that I just sounded like I should be part of a boy band from the nineties."

"Forgotten." He laughs though, putting me at ease. Pushing up, he stands and dusts off his pants. "I should probably go."

"Oh, okay." I remain seated, though I'm tempted to cling to his leg and force him to read to me again. Instead, I block the sun from my eyes and look up, not sure what to say.

"We're still on for tomorrow, right?"

"Yes. Three o'clock."

He nods. "Good. See you then, Singer."

"See you, Ethan." I watch as he walks away, looking at the phone in his hand.

Lying back, I pick up my book and find my place as if that gorgeous man didn't shake up my day in the best of ways. Finding it hard to concentrate, I watch him, a swarm of butterflies filling my belly. I close my eyes and shake my head, convincing myself to let the most amazing accidental run-in go. It's not easy, but then I remember how ridiculous I sounded about love. *Ugh!* Word vomit is never attractive.

Too distracted by real life to give a fictional hero my time, I decide to pack up and go home. It's not bad to be home on a Saturday night, or as Ethan mentioned, to be alone. It's only bad if you're unhappy, and I'm not.

Melanie and I have a penchant for Romance Channel movies and gummy bears. Add a glass of white wine since white goes best with gummy bears, and we're usually set for the night. Guess I'm flying solo with spicy ramen noodles and the bears for dessert tonight though.

We occasionally joke about sitting here sixty years from now—spinsters in our golden years. Until we've had a few glasses of wine and the image makes us sad. That's usually our cue to go to bed.

By the time the sun starts to set, I'm sitting crossed-legged on my couch, digging into my noodles, and watching a Christmas movie when it's still warm outside. My mind starts to drift to the encounter with Ethan today, and I call out to Melanie, who's getting dressed, to sidetrack my thoughts, "Are you almost ready?"

"I'm doing my hair."

"What time's the date?"

"Thirty minutes. I'm meeting him there, which means I'm going to be late since I'm not even dressed yet." Her apologetic tone doesn't hold sincerity. She's always been one to believe that fashionably late to a date is not a choice, but a requirement. It tests their interest. The bonus, she always has a few extra minutes to get ready.

Walking to the bathroom, I sit on the side of the tub. "Your makeup looks good."

"Thanks," she replies, concentrating on securing a pin on the side of her hair. The color of her hair almost matches mine when pulled back. I set my food down and replace her hands with mine, tucking a section in that she struggles to reach. "How was your day? What'd you do?"

Smoothing another section of hair and taking a pin from her, I keep my eyes on her hair to avoid the wide eyes I know I'll see when I answer her question. "I went to the park, but something interesting happened."

"Oh yeah? What happened?"

"Ethan happened."

"Ethan Everest?"

I don't have to look at her to see the excitement. Her voice pitching two octaves higher is all I need to hear. "The very one."

"That's weird."

"I thought so too. I don't see him much, but now he's everywhere."

"So coincidental. One could almost say *serendipitous*."

"One could, but one won't. I'll stick to coincidental."

"I expect no less." She laughs. "Anyway, and much more importantly, how'd he look?" With her hair in place, I step back so she can do a complete onceover with a handheld mirror.

"Does he ever look bad?"

"I don't think it's possible."

"He looked amazing."

"T-shirt and jeans?"

"Yep."

"Damn, that's rough. He looks good like that. He looks good in suits, too. Damn," she repeats.

"Totally." I feel my body heating either from the spicy noodles or the talk of Ethan. I'm thinking it's the latter, though I wish it were the former.

"How do you keep from jumping him when you see him?"

I laugh, loving that this is posed as a serious question. "Because I'm not a whore," is my not-so-serious answer as I follow her into her bedroom.

"I am. Proudly." She's not laughing at all. Taking a dress from the hanger, she holds it in front of her body and looks in the mirror. The best friend bracelet I gave her when we were fourteen still dangles from her wrist. Her half of a silver heart that has *BEST* engraved in it catches the light and shines. I don't wear mine all the time like she does, but when I do, I feel closer to her. I'm lucky to have her. I can't imagine life without her in it, even if she does push me to my limits socially sometimes, and my buttons other times.

"You're nuts, you know that, Mel?"

"I do. I also know that he is completely purr-licious."

"Purr-licious?"

"Yep. Purr-worthy and delicious. Purr-licious."

"Ah. Gotcha. Never change, my friend. Never change."

"I promise not to if you promise the same."

"That's an easy promise to make." Both of our pinkies pop out and

tangle together. "Pinky promise."

"Pinky promise. On a different note, are you ready for tomorrow?"

"I don't even understand what tomorrow is, so how can I be ready for it?"

"I'm telling you, Sing," she says, looking me directly in the eyes, "the man has a thing for you. Stop giving him all the power. Go, have fun, and see if there's any chemistry."

"Oh, there's chemistry, at least on my side. He makes me nervous and then I start with the word vomit or go awkwardly silent. I think I'll just think of it as two friends getting together to watch some football and drink beer."

"Baseball."

"Yes, that's what I meant. See? I'm nervous."

Once her dress is on, I zip her up. "There. I'll let you finish getting dressed. I have a date with some wine and a movie."

Five minutes later, I set my noodle container down, and say, "Wow, you are going to knock him off his socks."

"What does that even mean?"

"I have no idea. Maybe it's knock him *out* of his socks." I wave my hand. "Who knows? Anyway, you look great. Have fun."

Blowing me a kiss, she replies, "You know I intend to, so don't wait up."

"I have no intentions of waiting up." Her laughter subsides as she grabs her clutch from the table. I add, "I want all the details tomorrow."

"You've got it." The door swings open. "Love you like a sis."

"Love you like a sis."

When I hear her key twist the lock, I get comfortable on the couch, pulling a blanket over me. I still worry about her getting her heart broken, but we have to put ourselves out into the dating scene to find love. A broken heart is a terrible side effect, but finding love is a great reward. I guess I need to give her space and let her figure out her future. In the meantime, I'm ready to have my heart broken and pieced back together by this movie. Sure beats having it done in real life.

4

Singer

My feet stop as soon as I enter the pub, the door whacking me in the ass and scooting me farther inside. Something is cutting into my upper arm, so I reach up and yank the price tag off the shirt and tuck it into my pocket as I look around. I don't see Ethan, but I do see a sea of orange. *Shit.* Figures.

I start to back out, but my breath stops hard in my chest when I notice Ethan lean back from the row of people at the bar, smile at me while patting a guy on the back, and then come my way. *Damn.* The man can work a sports jersey and a pair of jeans. Pointing at my shirt, he says, "I didn't know you were a baseball fan."

"I'm not, but I wanted to fit in. I assumed we were going to watch the Yankees."

Eyeing me, he winks. "The Yankees never looked better." The man knows how to charm a girl. He then leads me to a booth in the corner. "I got here early so we'd have a good seat for the game."

"You did?" I slip into the booth.

"Sure," he replies, resting his hands on the table. "What would you like to drink?"

"I'll have what you're having."

"I just ordered a pitcher." The smirk that follows makes my tummy flip-flop in excitement.

"Great."

"Be right back."

I watch as he walks to the bar and leans over an open seat. Big smile and a headful of teased hair is happy to serve him. She's a flirty redhead, smiling a toothy grin while wearing an Astros T-shirt cut from the collar to the bottom of her cleavage. It's tied tightly underneath her breasts to show off her assets. She definitely knows her audience.

Turning my attention to the TV, the announcer says it's the bottom of the third. Astros are leading. When Ethan returns, he slides into the rounded booth and glances between the TV and me. I ask, "So this is where Astros fans hangout?"

He chuckles. "I think it's where everyone but Yankees fans hang out."

I squeeze the handle of my purse, ready to bolt. "Should I go home and change?"

"No." He blatantly checks me out, and I can't deny I like the way he looks at me. "I think you look great."

"Thanks." A soft heat warms me while he pours the beer. To distract myself, I point to his shirt. "Are you from the South? You're brave to be cheering for a Texas team in Manhattan."

"I'm a Texan, tried and true, but I moved here officially about eight months ago. I was here all the time before then."

"What brought you here?"

"My business. Things have"—he pauses, his eyes leaving mine momentarily—"changed, been restructured, so I'm working on some things that require me to be here full-time. It's complicated."

Wonder if that restructuring and change extends to dating as well. "What do you do? If you don't mind me asking."

He looks surprised and then pleased. "You don't google your dates?"

"I didn't know this was a date."

"Probably best on both accounts."

He takes a large gulp of beer, and I watch as his Adam's apple bobs. Because even *that* is attractive when he does it. Curiosity kills me, and I ask, "Why would it be best?"

A wide smile appears. "Because apparently the universe keeps telling me that relationships and me don't mix."

"You're a person not a cocktail."

That makes him chuckle. "True. Let's just say I haven't had a lot of luck

in the love department."

"I thought we were talking about dating?"

"Love and dating, are they not the same thing?"

"God, I hope not. Though one leads to the other."

"How about you? I've seen you with a few guys over the last year. No one serious?"

"No one keeping me from hanging out in a sports bar on a Sunday afternoon with you."

His grin grows. "Their loss. My gain."

The bar roars to life when the Astros score a homerun, and Ethan stands to get a better view during the replay. "Man, that was a great hit." He drops down and clinks his pint glass against mine.

I keep watching him as I take a sip, the butterflies returning to my stomach.

"As for dating," he says, picking up where we left off earlier, "practice makes perfect."

When I dare take a look his way again, my shoulders drop a little. "I get tired of the practice."

"I look at it like baseball." He glances to the TV again.

"Like a game?" I ask, following his gaze, then back to him. "I think most men do."

When his green eyes meet mine, he says, "No, not a game, but the practice. Practice is just warm-up for the game. A few great games lead to the playoffs."

"And the playoffs lead to?"

"The World Series."

I smile. "So every date moves you toward The World Series?"

Laughing, he says, "Well, no guarantees with that. I've been stuck in the minors for a few years."

With a new perspective, I realize just because the dates are bad doesn't mean they aren't valuable. I need to look at dating like this and put the fun back in *fun and games* when it comes to dating. "Maybe it's time we're recruited into the big leagues." I tap my glass against his this time and take another sip.

Our eyes stay connected over the lip of the pint glass. When he lowers his, his smile is broad and mischievous. "I'm kind of pausing my personal life for now."

"Why?"

"Things are complicated."

"So you keep saying."

Chuckling, he adds, "So I do."

I don't bother filling in the blank space. I want him to expand on that last comment, but his interest in the topic seems to have faded. His interest in me, seems to have picked up. Leaning a little closer, he asks, "How old are you, Singer?"

Taken aback by his question, I rest back, scoff, then laugh. "Wow, umm—"

"Sorry. I didn't mean to offend you. I'm just curious."

"How old are you?"

"Twenty-eight."

I know it shouldn't matter, but I like that he's older than me more than I should. "I'm twenty-five."

"You look younger."

"Is that why you asked me to *hang out* instead of *go out*?" I choose my words carefully even when joking.

"Ha! No. I'm glad you're older."

I burst out laughing. "Man, now I'm older?"

He's chuckling harder. "I'm screwing up here."

"You're doing better than you think, but I'm still curious to why you asked me here."

Our gazes hold a beat, then another until his lips rise up on the sides. "Our paths kept crossing—"

"Then maybe it was meant to be," I interject with a little grin of my own.

His smile remains, and if I'm not mistaken, maybe a little wistfulness is seen in the upturn. "Do you believe in destiny?"

"I don't believe in something controlling our lives. I own every bad decision I make."

Ethan chuckles. "Do you make many?"

"Enough to know that if destiny is in charge, she's out for revenge."

"If this is revenge, it sure is sweet." The bar crowd gets louder again, and he swears, "Shit. Tied game." He tops off our glasses and turns away from the TV as if it's offended him.

The other team scores again, dragging our attention back to the large screens hanging over the bar. "Are you into all sports or just baseball?"

"I like most sports, but baseball is my favorite to watch."

I twist the glass around in my hand. "Why is that?"

"I admire the patience, the skill, and the grace of the game."

I admire him.

I think I expected Ethan to be more arrogant and self-important, but he's not that. This Ethan is kind. Attentive. Charming. Well, I knew he was charming, but he's kind. He's so kind. And I find that I'm content.

I'm relaxed and having fun. It's easy to spend time with him because I don't believe I have to put on a charade. He asks about me, his interest genuine by his attention when I answer. I sigh quietly, still confused by what today is about. Is it a date or two friends hanging out?

Conversation doesn't lag and my enjoyment of the game has developed as he explains some of the plays.

By the eighth inning, we've worked our way through nachos, two hot dogs, and a bowl of popcorn when Ethan stands. "This game is over. Want to get out of here?"

"Sure. Where do you want to go?"

"Want to walk and see where we end up?"

After paying, we land on the sidewalk, and he lets me choose which direction. I'm not familiar with the area, but I know we're walking south. "Singer is an interesting name. What's the story behind it?"

"It's my mother's maiden name. She wanted to represent her side of the family, so they split the difference. First name from her side. Last name from my dad's. I wish I had a more interesting story."

"You make up for it."

"What do you mean?"

"I think you're interesting all on your own."

My instant reaction is to want to look down, but I don't. I hold my chin level and keep my eyes on him. "Thank you."

"You're welcome. I have another confession."

I clench my hands, bracing myself. "Okay."

As if the whole world is weighing him down, he sighs. "I probably shouldn't admit this."

Feeling antsy all of a sudden, I run my hands covertly over my jeans, nervous what he's going to say. "Ethan, just say it."

"I read your book."

"What book?" I ask, but quickly answer my own question. "The book in the park?" *The romance novel?* My eyes go wide.

His laughter is light, but it still gets my attention. "It was a little mushy in parts, but it was good overall. I bought the next one in the series."

With my hand to my chest, I feel like my heart might burst wide open from swooning, all because he read the whole book. "I haven't even finished that book. How did you?"

"I'm a fast reader. My time is limited so fitting things in for pleasure has become a struggle. I also might have stayed up late reading it to impress you."

"You wanted to impress me?"

"Sure," he replies, shrugging. "Did it work?"

Laughing, I reply, "It did, but I bet your date didn't like that." Fine, I'm testing the waters. I'm interested in him and nosy about his personal life.

"What date?"

"Last night."

"I didn't have a date, Singer, if that's what you're asking."

Dropping my gaze to the ground, I'm not smooth. That much is obvious. "Sorry. I should have just asked."

Lifting my chin, my eyes meet his again. "If you want to know something, anything, ask me." He looks down the street and nods for us to keep walking, so we do. "Anyway, I stayed home. I had some work to catch up on and then I read."

"But you're"—I wave up and down his body—"you. You didn't go out on a Saturday night?"

"Now I feel like a disappointment. Is it sad that I ordered pizza and stayed home?"

This news fans the flame of my staying-home-loving heart. "Not sad. I enjoy nights in. Pajamas, candy, and a good movie. That's a good night."

"Is that what you did last night?"

"I got takeout and watched a movie." Walking next to him, I ask, "Why did you really read the book?"

"You want the truth?"

Tilting my head, I deadpan, "No. Lie to me."

He has a great laugh. I let my gaze slide from his smile to his neck. He's so tempting to touch. I don't, but the desire is definitely there.

Still grinning, he replies, "I was intrigued by the part I read in the park. And, because I wanted to be able to talk to you about something you enjoy."

"So you really read it for me?" Trying to calm my crazed heart, I fail, and it begins racing anyway.

"I did."

Emotions for this man begin to bloom in my chest. "That's really sweet, you know that?"

"You're really sweet, Singer. I think that's why it's going to be difficult not to practice with you."

"Practice?"

Appearing shy for the first time in all the times I've seen him, he looks away. "Bad reference to our dating conversation earlier. Anyway, I liked the book."

Although he's quick to divert the conversation, I catch on to what he's really saying. He can't practice . . . *can't date me.* As much as I want to ask more about *practicing*, I don't. The mixed signals jumble my thoughts, and my stomach ties up in knots.

No dating. *But he wanted to impress me?*

He's said it, but why don't I believe him? Was he not flirting with me before? While his face is angled away, I stare at him, hoping to find an answer. His jaw ticks, his eyes focused on something in the distance.

I refuse to show him my disappointment, so instead of taking the time to untangle my emotional mess, I ask, "What was your favorite part?"

We stop at the corner in front of a colorful window display. Standing with our arms pressed together, our eyes meet in the reflection, and he says, "Her heart. Her heart pulses in her chest, every beat an answering response to my own throbbing question." My lips part and my breath catches as I listen to the lines of the book recited from memory.

My whole body heats, my feelings flamed by the words as I dare to look at him as he continues, "I want to kiss you until the clouds disperse and the sun sets. I want to hold you until the moon disappears into the morning light. I want to"—his eyes meet mine—"make love to you until your body falls apart and then piece you back together with the emotions I feel for you."

Hearts. Roses. A gamut of romantic feelings erupt within my soul. I want to kiss him. I want to kiss him *until the clouds disperse and the sun sets.* I want to touch him the way his words have touched me—heavy and deep. But hope is not something I can feel with Ethan. He's made his intentions clear.

No practice.

I start to think back at all the lost opportunities that seem too far gone to give us a fresh start—from last year on that balcony when he was so easily distracted to today's invitation to hang out.

Maybe we're not meant to be. All the questions start popping in my head, little light bulb moments reminding me to protect myself and my heart. *Why is he taunting me with pretty words when he's certain he'll never act on them?*

I can't let myself get sucked into another relationship that won't lead anywhere, no matter how attractive Ethan is, how he makes me laugh, how he brings out a smile just by smiling, or causes my body to react from only a glance. He's smart, charming, and attentive.

Damn him.

Deep inside, hope starts to frown.

Damn it.

I want to ask why he doesn't want to practice with me. The more time I spend with him is going to be detrimental in the end. I can't subject myself to the scrutiny of my contrary inner thoughts, so I pop myself in the forehead dramatically. "I just remembered. I need to wake up early tomorrow for a meeting. I need to go. I should get some sleep." I peek over at him to see if he's falling for my abrupt excuse.

His brows are bent in confusion when his eyes land on mine. "It's only five thirty."

"I have laundry. Lots of laundry." Which is the truth, though I have enough clean clothes to get by for a few days.

"Okay." His eyes narrow, and he looks perplexed as I

start to back away. My hand is up to wave, but I stop when he asks, "Did I do something wrong?"

"No," I reply, honesty getting the best of me. "You've done everything right." He has, which makes walking away that much harder, but what's the point in staying if he doesn't want to go out with me again?

Perplexed deepens into true confusion. "But you're leaving, and that's so wrong."

I now know that Ethan Everest is definitely someone I could fall for if I'm not careful. I can't fall in love with someone who doesn't want love in his life. *Doesn't want me.* And I must leave before more damage is done. "I need to go. I'm sorry."

Tucking his hands in his pockets, he nods. "Can I call you a cab?"

"I'll take the subway."

"You sure?"

"I'm sure. Thanks."

The early evening sunlight filters through the buildings as if seeking him out to shine down on. He carries a small smile on his face and stormy-green eyes that reveal a circle of gray at the moment. *Gorgeous.* "I enjoyed spending time with you, Singer."

"Me too."

"Maybe we can hang out again sometime?"

I take two steps back. "Maybe," I reply with hesitation. There's no crime with him being upfront on how he sees us. Thinking back on the last few hours, I did enjoy our time together. "Thanks for today."

"Thanks for coming."

More steps separate us, but the fun banter continues, "Thanks for inviting me."

"Can I ask you a favor?"

"Sure."

"Don't google me."

I pause, my eyes locked with his. Asking me not to makes me want to more than I did before, but I promise anyway. "I won't."

"Thanks," he says, sheepish. "Be safe getting home."

"I will," I reply, dashing off.

He says loud enough for me to hear despite the distance, "I'll call you."

Waving overhead, I keep moving toward the nearest subway station.

My first thought is that I forgot to ask how he knew my name last year. My second is how'd he get my number? But when I look back at him standing so strong in his stance, I realize I'm okay not having all the answers to this man just yet. Part of me looks forward to unraveling his mysteries, but the other part continues to be wary.

Why can't dating ever be easy?

5

Singer

With my head bowed and my hand cupped over my mouth, I whisper into the phone, "First, you don't come home until after midnight. Second, you avoided all the details. It must have been a great date."

Melanie laughs but catches herself and stops. She really does have an asshole of a boss, so she has to be careful about personal calls at work. "I'll tell you over drinks later. How was your time with the infamous Ethan Everest?"

"Is he infamous now?"

"Famous. Infamous . . . both work."

"What do you mean famous?"

"Stop holding back. Cough up the details. I have to go soon."

"Fine." I roll my eyes, but those pesky tingles take over and my excitement bubbles up. I have no idea why I torture myself like this over a guy I won't have a future with. "Sadly, it was better than any date I've been on in a long time. We laughed. We talked a lot. It was fun. Different."

"Why *sadly* then?"

My bubbles . . . every last one of them pop. "He only wants to be friends. He made it more than clear. He's on a love embargo, so things were left simmering after the boil of the first few hours."

"Oh, honey. Men don't know what they want. You'll just have to show him."

The door to the break room opens, and I whisper, "I've got to go, but text me later?"

"On it. Bye."

"Bye." I tuck my phone back in my pocket and push the espresso button on the fancy coffeemaker.

My boss walks into the break room—mid-twenties, manicured beard, and a custom suit I've not seen before. Chip Newsome's suits cost two months' of my rent. He oh-so-kindly let me know that once when we accidentally bumped together in the elevator after it jolted and my coffee spilled a drop or two on him. He's not hideous, but he's definitely not the type I'm attracted to.

Two things determine his Monday morning mood: if he got laid over the weekend and if his sports team won or lost. He can be a total asshole or a great guy. So I never know what I'm walking into until I'm already knee-deep.

"Good morning, Singer," he chirps.

He got laid.

He hands me my freshly brewed espresso and asks, "How was your weekend?"

His team won.

"It was good. And yours?"

"Fantastic! The Red Sox won, and I ran into an old *friend*. Someone I haven't seen in a while."

I almost giggle. I've got him nailed—well, I guess he got himself *nailed*—but I keep the inside joke to myself, not wanting to ruin his good mood. I also note the order in which he described his weekend—sports before pleasure. "Oh really? That's great."

He pours a cup of coffee and dumps in three packets of sugar along with two creamers. With both of us mesmerized by the stirring of his coffee, offhandedly, I say, "Sounds like a dream girl."

"Yeah." He keeps his eyes on the cup in front of him. "Let's hope we make it to playoffs."

"Yes. The playoffs indeed." I don't even know what I'm saying, but men are obsessed with sports, and he's making me think of Ethan with this sports talk.

He walks to the door and with his back to me, says, "Make sure you're ready for the meeting at noon."

"Will do," I reply not as chipper. As I burn holes into his back, I have no idea what meeting he's so *not* thoughtfully scheduled at lunchtime. No wonder I've lost ten pounds since starting this job last year.

When I return to my desk, a package sits squarely on top of it. I'm about to take it to Chip's office since packages that come to this department are for him, but I'm stopped when I see the name on top: Singer Davis.

My gaze darts to the return address first. It was sent from a store here in the city, but I don't recognize the name. Grabbing my scissors, I cut the seal. As soon as I lift the flaps, my smile is instant. Inside the box, covered with tissue paper is a navy blue hat with the Astros emblem on the front. Smiling too wide to hide my happiness, I sit down, rest the hat on top of my head, and pull the card out to read:

Singer,
Saw this and thought you could use the upgrade.
See you around,
Ethan

I'm not sure what to make of this present, but it makes me smile even bigger than I am already. I text Melanie: *I just got a gift from Ethan. A baseball hat.*

She replies: *Told you so.*

Me: *Nope. Just friends. 'I can't practice with you' = Only friends.*

Melanie: *I don't know what that means. We'll talk later. Boss called me into the office. Ugh!*

Thinking of bosses, I tuck the note back inside the box and open my calendar to prepare for today's meeting.

BY THE TIME I walk into the Mexican restaurant, Melanie already has margaritas in place with an extra bowl of salsa for me. I grab a chip as I sit down. "Thanks for being my best friend and knowing when I need tequila and when I need wine." I eat the chip and sip my drink.

"Crappy Monday?"

"Typical Monday."

"That's the worst. I almost walked out of the office three times today with no intention to return."

"What stopped you?"

"Remembering I have bills to pay."

"How did we end up doing exactly what we didn't want to do?" I ask and sip my drink. "We could have done this back in Boulder."

"We'd be living better there compared to the cost of living here." Melanie's the best at giving the real deal and laying out reality. "It's this city, Sing. I'm telling you." She sighs. "If I didn't have such a great date this weekend, I'd be moving at the end of the lease."

"So I'm not enough to keep you here, but one hot date and you're staying?"

"Two dates. We've set up another."

"It must have been some first date to get you to commit to a second last minute."

"It was." Her gaze gets all dreamy as she looks to the colorful lights covering the ceiling and smiles. When her eyes land back on me, she says, "I might be in love."

What? "Wait a minute. Back up. Umm . . . okay, slow down there and let me catch up. Love? Like L-O-V-E love?"

"One in the same."

As she goes on to tell me how Mike treated her like a princess and boosted her confidence in pursuing her dreams of blogging her way to success, I watch her. I watch how she smiles with sincerity tipping the corner of her lips, her eyes sparkling with excitement, and I hear hope every time she mentions his name. She's always been pretty, but when she's happy, the pretty shines from the inside. And if this guy makes her this happy after one date, maybe he's the one for her.

When she looks at me, her eyebrows go up in surprise. "Are you tearing up?"

I wave her off. "Ignore me."

"Aww." She gets up and comes to hug me. "Is it the margarita? What's wrong?"

"Nothing. It's happy tears. I'm happy for you."

She smiles as she sits back down. "Thank you. I'm happy, Sing. I feel like I've lost so much of myself to this city. It just eats up dreams and spits them out. But you always seem to be able to find the silver lining. I know it was my idea to come here, but it's your determination that's kept us here. And now with Mike . . . maybe he's the one."

"And selfishly, that means you'll stay here in the city with me."

"We make a great team."

"A dynamic duo."

"Enough about me," she announces. "Tell me everything about Mr. Everest."

Saturday in the park, Sunday at the pub, and I don't bother leaving out any details because I know she'd harass me for them anyway. I'd do the same to her, so all's fair in that department.

Her hand is over her mouth, but she still manages to gasp. "Singer, you have to be more than friends. You just have to. He's given you all the signs that he's interested. He asked you out *and* almost kissed you at that party last year."

The infamous almost kiss still haunts me.

Just as we're about to share what I feel like is going to be the first of hopefully many kisses to come, a woman pokes her head out the window and tugs on the sleeve of his shirt, pulling him back.

The air whooshes between us as our almost-kiss is interrupted. The model's icy aura giving me chills. She stares at me seemingly bothered by my presence. She's not a woman who's denied anything she wants, and she clearly wants Ethan. Turning to him, she says, "Come back inside. Keith is looking for you. We're doing shots and the game is almost over."

. . . "But this year, there wasn't a kiss or hug. There was barely a touch on my chin. But when it comes to Ethan, I don't want to get my hopes up." I liked that touch too much. "I had fun with him. He's different from most guys I've met." Crunching into a chip, I remember the end of my time with him. "There was no hug goodbye, not even a polite cheek kiss. Why didn't he touch me or want to make a move? I swear we were flirting at different times, and he complimented me. I could feel our connection, yet he acts differently from what he says." Hmpf. I rest my chin on my hand. "Oh Mel, I can't figure him out. He's an anomaly. He loves sports, but he didn't ignore me during the game like the guys did in college. We even left early. Yet, I think I've been friend-zoned, and you know there's no coming back from that."

"Don't say that. It can happen. You just have to stay in the game."

I give her the look. She knows the look well. I've never been afraid to call someone out on their BS. "You've friend-zoned guys before they were given a chance." To use Ethan's favorite metaphors to back me up, I say, "They didn't even get a first pitch. Heck, they never made it to bat, much less first base."

"Friend-zoned, Schmend-zoned. Look, if you want to go out with him again, do it. Or don't do it." She spins her glass around by the base. "It's your call at the end of the day, and I want you to be happy."

"Maybe I don't know him well enough to make the call, but I know when I look at the individual parts of the afternoon they don't match. He says all the right things, except when he says he won't practice with me. I can tell he likes me. Ugh. He's so frustrating."

"You're frustrated because you like him."

"You've seen him."

"I've seen him, but it's different when you speak of him. I can tell there's more than good looks that attract you to him. I knew that after you told me about the party last year." One perfectly shaped eyebrow rises in curiosity. "How close were you to kissing him again?"

"You play unfair."

"No, making you see that just because he says one thing doesn't mean that's the end of things."

"What do you want me to do? Chase him down like a stalker?"

Shrugging, she sips her margarita. "Whatever works for you." Her hand slaps down on the old wood tabletop. "Let's use the fictional world you love to live in—books—to prove my point. They're called friends-to-lovers romances for a reason."

"This isn't a fairy tale. If it was, he'd swoop me off my feet and whisk me away to his penthouse, and that isn't happening."

"You never know." She clinks her margarita glass against mine. "Mr. Ethan Everest might just turn out to be your Prince Charming."

"You're supposed to be the realist between the two of us."

"Love can change a girl."

6

Singer

And love did . . .

Melanie fell completely in love with Mike. It only took two weeks and she was ready for the white picket fence and two-point-five kids with him.

Her head is firmly in the clouds and her feet ten miles off the ground, walking on air. Her giddiness is usually contagious, but a certain person of the opposite sex has me all twisted, trying to decipher what the hell he wants with me—friend or lover.

As soon as Ethan returned from a business trip, he called to ask me to come to a sold-out game with him. With my wing-girl now occupied with her new boyfriend, I'm flying solo more than naught these days, so I readily accept the invite. *Practice or no practice.*

As soon as our eyes meet, his body starts shaking with laughter. I look down at my outfit and make sure there's not toilet paper hanging from my jeans or some weird wardrobe malfunction. Everything appears fine. But he's still chuckling. Instead of hello, I ask, "What?"

Facepalming himself, he shakes his head, then laughs again. "Are you trying to get my ass kicked?"

Totally confused to what is so funny, I confess, "I'm lost."

"An Astros hat with a Yankees shirt?"

"I thought since they were both playing that I could support them both."

"It doesn't work like that." I raise an eyebrow when he goes on to explain, "You have to stand by your team. Through good and bad, thick and thin—"

"Hell or high water?"

"Yes," he replies, amused. "You have to remain steady in your support. There's no fair-weather friends in sports. You have to be all in for your team."

"You've got to do it for your country," I joke.

He tips the bill of my cap down. "Ya goofball."

"But *you* gave me the hat." His passion over the outfit morphs into a broad and gorgeous smile. He uses it like a weapon, hitting me right in the . . . I fan myself. Damn him. "So what you're saying is I need an Astros shirt now?"

"Yep. C'mon. My treat."

Thirty minutes later, I'm wearing a new Astros jersey and my Yankees shirt has been stuffed inside my purse. "Looking good there, Davis."

"Thanks," I reply with a wiggle of my shoulders.

The fans around us are not as amused. When we get a few dirty looks as we head for our seats, I ask, "Are we going to get our asses kicked for wearing these shirts in enemy territory?"

"Let 'em try."

His biceps flex; I'm not sure if he's aware that they do,

but I sure am. Sculpted muscle that takes time to define peeks out from under his sleeve. "Beer?" he asks.

"Yeah, sure." My throat's gone dry. "I'm thirsty."

"Hey, you still with me?" Brushing against me, he asks, "Where are your thoughts?"

In the gutter. It's not fair to react like this to a man who's currently captaining a love embargo, but he sure makes it hard not to. "Just excited to be here." *With you.*

"I've been looking forward to it all week."

"It should be a good game. Even though they're playing away, the oddsmakers have the Astros. I hear that's uncommon." I might have studied a few sports sites to get caught up on what's happening with the two teams.

"I meant seeing you." He chuckles. "But yes, it's uncommon for the Astros to get any support. They're scrappy this year."

Our gazes hold a few seconds before I start to ask, "Yeah, scrappy . . . What happened to just being fri—" I'm knocked sideways as some guy sideswipes me to the right when he barges between Ethan and me.

A strong hand grabs my wrist before I fall back any farther. I'm righted and my hand goes to cover my chest, which hurts from the impact. Concern—a deeper shade of the usual green—colors his eyes as they peer into mine. In a swift move, he closes the distance to the guy and knocks him on the shoulder. "Watch where you're fucking walking."

The balding Yankees fan is a few years older and bigger than Ethan in size, though not in height. "What'd you say to me?"

"You knocked my girlfriend. Watch where you're walking."

Girlfriend rings in my ears, so loud that I almost don't hear the other guy.

"Fuck you, fucking Astros." The guy spits at Ethan's feet, his buddies laughing.

"Be careful how you speak to me. Your insubordination will not be tolerated."

"What the fuck?" the guy mutters, confused as he looks to his buddies. "Insubordination?"

"Apologize to her and then watch where you're fucking walking next time." The growl in Ethan's voice rumbles from his chest, anger tightening the muscles in his neck.

The man must realize he's met his match because he looks at me, and says, "Sorry about running you down. I wasn't paying attention."

Still holding my chest, I nod and shift uncomfortably under everyone's attention. Ethan says, "Thank you."

"Whatever," is heard as the guy walks away.

"Are you okay?" Ethan asks, approaching me.

"Fine. You didn't have to do that."

"I did," he replies lighter in mood. "He'll keep plowing through the crowd if someone doesn't stop him."

We start walking again, and I peek up at him. "You called me your girlfriend," I whisper.

I see the small smile before he restrains it. "You're a girl and you're my friend."

"Ahh. Well, an asshole move on his part isn't worth getting in a fight over."

Ethan comes to a stop, a hand finding my hip while his eyes roam over my face appreciatively. "It wasn't about him. It was about you and making sure he knew he can't get away with hurting you." Taking me by the hand, he adds, "C'mon. Let's get that beer and head to our seats. The game's going to start."

Thoroughly confused, I tug him to a stop. "Ethan, what's going on?"

He looks back at me quizzically. "We're going to watch a baseball game."

"No, with this?" I lift our hands up between us.

My hand is released. "Sorry, just protective, I guess. I know you can take care of yourself." Nodding toward the direction we're heading, he starts walking.

I remain in place watching him, more perplexed than ever about what this is between us, what we are to each other, and what tonight is really about. *He said he'd been looking forward to seeing me.* So many questions and he's still walking away, so I jog to catch up, leave them to ask another day, or at least when we're not on a mission for beer before a playoff game.

With a beer in hand ten minutes later, I stand next to him in front of an elevator. "Where are we going?"

His eyes are trained on the floor number above the door. "To the suites."

"Really? How'd you score that?"

"I have rich friends," he replies while glancing down at me.

"I need some of those. Why'd we buy beers at the concession stand?"

Looking over the lip of my cup, he sees that I've already drunk almost half. "Thought you might be thirsty."

"Guess I was." Nervous is more like it, but I'm good with him thinking I'm thirsty.

When we arrive in the suite, I'm in awe. Taking me by the elbow, he shows me to the seats. I'm too busy staring at the field and this vantage point to worry about my seat though. "Rich friends are *very* good to have."

"They sure are." And there's that sexy wink again.

Four innings in, and I'm stuffed from all the good food and candy. The suite life is definitely the sweet life, except

Ethan's been busy the whole time talking to some men sharing the box. When he returns and finally sits down, he asks, "How's the game?"

"Good. You should watch it."

His laugh has become one of my favorite sounds. "Hint taken."

"No hint. Just a little lonely."

His hand covers mine on the armrest between us, and he squeezes lightly. "I'm sorry. I didn't expect to run into them and they had some business to discuss. I'm all yours for the rest of game."

All mine. My bottom lip gets tugged under my teeth just thinking about the possibility. My gaze dips down, lingering on the strong lines of his hand and wrist, the veins prominent and strong. He was ready to fight for me. That might be a turnoff if another guy angers easily, but knowing Ethan was defending me is a whole other story.

He leans back in his chair, and whispers, "I'm glad I'm here with you."

That makes all the difference in the world to me, but I'm not willing to put that out there. "That's nice of you to say." My annoyance isn't kept at bay this time.

His hand disappears too soon from mine, but I leave mine there in case he gets the urge to return his. "What's wrong?"

"Why do you say things like that?"

"I say what I feel."

"You put words carelessly out there without regards to how they might make me feel."

Shifting in his seat, he comes closer, and whispers, "How do they make you feel?"

"Like there's hope for us when there's not."

His eyes return to the baseball field. When they return

to me, he sighs. "I like spending time with you. I'm doing the best I can right now." Running his hand through his hair, he says, "My life is comp—"

"Complicated. I get it, but you're making my life complicated."

"I'm sorry. I don't mean to, Singer. I know it's selfish to leave you with vague answers, but there's no hidden agenda here. I just thought it was time we get to know each other. We seem to find ourselves in the same place quite often."

"But why now? It's been a year."

"Because I'm finally free to do so."

"You're not as free as you think you are if your life is too complicated to consider more." *More?* I sound like a whore begging for sex. *Ugh.*

A small smile appears, some relief found in his eyes. "I want to get to know you. How about we start there?"

Seems I'm not going to break through that wall of secrets he has raised high around him. I have to make a decision. Do I want a friendship with Ethan, or do I cut my losses now and walk away?

I start to stand. My hand is instantly pinned to the armchair. It doesn't hurt, but it gives his real feelings away. "Please stay, Singer."

"Why?"

The stress crinkles at the corners of his eyes as a debate rages inside. "Because I may not want to involve you in my *complications,* but it doesn't mean I don't want to involve you in my life."

I stand there looking at him, the truth not only heard in his words, but written all over his face. I sit back down. "Okay."

"Let's start again."

I agree and ask, "What do you want to know about me?"

"Let me see . . ." We watch a few plays, then he asks, "You work at a financial firm. What do you do there?"

"I work for a financial advisor. I'm an assistant. I edit all the documents that go out and pretty much run his career while he makes the big bucks."

"So you're not happy doing that?"

"I'd rather work in publishing."

Interested, he asks, "Oh really? Doing what?"

I feel silly voicing my career goals to someone who seems to have his life together in spite of some complications. I do it though. I give a voice to my dreams and send a wish into the universe. "I want to be an editor of fiction, specifically. I love getting lost in a good book."

"Why don't you do that currently?"

"Because I need to pay rent. I keep on top of the market and send out my résumé when I see opportunities. It's a small industry so the jobs are hard to come by."

"I have faith in you."

"You and Mel. Lately, I've been starting to wonder if it's time to face reality and settle into a career that's reachable."

"Doing something that's reachable isn't a dream. It's just, I don't know, life. Don't give up."

"I think some days I'm just tired of the struggle."

"To pay rent?"

"To pay bills, make ends meet, rent, food, going out. I'm broke most of the time." Rolling my eyes at myself, I add, "This is probably not considered an attractive quality."

"Being broke?"

I laugh. "Yeah. I don't need someone to rescue me—"

"I can tell. You're a strong woman, Singer. Just hang on a little longer. Your dreams might come true. Speaking of selfish, I really would like you to stay."

The intensity behind his words and in his eyes hits me,

and my throat goes dry. When I finally exhale a long held breath, I say, "I will, for now." I only receive a nod in return, but what do I expect him to say? "What about you?" This time I'm not feeling so shy. "I don't know much about you either. Tell me something your mother doesn't know."

Chuckling, he replies, "My mother doesn't know a lot about me. It's probably best to keep it that way." He settles in. With his eyes on the field, he kicks a foot up on the wall. His gaze works its way back to me, reticence in the comforting greens. "You didn't look me up."

"You asked me not to." I shrug. "Anyway, I like to get to know a person from talking to them. Why waste my precious youth googling someone who said he can't *practice* with me?"

"All good points." He chuckles. "I agree that I'd rather get to know you from spending time with you as well. So if it matters, I didn't look you up either. I also didn't ask our mutual friends, though I'll tell you, I was tempted a time or two."

"Why don't you just ask me?"

A small shrug is followed by a smaller smile. "I don't know. I'm afraid to mess things up."

"With us?"

"Yeah, I like that it's easy to talk to you. And I like the way you look at me like—"

Some man grabs his shoulder and shakes it. "Good to see you, Everest. Call me on Monday, and we'll wrap things up."

"Yeah. I will. Thanks." He shakes his hand then turns back to me.

I'm still hanging on his last words. "Like what?"

"Huh?"

"You said I look at you like . . . and then you were interrupted."

He smiles and it's as bright as the lights over the stadium. With a gentle elbow nudge, he says, "Maybe I spoke too soon about practicing with you, but I like hanging out and don't want to screw this up by having sex with you."

Is my mouth hanging open because it sure feels like a gaping hole after hearing that statement from him? Hinging my jaw back up, I could analyze what he said for hours, but right now all I can say is, "You're very comfortable talking about having sex with me."

"Sorry. Too much? I'm trying to be upfront with you."

"I like that you're honest. I just . . . I don't talk about it so freely. I'm kind of a prude when it comes to that."

"To sex or talking about it?"

It's not lost on me. Ethan Everest wants to sleep with me. It's also not overlooked that he likes our friendship. I do too. My cheeks are on fire, way beyond friendship and deepening into lust. I whisper, "Talking about it."

"You don't come off as someone who blushes from the drop of a little sex talk."

Scoffing, I reply, "I might take offense to that."

He laughs. "No, no offense intended. You just seem open. Maybe it's that you're easy to talk to, so I open up."

"Okay, that's not so bad. Good save by the way. And since when does sex screw things up?"

After the laughter stops, he says, "Maybe that's only with me."

"Sex with you screws things up? Maybe you're having sex with the wrong people then." Even though I return my focus to the game, I can feel him staring at me. When I glance over at him again, his gaze is heavy, but his eyes seem to carry the weight of the world. *Why?*

"I think you could be right." He turns back to the game, the conversation over by the looks of his attention toward the field, and the posturing as he grumbles because of a bad play.

I sit back and drink my beer, though all I want to do is talk more about sex with the right and wrong person and why he thinks he spoke too soon when it came to me. So many questions, but I don't ask them because *I'm* afraid to screw up whatever this is with him.

THE ASTROS LOSE, but we still walk out proud supporters in our shirts and hats. No fair-weather friends here. Nope. We'll show our support even through defeat, and joke about it along the way. Outside on the sidewalk, he stops and looks at me. With a tug to the bill of my cap, he says, "You look cute."

First it was good. Now it's cute. I think this might be progress. And as I start analyzing what he actually says, I think he's going to continue with *in this hat* or *in this shirt*, but he doesn't. He just leaves it right there with "you look cute." And my smile couldn't get bigger. I tug on the bill of his hat and say, "You look cute, too." *So cute, handsome. Knee weakening. Panty dropping . . .* He reminds me of Sam Hunt with his boy-next-door charm and happy-go-lucky attitude. "So where you taking me now?"

"Who says I'm taking you anywhere?" He tries to hold a straight face, but fails. "Come on, let me buy you a drink. Us defeated fair-weather friends have to stick together." He wraps his arm around my neck, and we start walking. My heart is racing and the buzz I was feeling earlier is gone. I'm sobered by his touch, his smile, by his body pressed against mine.

My feelings are jumbled by what he says, and my body reacts to every little smile he sends my way. I'll wholeheartedly blame the alcohol. It's easier than blaming myself.

Singer

We can't catch a cab dressed like this. Not in Yankees country.

For ten minutes, Ethan's waved an arm, whistled, and even stepped off the curb to get a cabbie's attention until I pulled him back. With the crowd pouring out of the stadium, it will only get harder to get a ride, so Ethan calls a private car service instead.

Sitting in the back, I run my hand over the upholstery, appreciating the fine leather. "What a score, huh?"

He nods. "Food or drinks?" And then he yawns.

He looks exhausted, so I suggest, "We can call it a night if you're tired. It's late anyway."

"Sorry. It's been a long week, and I never sleep well when I travel."

"Is it the bed? I always sleep better in my own. It sucks on trips but makes coming home that much better."

"Not sure. When I think about it, I don't sleep that well at my place either." He scrubs his hands over his face.

"You're probably right. I can tell I won't be much fun. I've not had a good week. The Astros losing just adds to the tally."

"I'm sorry."

"Don't be sorry. You were the highlight."

Our shoulders knock together. "I had fun. Thank you for taking me. We can just ask the driver to go to the nearest subway station. Then I can take the train home."

"No way. Not at this hour."

"It's fine. Really. I do it every weekend."

"I'll see you home. Where do you live?"

I hesitate. As soon as I say it, he's going to find out just how broke I really am. We've always seen each other at nice restaurants or upscale bars. He's seen the best of me. Am I ready for him to see the worst . . . the truth? Taking him downtown is going to be a bad ending to a night that's been so good.

Leaning back, I drop my chin, and whisper the address. As soon as I tell him, he tells the driver. There's no judgment in his tone. His fingers touch mine on the seat between us, and I leave my hand there, liking the connection, a little heat of comfort. A few blocks pass before he says, "You shouldn't be riding the subway at night."

"I can't afford private cars, or cabs for that matter." I don't mean to snap at him, but my defenses have already shot up.

"Don't ever be ashamed of how you live. You work hard. Good will come of that."

"I'm surrounded by friends who are doing all these great things and moving up in their careers back home. But Melanie and I can't seem to get solid footing here."

His eyes are on me and the lights outside the window flashing by make them shine. "You took a risk moving here to pursue not only a career, but a dream. That's admirable, Singer."

"I try to remind myself that staying in Colorado would have been easy. I'm paying my dues for taking that risk; I don't regret coming here." Glancing into his eyes, I say, "I'm a different person here, not boxed in by expectations, or held back by small-town thinking. I love being in New York, but it's hard sometimes."

He smiles as if to himself. "You say you're different here, but I think you would be different anywhere you go."

"Should I take that as a compliment?"

"Definitely. From your name to the way you dress. You are uniquely you. I like that."

Flattered by the compliment, I ask, "You like the way I dress?"

"Yes, you don't dress for others. From the dress with the dots to that Yankees shirt that looked like you wore it straight from the store. Your clothes reflect your personality, which is how it should be. Genuineness is a rare thing in Manhattan."

I take a minute to recover from the fact that he remembers what I wore that first night in the Bronx over a year ago. When I do, I angle toward him. "I did."

"You did?"

"I bought that shirt on the way to meet you. I had no idea who was playing, but I wanted to fit in."

"Fit in with what?"

"Fit in with you, Ethan." Laughing lightly, I feel embarrassment creeping up my chest, but I have nothing to lose. "I figured it would probably be the Yankees playing, but I'm glad it wasn't."

"Why is that?"

"Because it kept you just as unpredictable as you've always been."

Stealing a glimpse, he looks up under dark lashes. "See? That's where I see things differently. I think I'm quite boring. But I like that *you're* unpredictable."

"You date models and travel for work. Nope, not predictable at all."

Grimacing, he says, "I have *dated* models, but only occasionally. I've also dated women in other professions—lawyers, doctors, an actress, a bartender, waitresses, and a preschool teacher, but everyone seems to only remember the models."

"Which do you remember?"

"I'm not sure any have been worth remembering or I'd still be with them."

"Good point." The mood lightens between us. I don't think I could list the professions of the guys I've dated.

"I really don't think you should ride the subway at night, Singer." He turns his attention and looks out the window.

And just like that, his heaviness creeps back in and I nod, unaware if he can see me or not. "It's okay to change the subject, but if we are, can I ask you something first?"

"Okay."

Thinking back to our time on the fire escape, I don't remember if it was baseball, basketball, or football season. Maybe it was all three if that's possible.

What I do remember is how Ethan turned away from me and exhaled a shaky breath. I remember the way he gripped the railing, turning his knuckles white, and the way he reluctantly stood up. I remember all his ways, but I also remember that almost kiss like it was yesterday, an hour earlier, or maybe it was merely seconds before by the way my lips still tingle in anticipation.

I remember his reluctance to leave me, and then how he looked back, smiled, and said, "See you around, Singer Davis." I'd never heard my name sound so seductive, so smooth. It struck me that he had known my name without me giving it.

"How'd you know my name last year when we had never met?"

"I asked."

He asked.

He asked others about me. Just that simple, and now I'm smiling.

The car comes to a stop in front of my building and an unsettled silence surrounds us. I'm not sure what to do, how to say goodbye to him. Open the door and dash, or leave it open to see what he does? Dashing is the most appealing right now, so I turn toward the door, but stop. "So this it."

With his hand on my arm, he says, "I'll walk you up."

"You don't have to."

"I want to." He opens the door and slides out, but reaches back in for me.

I take his hand and when I step out, I'm brought face-to-face with him. I lick my lips, and then drag my bottom lip under my teeth. His eyes latch on to the action and my body curves in, bringing me even closer. With our bodies so close, the heat emanates between us. I don't think I can stay just friends with him. The chemistry I feel between us is too potent, too combustible.

Stepping to the side, I look over his shoulder at the door to my building. But his hands are still on me, a fire ignited despite my better judgment, so I glance back. "I should go inside."

"I CAN WALK you to your door."

"No, this is fine." If I invite him up, I'll want him to come in, and then I'll want more . . . *Seems like the theme of my life.* More. "Thank you again for tonight."

With a tip of his chin, he follows it with, "I'll call you soon."

I take a few steps away from him, putting distance between us, and fighting myself to not offer him a drink. When I look back, his eyes are still set on me, which part of me I'm not sure, but they're scanning upward when I catch him. I turn all the way around and laugh. "You keep that car waiting much longer and it's going to be awfully expensive."

Fidgeting with his baseball hat, he finally takes it between his large hands and spins it backward on his head appearing bashful and chuckling. "I think it'll be okay, but thanks for looking out for my wallet."

My head tilts to the left, and I smile. "For someone who was yawning, you don't seem so tired now."

"Second wind." He comes closer. "I spoke too soon."

"About?"

"Us. Tonight. You still up for a drink?"

I try not to jump at the offer to spend more time with him, but I suck at lying. "I am."

His arm waves toward the car in a formal invitation. "I just so happen to have a car waiting."

We settle back in and Ethan tells the driver to surprise us. The driver has kind eyes when he smiles. "You got it, sir."

I didn't expect a can of root beer and a hot dog from a stand down near the river. The street lamps shine enough light to feel safe, and there are other couples with the same plan in mind wandering around. We sit on a bench and look out at the water. "It's a beautiful night," I say. "Stars as far as I can see."

"A rarity in the city."

"This is nice."

"This *is* nice." His voice causes me to look his way.

I ask, "Are you dating anyone?"

"Wow, that came out of left field." Balling up his trash, he shoots it toward the trashcan and makes it. He leans forward on his thighs and looks at the water before us.

"I'm sorry," I quickly add. "Was that rude to ask?"

"No. Don't be sorry. I know this is . . . weird, but I'm not seeing anyone or I wouldn't have asked you out." Turning to greet me with eyes that shine with an inner light, they contradict the night sky. "Can we just go with it?" This time I turn away, my lower lip finding the edges of my front teeth. When I don't answer, he adds, "I promise you I'm not dating anyone right now." He's too tempting to keep my eyes away for long, but find a straight line across his face when I prefer a smile. "If someone asks you out though, and you want to go, you should."

"Why are you saying this?"

"Because I have a lot of shit going on, and you're too good to drag into it."

"You said your personal life was complicated. And your business life?"

"My personal life is my business. That's why I don't want you mixed up in it."

I exhale and sit back, watching as the moon casts reflections of dancing light across the choppy water. "Can I be honest with you, Ethan?"

"I always want you to feel free to speak your mind, Singer. I hope I can with you as well."

"You can. I figure it's better to be honest upfront than hurt someone down the road through misunderstanding."

His eyes are fixed on me. "What do you want to tell me?"

"Sometimes the quiet that surrounds you makes me think you're not having a good time." He's about to say something, but I place my hand on his leg to stop him. "And then your lighthearted, playful side puts me at ease."

He rubs a hand across the light scruff of his jaw and says, "I've had a lot happen over the last year. Stuff that drags me down. When I'm around you, I feel more like my old self."

"Is that why you asked me to hang out?"

The corners of his lips lift, and he confesses his own secret, "Selfishly, yes. You're not tangled in my professional life. I like that. I'd like to have a friend who is separate from that world, someone who I can be me with and just have fun."

He wears confidence like a second skin, but I see that's for the world. He's bashful for me, and it's stinkin' adorable. "Are you asking me to be friends with you, Ethan?"

"I thought that was understood from the pub."

"No, that was you *telling* me we had to be friends because of your complicated circumstances. *This* is you asking me."

"I'm asking because I like spending time with you, and we have a good time when we're together."

"Then I accept," I say, holding my hand out.

He takes my hand and we shake on it, confidence returning to his eyes. "I don't have to pretend with you, Singer. You don't know how much that means to me."

"Why do you have to pretend at all?"

He stands, sighs, and then offers me a hand up. "We should go."

I'm becoming familiar with his modus operandi. When I get too close to his heart, he shuts down. Although I hate that there are walls that divide us, I feel I don't have a choice but to accept them. *For now.*

I respect him enough to enjoy the parts he shows me

and wait for the rest. We're not in a race to the finish, but a gradual getting to know you stage. I take his hand and stand up, not pushing him for more. *Again, for now.*

Inside the car, the tension is growing between us, and the ride is much quieter this time. I'm not sure I'm built to withstand the back and forth, and I debate if I should call the whole thing off. The friendship. The hanging out. Whatever else this is.

He's one of the most handsome men I've ever seen, but attraction doesn't guarantee a love connection. He's open and then closes just as fast. I sigh to myself while staring out the window. Honestly? I don't enjoy not knowing where I stand when it comes to the people in my life, and with Ethan I'm adrift in a sea of darkness.

Then he reaches over and takes my hand . . . and there it is. *That's* what keeps me here. He's strong and has so much going on in his life, but the gesture is simple. Sweet.

Rationally, I know better.

But I'm struggling to tell my heart the truth—we may never be anything more than friends who hold hands. *Am I okay with this?* It's something I'm really going to have to consider once I'm alone and can think clearly.

When we arrive at my building, he offers to walk me in despite my protests. I decline again, and punch the code into the security keypad.

"Hey, Singer?" he calls from the curb, hanging back after I insisted.

"Yes?"

Running his thumb over his bottom lip, his chin is tilted down, but his eyes are solely on me. "I like you the way you are."

"Really?" I ask, smiling.

"Really. As for the pub back there, it doesn't matter what you wear, you'll always stand out in a crowd."

"Is that a compliment, Mr. Everest?"

"Yes. Don't ever try to be someone you're not."

"And what am I not?"

"Expected."

The comment hits me right in the heart—the emotions from being so sweet start bubbling over. And just like that, I'm sucked back into his orbit. Heart be damned. Smiling, I give another wave and go inside without looking back this time. The door slams, and I lean against the wall and take a deep breath to calm the beats of my racing heart.

That man.

I'm weak to that man when I need to be strong.

Just friends.

A gentle reminder whispers across my mind.

8

Ethan Everest

I'm no expert on New York but I can tell by the graffiti on the buildings and the hookers at the corner this is not where someone like Singer should live.

What is she thinking? I don't even like driving here, much less leaving her behind. Despite where she lives, she's not the kind of woman to play the damsel in distress, even if it's for her own good. I may not know her well, but I've learned over the last year of watching her to know she doesn't need saving.

Still. Her embarrassment over where she lives sucks. She's doing the best she can, and works hard by the sound of it. Fuck whoever thinks less of her for that. I just wish she didn't feel that way around me. I hope *I* don't make her feel that way.

For my own peace of mind though, I'll make an effort, and package it as a friendly gesture. I don't want to come on too strong. Not with her. Ever since I saw her lost in her thoughts out on that fire escape, the pretty brunette with golden highlights has become a fascination of mine.

Her quirky style and sweet smile.

Beautiful green eyes that hold more innocence than naïveté.

People underestimate her. I see the way they overlook her for someone more obvious, someone more pretentious and needy.

She's none of those things and revels in blending in, being able to sit back and watch, to observe life around her, *to observe me*. She thinks I don't notice, that I never did. But I see. I see how she looks at me. I see how she cares.

I care about her, too, more than I should for a woman I barely know. I also never saw her coming. At that party last year, she was unexpected and entirely irresistible. I can't believe I almost kissed her after hardly talking to her. She's unassuming and shy, even more so when sitting between two women who were vying for anyone's attention that night and zeroed in on me at different points.

I pretended Singer wasn't there. It was easier to carry on casual conversation, but there was nothing casual about that night. A night of bad decisions led me to months of regrets. Now, almost a year after meeting Singer, my life has changed for the worst. What once was living the high life had flipped to being buried in legal drama, my life flipping on me like my friend did.

Why'd I ever go back inside? Why'd I leave her on that fire escape? Why'd I let her walk out without getting her number? I'd already made the effort to get her name. I hate that someone so easily distracted me. I didn't want easy, but I was easily swayed away.

I want Singer's complicated emotions mixed up with mine. I want to see that blue dress on the floor at the foot of my bed. I want to mess her hair from kisses that become entangled in my white sheets. I want to wake up with her red lipstick marring my pillow and marking me.

Singer flew away that night, and I let her. *Foolishly.*

I won't make that mistake twice, but on the advisement of my legal team, I'll keep it light, keep it friendly. I'll keep her at a distance until this situation with Dariya is settled.

And then I won't.

Then, I'll go after her until she says yes to trying something real.

The car pulls into the underground garage and stops in front of the door. My driver, Aaron, turns around and asks, "Would you like me to go up with you?"

The seriousness of his tone reminds me of the reasons I need security. "No, I'll be fine. Lars will be there." As if a ghost, Lars appears and opens the door.

When I get out, he greets me, not with a smile.

"Good evening," I say, moving inside the elevator, standing at the back.

He steps inside, standing in front of the door, and pushes the button to my floor. "Good evening, sir."

His back is to me and I sink against the stainless steel paneled wall. "Anything I should know about?"

"No, sir."

"Good." I run my hand over my face as exhaustion sets in. "What are we going to talk about when all this business is settled?"

He turns and looks over his shoulder with a small smile on his face. "Baseball?"

"Maybe we can catch a game together."

"Only if you let me enjoy the perks of those box seats."

"Maybe I'll let you call me Ethan, too," I joke. He refuses

to call me by my name. He's all business all the time, even when he laughs, like now.

Stepping aside, he says, "Good night, sir."

"Good night."

Walking down the black painted hall, I glance at the framed art that lines the walls. They're not my photos, but other peoples' work I admire and collect. Most of the art has no value but to the buyer who's willing to pay for it. I paid more than the asking price because these pieces spoke to me—haunting, happy, sad, joy, ambition, depression. So many emotions are expressed in the photos.

The view of the city greets me through the wall of windows ahead. Lights from a skyline of buildings dot the nighttime scenery like little stars here on earth. I head to the bedroom and am welcomed by more windows. With the push of a button, the curtains begin to close, the lights dimming along my path.

The apartment is too big for me. I used to think I could grow into it. Now I realize it's best to be alone. Everyone wants something from me. No one is genuine when they know you have money. It's as if people feel entitled to a share of something whether they helped make it or not.

Like most nights, I lean my hands against the bathroom counter after my shower and stare into the eyes that have lost a lot of the life I used to love. Things were good before. I was happy, having the time of my life. That's what my twenties *should* be about. Living large and being in charge.

I took my eyes off my goals, trusted people I shouldn't have. I should have paid closer attention to the people I let in and the people influencing my ex-best friend, ex-business partner. So many exes tied up in him. It's a quandary really. I miss Keith sometimes, yet at other times, I wish I'd never met him. Money has changed us all. Happiness now comes with a price, and I'm not sure if I'm willing to pay it anymore. *Does that mean I'll be eternally lonely and unhappy?* Although this is not how I saw my life going, I'm not sure I have a say in the matter anymore.

When I reach my bedroom, I crawl under the covers and bring my phone to life. It doesn't take long to find the photo I'm looking for. Blue dress, red dots. Ponytail high on her head. Tempting red lips. *Singer.* It's taken all of my willpower not to kiss them, not to kiss her.

I scroll through the other photos I've taken of her. She only knows about the one I took at the park and the selfie we took together at the pub. The others I took when she was being magnificent and unaware. Call me a creeper, but I love a candid, especially of her. Her eyes hold a soul that sees the good in others. She sees the good in me.

While looking at a photo of her in jeans and a jersey from last week at the bar, I can see the difference in her figure. She's thinner than last year. I enjoyed that she drank beer without counting calories. I appreciated that she had tits. Real ones. Full. A good handful. The shape of her waist and the way it flowed wider to her hips in that dress had every guy staring. She looked sexy. Yet she had no clue how many men watched her. She certainly didn't need to lose weight.

She's still just as stunning, but seeing where she lives makes me wonder if she's lost weight by choice or because she couldn't afford to feed herself. *Fuck.* I have enough to worry about. Now I'm worrying about Singer Davis and her eating habits. I sound like a fucking psycho. I hate that life is so fucking convoluted.

When did my life get so complicated?

Oh, that's right. The day my share in the hottest social media site in the last ten years made me a billionaire at the age of twenty-six. What started as a fun way for my friends to connect in high school without our parents knowing, developed into an online community by college. I took this company to the next level. Nobody had interest in it until it was turning a profit. When it became monumentally life-changing, that's when things went awry. Even today, I can admit the setup wasn't obvious. I didn't know *friends* were capable of screwing me over so cleverly. He'd been so . . . calculating. Our friendship had meant nothing. Thanks to Keith, I learned that loyalty and friendship came with a multi-million dollar price tag.

Greed being his sole motive, I was officially fucked over by my best friend. Our friendship sold to the press. Photos leaked. My name was splattered across headlines—TV, newspapers, trash rags, online—calling me incompetent. The ultimatum was either I step down as CEO and become a very silent partner or I let them buy me out. My own company. *My idea.* I created the site from the ground up. Ten years later, I was forced to walk away. I still own my shares, my role and buyout price still in negotiations with a team of lawyers representing each of us.

I left my company behind when I walked out that door. The life I knew in Houston was over. People picked sides and unfortunately, a lot chose to believe his lies. I have my family—my mom and dad—but that's it. My mom stood strong for a while, but the pressure of the reporters became too much. When she asked if the rumors were true, I knew it was time to leave. I don't blame her for being curious, but it was a shot to my heart that she even had to ask.

Houston society is like any other major city—full of social climbers and fakeness. To spare her any more embarrassment, I took off.

With a remote office in New York, I was used to the city.

The apartment was here, and I wouldn't have to see Keith. He stayed there. I came here to focus on my other investments. I'm not stupid. I built an empire once. I can build another, and I'm off to a damn impressive start. As a venture capitalist I have a hand in all kinds of great moneymakers instead of only one.

It's good to stretch my muscles in new ways, to reinvent myself, to show I'm more than an overstated dating site, and find success again. This time I don't have partners, but I do have advisors. Damn good ones, too.

Yeah, I don't need others. I'm doing fine all on my own.

Friendships are now kept at bay. Until Singer. She makes me confess my secrets and inner thoughts. I overshare with her, yet I don't know why. *Is it because she actually listens?*

The only foreseeable problem is that one day she'll know the truth about me. I have a past the media loves to drudge up. She'll see the leaked photos and articles that painted their own story, a fake one to fit their agenda, and to sell their content space. No matter how much I hate it, I can't change it. Money can't buy everything. I've learned that the hard way.

What I can do is show her who I am on the inside and hope she can trust what she sees. It's the only defense I have to fight the lies she'll read about me.

Two a.m. I can't sleep, so I give in to my racing mind and give up trying to rest. I go into my office, grab my laptop, take it to the dining table, and sit. I like the vast darkness outside the wall of windows. I like seeing the city at this hour with only a few lights to draw the eye. It's the only time this city gives the impression of peace, and I like it. The quiet.

I download the photos from my phone I took in the park, the photos of Singer, and enlarge one where she's looking up at me, the sun in her eyes, eyes speckled in a variance of greens, gold, and brown with just a tinge of blue. When I see her, my mind always wanders back to the what ifs . . .

What if I had stayed on that fire escape?
What if I had kissed her that day?
What if?
What if?
What if?

I'm tempted to break the promise I made her commit to me. I've had her name in the search box more times than I can count, but I never clicked the button.

Shit. *4:16 a.m.* The hours have slipped away. I drop my head into my hands and use the pad of my palms to rub my eyes. I hate the way my mind tortures me in the early hours before the sun rises. As if the daylight hours weren't bad enough.

I step into my comfort zone—work. The priority emails are sent responses before I sit back and spin toward the windows. The sun's still asleep and the moon's shining high. It's a life of luxury . . . but a lonely one. When I walked away from everyone, I thought I would find myself, but I haven't. I'm lost. I concentrate on the things designed to distract me, things I can control.

A certain green-eyed, honey-haired beauty keeps clouding my usually focused mind. I'm bothered by her neighborhood. Singer deserves a better place to live than one covered in grime and surrounded in danger. I get that she wants some independence and that's all she can afford, but is her safety worth it?

Before I head to bed, I send a text to Aaron. I wonder how she'll react tomorrow when she sees him. I wonder if she'll call me. I've been warned to stay clear of entanglements for the time being, which includes Singer, but I can't seem to stop myself when it comes to her.

In the time we've spent together, I know she deserves someone worthy, someone not buried in indecency and threats. I'll only cause her pain, damage her vibrancy, and take her good until nothing but the bad remains.

Can I keep my distance? When I'm alone it's easy to say yes because my thoughts are clearer. I know my enemies and the lowball tactics they use. They'll drag her through the press with fake "facts" and exploit her goodness, making her appear bad. They'll sully her sweetness. I should listen to Reegan. His two-word warning—stay away—is meant to protect the innocent. But it's her purity that draws me to her.

The "Bad-Boy Billionaire" mired in lawsuits shouldn't tarnish her good girl-next-door image. I'm not sure how she hasn't heard of me, but I'm thankful she hasn't. I like that she sees me for the person I am and not the image sold to the highest bidder.

Singer still sees the carefree guy she met on a fire escape, the one with the world at my feet. Keith and Dariya destroyed him like they're trying to destroy my company.

The only way to protect her is to walk away from her. How do I do that now that I've glimpsed how good it feels to be with her?

9

Singer

I'm confused.

The driver patiently holds the door open for me as I try to figure out what the hell is going on. When I look at his face, he seems familiar, just like the car he's in front of. "Did you drive me home last night?" I finally ask.

"Yes, ma'am." He nods, keeping his head held up.

"Why are you here today?"

A friendly smile entrenches itself into the creases of his cheeks. "I'm your driver."

"What do you mean?"

"I'm here to drive you anywhere you'd like to go."

Despite my narrowed eyes, he doesn't explain further. Stepping closer, I say, "I can't afford to pay you to take me up the street for coffee, much less to work."

"That's already been taken care of, Ms. Davis." Tapping his watch, he adds, "I believe you need to be at work by eight?"

Not a hint, but a direct reminder. I glance at my watch.

He's right. I need to get going or I'll be late. Then the one connection to this man I have dawns on me. "Did Mr. Everest send you?"

One nod confirms my suspicion, but leaves me stuck in the middle of what to do. Do I take the gift being offered? Or walk away, effectively snubbing Ethan's thoughtfulness?

Really, there's no debate.

I get in.

As soon as the door shuts, I try to act cool, because I don't want the driver to think I'm unsophisticated when it comes to the finer things. "Hi, I'm Singer."

"Yes, Ms. Davis. I'm Aaron."

"Hello, Aaron. It's nice to meet you."

"You too, ma'am."

Leaning forward, I take hold of the leather seat in front of me. "Can I ask you something?"

"You can ask me anything."

I ask what I've been most curious about since I walked outside this morning, "Last night wasn't a coincidence when you showed up to take us home, was it?"

"No, ma'am."

"So are you here for more than just this morning?"

"Yes, ma'am."

"For a week or longer?" I'm giddy from the thought, at the luxury of having a driver.

"Longer, ma'am."

"You don't have to call me ma'am. Singer is good."

"Yes, Singer."

When my eyes meet his in the rearview mirror he winks playfully.

"You don't have to use my name every time either."

"Yes, ma—"

He catches himself. I smile and ask, "So how long are you assigned to drive me around?"

"For as long as you wish."

"Wow. That's quite an offer."

"Not an offer."

"You're right. He didn't ask me. He just sent you. So you're a gift?"

He chuckles. "Yes, I guess."

My back hits the leather when he starts driving and I check out the interior in the light of day. It's nicer than I could see last night in the dark. I run my fingertips over the wood grain detailing, not sure how to process that I'm sitting in the back of a very expensive car in Manhattan being driven to work. And he'll be back to pick me up at the end of the day to boot.

Leaning forward again, I ask, "Did Ethan say why he sent you?"

"He didn't."

"And you didn't ask?"

"I don't ask why."

I'm not sure how I feel about any of this, so I do what I always do. I text Melanie, who left for work early to get in some overtime: *Ethan Everest sent a car to take me to work.*

And then I wait . . .

All of ten seconds.

My phone is ringing, and with a goofy grin on my face, I answer in my mock-fancy bad English accented voice, "Hellooooooo?"

"What do you mean he sent a car? I need more than that."

I laugh as I set my cardigan on the seat next to me. "I walked out this morning to head to the subway and there was a car waiting for me."

"What the what? Why? Why would he do that?"

"I haven't asked him yet. I'm not sure what to do." I run my hand over the smooth upholstery again. "The car is really nice, Mel."

"Is this just for this morning or what?"

"Aaron said it's for as long as I want him."

"Who's Aaron?"

"The driver," I reply as if she's ridiculous for not being able to read my mind. Most of the time it seems she can. She's honed her telepathy skills over many years of friendship.

She audibly gasps. "You know the driver's name?"

"Yep." The buttery leather makes me sink into the seat like it was custom-made for me. "This is the nicest car I've ever been in, including the limo we took to prom. But I'm not sure what to do—"

"I know what you're going to do. You're going to be driving me home from work today is what you're going to do."

Giggling in response, I say, "I think I can do that. I'll ask Aaron, but should I call Ethan to thank him or text him or not? Will I seem unsophisticated if I'm excited about this?"

"Definitely call him. No text. This is huge and deserves a call."

"How do I say thank you for this kind of gift?"

"Sex."

"What?"

"Yes," she replies with all the confidence in the world. "This is a sex-worthy gift. Better than a third date."

"Oh my God, Mel. I'm not having sex with him as a thank you."

"You act like it would be torture to have sex with Ethan Everest."

"Sex with Ethan would be nothing short of incredible," I say, realizing too late that Aaron can hear every word I say. Ugh. So mortifying. Holding my hand to block my lips from being read, I lowering my voice, "Can I keep Aaron? I really want to keep him."

"I'm not sure, Sing." She laughs. "You need to talk to Ethan though. What if he's paid for like a week and then you're supposed to take over the payments. How does having a driver even work? Is he salaried or paid hourly? By each trip or miles? Hey, I thought you guys were *only friends*?"

"Me too."

"I love you to death, but I wouldn't give you this kind of gift as a friend. Just sayin'."

"I know. It's extravagant and luxurious, but unfortunately it's a luxury I can't afford."

"Sounds like you need to make a call, but can I ask a favor first?"

"Sure."

"Can you make the call after you drive me home tonight?" She breaks out in laughter.

I roll my eyes before cracking up too. "Ha ha! I'll keep that in mind."

"I need to go. Let me know how it goes."

"You know I will. Have a good day."

When I hang up, I debate if I should call or text him, not knowing the protocol for this kind of thank you or if it's too early, so I start my own investigation into the mysterious Mr. Everest. "Aaron, do you know what time Ethan wakes up?"

"He's asleep if that's what you're asking. He went to bed at five."

"In the morning?"

"Yes."

"Does he stay up that late every night?"

"A lot of nights."

I might be crossing a line, but Aaron will tell me if I am. I can tell we're going to be fast friends. "Do you know if he was alone after he dropped me off?"

In the mirror, I see Aaron's eyes crinkle at the sides followed by a smile. "Yes. He was alone. All night."

See. Fast friends. "Oh, but don't tell him I asked you that. Okay?"

"It's our secret."

Looking away, I try to hide my smile, but when I peek back, I see him still smiling.

It's gone quickly when I think about why he was up all night. He mentioned troubles and not being able to sleep well in his own apartment. A deep-seated sadness seeps in. We've hung out several times now and he's always in a good mood until he lets his mind wander and exposes his worries through his silence and distance. When I've seen him out with our mutual friends, he's smiling and having a good time. Is he putting on a front to hide his true emotions? Am I seeing the real man beneath the handsome surface or is it just a façade for show?

The car pulls to the curb. "We're here." Aaron dashes around to open my door.

I'll call Ethan later and thank him. For now, I'll let him rest. When I step out, I say, "Thank you. So—"

"Yes, I'll pick you up at five this evening. And then we'll pick up Ms. Lazarus. Have a good day."

I'm tempted to ask how he knows Melanie's last name, but I'm trying not to look a gift horse in the mouth. "Thank you. You too."

The hands of the clock drag, each minute feeling like forever while I wait for an appropriate hour to call Ethan.

What is an appropriate hour when you hit the bed at five? Remembering my college days, I'm thinking after one p.m.

Chip has me off to get a "barista made" coffee at ten for an energy boost. Apparently mine aren't up to coffeehouse standards, and this does not bother me one bit. I run out to get lunch at eleven thirty from the deli down the street and then I'm stuck in another lunchtime conference call that lasts past two. I keep checking my watch as if that will speed things up. Before I have a chance to make the call I want to make, a stack of statements lands on my desk that need to be entered into the network accounting system immediately I'm told, and this keeps me busy until after four.

Despite the endless numbers and distractions, Ethan hasn't left my mind. My first real break finally comes, and I figure I should do the deed. I push down this anxiety lumped in my throat and take my phone to the women's restroom to hide from Chip.

One ring.

Two rings.

"Hello, Singer." His voice is smooth and much too seductive for four in the afternoon when I'm dressed in a conservative blue dress and yellow cardigan.

"Hi." I stop, suddenly forgetting the reason I called. My name the only thing I want to hear him say, again and again.

A chuckle infiltrates the connection, and he asks, "Are you there?"

"I am. I wanted to call you—"

"I like you calling me. Why is it echoing?"

Turning and covering my free ear, I say, "I'm in the restroom. I'm not allowed to make personal calls at work."

"And yet, you called me, you rebel."

Biting my lip, I close my eyes and listen, his words warming me. "I want to thank you for Aaron."

He laughs again. "I didn't give you Aaron, but he's a perk of the package."

"For sending him to drive me. Don't tease," I say, my happiness lilting my tone. "And if I'm being honest—"

"And I hope you always are."

"I'm not sure what I'm supposed to do with this gift, Ethan, or why you did this for me."

"Can I be honest with you?"

"I hope you always are." I repeat his line with a goofy smile on my face.

"Would you believe that I did it for selfish reasons?"

"You and your selfish reasons," I tease. "Spill. What are they?"

His breath deepens as if he's relaxing back, then he replies, "I don't want you taking the subway anymore. I don't want you walking around that neighborhood. There has to be other options for you."

I try not to take offense—to feel judged—but he's not the first one to say this. I'm trying to make it here, so it is what it is. "You have money to toss around apparently, but I don't. I'm sorry you don't approve of where I live, but I'm doing the best I can. One day, I hope things change, but for now, I carry pepper spray, and I'm careful."

"The car came from a good place." He sounds like he's struggling over his thoughts. He sighs, and confesses, "I worry about you." *He what?*

I whisper, "Since when?"

"Since the night we met."

My breath catches in my chest, and I look around to make sure I'm still alone as tears fill my eyes. I don't even know why that makes me emotional. I don't understand why he says such things, especially given his choice about us. *Or the lack of us. This is so confusing.*

What I do know is that I like him. I liked him that first night, but since I've gotten to know him a little better, I'm even more enamored.

"You know I'm struggling to accept this gift, right?"

"I know, but I hope you do."

"I can't repay you."

"I don't want you to. I want you to be safe."

I ease up on the heaviness of the conversation, and say, "Thank you."

"You're welcome."

"Now that I have a car and driver at my disposal, how about I take you to dinner sometime to show my gratitude."

"I'd like that." He chuckles. "What day do you have in mind?"

"I promised my best friend a ride home tonight. We live together and she's fully impressed with the car situation."

"Glad to hear it," he replies, and laughs again.

"How about Aaron and I pick you up tomorrow around six? I take it he knows the way?"

"Yes, he does. I'll see you then."

"Goodbye, Ethan."

I hang up and hold the phone to my chest. When I see my reflection in the mirror, I tilt my head down and continue smiling.

That man.

He's affecting my head and my heart. That only means one thing—*Trouble.*

I WALK out of the building at five after five. Aaron nods and opens the door for me. "Hello," I greet.

"Hello, Singer. How was your day?"

"Not worth mentioning. Yours?"

"Busy."

I like that he's letting his guard down. "And yet you're here."

"You're a priority."

The ultimate professional in him returns so quickly. "Thank you."

After telling Aaron where Melanie works, I call her. "We're on our way."

"I'm already outside. I couldn't take being in there any longer. Up for drinks?"

"Yes. Always. You decide and Aaron will drive." I catch his eyes in the mirror, and by his silent laughter, he seems amused. I laugh too. Might as well enjoy it while I have it.

When I return to the call, she says, "I like this chauffeur business."

"Don't call him that. It makes me feel weird."

"You should feel weird," she teases. "There's nothing normal about it."

"*Huuusssh*. See you in a few."

When the car arrives and Aaron hops out, I lean my head out and say, "Aaron, this is my friend and roommate, Melanie. Melanie, this is Aaron, best driver in the city and great with advice."

He chuckles under his breath. "You don't need my advice. As for the driving, it's a pleasure to drive you around town. Nice to meet you, Ms. Lazarus."

"Oh no," she replies, tugging the bottom of his tie. "Just call me Melanie, or even Mel, if you prefer." She slips into the car after I move back inside but peeks out and says, "Nice to meet you, too, Aaron."

Melanie is dressed to kill—fitted pencil skirt, tailored blouse, and sky-high heels. As soon as the door is closed, I wolf whistle. "How have you not gotten a promotion when you dress like that?"

She bumps me with her elbow. "Because I won't sleep with my boss . . . no matter how many times he hits on me. You know I have standards. Not many, but a few."

"I'm sure it's hard to a be woman of integrity when you're gifted with a perfect-ten body and offered a life of leisure on a daily basis."

It may be true, but it's our inside joke. Her heart's too golden to be traded for financial security. She wants love, the real deal. Money too, but only with someone she truly cares about, despite all the stuff she says otherwise. In the meantime, it doesn't hurt that she looks like a bombshell—a knockout beauty with a heart.

"There is nothing about him I'm attracted to. Anyway, I have a date with Mike tonight, and I had intended to talk you into going out for drinks already."

"*Ahh* now I understand the outfit."

"Exactly, or I'd be home tonight in sweats. So where are we going?"

"If you don't mind, I have a suggestion," Aaron says.

"Of course not," I reply. "And we'll do one better. Surprise us."

"Yes, ma'am."

"Singer, please."

He smiles in the rearview mirror. "Yes, Singer."

"Thank you, Aaron."

When I turn to Melanie, her mouth is hanging open. "You've adapted quickly to the good life."

"Stop." I laugh with her though, because maybe I have.

Aaron pulls to the curb and points us to his recommendation a few doors down. When we walk into the swanky bar, I feel underdressed. Melanie, on the other hand, fits right in with the happy hour crowd. She's great like that. She blends in with her attire and her social nature. I follow as she beelines for the bar and scores two seats for us.

Scents of the ocean—musky amber mixing with masculinity—fill the air. Only one man has the ability to make my knees go weak when I'm already sitting down. I take a breath, inhaling Ethan Everest deep into my body while words are whispered in my ear, "Singer Davis. To what do I owe the pleasure?" He turns and leans his elbows on the bar, putting us face-to-face.

Good Lord, this man is gorgeous. In shirtsleeves and a vest, he's a real lady-killer. I don't think I'll ever handle seeing him in a full suit or tux. I make a mental note never to go anywhere formal with him.

Some of his hair has fallen over his eyes, freed from the gel that held it in place earlier in the day. His jaw is covered with a five o'clock shadow almost as if the hour commanded it. The knot of his tie is loose and the top button of his shirt open.

Pressing my hands to my lap to steady them, I feign nonchalance to how stunningly handsome he is. "I'm starting to think I was set up by a certain driver."

The right side of his mouth slides up. "Remind me to give Aaron a bonus."

To distract me from staring at his mouth and the naughty thoughts crossing my mind, I wave my hand next to me. "Have you met my friend, Melanie?"

His eyes leave mine, and he smiles. "Not officially." They shake hands and he says, "Ethan Everest. It's a pleasure to officially meet you."

"Melanie Lazarus, and the pleasure is all mine."

"May I buy you ladies a drink?"

With the bartender standing by, I reply, "I think I owe you a drink or twenty."

"Dinner tomorrow will do." He winks, and I melt a little more into this barstool. Damn him and his sexiness.

Melanie orders, "Dirty martini—vodka, extra olives."

Although I want to ask her when she started drinking martinis, I don't blow her cover. "A glass of sauvignon blanc, please."

Ethan turns to the bartender and says, "Put it on my tab."

"Gotcha," he replies and is off to make our drinks.

Pushing off the marble bar top, Ethan looks at me. "I'll let you enjoy your time with your friend. It's good to see you."

I tighten my shabby cardigan around me, well aware that my attire doesn't live up to the standards of this place and shouldn't be in the vicinity of the infamous Ethan Everest. "Good to see you," comes rushing out.

A bony elbow spikes my upper arm that kills my Everest high. "Ouch."

Melanie asks, "What are you doing?"

"What do you mean?"

"Why are you bundled up like it's thirty degrees in here?"

"Because I feel ick dressed like this. I look terrible. I look like a low-paid secretary."

"You *are* a low-paid secretary, but that's nothing to be ashamed of. You work hard for your money." I glare at her until she asks, "What?"

"I was waiting to see if you were going to break into song about working hard for your money. And don't think I didn't notice the lack of compliment for my outfit."

Our drinks are set down and we each take our glass in

hand. She says, "I'm struggling to compliment that sweater." She clinks her glass to mine. "But no matter what you wear, you're good enough for Ethan Everest. No matter how damn sexy and swoon-worthy he is, so don't doubt the person you are. You're beautiful inside and out."

"Thank you." I take a drink and then ask, "You really think this sweater is ugly?"

"The worst, but I still love you. And apparently so does Mr. Fancy Pants." After sighing, I vow to donate the sweater to someone who will give it the good home it deserves. I know she cares about me and only wants what's best. Her gaze leaves mine, and I follow it over my left shoulder.

Ethan is bogged down in what appears to be a serious conversation with two other men, but his eyes are on me.

He smiles.

Just for me.

And I return one.

Just for him.

10

Ethan

There's something about Singer.

Every damn man in this place is taking notice, too.

I'm no different.

It's easy to imagine they're eyeing her friend by the way she looks in her outfit, but I see where their eyes land. Singer doesn't need tight skirts, low-cut shirts, fuck-me heels, or heavy makeup. Neither does her friend, though every man here appreciates the effort.

But there's something about Singer.

She's in a league of her own, and she doesn't even realize it. Our eyes meet across the sleek marble bar, ten or so people separating us. I smile not only because she makes me grin like a fool when I see her, but because I like to see that delicate blush cover her cheeks when I do.

There it is.

Satisfied for the time being, I mentally rejoin the conversation I really should be more invested in since it's about my business endeavors. ". . . for tax purposes," Reegan, my lawyer, says. "Just think about it and let me know what you want to do." I look at him, and I guess my expression tells him everything he needs to know in return. He laughs and adds, "Has this whole conversation been pointless? How about I detail it out and send over an email?"

"That works," I reply, not even a little embarrassed to be busted.

Reegan looks behind him, and I use the opportunity to glance back at Singer again.

When he turns back, he says, "Be careful."

"I don't have to with her. She's everything Dariya isn't."

"Until she wants her piece of your pie, too."

"She's not like that." I'm defensive when it comes to Singer, a girl I really don't know that well, but one who deep down I feel I can trust. "I know her well enough to know she's not like that."

"Don't trust anyone, Ethan." With a finger wagging in front of me, his tone is pointed. "You were fucked over by your best friend. Strangers don't give a shit about you. They do care about your money though. So protect yourself until the case with Dariya is settled. Shit, protect yourself always. How about that for some free advice?"

I pat him on the back and chuckle. "I like your free advice. It's the six hundred dollars an hour advice I don't like."

Matthews laughs, catching me off guard. He's my chief financial officer, and the only one who moved over to work with me, other than my secretary. He's young like me, but he knows numbers and gets shit done. He turned down a partnership with Keith, took a pay cut, and came with me to New York. I don't trust many anymore. Being burned will do that, but I trust Matthews and Reegan. I say, "I'd almost forgotten you were here. You've been too quiet."

Reegan chuckles too. "Yeah, that's not like you at all. No smartass comment?"

"I was waiting. You two sure are chatty chicks today." He finishes his beer and adds, "No one's saying you can't"—he clears his throat—"take care of business. Just don't get involved."

Reegan adds, "And by involved, no dates. No romancing. Score, then hit the door."

Shaking my head, I reply, "If that's Reegan's version of dating, no wonder he's alone. You've got no game."

He laughs. "I've got more game than you give me credit for."

Matthews says, "Dude, don't even go there because then I'm going to have to throw down a bet, and the last thing I want to see right now is you trying to hit up on some chicks. Cuz if that happens, then we'll be picking you up after they shoot you down, and I don't have the energy for that tonight."

Matthews and I bump fists, but Reegan says, "Fuck you. There's going to be a bet all right, but it starts over the weekend. I need to get home and sleep for a week. This bastard"—he points his thumb my way—"is working me way too hard."

"You mean earning your pay?" I correct before finishing my beer.

"Yeah, that."

Matthews eyes his prey, but we need to get rid of Reegan first before we approach. He's not the best wingman. "Go home. Email me tomorrow."

Loosening his tie, he says, "Yeah, four nights in negotiations has kept me up. I need sleep. I'll catch up tomorrow." He starts to walk away but comes back and signals toward Singer. "Stay out of trouble and steer clear of any photographers in the area."

"Got it." I salute.

"Night."

As soon as he's out of earshot, Matthews elbows me in the ribs. "Introduce me to the friend."

My lack of reaction might prove the point I'm making. I just hope he gets it. "One condition. Keep your eyes on the prize and don't let them wander to the other."

"I get it, Everest. I'll keep my skills in play on her friend."

"You sound like an asshole. You know that, right?"

"Pretty much."

Stealing a glimpse of Singer over the heads of the other patrons, I see two jerks sidled up to them. *Fuck that.* No use fighting it. It's only an interest in the woman. *Interest* is not marriage or anything. "C'mon." I walk with purpose behind a long row of barstools and work around people standing in groups. When I reach Singer and Melanie, I don't bother with the asses drinking—oh good fucking grief—*Is that a daiquiri?* Banana, at that. No. Not happening. I step right in front of them and kiss Singer on the mouth.

This is my first mistake.

When there's no response or movement, I open my eyes.

Her eyes are wide. Her body is tense. Her lips glued closed.

I lean back to see the horror I felt in that kiss, her shock in the way she's staring at me.

Geez, it's not like I shoved my tongue down her throat.

My second mistake—trying to explain, instead of owning it. "Looked like you could use some help."

She doesn't say anything. Her lips are parted, her breathing has picked up, but she's still staring at me. Her arms are in the same position they were when I jumped in here and kissed her like a fucking idiot.

"You kissed me," she says.

"I'm sorry." *Sort of. Not really at all.*

"You kissed me." Her expression softens and her gaze lingers on my lips. Reaching out, she runs the back of her fingers across my lips. "You have lipstick on you."

"It's okay."

A smile pops onto her beautiful face. "It is?"

I nod, suddenly very aware that my heart is pounding more quickly in my chest. I exhale and she whispers, "Why did you kiss me, Ethan?"

This is starting to get really fucking embarrassing. Matthews is in full laughter mode behind me. Pivoting my gaze a few inches to the right of Singer, Melanie has a raised eyebrow and one of those all-knowing smirks women get when they're right and they know it.

Leaning in, closer to her ear, I whisper, "Saving you."

"From what?"

"These banana-daiquiri-drinking fools."

The softest of giggles fills my ear and I turn to catch sight of her again. Her head is tilted back with her eyes closed. Her neck is lean and so very tempting to kiss.

Singer's hair falls behind her shoulders in waves, and again, she's completely immune to the many eyes watching her. I want to cover her with my body, hide her away from the prying eyes, absorbing the sweet sound meant for me alone. When she looks up, her hand grazes across my cheek before sliding down to the back of my neck. My skin is electrified, my body wanting more of her touch, of the warmth of her hands on me. It's gone too soon when she drops it back to her lap. She no longer looks surprised, but . . . amused. Happy. "What has gotten into you, Everest?"

You, Singer Davis. *You.* I glance over my shoulder at the chumps who aren't as happy as Singer that I'm here. When I turn back to her, I grin, liking her attention. "I never took you for a daiquiri girl."

"You're probably right, but isn't that for me to decide?" She bats her eyelashes. "Hint. Hint. You're scaring away the customers."

Now I laugh. She's stinkin' adorable. I sidestep right out of their way. "My apologies, gentlemen."

I'm about to take off, but slender fingers wrap around my wrist. "You're leaving already?"

"I was thinking about it."

Her green eyes shine in delight, her smile beaming. "Stay awhile." *And my choice is made. Two words from Singer and I stay. What is she doing to me?*

Glancing to the daiquiri drinkers, they look annoyed. The taller of the two, and when I say tall, that's a stretch . . . I laugh at my own pun. He interjects, "Hey buddy, we were kind of here first."

My head bolts back. Did he just stake a claim on my Singer? "Here first? Like you have rights to the ladies because you were standing here striking out?"

His chest puffs out matching his daiquiri belly. "Get lost, will ya?"

"No. I won't unless the ladies want me to." My gaze connects with Singer's. "Do you want me to get lost?" The question isn't *lost* on me. It's a feeling that's consumed most of the last year. Being around Singer the last few weeks has me feeling a little more *found.* So I'm not ready to leave just yet.

Matthews angles his head up, waiting like me.

She says, "I was hoping you'd stay."

Daiquiri douche hits his friend in the chest, and says, "Dead end. Time to move on," and they walk away without so much as a goodbye to the girls. *Assholes.*

Singer's lips twist. "Bet you're pretty proud of yourself, aren't you?"

"Proud as a peacock." I point to Matthews. "This is my friend Rhett Matthews." Looking at the girls, I say, "Singer Davis and Melanie Lazarus."

He shakes their hands, and I can tell he's using that voice he thinks is smooth when he says, "What are we drinking?"

We get another round and find a table that's not in the middle of the crowd. Melanie talks to Matthews about his occupation. As they make the typical conversation, I move the tip of my shoe against Singer's to get her attention, but leave it there just because I want to. "What are you doing after this?"

Her lips bloom into a smile. "Going home. There's a Romance Channel movie on tonight I want to see, and then I thought I'd finish reading my book."

"You still haven't finished it?"

"No, I've been distracted." She winks. Damn, she's going to do me in.

"In a good way or bad?"

"You tell me, Everest."

"I think the wine's making you feisty, Davis."

She scoffs, but the smile remains. "I prefer sassy." Her smile begins to fade as she lowers her chin. Her eyes stay on mine while she takes some of her hair that's fallen forward and fidgets. "Why are you looking at me like that?" *Why does she notice everything?*

I grab my beer and take a long gulp. It seems her opinion is something I care about, especially what she thinks of me. When I set the glass down, I reply, "I didn't know I was looking at you weirdly."

"I didn't say it was weird." She licks her lips, and I lick mine. *I want to taste her again. I want her to want me to taste her again.*

But I won't.

"I probably need to go."

Sitting upright, she's surprised. "Already?"

Matthews and Melanie stop their conversation abruptly when I stand up. Rubbing the back of my neck, I lie, "I have a lot of work to do tonight." I look to the bar. "I'll pay out. Drinks are on me. Stay as long as you like."

Melanie says, "I can't stay. I have a date."

Matthews doesn't take that news well. She stands, and he stands. He says, "It was really nice to meet you."

Melanie's not immune to compliments and seems comfortable in receiving them. "It was really nice to meet you, too. Maybe I'll see you around."

"I hope so."

Damn, he's laying it on thick. It works because she smiles.

"I'll see you tomorrow," I say just for Singer.

Grinning, she nods. "Thank you for the drinks and the sweet ride." But it's not her truly relaxed grin. It doesn't surprise me really. I kissed her, for fuck's sake. Just because I wanted to kiss her and to claim her in a primal way. To her, it was a kiss of convenience to send the assholes away. I hate keeping her at a distance. I don't want her to think I'm jerking her around. The advice of my lawyer bounces around my head, but it also goes against everything I'm feeling for her. She's good inside. Genuine. Ah, fuck it. "Sing—"

Matthews fist-bumps my hand as I raise it. "Thanks for picking up the drinks."

"Yeah. Yeah," I reply, watching Melanie and Singer hug. I notice she slides Singer's hair behind her shoulders, and then whispers something in her ear. They laugh, and I can see how much they mean to each other.

It's probably better I didn't get to finish what I started. I walk to the bar and hand over my card. After signing the tab, the ladies joins me, and I follow them outside. Out on the sidewalk, I say to Melanie, "It was nice to finally meet you."

"Yes," she replies. "We have so many friends in common, I'm surprised it took so long."

Singer smiles. "Can I hail you a cab?"

She's a tease. A gorgeous one at that. "I think I can handle it."

I step off the curb and put my arm up, spying Aaron on a side street waiting a block down. I'm used to having him at my disposal, but he's Singer's for now. He gestures a small wave, and I acknowledge him back.

When a cab pulls to the curb, I open the door, and lean in. "Give me a minute."

"You got it, bub."

I step back and eye Singer. Her shyness shines through and she looks down. "I'll see you around?"

Nodding, her smile returns just before Aaron pulls to the curb. I open the door, and add, "Goodbye, Singer."

"Goodbye, Ethan." I was as she slips inside.

Before Melanie slides in, she looks up at me. "Singer is special."

I like her. She's protective and loyal. I'm glad Singer has

a best friend like her, one who has her back. I miss that. "She is."

"Make sure to treat her that way."

"I will," I reply to ease her concerns, and because this time I don't lie.

11

Ethan

I blame Singer.

She's got my thoughts all twisted.

If only things had started off differently than they had with her, then I wouldn't be embroiled in the mess I am.

But Singer Davis stunned me in the most unassuming way.

I've already been here an hour and still not had the balls to go up to her, much less talk to her. She's different from the other women here—quiet, a little reserved, gorgeous with long hair twisted into a ponytail that sweeps back and forth across her neck. Her eyes are the prettiest green, reminding me of brilliant emeralds.

She's intimidating, and I'm the kind of guy who's never intim-idated in business or life. I've paraglided over Paraguay. I've bungee-jumped in South Africa. I swam in the Amazon and created a multi-billion dollar company. I don't have to use lines on women. I just have to show up.

So while there's a myriad of opportunity circling around the room trying to get my attention, I don't go for the obvious. I go for the intriguing. The fascinating. The demure. The beautiful. "Who's that girl in the blue dress?"

Keith, my best friend since I was ten, looks over his shoulder. "Not sure, but check out the legs for days over on the couch. She's been staring at you since we walked in." He pops me in the chest. "Fucker. You get all the hot ass."

"Hot ass," I grumble, remembering his words. Pacing is something I seem to be doing a lot more lately. I stop in front of the windows that frame a view of what feels like the whole city. This view was worth every penny I paid for it. I just wish I could enjoy it.

My gaze shifts from "legs for days" to the blue dress. An audible moan is heard rumbling from the guys watching the game. The Yankees are down in the seventh, but I'm too distracted to care. Standing with this group of strangers, I ask, "Hey, you know her name?"

"Singer."

I want to see her again. It's only been a few hours but it feels like days since I've seen the sun, a year since I felt her heat.

Why did I allow myself to be distracted? Dariya didn't drag me inside to watch the game. Keith wasn't concerned about a possible scandal.

The whole setup makes me sick, but knowing I fell for it, makes me regret so much more.

I pour more bourbon and sit at a table that seats twelve, but has only ever hosted one. Maybe I should go out, find some entertainment for a few hours, bury myself deep in a different kind of regret. It gets lonely, and pretending I'm not isn't easy.

Picking up my phone, I press Aaron's number. He answers after one ring. "Good evening, sir."

"Did Ms. Davis make it home safely?"

"She did. I'm just leaving her street now."

As curious as I am to what she's been up to since I left, I don't ask. I didn't send Aaron as a spy, but I'm weak and ask, "Is she in for the night?"

"She said she was, something about a movie to watch. She told me to go home. Can I take you somewhere, sir?"

"No." My answer comes too quick, considering I want to say yes. I need relief. *Want a distraction.* "Go home. We'll speak tomorrow."

"Six?"

"Yes."

"Have a good night, sir."

"Stop calling me that, Aaron. You know I'm fine with Ethan."

"Sorry. Habit."

"Break it," I reply, but still respect his integrity.

He laughs. "Good night."

"Good night."

I take one more shot of courage and get up from the table. I'm tired of this. It's bullshit, and I'm over having to sit alone every night.

With a text from Matthews calling me back out, I decide to go.

After showering, I get dressed and leave. As soon as I get in the cab I'm tempted to tell the driver to take me to Singer's, but Reegan's warning replays in my mind. Until this case is settled, Singer's red lips are off limits. *Keep it casual.* The paparazzi can twist the simplest photos into something seedier, but not if I don't give them anything to run with. I've been lucky they haven't tracked Singer and me so far. The pub in the afternoon and the game. Both were cleared before I arrived. I was told to keep it friendly.

Singer Davis makes that an almost impossible task.

But after six months of sainthood, the stalker media is finally losing interest in my personal life. I need to be careful not to feed the beast.

I entered through a private back entrance, making my way through the club to the VIP area, where no cameras are allowed. Just past eleven, a woman's hand is on my thigh—red nails that come to a dull point—rubbing over my jeans. Her ample but hard tits are pushed against my bicep, her lips at my ear. I don't think I've heard anything but *maybe* every third or fourth word.

This place is loud, and my mind is stuck on a walkup twenty minutes south of here. Matthews has his hand up the skirt of a redhead he met less than an hour ago. He'll be leaving with her soon, leaving her friend attached to me. He always opens his big mouth to brag about the company when all I want to do is forget about work for a while. So I'm not really falling for her advances, they come with a price tag I'm not willing to pay.

She whispers, "Maybe we should go to your place?"

My place? It's my safe haven. "No." I stand and reach for my wallet. All three of them watch me. I avoid her eyes because I don't want to see the need in them. They'll conjure my own needs and then I'll be stuck in that regret from earlier, trying to politely get her to leave the penthouse.

Matthews knows when I'm not into someone or something. He's learned my telltale signs. Earlier, I left to save Singer the trouble. Now I'm leaving to save myself. He says, "I've got it."

"Thanks." I tell them and walk away before I'm shamed for bailing on her.

Outside, I get a cab fairly fast, considering the busy

night. The address rolls off my tongue. Not a true slip, but one with motive behind hit.

I'm a foolish fucker for doing this, but courage has kicked in, so I sit back and think about how I'm going to explain why I'm there when I see her. Twenty minutes. I have twenty minutes to figure my shit out.

Any other day or night in the city and I'd be sitting in traffic. Not tonight. Destiny has cleared the path like a runway for this taxi to takeoff, and we make it to her place in record time.

Standing outside Singer's building, I scope out the surroundings and her building in the middle of the street, and then shake my head. *What the fuck am I doing here?* I pace, checking the time and try to talk myself out of doing what I know I'm going to do.

"Got a spare ten?"

My eyes are drawn to a homeless man who has his stuff neatly piled around him. He doesn't look too scruffy, though I'm not one to question him. I reach into my pocket and pull out a twenty. Handing it to him, I say, "What's your name?"

"My friends call me Frank."

"What can I call you?"

"You just gave me a twenty when I was gouging you by asking you for a ten. You can call me Frank."

Kneeling down, I chuckle. "I thought twenty might be the going rate, Frank."

"Don't get conned, mister. Most of the guys down at the shelter admit they'd be happy with a dollar."

"A dollar's not gonna buy much these days."

"It's enough to get something to eat, something small, or a coffee at the corner to warm the insides."

I reach out and introduce myself, "I'm Ethan. Good to meet you."

"Good to meet you," he says, shaking my hand. "Who are you here to see?"

"How do you know I don't live here?"

"The doubt that keeps you walking back and forth out here instead of going in there. The debate you have going on in your head, most likely concerning the time, or the girl—"

"Hey hey, Frank. Ease up there. I thought we were friends."

He leans his head against the brick and laughs. "We are, but I know the look of questionable intentions when I see them, and you have them written all over your face."

"My intentions are not questionable."

"What are your intentions then?"

Taking a minute to think about it, I start to wonder if my intentions are questionable when they concern Singer. I stand up and sigh. Running a hand through my hair, I reply, "I don't know. She has me all messed up."

Laughter echoes from deep within him, and then he says, "That sounds like a woman you should marry."

"What?" I'm shaking my head. "No. I don't know her well enough for that."

"I'm telling you. Save yourself the disaster that lies ahead and marry her. Skip the pacing and just go forth, young Ethan."

He makes me laugh again. "You might have a valid point, but how about I get to know her first?"

"That's a good idea, too, but you should do it before some other guy marries her while you're busy getting to know her." He taps his wrist though he's not wearing a watch. "Best get to it. It's getting late."

I step toward the building buzzer, but pause with my finger hovering above it. "Hey Frank, do you think it's too late to knock on a woman's door who you're interested in, but haven't told her yet?"

He looks far off into the sky. "It's almost midnight. Might come off like a booty call. You don't want that for the girl you're going to marry."

"Stop saying that." He shrugs, and I add, "Yeah, I don't want her to think I'm just stopping by for . . . well, you know."

"I know." He points at the corner. "If you're needing a ride home, you can catch a cab down there a lot easier than this street."

"Why'd you pick here to make camp?"

"Quiet and safe, I reckon." Shrugging again, he says, "Anyway, I look out for the tenants when I'm around. They're some of the nicest I've met."

"They're lucky to have you." Reaching into my pocket, I pull out another bill. It happens to be a fifty. I hand it to him and he graciously accepts. "You looking for work?"

"Always."

"I'll ask around tomorrow."

"I'm a people person, so don't be shoving me in some old basement to sort mail."

Laughing, I reply, "Duly noted."

"So you want me to tell Miss Singer you stopped by?"

Taken by surprise, I ask, "How'd you know I was here to see her?"

"I didn't, but figured. She's the only single tenant in the building who's not dating anyone other than crotchety Mrs. Kelso, and Kirby, the landlord."

"The power of deduction."

"You have good taste. She's a lovely woman." *It doesn't surprise me that he knows Singer well enough to say that.* No doubt she won his heart by simply being her.

"Yes, she is," I reply. Looking up at the building once more, I sigh. "Guess I should get going. Have a good night and a good meal, Frank. Nice chatting."

"You too, Ethan. Next time I want to see you in the daylight."

Laughing while walking away, I reply, "Okay."

I may not have accomplished what I came here to do, but the trip wasn't a loss. In fact, I consider it a win. I met another person completely under Singer's thrall, and somehow, that makes me feel a little better. Her friends are loyal and love her dearly. I may not ever get to have her, but she'll never lack for people to adore her. *As she deserves. As she'll always deserve.*

12

Singer

7:38 a.m.

Late.

I'm going to be late.

The only positive I can find on this dreary Friday is I have Aaron waiting to drive me to work. We'll make up some time since I don't have to run four blocks to the station, but only if traffic is flowing. And if I find this damn shoe. Either way, if a miracle doesn't happen, I'll be late.

I find the shoe under a pile of dirty clothes and hold it up like I'm celebrating a World Series win. Baseball seems to be on my mind more than ever. Ethan's rubbing off on me when I really wish he were rubbing *on* me. My mind goes to the gutter a lot faster the more time I spend with him as well.

Girlfriend.

Days later, just thinking about when he called me his girlfriend does things to me. He tried to cover, but I see through him. It made me feel closer to him, protected in some caveman way I shouldn't admit to other women. I'm strong all the time. It would be nice to find someone to carry some of the burden sometimes.

7:42 a.m.

Shoot.

I'm definitely going to be late.

I quickstep to the kitchen and slip my bag onto my shoulder. I grab the two coffee cups and head out. Skipping down the steps and out the front of the building, Aaron is standing there with a smile on his face. "Good morning, Singer."

"Good morning, Aaron." I hand him the cup. "I thought you might like a cup of coffee."

His strict stance is shaken as he takes the travel mug in hand. "You brought me coffee?"

"It's not the fancy Starbucks kind, but I think I make a decent cup."

"I'm sure it's more than decent. Thank you."

I find immense pleasure that I could crack his staunch façade. Now we can be real friends. "You're welcome."

I reach for the car handle, but Aaron says, "Someone would like to speak with you," and signals behind me.

When I turn, Frank is leaning against the lower brick of the building. Some mornings he's not here, but it's always good to see him when I do. He has a heart of gold and has been around for as long as I have. With a keen knowledge of the area, our building, and the tenants inside, he's fun to chat with.

Despite the condition of his life, he remains positive and respectful. I've never felt unsafe around him. He's our personal neighborhood watch. I really wish I could do more than I do for him. With finances being tight, I give what I can but sometimes that's only a dollar or two. He's always grateful, though I suspect that sometimes he gives the money to other people more in need than he is. It wouldn't surprise me. "Good morning, Frank."

"Morning. I came by to let you know that a man was here to see you last night."

"Really? Who?"

"Ethan."

"Ethan?" I ask, shocked to hear this.

The smile on Frank's face grows as if he has the secrets I want, which I do. "That's the one."

"What did he say? Did he say why he was here?"

"He stood at this very spot looking at the building and mumbling to himself. Lots of pacing, his steps matching his thoughts, I suppose."

Aaron is laughing behind me, so I shoot him a glance, and silently ask why Ethan was here.

Frank adds, "He introduced himself and shook my hand."

THAT SOUNDS LIKE ETHAN. He looks both ways down the sidewalk before lowering his voice and saying, "A little warning though. You should look out for him. This city's going to take advantage of him if he's not careful."

Now I laugh. If there's anything I've learned about Ethan Everest, it's that he knows how to take care of himself. "Duly noted."

"I had a good meal last night because of him. I'll have a better one today."

As much as I love to hear that Frank's getting good meals, my mind is still stuck on the fact that Ethan was here. "When?"

"Breakfast and lunch. I might even squeeze in brunch."

"No, I mean, when did he stop by?" I glance back to Aaron who shakes his head no. So he came by cab. "What time?"

"Around midnight. I told him that you deserved better than a booty call."

My eyes go wide. "He came here for a booty call?"

Aaron clears his throat and interrupts, "We should get going, Singer. You're already going to be late."

"Okay." Turning back to Frank, I say, "Thanks for letting me know."

I hand him my coffee, but I wish I could help him get a home. "I'd like you to have this."

His expression softens as he takes the turquoise coffee cup. "Thank you, Miss Singer."

"Thanks again and have a nice day."

He holds the cup up and returns to his belongings. The car door is opened and I slip inside. As soon as I'm settled inside, Aaron rushes back inside, and says, "I'll try to make up some time. Would you like this coffee?"

"No," I reply, shaking my head. "I made that for you." I stare out the window, still in shock to learn that not only was Ethan here last night, but he was here on a booty call. That man is going to drive me nuts with curiosity. Why would he come to see me for a booty call when he says we can't date? He makes no sense at all. Leaning forward, I ask, "Did you know about Ethan coming here last night?"

"No."

"What do you think he wanted?" A million things run through my head. His gaze reflects in the mirror and I know he wants to say what I struggle to believe. "You really think he came here on a booty call?"

"Mr. Everest has never been the booty-call type."

"But?"

"No but."

"But I feel like you have thoughts on the matter. Care to share?"

"I do think it's odd he traveled here just to turn around and go home." *Especially at midnight. Was he already out? Had he not gone home and worked like he said he would?*

Flopping back on the seat, I find it odd, too. "Please tell me what to think before I drive myself mad, overanalyzing this all day."

He steals a glance in the rearview mirror before returning his eyes to the road. "I wouldn't assume the worst. Mr. Everest tends to surprise people."

"Well, I'm surprised all right. That's for sure."

I think Aaron is intuitive. He knows when to drop a subject and he does though I'm sure he could defend Ethan until the end. It's probably best if I follow his lead and not overthink the late-night visit.

I'm twenty-five minutes late when I walk past reception. Chip is sitting at my desk, rummaging through my personal effects. "Sorry, I'm late. Traffi—"

His hand goes straight up to stop me from talking as he turns toward me. "No need. I have a favor to ask." *Oh great.* I take the bag from my shoulder and set it on the ground as he stands up. Eyeing my desk to make sure he's not found any incriminating evidence that would get me fired— receipts from sneaking out to the café for an afternoon cupcake, phone bills showing I talked to Mel during work hours, my candy drawer. Before I have a chance to speak, he says, "I need you to accompany me to a dinner tonight."

"What?" I look around hoping not to get any attention from my coworkers. Or him for that matter.

"I know this seems potentially out of line—"

"Potentially?" I whisper, cocking an eyebrow up.

"Okay, a lot out of line, but so is being late, and if I'm not mistaken, this tardiness might be your third, which means a written warning."

My jaw hits the floor. "You're blackmailing me?"

"I can't show up alone," he whispers. "My ex will be there."

"Then why are you going?"

"My ex is a client."

My head jolts into a double take. "You were dating a client?" My lips contort from pursed to cat who ate the canary.

"Yeah, keep it down."

The tides have shifted . . . "That's against company policy, Chip," I tease.

"This is why we can call it even."

"Blackmailing is against the law, you know. So I really think I'm in the power position right now."

He huffs, but I see the smile trying to peek through. "You are. What do you want?"

"What time's dinner?"

"Seven."

"I'll never make it home and out again with enough time to change." I pull the front of my cardigan out. "I'm thinking this isn't the right attire for dinner?"

"No. Do you have anything designer?"

Tilting my head, I glare at him. "I have *a* dress."

"Perfect. What if I let you leave early?"

I grin so big, it's almost unbearable even to me. "Deal."

"That was easy. I was going to let you out of getting my coffee from down the street too, but you drive a soft bargain."

"Damn it. Agreed too soon," I joke. I reach for my wallet, but he takes my wrist. "I'll buy yours today."

"Wow, speaking of soft."

"Just don't tell anyone. Okay?"

Laughing, I agree then take his money and my phone before heading for coffee. On the way to the coffeehouse, I text Aaron to pick me up at four instead of five. He's quick to respond, but I still need to text Ethan. It's my job or dinner, so I'm sure he'll understand. It's disappointing I won't get to see him and ask him about his late-night visit. Shaking my head, I'm still surprised he came by so late.

A booty call?

Really? I would have never thought him the type, but he's a man, so maybe I've been giving him too much credit.

Touching my lips, they tingle under my fingertips, his kiss still lingering. Who cares if it was for show or staking some claim? I liked it.

His jealousy clearly got the better of him, but yet, his complications are the sole cause of us not dating.

And who is Ethan Everest to judge who I spend time with or have sex with? *Does he have no faith in my taste?* The second they ordered those drinks, the option for anything further was automatically off the table.

I open the door to the coffee shop and get in line to order, finishing my recap of last night. Looking down, I'm in a different sweater, but it's still pilling at the sides and inside the elbows. No matter how I attempt to justify it, my wardrobe has become shabby. I don't want to be seen as shabby or easy and desperate. Mel has been dying to take me shopping. Maybe it's time I give in.

When the barista calls out, "Singer," I pick up my order and head back to the office. After delivering Chip's coffee and his change, I sit at my desk, pull my phone out, ripping the Band-Aid off and text Ethan: *Hi, it's Singer. I need to reschedule dinner. I had something come up.*

Seconds. It's only seconds before I see the three little wavering dots appear and my heart starts to race waiting for his reply. *That's too bad about tonight. I was looking forward to it.*

Me too, but I wonder if it's for the same reasons. Another message pops up from him: *How does your schedule look tomorrow?*

Is he asking me to take him out on a Saturday night? Is this a real date or a booty date? *Is there such thing as a booty date?* How did we go from just friends to . . . my spirits perk up—to *friends with benefits?* Maybe I rushed to judgment, so I type: *You want to go out on a Saturday night?*

Ethan: *Pen me in.*

Cocky. So cocky with the permanent ink. I reply: *I've penciled you in.*

Ethan: *Faith, my dear Singer.*

After my tummy stops somersaulting from him calling me "dear," I type: *I have plenty of faith. It's hope I'm currently lacking.*

The dots don't come. Another message doesn't appear. I'm left hanging. Should I have not been so honest? Is it too soon for that? This is what I've been afraid of. He has me all mixed up inside, second-guessing everything when it comes to him. Cautious. I need to be more cautious when it comes to Ethan Everest.

I set my phone on the desk and turn on my computer. The first email opens just as my phone buzzes across the beige laminate desktop. Caution flies out the window, and just like that, my hopes leap right back into the front seat.

Ethan: *I have enough for the both of us. See you tomorrow, Singer.*

I'm a fool for allowing hope back in, but, like Melanie, deep down I'm a fool for love and those damn happily ever afters as well. I'm not a teenager or in college, dating boys anymore. Smiling, I close my eyes and daydream of the man himself.

Ethan Everest is no boy.

He's all man.

And it doesn't matter what's happened in the past. Love is worth the risk. There's no way to find out if there's more to us unless I step up to the plate.

Batter up.

Running my hand over a few loose threads, I worry about the seam. "This dress is starting to show some wear and tear." A year ago, Melanie and I decided to put our money together to buy a designer dress, one that would last years instead of wearing it once and tossing it. We've both worn it at least twice, if not more when I include New Year's Eve last year when she wore it the last minute.

Black satin with folds that accentuate curves or creates them if you're lacking. Fortunately, I'm not. The sweetheart neckline highlights my cleavage while still coming off as classy. It's perfect for tonight's event.

She bends down and carefully tucks the threads in. "Hold on." Disappearing from the bathroom, she runs to the kitchen. I can hear her digging through the junk drawer, then she's back in a flash. "Let me trim these." After she performs minor surgery on the dress with scissors, she admires her work. "There. Perfect. Like you."

I'm accosted the second I walk into the restaurant. While

we walk to the private dining room in the back, Chip is speaking at the speed of light, "There's something I haven't told you, and I need you to be open-minded."

He doesn't even acknowledge how I look, or that I dressed up for dinner as he requested. "I'm always open-minded." I'm not sure that's entirely true, but I try to be. "What is going on?"

I wait for him to say whatever it is he's trying to say. "This dinner is important. He's brought his team together along with some other people. I need to make a good impression. There are account opportunities in this room tonight, so do your best to land them. My father is expecting a big fish to come tonight."

My glare goes flat. "I know how to behave."

"I know you do. That's why I invited you." His hands go up. "I'm just nervous."

"Speaking of behaving, am I your fake date or your assistant tonight?"

"How about both? Just have my back. I talk too much when I'm anxious."

The door is opened, and we step inside. "It will be fine. I promise." I instantly recognize Umberto, one of our larger clients. We handle his holdings here and in Italy. He's gorgeous and very memorable. Every girl at work makes sure to have on fresh lipstick and look their best when they know he's coming into the office.

He greets us with a smile and open arms. "*Buona sera*." He kisses me on each cheek before turning to Chip. His tone turns, the happy held captive in his eyes as he says, "*Buona sera*."

Chip says, "*Buona sera*."

Umberto turns to me, his smile returning. "Bella Singer.

So glad you could join us tonight. Prosecco is being served. I hope you like bubbles."

"I love Prosecco. Thank you."

"The waiter will bring you a glass," Umberto says, his voice formal, stiffer as he looks Chip over. "It's good to see you, Chip. I think we shall have business to discuss further, maybe over Scotch later?"

"I'm free. Yes, business later." Chip is reserved, not like himself at all.

"Enjoy dinner." Umberto excuses himself to greet more guests, and I turn to Chip.

"*Grazie.*" Chip's accent is on point.

"Wait a minute." I gasp. "Your ex is a man?"

Nodding, he says, "Yes, and he's gorgeous."

Holy wow is Umberto ever so gorgeous. "Incredibly," I reply, turning my gaze back to Chip.

"Yes, he's all man." Chip rubs his temples and closes his eyes.

Again, I'm quick to note, "He's a man."

When he returns my gaze, he whispers, "You're quick with the two plus two, Singer."

"I think we're talking about one plus one. Are you gay?"

He exhales a long breath, his eyes admitting the truth before he says, "Do I have to answer?"

"No," I whisper, leaning closer and rubbing his arm. "You don't have to hide who you are from me."

"I hide who I am from everyone except . . ." He glances to Umberto.

"Why were you always talking about women if you're not into them?"

"A cover," he replies.

I don't know why this surprises me, but it does. Then I

realize why he lied—*the owner of the company*. "Your father doesn't know, does he?"

"No," he scoffs. "He'd disown me."

"You're living a lie for what? Money?"

"I'm living, and very well-off I might add. That's the most important part. I've got it made at the company, and what my father doesn't know won't hurt him."

My heart hurts, sadness swarming my chest. "What about love?"

He sighs. Taking me by the elbow, we turn our backs to the other guests. "Love is nothing. I can find happiness without dragging unwanted emotions into it."

"Chip, you dragged me here as a front because of those unwanted emotions you think are so unimportant. You care about him more than you're willing to admit." I take a deep breath after that long-winded response.

"Look, Singer, I need your help tonight. If you're not willing, you can go and I won't report you for the lateness. But if you're willing, I'd appreciate it."

Our eyes stay fixed as seconds tick by, and I debate what is best to do. I look over my shoulder and see Umberto laughing with an elegant lady in a silky burgundy gown. I also see Chip's eyes glued to them, an uneasiness in his ex's eyes when he glances our way. It makes me wonder if he's feeling the same about Chip right now. I'm a sucker for a love story, so I make my decision. "I'll stay."

That arrogant smile Chip does best appears. "Thank you."

"You're welcome."

We pick up our glasses, and I remain against the red velvet upholstered wall while Chip, in work mode, walks around the table like the shark he is. Who will his prey be? While everyone else in the room is mingling, he switches three nametags opposite ours as the maître d' rings a small silver bell and announces, "Dinner is served."

The table is set for ten and covered in deep red roses, crystal glasses, and gold-edged plates. Chip joins my side and says, "We're over here."

We're seated next to each other at the center of the table that Umberto heads. After I take my napkin and drape it across my lap, I look up and right into the stormy greens of Mr. Booty Call himself.

13

Ethan

Is this a coincidence or a setup?

I doubt it could be a setup, considering Umberto is hosting the dinner. If it's a coincidence, have I screwed up royally by showing up here with Nicolina? It doesn't look good that I'm here, last minute, with another woman. It sure as fuck doesn't look good that she's here on a date with some asshole that's not me either.

Trying to control a deep exhale, I steady myself after seeing Singer—surprise in her eyes she tries to hide, black dress that hugs her curves in all the most enticing ways, lips the color of ripe strawberries.

Fuck.

Some things need to be clarified before we both jump to the wrong conclusion. I'll try to give her the benefit of doubt, but I'm not sure she'll give me the same. I may be a plus-one tonight, but Singer needs to know I only have eyes for her.

If only I could tell her why I've not kissed her with

passion, kissed her deeply until we roll into bed, kissing even more. Fuck. I'm sitting here with Nicolina like I can't go one night alone. This looks really fucking bad.

Lifting my eyes to the woman seated across from me, her eyebrow rises and a grin tickles across her lips as she attempts neutrality. *She's not upset with me?*

She's amused?

Who is this goddess?

Singer Davis.

I let one side of my mouth ride up and lower my voice. "Good evening."

"Good evening," she replies in a whisper just for my ears alone.

The sexy siren.

The combination of that black dress and those damn tempting red lips, teases my cock, making my pants feel tighter. Despite the vixen image she's exuding, I want to see that demure smile that drives me wild. I'd do anything to watch it grow just for me. It's become my night's new goal.

My attention shifts to her left when a man breaks our connection. "Mr. Everest, it's good to finally meet you. I've been meaning to contact you. I'm Chip Newsom of Newsom Manhattan Financial."

"About?"

"Handling your finances and looking into your assets and holdings."

I glance to Singer who is attentive to the conversation. All business. I hate it. I want to hear her laugh over baseball metaphors. I want to see her look at me like she did after I made that guy apologize for running into her, that delicious mix of seeing the me I used to be and the predator looking upon its prey. It's heady and levels me every time because I can't act on my feelings for her.

Chip goes on, "I've called your office, but unfortunately, you were traveling at the time. Maybe we can schedule something now?"

My assistant had the portfolio on Chip Newsom delivered right before the drive over—Singer's boss, old money from Dick Newsom, his father, and Richard Newsom, his grandfather. Not impressive on paper and a class-A jackass on the social scene. I glance at Singer, who is still focused on him and a growl rumbles through my chest. I can see now that this is a work dinner, so I shouldn't feel put out. *But yet . . .*

I want her time.

I want her eyes on me.

I want her smile, and I don't want her to learn about who I really am from this guy. I just want to be Ethan to her Singer. "Give Rhett Matthews a call. He's the CFO."

Chip puts his elbows on the table while the first course is being set down. "Great. Does next week work for you and Mr. Matthews?"

I try to keep from sounding curt, but I'm not sure if I succeed when I say, "As I said, contact Rhett. He takes the initial meetings on behalf of the company."

Singer's slender fingers reach over and touch his forearm, and a breath fills my chest. Fuck. I hate feeling jealous, and that's all I feel when she touches him. She should be touching me. She whispers to him, "You have the name of the CFO. Let Mr. Everest enjoy his meal."

Chip nods and removes his arms from the table as his soup is served. As hungry as I was, my jealousy is spiking to another level. *Is she on a date with her boss?* I told her to date others . . . Fuck. I hate feeling confused.

It's hard to play it cool. It's even harder to not lunge across this table to pummel him. My ego is dented and my pride is wounded. I should have never fucking told her to see others. I thought she should count me out until my case is settled, not rely on me for more than a few friend hangouts. But this won't do.

She's mine.

Motherfucker.

Chip is engaged in a conversation to his left, going through his cheap spiel again, but this time, she lets him. An opportunity arises. He becomes secondary to my main concern, which is Singer. The beautiful woman across the table won't look at me, and I'm struggling to read her mood. She seems discontent.

"Pasta e Fagioli is one of my favorite soups," I say, making small talk, saying anything to bring her attention back to me.

She bursts into sweet laughter, seeing right through me, until Nicolina, who is sitting next to me, comments, "Mine, too." Singer's laughter comes to an abrupt halt.

Nicolina is stunning and from a family of well-known blue bloods, but she has one dirty little secret—a penchant for a blue-collar construction worker in Brooklyn who likes to get as dirty in the bedroom as he does at work. She told me about him one night when she was wasted on dirty martinis. The drink apparently reminded her of him. Although she keeps him under wraps from the public, she's always very open with me.

Her brother, who has a closet of his own secrets, bailed on her and hopped a flight to Mexico with his new boyfriend. She told me he was interested in our host, but Umberto isn't open to new relationships at this time. Since she hates breaking her commitments, she called me. We're only friends, the spark never there for me. We enjoy each other's company, so here we are.

How Singer and Chump play into this night, I have no idea, but I plan to find out. Nicolina introduces herself to Singer. "We were not introduced. I'm Nicolina Luchesa."

"Hello." She sounds meek, and it's all wrong on her. Come on, Singer. Show her the woman full of moxie and fun. Then she adds, "I'm Singer Davis."

"What a unique name." Nicolina sets her sights on Singer, narrowing her eyes.

"It was my mother's maiden name."

"Oh." Nicolina voices her disappointment with a sigh.

I'm quick to say, "It's unique like Singer herself."

"You know each other?" Nicolina's gaze bounces between Singer and me.

Singer's are set on me, a slow blush blooming. I add, "We've met before. She has a quick wit and a creative sense of style."

Nicolina's smile is tight. "You seem to know each other *quite* well to know such details."

She doesn't ask the question, but it's inferred. My legal team has "approved" Nicolina as someone to be seen with. She's a socialite and someone Page Six loves to write about, but she's scandal free and apparently makes me look good.

I would think by that definition, Singer would make me look like a saint. But it's not about how she'll make me look, but how I'll make her look. Fuck. I should have kissed her last year when I had the chance.

Singer shifts in her seat, readjusting her napkin in her lap. I slide my feet forward until they bump into the tips of her shoes. Nicolina is pulled into a conversation on the other side of her, so I speak only to Singer, "You cancelled on me."

Taken aback, she whispers, "I had to. I was given no choice."

"You had a choice. You chose him."

"No, it's my job."

"What is?"

"Can we talk about this later? Please?"

Strands of her hair have come loose, framing her face and distracting me. She's even more stunning, but she quickly tries to smooth them back in place.

Without thinking, I say, "I like your hair down."

Her hands freeze in place as her lips part. Her hair is unpredictably wild and free, so much like the girl I've discovered her to be. But tonight she's reserved, and her bright greens are shadowed in the candlelight. I like her brave and bold, carefree and smiling.

Nicolina whispers, "You haven't taken your eyes off her since we arrived."

"I can't." This time I speak so Singer can hear me, "The first time I met Singer she was wearing a navy-blue dress that had red dots all over it."

"That must have been quite a sight," Nicolina states distastefully.

"She was. Quite the sight," I add, staring into Singer's eyes. "Every guy in that apartment had their eyes on her."

"Maybe I should wear more polka dots," Nicolina teases, and then sips her red wine.

"It wasn't the dress."

Nicolina sets her glass down, the sound of crystal colliding catches everyone's attention. "I thought we were talking about fashion."

Singer's staunch disposition softens and her feet lift. I slide mine forward until her shoes are resting on mine. A small smile appears on her lips and damn, I wish I could taste those instead of the second course placed before me.

"Who was the designer of this special eye-catching

dress?" Sarcasm drips from Nicolina's lips, which is unlike her normal tone.

Singer's smile fades and her bloom begins to falter. "Nicolina," I warn.

"It's a simple question. The way you speak of this dress intrigues me. I'd like to see the full collection."

I glance to Singer, who has just finished her drink and is now filling her mouth with lettuce, I'm assuming to keep from saying what she really thinks of Nicolina. To save her the trouble, I respond, "It was Singer—"

"She made the dress?"

"No, all eyes were on Singer. The dress didn't matter."

A fork clatters and Singer stands. "Please excuse me."

I stand automatically. When Singer starts to leave, Nicolina touches my hand, wrapping it around mine. "You can sit down, Ethan."

"Please excuse me." I walk out the door, trailing Singer a good fifteen feet or so. I catch up to her before she has a chance to disappear into the bathroom. "Hey."

She stops and looks back but keeps walking. "Hey."

Maneuvering in front, I put my arm up to halt her. "I wasn't expecting to see you here."

"I wasn't expecting you either, but here we are." Her tone is off, her eyes everywhere but on me.

"I'm not your enemy, Singer."

She leans against the wall, her hands twisting together. "Then what are you? Because I really have no idea."

"I'm just a guy." I check to make sure no one is coming down the hall and lean forward, resting my hand above her shoulder. I move a foot between her feet and press my body to hers. "You're just a girl. Togethe—"

"What are you doing, Ethan?" Her breath catches.

"I meant what I said back there."

"Which part exactly? I'm starting to feel like I'm a pawn in a game you're playing. A challenge you took a year ago that you're ready to end and claim victory."

"The part about not being able to take my eyes off you then or now." I may not be able to be completely open about everything, but I need her to know the truth about how I feel. "You're not a game. Not to me." My breathing picks up, matching hers. Like my heart, my chest feels open, my emotions wanting to pour out.

She makes me feel too much—vulnerable, bare, but important. I should push her away, but I can't. I press my middle to her, exposing my physical attraction to her. Her dress is thin, and my body naturally reacts to the feel of her anger, her heat against mine.

I move my lips closer as one of her fingers hooks around a belt loop, holding me to her. She asks, "Are you drunk?"

"No. Why?"

"Because you're looking at me like you are."

"I want to kiss you, Singer Davis."

She sucks in a breath and says, "Then kiss me, Ethan—"

"Everest?"

Fuck. When will I get to kiss those lips that linger in my mind late at night? Pushing off the wall, I stand and straighten my suit jacket while Singer's hand falls to her side. "Chip."

He comes toward us. "Singer, everything okay?"

"Fine," she replies.

"The main course is served. I wanted to make sure you were all right."

She tidies some of her hair that's fallen again, this time tucking it behind her ear. "I'm fine, Chip. I'll be right there."

"You coming, Everest?"

This guy's overprotectiveness makes me wonder what

the fuck their relationship really is. I catch Singer's eyes on me, concern shading them darker in the dim light. I want to smooth away the worry from her forehead and kiss the lips that have twisted nervously. But that will only make it worse, so I reply, "Sure. I'm coming."

Like an asshole, he stands there with his arms crossed like he's won the war while waiting for me. *What's he's so worried about?*

I walk past him and back to the dining room. As soon as I sit down, Nicolina says, "She's not your typical type, Ethan."

"That's why I like her."

The bite she's about to take hovers in mid-air. "Ethan?"

"What?"

"You just said you like her."

"And?" It doesn't dawn on me at first, the response coming so easily, but when I look over, I see it. *Hurt.* Fuck, I hurt Nicolina.

"You like her," she repeats, the words sinking in as a revelation seems to cross her face. She lowers her gaze to the table. She drops her napkin to her seat and grabs her purse. Clearly upset, she hurries to the door.

I've managed to upset two women in the span of ten minutes, and I don't know how. When I look down the table, Umberto is watching me. *Shit.* I dash through the restaurant, catching up to Nicolina before she reaches the sidewalk. "Nicolina, wait."

The door opens, and she rushes out with me fast on her tail. Outside, I reach for her just as she takes another step, slipping through my fingers. "Don't, Ethan."

"Please talk to me."

"You know why I'm upset," she says. I do, but I've pretended I didn't for a long time. Stepping closer to me, she looks at the valet before turning to me. "I know I shouldn't be. You've always made your feelings for me clear, but deep down I always thought maybe we might find a way to each other."

"I'm sorry."

"You don't have to be. You did nothing wrong." When she looks down she closes her eyes and takes a deep breath before looking back up at me. "She seems very lovely. If not me, she's exactly the kind of woman I want you to be with." Reaching up, she touches my cheek. "I'm hurt now, but I'm happy for you, too."

I step forward and we embrace. "You've been a good friend to me."

"I still am. I think I just need to get some rest. I'm tired from the long week."

"Brooklyn's not that far."

The reflection from the streetlamp sparkles in her eyes. "No, maybe I'll detour."

"Maybe you should consider doing more than detouring. Maybe stay awhile."

Shaking her head, she replies, "He'd like that. He always asks me to stay the night."

"Why don't you?"

"What would my family say? What would the papers write?"

"That you followed your heart."

"Are you going to follow yours?"

I can't see Singer while standing outside the restaurant, but she's starting to feel like a part of me. "I don't want to hurt her."

"So you'll hurt yourself instead?"

"Yes."

"I was wrong before."

"About?"

"You don't like her."

"I do. Very much."

A soft smile slides across her face. "No, Ethan. You don't like her. You're in love with her."

My mouth falls open and my eyelids tighten as I stare at her. "I don't love her." The words feel wrong as soon as I say them.

Nicolina's grin expands. "Okay. You don't love her." She signals for the valet to call the next cab. "But remember, while you're busy *not* loving her, someone else will. Then you'll be wishing you had listened to your heart instead of your advisors, who have your business in mind and not your life."

The valet opens the door to the cab, and she starts to go. She stops and looks back. "I think I'll head to Brooklyn and surprise him. What are you going to do?"

"The only thing that feels right."

"Good for you." She gets into the cab and rolls down the window. "Take care, Ethan."

"You too."

When I return to the dining room, dessert has been served. Singer's dish remains untouched, and she's restless. Chip has given her his full attention, and though she doesn't seem to be listening to him, she refuses to look my way.

As soon as I sit down, I whisper under my breath, "Look at me." I don't care if Chip or anyone else hears anymore. I only care about her. When she looks, I add, "She's a friend. Who is he to you?"

"My boss."

"Is that all?"

She snaps, "You're out of line, Mr. Everest."

"Am I?" I challenge.

"Yes, you are. You have made yourself more than clear on several occasions that not only can you not *practice* with me, but how you feel about me."

"See, that's where you're wrong, Ms. Davis. I may have said we can't *practice* together, but I've never shared my feelings. Though I should have, from the beginning."

My breath comes short as I hold the weight of everyone's eyes on me. But as I stare into the only eyes I care to see, I realize what I've done. Standing, I back away from the table. My confession leaves Singer staring at me. "If you'll excuse me."

I leave the room and in seconds reach the valet. Where the fuck is Aaron? Shit. He's driving Singer. I raise my arm just as I hear, "Ethan?" The melody of my name draws me to look back. When I do, she says, "Tell me how you feel."

I struggle. Voicing my feelings for her is selfish in many ways, but risks her life in others. However, keeping my emotions to myself will surely send her away.

She pleads, "Please."

The words don't come. Instead, I'm moving. My hands wrap around her waist, and I spin her to the side. Just when her mouth opens to speak, I cut off her words and replace them with a kiss.

Delectable, plush caresses, pillow talk at night, sex in the morning. Fuck. I'm hard. I want her. I want her so fucking much, so when the kiss crosses that imaginary line where we should stop, I keep kissing her because she tastes too good to stop.

But we have to. Our lips part, and I say, "I may not be able to do everything I want with you, but I can't resist your lips any longer."

"I don't want you to resist. I want you to want me."

"I do, Singer. From the moment we met, I've wanted you."

"Then why won't you take what you want?"

I turn my back. I can't think clearly looking into her green, hopeful eyes.

"I'm tired, Ethan. I just want to go home, get out of this dress and these shoes, and take a bath."

Trust me, sweetheart. That's all I want, too. I'm determined to help keep her faith. I promised I'd keep her hopes alive. "Let me make tonight up to you. Come to my place. I have an amazing tub that never gets used. I'll explain everything if you'll just give me a chance. In private."

With wide eyes, she tilts her head, her gaze piercing mine. "You want me to use your tub?"

"I want you to use my apartment. It's yours for the night. You can be my guest."

Despite that her forehead is crinkled incredulously, she asks, "What about sleep? Where will I sleep?"

Present tense. That means she's halfway there. "I have guest rooms."

"Rooms?"

"Yes, Singer. Rooms. Spare rooms. Several." *Not to brag or anything . . .*

"You live in a fancy apartment . . . I now have a driver on call . . . Chip wants your business." The pieces connect as she stares at me. Discovering I'm rich isn't the secret I'm trying to keep from her. It's the other stuff that I want to hide.

"Yes," I reply quieter. "Can we please talk in private, at my apartment?"

The question seems to break the ice. "And I can bathe?"

"Yes, absolutely. You can bathe above the city lights."

There's the smile I've wanted to see all night. Goal

achieved. A shiver zips up her spine, and she rubs her arms. "It's getting chilly. How far do you live from here?"

"Ten minutes. Max."

"Your place is nice, isn't it?"

"The apartment is amazing."

"I meant the tub," she says, smiling.

"The tub is incredible, and you'll be the first to use it." I see the fight leave her shoulders. She wants to give in, and damn do I want her to. Stepping closer, I say, "Please."

"Well, tomorrow is Saturday, so it's not like I have to wake up early. I love a great tub. And you did say you'd tell me all your secrets. That's very tempting. Does that still hold true?"

"Yes." Taking her wrist, I pull her gently toward me. "Say yes to me, Singer." I have never wanted to hear one word more than I do now. I've never craved someone's answer as much as I desire hers now. If only she could see how much she means to me. I'm wearing my heart on my sleeve, my soul exposed.

Looking into her eyes, I silently plead, "You've fucking reduced me to this." Yet surprisingly, I don't feel vulnerable. I feel empowered around her. I feel like me again for the first time in a long time, because she accepts me as I am. *Please say yes, Singer.*

With her gorgeous eyes ablaze, she answers my prayers. "Yes."

14

Singer

The heat of his gaze warms my skin, making my heart beat faster. His knee is bumped against mine, claiming most of the backseat. The tips of our fingers touch on the smooth leather between our bodies, and I can barely breathe.

In the few words exchanged over dinner with Chip, it seems Ethan is quite the catch in the world of finance. I've never seen Chip basically beg for a meeting. I peek over at the man next to me, the man I promised never to search online. It's clear his secrets aren't so secret, except to me.

By the respect he received from others at dinner, it's clear that Ethan commands boardrooms. But he also seems to command the air in the back of this car. His voice is low and domineering, and I'm not sure if that is hurt I hear in his tone. "Why did you have to attend tonight's dinner?"

When I dare look his way, the storms have become hurricanes with emotions twisting in his eyes. "What do you mean?"

"You cancelled on me tonight. I felt like an idiot when I walked in and saw you there *with* him."

"An idiot? I was there for work. You, however, were there with one of the most beautiful women I've ever seen, Ethan. So perhaps you were going to cancel on me anyway."

Despite the rising emotions, our hands haven't moved, his knee still steals my space, and the heat from his touch spreads lower in my body. *Or is that from the kiss?*

"Your job requires you to go on dates with your boss?" *What the hell is wrong with him tonight?* It was a work dinner. He was there with another woman.

"Screw you." I turn my head and look out the window. "Please take me home, Aaron."

"No, Aaron. We'll be going to my apartment."

My head almost falls off from jerking so hard to the side. "Don't override my request like I don't have a say in the matter. To my house, Aaron."

"Don't start a fight where there is none. My apartment, Aaron."

I hear Aaron sigh while I release my irritation. "Listen, Mr. Everest, you don't own me. I don't care what business you have that has Chip tripping over himself to win your account. I don't care if you can afford fancy drivers or if you send me cars to cruise around the city. What I care about is kindness and decency. You treating me like a whore is neither of those things."

"I didn't."

"You did. When you inferred my job requirements included fucking my boss."

"Don't twist my words. I was clarifying what exactly your job is that you have to date your boss."

My anger boils. "I was late to work. Three strikes and I'm

out. He made me a deal. Escort him to this business dinner and no strike."

His disgust is seen as he narrows his eyes. "He blackmailed you into a date?"

"It wasn't a date. It was an arrangement that was mutually beneficial." Looking out the window, I realize this is not the way to my house. "Aaron, I'd like to go home please."

Aaron's eyes dart to Ethan's in the rearview mirror. Ultimately, Ethan holds the power. I'm not sure how I feel about that. I start to move my hand away, but it's captured before I can retreat. "I'm sorry."

Ethan's handsome face is contorted into a bevy of remorse and sadness.

"Why are you sorry?"

"I didn't mean to insult you or your integrity. I was trying to save you from my troubles, but all I've done is cause you more. Tonight has been trying. I'm sorry, Singer."

"For us both. Do you think it was easy to see you with that woman? I'm tired of pretending I don't have feelings for you. I do. That's the truth, maybe the sad truth. I know you feel something for me, maybe more than friends. You promised if I came back with you, you'd tell me the truth. You'd tell me what's keeping you from seeing me as more than a friend."

"I did, and that still holds true. Will you give me another chance? Will you let me explain?"

"You're asking me to come to yours still? Why can't we talk at mine?"

"Because you have a roommate. Because I can only imagine the walls are thin and the space not private."

He's right. "And your place has all the wide-open space you need to talk to me? Don't you see, Ethan? I'm right here. You can always talk to me. I don't know who hurt you or why you don't trust me, but I don't think it's fair for someone else's wrongdoings to be held against me."

"You're right." His hand tightens around mine as if I'll slip away. "If you want to talk at yours, we can. Aaron, please drive to Singer's apartment."

"Wait." Aaron looks at me in the mirror. I look to Ethan. "What about the tub?"

"What about it?"

"I've changed my mind. We can talk at your place."

"Because of my tub?"

"Yes. Aaron, we can go to Ethan's instead."

"Yes, ma'am," he replies.

Ethan shakes his head. "I will never understand women."

"You don't have to. You only have to listen to know what they want."

A small smiles plays on his lips. "So the tub is the magic key?"

"No, your apology was. The tub is just a bonus."

We enter a parking garage, and I realize I don't know where I was driven, too busy being caught up in Ethan to notice the rest of the world flying by. Bringing my hand to his lips, he kisses it slowly, his eyelids briefly falling closed. "Stay close to me."

His words sound ominous. His door is opened, and we're ushered out before I can question what's happening. A large man with downturned lips and a scowl that looks embossed onto his face, speaks to Ethan, "All's clear. Two paps earlier, but they left after we sent them an anonymous tip in the wrong direction."

Ethan chuckles lowly. "Good to hear, Lars."

When the elevator door opens, this Lars guy guides me

inside ahead of Ethan and then joins us. "Good evening, Ms. Davis."

The door closes, and I reply, "Hello." *This is awkward.*

Ethan leans against the corner and unbuttons the top button of his shirt. "This is Lars. He's head of my security."

Security? Head of, no less. "Ah." I play this off like it's normal. It's not, so I stay quiet and hold on to the railing. Lars faces forward, leaving Ethan and me on opposite sides of the elevator. I wish there was music or something to break the tension swallowing this confined space. I let my gaze run along the floor to the expensive shoes I failed to notice earlier and up the legs of a suit that can rival any Chip has bragged about owning.

Farther up, I get a glimpse of what I felt earlier in that dark hallway. My eyes flash to see his set on me. My lips part and my chest rises and falls with quickened breaths. His fingers wrap around the railing, his knuckles whitening. He licks his lips, and my body feels bare under his gaze.

The elevator stops and the door opens. Lars silently steps out, but Ethan waits for me to exit first. I only take a few steps into the dark hall lined with art and wait for Ethan. Behind me, he says, "Good night."

"Good night, sir."

The elevator and Lars disappear, leaving us alone, but I'm too stuck on the apartment or should I say mansion in the sky. "This is your place?"

"Yes."

"Is this the penthouse?"

A small shy, maybe even a little embarrassed, smile crosses his lips. "Yes."

I don't know why I'm stunned, but I stare at him, unable to understand. "What do you mean?"

His smile smirks on the right side. Taking my hand, he

leads me down the corridor. "What do you mean what do I mean?"

"I thought you were normal."

We stop and his head jolts back. "I am normal, Singer."

"This is not normal." We start walking again. "There is nothing normal about walking straight into an art gallery from the elevator and calling it home."

He stops in front of me and cups my face. "What about expansive views and a custom-built coffee machine? What about an infinity tub that overlooks Central Park?"

"No. Nope. None of that is normal."

"So what do we do then?" He kisses my cheek so lovingly that I close my eyes to savor his lips on my skin. I slide my hands under his jacket and hold on to his midsection. Whispering, he says, "Would you like to leave?"

My eyelids fly open. "No. Who needs normal when you have a built-in coffee machine and an infinity tub over-looking Central Park?"

Laughing, he releases me and turns to walk ahead. Looking just beyond him, I finally take in the place.

Oh. My. God!

"You've got to be kidding me."

Standing in the middle of the large expanse of a space with his arms held wide, he says, "Welcome to my home, Singer."

My feet are grounded to the spot and my mouth hangs open while my eyes feast on the awesomeness of this apart-ment. "You live here?"

"I do." The answer seems to make him smile again, and he shifts. "Can I get you something to drink? Wine, cham-pagne, anything you want."

"Whatever you're drinking."

He walks in the opposite direction of the kitchen. "How about I surprise you?"

"I like surprises."

"Come with me." He leads me down a hall to a bedroom at the far end. The door is open, and he peeks back as if to make sure I'm still there. "The tub. You have to see this bathroom and tub."

His smile is magnetic, his excitement contagious. He has me hook, line, and sinker, making me forget all about the earlier argument. When he reaches back for me, I readily take his hand. He pulls me close and says, "Don't fall in love."

"Don't flatter yourself."

"I meant with the tub." The repeat of my earlier words make me laugh.

We turn a corner and he slides open a huge door on an exposed rail. I'm about to have an extremely witty comeback, but my whole body freezes when I enter the Mecca that is his bathroom, or more appropriately called, the spa. "Holy mother of relaxation." I pirouette across the marble floor because I can. "Where have you been all my life?"

A chuckle grabs my attention and I look back. Ethan, in all his sinfully sexy glory, is leaning on the doorway grinning at me. He looks as carefree as I feel. "What are you looking at?" So what if I flirt and shake my hips. He looks as delicious as the dessert I regrettably didn't have tonight.

"You. You're beautiful. You know that, Singer?"

I'm not quite sure how to reply, but my cheeks feel flush, so I look down. "What's gotten into you, Ethan?" Aaron was right. Ethan's unpredictable. He makes me feel unsteady.

"We're alone." He runs his thumb over his bottom lip and watches me. "I like being alone with you."

"We've been alone before."

He comes toward me. "We've been surrounded by thousands of people before. That's not alone. That's biding time."

"Until?"

"Until now."

Standing in front of me, he tilts my chin up, and I ask, "What happens now?"

"Whatever you want to happen." He kisses the corner of my mouth then whispers, "What do you want to happen, Singer?"

For you to touch me, to kiss me, to—"To take a bath?"

"I'll start the water." I watch as he walks to the large tub and turns the knobs. His fingers dance under the water as he finds the perfect temperature. I can't wait to find out what that might be. Glancing back at me, the smile is still present. "You're gonna love this."

"I already do."

That same grin tempers toward cocky when he turns back to the faucets. I set my purse on the counter before walking to a door. "Is this the closet?"

"Toilet."

"Ah. Where's the closet?"

"Are you trying to get a gander of my underwear?"

"No." I laugh, though I am curious about what he wears. "I can only imagine how amazing the closet is if this is the bathroom."

"It's enviable and way too big for me."

Leaning against the marble counter, I say, "This place is too big for one person."

"I'm hoping for more one day."

"Me too."

When I say that, his eyes are drawn back to me. "I think it's ready. I'll get you something to drink. There are bubble suds over there and a towel here."

"Did you just say bubble suds?"

"Yes, the stuff that makes it all white and bubbly."

"Bubble suds?" I repeat again this time letting my laughter take over. "That is adorable."

"What's so funny? That's what my mom called them."

"What, when you were five?"

He shrugs lightheartedly. "Pretty much. That's probably the last time I took a bath."

I usher him toward the door. "You're missing out then. Baths are a glorious thing, and I intend to soak up every second of relaxation I can in here. Pun intended."

"I want you to enjoy the view and bath for the both of us. I'll close the door and give you privacy."

"Do you have a robe I can borrow for after?"

"I've got you covered." *I bet he could cover me in all the right ways.*

"Thanks." The door closes and I walk to the tub. It's an incredible tub, just as he promised. I've never seen an infinity tub, but I cannot wait to get in. The view of the city and park adds to the magic.

Slipping off my shoes, I dim the lights on the wall panel. I take my clothes off and hang them on a hook near the door before returning to the tub.

The tub, warm and inviting as I step in, eases my aching feet from my high heels and the tension in my shoulders. I pour some of the bubble suds and giggle. That was so cute and showed me a whole new side to Ethan—the at-home Texan who relates to his roots—instead of the strong, quieter, broodier man I see sometimes.

While the suds foam and the tub fills, I look out the window. The sky is clear up here. The buildings are far enough apart to avoid spying on neighbors. It's like floating in heaven.

I hear his knock on the door, so I call, "Come in," while making sure the bubbles cover all the important parts.

Ethan walks in with two glasses of champagne in one hand and the bottle in the other.

"You came prepared," I note, leaning back on one side of the tub.

"I thought I might join you." He waggles his eyebrows.

I giggle and reach for a glass. "Come on in," I reply and wonder if he will really take me up on my dare.

He sets the bottle and his glass down on the side of the tub. His tie was removed before he came in and I notice his shoes are long gone, along with his jacket. When he starts on the buttons of his shirt, I sit up, scooping suds over me. "Wait, for real?"

"Yep. I think that tub's big enough for the two of us."

"But you said you don't take baths."

"I also said I've never used this one. Seems like an opportune time."

"But I'm naked," I say, worried about everything—his body naked next to mine, not shaving my legs before I went out tonight. My mind flickers through my flaws. Ugh. No. Just no. Not like that. That stuff should be shared in the dark of a bedroom under the influence of alcohol and desperate sex. We're too sober for this. *I'm* too sober for this. What does he possibly see in me when he has women like Nicolina waiting?

He's more than I've imagined, and in some senses, it scares me. He's the sort of man women like Nicolina land. For once though, it was as if she saw me as competition. *The feeling is exhilarating.*

"Like I said, seems like an opportune time."

His shirt is dropped, his undershirt following quickly behind. Good God Almighty. What does a guy who looks like that see in me? "I see you like to work out." I clear my throat and want to bonk my head on the side of the tub for saying it out loud.

Chuckling, he says, "I have a gym down the hall. It's how I relieve stress."

"I thought that's what sex was for." I gasp and cover my mouth, wishing I could keep my crazy thoughts in my head where they belong instead of on my tongue. His eyes are heavy, a smirky smirk restraining a laugh. "God, you cannot let me talk when I'm nervous."

"If this is what happens when you're nervous, I'll make you nervous more often." His pants come down and my curiosity is answered. Tonight he's in boxers. When he catches my eyes on his package, I'm thankful I'm wearing waterproof mascara because I immediately go underwater. Screw my makeup. It's really the only way to keep my mouth in check at this point. I count to five and then pop back up. With my hands covering my boobs, I ask, "You're really coming in?"

"Yes, scoot over."

Good God Almighty.

15

Ethan

Her eyes are wide, her arms crossed over her chest though the suds cover everything I wish I could see, and now because of her sudden dive underwater, the makeup on her eyes is now around her eyes and sliding south. "I won't come in if you really don't want me to. Tell me what you want, Singer."

She slides to the far side, and says, "I want you to come in. Just no peeking. Okay?"

"I can't make that promise."

Rolling her eyes, she laughs. "Fine. C'mon anyway. But remember, that means I can peek, too."

My cock hardens from the thought of her gaze on my body. "That's fair."

I step inside the tub, and she protests, "No fair. You have your boxers on. You have to take them off."

"Why, Singer Davis, you sure are demanding for someone naked in *my* tub." I strip my boxers down, and she hides her eyes.

"Good Lord."

"Good works. Incredible. Amazing. Awesome. Works better."

"Oh God."

"About that. I know this might be a religious experience of sorts, but you can still call me Ethan."

"Ugh. Stop all right already and sit down."

I sit, and the water splashes over the sides so I turn it off. The water's warm and she's right, relaxing. "You can uncover your eyes. Nothing to see here but white bubbles." I stretch my arms wide over the edge.

Her hand dips into the water and she leans her head back. "This is the best bathtub ever. I thought you were just trying to get me to come back with you to have sex." Her sweet smile is full of mischief and is very contagious.

"And yet, you still came."

Shrugging, she replies, "Busted." She picks up her glass and leans forward. The damn bubbles are thick, guarding her body from view. "To this tub."

"And devirgining it," I add.

"Is it de or un?"

"I went with de. How about you, Singer? When did you first get de-ed?" Not sure if it's the heat of the water or the questions that pink her cheeks, but the color is there and she's beautiful.

She takes a sip, and sets her glass down. "When I was eighteen."

"No juicy details?"

"Why are we talking about this again?"

"We're getting to know each other." I'd like to get to know her body on top of mine better.

"Fine. It was the first time for both of us. Trust me, there are no good details to share. It was fast and awkward. I think it was over in less than five minutes."

"Yikes."

"You?"

"Seventeen after we won the regional championship in football."

"There's more to that story for sure."

She makes me laugh, something I haven't done much of in the last year. "Same old story—cheerleader, star football player, one cold Texas night in December."

"I didn't know it got cold in Texas."

"It was like an inferno in that truck bed."

"It was in the back of a truck?" Her cute little nose scrunches, but she leans back again and drinks more of her champagne.

"It was a nice truck with one of those hardtop covers. I had blankets and an air mattress that filled the bed. No candles for obvious reasons, but a sky full of stars and Sarah McLachlan playing through the speakers."

"I didn't take you for a Sarah fan."

"My girlfriend was a huge fan. It was my way of romancing her."

She stretches her legs forward, the length against the side of mine. Her foot rests against my hip. I slide my hand under the water and run my palm down the side and take hold of her foot, rubbing the arch with my thumb. She moans in pleasure then asks, "Do you remember what song was playing?"

"Fallen." I match her position and lean back, remembering those times. They were so much simpler.

"I don't know if I remember that one."

"It should have been a sign we wouldn't last."

"That happy, huh?"

Moving my hand to her ankle, I slide it farther when she doesn't move away. "Mistakes and paying the price."

I look her way when her hand matches my movements on my leg. We're both still, our gazes steady on each other. The bubbles are starting to dissipate, and I can't take my eyes off her. Wrapping my hands around both her ankles, I tug gently causing her to slide down just a little. It takes her by surprise and she bursts out in a laugh. "You better not, Everest. Paybacks are hell."

I tug a bit more, her mouth going under as her arms fly out to grab hold of the edge. I don't give her time and pull all the way. She disappears under as the water and the remaining bubbles drain over the edge. When she pops up, I have her on my legs. Her mouth opens wide, matching her eyes. "Oh my God. I can't believe you just did that."

Twisting to the left, her hand misses my arm and hits the water, splashing some onto her face. She huffs and splashes as she scoots back. I'm too busy laughing to care about getting wet. I'm in a bath for fuck's sake. I kind of expected to get wet. But my laughing ignites her temper.

Singer Davis fired up is a sight to see. Her eyes blaze with passion that she tries to restrain, to hide from the world when it's what should always be seen.

"I'm going to get you, Everest. When you least expect it." Her threats are wrapped in laughter, but then something comes over her, maybe the realization that our bodies are exposed if we look through the crystal waters.

She slides through the water and rests her arms on the side facing out the window. The tub is too large. It could fit four people, but I wish it were smaller. I wish it was like the one I grew up with where our bodies would be wrangled together and my arms would be wrapped around her, holding her close.

I test the waters of her emotions and touch her back, letting my fingers run down her spine. She glances over at me but returns her attention to the city outside.

It's not a view I take the time to appreciate often, but when I attempt to now, the beauty before it eclipses it in every way. "The view is stunning."

She continues to stare out the window, her gaze lost in the distance. "It is, isn't it?"

"I'm not referring to the city." Seemingly caught off guard, she looks at me. "Yes, you. You're very beautiful." She looks down and all I want her to do is look up. "Something is wrong with the world that you don't feel it, that you don't feel beautiful on the inside. Why is that?"

"You can have any woman you want, Ethan, but somehow I've been caught in your web. You're making my head spin, but my heart already feels like it's held captive."

"I will never hurt you."

"I can't think clearly around you. I shouldn't tell you this. Being upfront with you so early into . . . *us*, but I'm not good at hiding my feelings." *Oh.* This time she comes closer. Her breasts full and weighted even in the water though her breath floats to the surface of her lips—heavy.

"You don't have to hide your feelings with me."

"You ask me why I don't see things the way you do—"

"No. I asked why you don't see yourself the way I do."

The smallest of smiles appears, but it's there. The tips of her nails walk across my thighs and higher over my stomach. Her legs are brought around until she's straddling me. She's farther back than I'd like, but I need to find patience in the moment. She continues and says, "You treat me as if I were you, but I don't have the same power you carry into a room."

"You do. You're just not paying attention. You don't need the daiquiri douches or the Chump."

"What power do I have, Ethan?"

"Can't you see the power you have over me?"

Moving of her own accord, our bodies entangle in dangerously sexual territory. "If I have these so-called powers over you, why didn't you kiss me that Sunday after the pub or when we said goodnight at my place?"

"I kissed you last night. I kissed you tonight."

"You *claimed* me, Ethan. There's a difference."

Her words are a sucker punch to my heart. She's right, but I'm the asshole being called out on it, and it makes me feel like shit. "True. I'm sorry."

"I don't want you to be sorry. I want it to be real."

I thought I was wearing my heart on my sleeve. I wasn't. Not really. Not like she is now. She exposes herself in ways I used to before I was burned for doing the same. I don't want to be the one she remembers burning her. "It is real. It was, for me, but it was also a mistake I made, something I shouldn't have done in front of people."

"Why? Are you embarrassed to be seen with me in public?"

In public.

She's got it all wrong. So wrong. My breath comes harsher when I gently take her by the waist and confess what I know I should hold back. "Never." She starts to slip away but my grip tightens, holding her in place. "God, no. I would kiss you all the time if you were mine—in public, in private, inside, outside, and all over your body shamelessly."

"But you just said—"

"I've been betrayed before. I'm dealing with shit from my past, so I have trust issues, and as much as I want to get to know you, I can only let you in so far right now." I stare into her eyes, wondering how far I can go, how far I can open up. *Do I mention the case?*

Her hands flatten on my chest, and she leans down putting her cheek against mine. Whispering, she says, "I see how you struggle, how you carry the weight of life on your shoulders. I'm not here to cause trouble or damage you in any way. Keep your secrets if that helps ease your mind, but know"—she lifts up to look into my eyes—"I will never betray your trust."

My hand covers her right one. "I know you won't. Let's just take things slow if we can."

"By slow, you mean not being in a tub naked together?" The corners of her pretty lips tilt into a smile.

"Not that slow. Will you stay the night?"

"I'll stay."

Fuck, she's amazing. I reach up and grab her by the back of the head, my other arm wrapping across her shoulders to spin her under me. With her body pressed to mine underwater, I kiss her lips as laughter escapes.

I want to fuck her so badly, a craving that consumes me daily. She's naked beneath me, and I can't have her. The torture batters my soul.

Her fingers weave into my hair, and she pulls me to her. "I want you, Ethan."

Dollar signs don't shine in her eyes. I see nothing but sincerity. "I want you, Singer." Is she worth taking a risk again? Opening myself up to being used? Would she do that? I kiss her cheek and then lean my head against the same spot. Her skin is so soft, her hands so gentle.

I drop my head to her shoulder. I was prey to Dariya. *What am I to Singer?* I trust her. I do. Maybe it's wrong, but my heart is beating, pounding to be with this woman. I feel like me for the first time in forever. She accepts me for who I am with no expectations of more. Do I tell her? Do I expose my vulnerabilities and open myself to possible hurt? Do I kiss her and risk bursting the bubble that protects us, protects this moment and the innocence that created it? *For Singer, I do.* "Leaving that fire escape, walking away from you that day was the biggest mistake I've made in years."

"Why did you leave? Why did you leave me for her?"

I lower my gaze, feeling shame rolling through me. I look toward the window. "I don't know. It was like the moment passed us by, this bubble that surrounded us popped in an instant."

"It didn't for me."

Looking over at her, I say, "You had enough hope for both us back then, but I lost faith."

She's not embarrassed or shy, but confident as she sits on my lap and takes my face in her hands. "We don't have to change the world in one night."

Sitting up, I settle her where I want her to be. She sucks in a quick breath. "One night with you will change me."

"Maybe this is our second chance."

"You make a convincing argument. I always thought you'd be more reserved when it came to sex."

"There's something about you I trust."

I laugh. "I'm probably the last one you should trust. Haven't you heard?"

"No, I haven't heard. Why can't I search your name online? What will I find, Ethan?"

"Lies." I look away. "*Some truths.* Some lies."

"Don't shut down on me. Please. I'm here," she says sitting up, her perfect breasts fully above water for the first time, one of her hands tapping gently on my chest. The location warms over my heart, and the beat in my chest is strong. "There's no hiding when we're like this. You think this connection we feel is only physical. Physical attraction may be the reason you kissed me, but it was in here that we bonded. Don't discredit us. Don't treat me like you treat some woman hanging on your every word at a bar. I've kept my distance for so long in hopes that when the time was right, we would have another moment and it wouldn't evaporate into thin air. So stop trying to end us before we even begin."

I want to believe her so badly. In an ideal world, this would be easy. I'd kiss her. We'd date. We'd fuck. Make love. Go out for dinner. Stay in and watch movies. Normal dating stuff. But I don't live in an ideal world. I touch her cheek and look into her eyes. "You're too beautiful to be dragged into so much ugly."

When her fingers wrap around my wrist, she says, "What if I come willingly?"

"Then you're a fool."

"Then call me foolish because I'm taking my chances." She leans down, her nipples brushing against my chest, and she kisses me.

And then I kiss her right back.

16

Ethan

Lips that taste this good should be forbidden. We leave the water behind, and I wrap her in a towel. Standing in the middle of the bathroom, she shivers, so I kiss her until she's heated and a sinful pink creeps over her chest. Her body gives her mind away. Wicked words from her mouth may elude me but her body exposes her lustful thoughts. I scoop her up to a delighted squeal and carry her into the bedroom.

Just before I set her down, I ask, "What do you want, Singer?"

"What *do you* want?" She bites her lip and waits as if I'd ever turn her away.

"You."

She kisses me, but I have plans, plans that involve her body molding to mine as we fuck. I kiss her quick, eager to get to the action by tossing her on the bed and capturing her towel.

"Ethan?" Her protest leads to laughter as she lands.

She is naked before me, and the game I was playing no longer interests me. *She does.* My muscles tense. My cock hardens. My heart clenches as my gaze roams her body. In awe of her beauty, my body stills as I stare. She's my Aphrodite. Goddess of Beauty. "All's fair," I mumble, trying to pretend she doesn't affect me like she does—deep down to my core.

I strip my towel from my waist and turn to toss both behind me.

"I like the view." She slinks under the covers, shyness with a bold smile on her face.

I don't stare, though seeing a flash of her naked body makes me want more. "Touché, Ms. Davis."

"Will you get in bed with me?"

Her need to hide away bothers me. Does she really not know how stunning she is? How is that possible? How is she even single? She's witty and clever, gorgeous and perceptive. Her body is killer. Her eyes captivate my soul.

When I climb into bed, we lie there, sticking to our sides. Glancing over, Singer's gaze reaches the window and she stares out into the inky night. The room is dark, the windows of the skyscrapers outside lit up like little stars. When she turns back, a small smile appears.

This is what I've been missing. I knew it a year ago and ignored this deep desire. Now it courses through my veins. She courses through my soul. I care. I care about this woman. It threatens the firm foundation of my usually steady life, but I welcome it. I welcome the change. Before I lose myself in a confessional of commitments I shouldn't make to this beauty, I ask, "Do you like strawberries?"

"I do. I also like pretzels," she says, reaching to the nightstand where I had left a bag from my earlier excursion to the kitchen. "You don't mind crumbs, do you?"

"I do," I say, getting up to grab the champagne from the bathroom. "But not from you. Pretzel away."

She crunches, and I would normally cringe, but when I return she's so cute eating them I can't be mad. After sipping the champagne I hand her, she asks, "Why did you bring me here, Ethan? To champs and pretzels, to show off your fancy-schmancy tub and apartment? Or maybe"—she leans forward when I sit and taps the end of my nose—"you have something more scandalous in mind?"

"I have enough scandal in my life. How about I go with the other options?" Settling against the headboard, silence surrounds us. She discards the bag and turns to me, her fingers touching my chest as if she does it all the time.

A strange emotion fills my chest from seeing her in my bed. I've imagined her here so many times, but it all pales to actually having her here. Her presence lights up the whole room. Possessive. That's how I feel, and it's something I've not been allowed to act on until now.

Sliding down, I maneuver my arm under her. Her body molds to mine, her arm over my stomach, and one of her legs draped over mine. Whispering, she asks, "What are we doing?"

"Such a loaded question." I run my fingers over the smooth skin of her back.

"I like this."

"This?"

"All of it. Tonight. You. *You* being here."

The tips of her fingers stroke my neck and higher until her palm warms my cheek. "I like being here. I like *this* with you." Checking the time over my shoulder, she says, "It's almost eleven."

"Are you tired?"

"I usually go to bed around this time." Looking up at me,

she smiles. There's no fear in her eyes, no hesitation to be found. There's nothing but a green light for go.

Running my hand over her hip, I marvel how the very act is more intimate because she's trusting. She's so trusting with me, in me.

"We haven't eaten a strawberry, and you went all the way across the palace grounds to get them. That was quite a trek to set this all up."

"Very funny." I chuckle, but quickly grab hold of her hand and roll on top of her. I wiggle, and her legs part for me, allowing me to settle between them. My hard against her soft. Kissing her quick, I say, "I think you're right. I think we should eat strawberries."

I reach for one as I hover over her. When I turn back, my breath escapes in a harsh release. She stuns me in this moment, her beauty wrapping me up in twisted feelings that started in my gut and have taken my heart hostage. This isn't as casual as I've led her to believe. This means something, more than I kidded myself to believe. But tonight feels too good. *She* feels so good. I take a risk that feels like a dare, daring myself to take what I want.

I've been with women, plenty of them, but Singer is . . . she's different and there's no denying this means so much more than a quick fuck or a one-night stand. *Nicolina thinks I love her. Do I?*

Exhaling slowly, I know I need to get out of my head and back to what's right in front of me instead of thinking through everything. Touching the berry to her skin, she sucks in a breath. I smile, and in a low voice I remind her, "Breathe, Singer."

Her nipples are pert under the sheet, causing my breath to match hers. *Why am I nervous?* I'm never nervous. I'm always in control. I am in control now. I blow across her skin where the juice glistens. The strawberry moves slick, dipping in and following the contours of her collarbone. My eyes meet hers before I lower and touch my tongue to her, licking the sweetness from her skin.

Her hips move against my cock, and I press right back. I want to sink inside her, forgetting who I am and the life I've created. I want a redo with this woman. I deserve it, just like I deserve the truth to unchain me.

I've lost touch with that guy Singer met a year ago. The one who knew who he was and where his life was going, the one who saw a beautiful and intriguing woman and tried to kiss her on a fire escape. But when she looks at me, I see him reflected in her eyes. I can almost feel him inside me under her gaze. She makes me want to be that man for her. God, I want be that man for her.

I want to be that man again *for me*.

The taste of her skin is sticky sweet, and intoxicating, a flavor that will linger long after she's gone. I toss the strawberry back into the bowl and start to devour her instead. I'd love to give her slow and steady, but not this time. Not possible the first time with this woman.

The woman tempts my body to do dirty things. My soul gravitates to her blind trust in me. The press openly talks about the *bad boy* I'm supposed to be, and her shy, vulnerable side definitely attracts that side. With Singer, I want to take what I want instead of asking. She brings out the devil in me.

Taking a deliciously pink nipple between my lips, I move my hand to the curve of her waist. My middle moves against her, her legs widening for me in a welcoming embrace. I'm so close to fucking her, even though I know I shouldn't. I know she shouldn't be here at all.

Lust.

Easy.

Betrayal.

My demise.

I close my eyes, squeezing them tight.

Fuck the past.

Focus on the present.

Nails graze against my scalp, and fingers caress my jaw, lifting it up. Looking up, even in the low light of the room, her eyes make me want to be everything for her. "Be here, Ethan. Stay right here with me." *How does she know I need those words to bring me back?*

She sees through me.

I think she always did.

Moving higher, I keep my body against hers and brush my fingertips over her cheek before kissing those red lips. Lowering my hand, I rub the inside of her thigh. Goose bumps rise under my fingers, her reactions an aphrodisiac, feeding my cravings for her.

Magnificence.

Acceptance.

Truth.

My beauty.

"I want to make you feel so good. I want you to feel how you make me feel."

She smiles, her finger tracing my upper lip. "I do. Look at me. Really look at me. I'm here. The quiet that steals your thoughts and causes you to shut down on me, I need you to fight it. I don't want to feel doubts when I'm with you, so I need to know I don't cause them."

"You don't. You make them better. When I'm with you, it's easier to believe there's still good in the world." She kisses me. Her hands are strong, wrapped around my shoulders, and they bring me back against her. With my fingers finding that sweet spot between her legs, I watch as her mouth opens, and a desire to fill it emerges.

The way she moves beneath me, the soft mewls, and her fingers pressing into my skin, I know she's already close, but I need more, more of everything with this stunning creature. I lean down to take her breath and make it mine. "I want you so bad."

"Then take me, Ethan." Her breath comes hard, her words punctuated on the tip.

I've always prided myself on self-control but my limits are shredded. I rest my forehead on her shoulder and enter her softness with two fingers, her warmth spreading through my body. My hips move, trying to push my release forth. My fingers fuck, and mewls become moans, a siren's call that sings to my core.

I need her to find that place that gives her mind peace and makes her body mine, so I watch her reactions, and feed her frenzy. I kiss her again and deeper, using my tongue to taste her orgasm just as she peaks. When I release her lips, my name tumbles off her tongue, and I'm locked in a tight embrace.

"I want you so much," she says, her words pulsing through like her pussy is around my fingers.

Reaching over, I pull the drawer open and grab a condom. I hate to ruin the moment, so I'm fast. Once covered, I'm over her and positioned. Wild eyes beg for more, and I lean down to kiss her as I push in. My head drops down as her heat envelops me, searing me, easing my soul from the daily burdens. My mind focuses on her— pinpointing every gyrate that elicits a moan, every scrape of her nails that urges me on. "You feel . . . you're amazing, Singer."

I want to fuck. I want to thrust and pound.

Restrain. I keep the reminder on a loop as I make love to her slowly. She deserves love. It's easy to get lost in this woman with her intrigue and smiles. Her honesty and innocence. Her body moves with mine and then urges me for more. I give in and move on instinct to feel—*God, she feels so good.*

Hands roam freely over my back and squeeze my ass. I push up higher and thrust while watching her. When she opens her eyes, a sly smile rolls across her lips, and she murmurs, "I want more."

I fuck her with my mind and my body, my soul bonding to her angelic being. I fuck and I fuck until she's crying my name in completion, as if another name will never be uttered from her lips. I fuck until I lose this world and live in hers, the blackness full of stars. I reach out until I grab hold of hope again, falling back to reality.

"Ethan?"

Opening my eyes, hers are already trained on me. "Yeah?"

The palm of her hand presses to my cheek, and she says, "You feel so good."

Staring into the sun has a way of making you look inward. Her light of blinding purity penetrates the icy walls I constructed to protect my heart, and they begin to melt at her feet. Stealing one more glance, I now see. I see how she so easily accepts me. The gold flecks in her eyes shine in the dark, just like her sincerity. I tilt my head down and kiss her shoulder. "You've made me believe again."

Her nails gently scrape through the hair behind my ears. If I weren't so caught up in awakening emotions, it would tickle.

"Believe in what?" she whispers.

"In living this life to the fullest. You gave that to me."

A gentle giggle lifts from the lips and the sweetest pink threatens to cover the light freckles on her cheeks. "That sounds like a heavenly experience."

"It was." My heart thuds against my chest and I wonder if she can feel it. I discard the condom quickly and pull her close until she's tucked against me. "I'm afraid I'm not going to be able to let you go come sunrise."

Squirming around until she's comfy, she takes a deep breath and exhales, her body free from tension. "That's okay," she replies sleepily. "We can sleep long past sunrise. Tomorrow is Saturday."

I'm fading fast, peace washing over me as my eyelids grow heavy. "Good point, Singer Davis."

A sweet little kiss is pressed to my chest, her voice growing in distance. "Good night, Ethan Everest."

17

Singer

Life is blissful.

But I try really hard to keep my happy sighs contained. I don't want to scare Ethan and have him thinking I might be some crazy girl with lofty intentions. That's the thing with him. He's temperamental. Not how I originally took him, but the year has changed him. I didn't know him at all last year, but the wide smile I saw that day has faded over months. Noticeably.

Standing in the living room of this huge apartment, I wonder who tried to extinguish the fire I saw in his eyes the first time we met. Who turned it from a flame to a flicker? From what he's shared tonight, can I ignite him back to life?

He has trust issues, but he seems to want to trust me. *Why?* How am I different?

This castle is amazing, but even with him in the other room, I feel so alone in the expansive space. Does it affect him the same way? It seems so opposite of who he's struggling to be around me. The walls around his heart feel impossible to climb. He's built them to the sky. But maybe, for me, there's something hidden, a ladder or a secret staircase that will let me climb inside.

This isn't a home. This is a place to sleep and eat, stiff like the furniture—sterile—not lived in at all. My apartment has poor lighting, but it's cozy and comforting.

It's drafty here. I take a blanket draped over the couch like a designer placed it there when he moved in and it's not been touched since, and wrap it around me. The T-shirt I stole from a shelf in the closet is not enough to keep me warm.

"I thought we were going to sleep in?" he says across the stark light-colored wood floors.

"Did you miss me?" I turn to look his way.

"I did." Standing just outside the hall, his incredible upper body is on display. Sleep pants hang low, teasing me with that V made of muscle and dirty thoughts. I lick my bottom lip, and then say, "I'm forever trained to wake up early. My body has set its own alarm clock, but I was hoping you'd get more sleep."

"I slept. That's saying something." His words say everything and mean more to me than he knows. He comes to me, cups my face, and kisses me. "Do you want to try to sleep longer or can I make you coffee?"

"I slept soundly. Coffee please."

"You got it." Taking my hand, he leads me to the kitchen.

"I tried to figure out the coffee machine but it's serious business."

That makes him chuckle. "What would you like? A latte, espresso, café mocha? It can make practically anything without letting me screw it up too much."

Setting the blanket over a barstool, I slide onto the large island behind him. I make sure his shirt is pulled low protecting the back of my legs from the cold marble. "Ohh. A café mocha please."

"You got it." I watch as he takes milk from the fridge and adds it to the compartment before pushing a combination of different buttons. The machine is off and buzzing when he turns around with a smile on his face.

Content.

He looks content, and content looks so good on him. Casual and relaxed, the burdens he carries not currently a weight on his shoulders. His ease comforts me. When he touches my knees and slides his fingers underneath to tickle, I laugh before I'm pulled to the edge, my legs around his middle. I lift and cross my ankles behind his back and take him by the face. "I like you, Ethan. I hope you're okay with me telling you."

"I'm glad to hear it. I like you too. A lot."

His hands warm my hips and if I'm not careful, he's going to have me orgasming right here on his kitchen island, so I kiss him because nothing sounds more amazing than that right now. Warm hands slink under the T-shirt and around my ass. I'm bare, but he brings me closer until I'm pressed against him.

My body wants his hands all over. I stopped worrying about what he thinks and just let him feel, allowing myself to feel everything he wants to do. When he pushed them inside me last night, he made me come so fast.

I don't think I'll last long now, either. Everything about him—from his body to his lips to his words and the way he looks at me—it's as if he was designed to be my weakness.

I will give in to him every time.

Damn him.

The machine chimes and Ethan pulls back. I like that I affect him. I like watching his chest rise and fall faster than before. I like that he's disappointed we were interrupted. "You, Ms. Davis, were saved by the bell."

"Saved from what?" I ask as he turns to retrieve the coffee.

"From being ravaged right here on this cold counter."

"I'm not happy one bit about being saved now that I know ravaging was on the table." *Literally and figuratively.*

He sets the tall mug down next to me. "The table can be arranged." We both look at the long dining table nearby. "If you're into that sort of thing."

"I could be tempte—"

Before I finish my sentence I'm scooped into his arms and carried to the long table. It's wooden and appears old, but I'm sure he spent a fortune on it like everything else in this penthouse. I'm set down and the blanket is retrieved. He spreads it out and then lifts me on top of it. "We don't want to risk splinters."

"That's for sure." Our gazes meet. Our smiles lighten. The intensity brewing between us builds as he leans forward, resting his hands on either side of me. Leaning back on my elbows, I close my eyes right before our lips touch. The pressure is light, the feel matching the morning as the sun rises outside the picturesque windows.

My legs are spread, and his fingers gliding up the inside of my thigh. The air is thick with desire, the whole apartment feeling a few degrees hotter. "I think you might even be sexier at sunrise than you are at midnight. I might have to hold on to you for a few days just to see the variance."

"Like the hours, it's not about the minutes that make them up, but the moments that make them memorable." Sitting up, I kiss him. I kiss him because this man is almost too handsome to look at, and his sweet words are arrows of beauty straight to my heart.

When our lips part, he inhales and I think he takes a piece of me with him. "You make me want to experience every second of your day." The heat of his hand moves to press on my most sensitive area and his fingers begin to circle. My breath is jagged on the tail end of a sharp intake. I lie all the way back, but keep my eyes open, staring at the way he bites his lip as he watches his hands move over me.

When his gaze lifts to mine, I can't find the normal troubles in his expressive eyes. I suck in a breath. He allows me room to feel instead of think. He allows me to be the woman he believes me to be. Pliable to his touch, but reacting to every coax and caress, I whisper, "I want you inside me."

"Say it again, Singer. Just for me."

"It's only for you." I push my hair back, feeling restless from the cravings he's awakening. I repeat it, quieter and heavier this time, just for him again. "I want you inside me, Ethan."

He pulls the blanket toward him until my knees near the edge, and then kneels before me. "Can you stay still for me?"

I shake my head well aware of my limitations when it comes to this man. "No."

His laugh is deep, buried in his chest. "Well, try. All right?" This time I nod. "Just lie there and enjoy."

"What about—"

"Shh." A large hand takes ownership of my stomach. "I want to do this for you. Will you trust me?"

"I do trust you," I whisper, but it's so quiet I doubt he heard. Closing my eyes, I want to silence my racing thoughts.

With his mouth between my legs, my body feels combustible. I've never felt more vulnerable than I do right now. This is new.

The vulnerability.

The position.

The man.

The relationship.

I rest my arm over my eyes, hoping to block out my fears. What if he finds out that he's the first? Should I be doing something? *Oh my God.* My eyelids close as my back begins to arch. I reach for his head and grasp at his hair, needing something to hold on to, but I need something solid, so I reach to the sides and hold the edge of the table with both hands before I float away.

Ethan secures me to the blanketed surface, but my hips buck involuntarily to the swift swirling of his tongue. As soon as his fingers slide inside, I'm lost to the same oblivion, my body tensing, my voice not my own when I cry his name in ecstasy.

I release the table and let my lifeless body lie in recovery while he kisses up my stomach to my chest, tenting the shirt. When he kisses and licks, naughty man, between my breasts, I laugh. "You are positively great for me, but let me be great for you. Make love to me."

"Making love isn't for tabletops." An eyebrow is cocked. "But fucking is."

His warm breath sticks to my already dewy skin, and I know the words I chose don't mean the same thing as what I want. I may not have been with many guys, but I'm not inexperienced. I know what I like and what I want, and with him I welcome the sexual onslaught. My guard is down, so I whisper, "Fuck me, Ethan."

Not two minutes later, his arms have caged me as he leans above me, thrusting. That bottom lip is still trapped beneath his teeth. His eyes are closed and his muscles strained with tension. There's so much beauty in the pain written on his handsome face. That I cause this man to fall to his knees turns me on even more.

I close my eyes and my back lifts to lower my hips as he gets a better grip, using my body to drain away his burdens. His release comes fast and is punctuated with a groan of pure ecstasy.

The weight of his body presses down on me and he relaxes. "So good," he mumbles. "So damn good."

He doesn't stay long enough. When he stands, I lift back up on my elbows and ask, "Is it wrong that I don't feel any guilt about this?"

"Fuck, no. You shouldn't feel any guilt. What's the fun in having sex if you can't enjoy the pleasure of it?"

I close my eyes and lie back down. "Good, because I feel so damn amazing right now."

"Do you normally feel guilty?" Coming back to the table, he sits on a chair and runs his hand over my breasts and lower.

"Kind of."

"Why do you feel guilty?"

Fingertips dip between my lower lips and I exhale harshly. "I was always told to save myself . . ." My lids close and my body begs for more.

"For what, Singer? Save yourself for what?" Angling around, one of his hands steadies my thrusting hips, wanting more already, wanting more again.

"For marriage or at least keep my number of partners low."

"Fuck that." Two fingers slip into me, his thumb pressing delicious circles over my clit.

"Oh God." I force my body down, my mind struggling to hold on to the conversation we're having.

His lips are at my ear, whispering, "If someone doesn't

want to marry you because you enjoyed life before you met, they don't deserve you, baby." He kisses me, stealing the moan of pleasure right from my mouth.

Clenching.

Tightening.

Blissful relief.

When my breath steadies and I open my eyes, he asks, "How do you feel right now?"

"I've never felt this good."

"Good. That's how you should feel after a night of making love." His shoulders are broad, the muscles of his shoulders and arms defined by confidence. As his hands roam over my middle, his eyes alight with mischief.

I want to enjoy him in his sexy glory, but I'm still stuck on the table with the words "making love" dancing through my head. *Yes. Ethan. Love.* I feel it so much in the afterglow.

"Hey, beautiful?"

"Yes?"

"Let's go."

"What? Where?"

"Let's get cleaned up. I'm taking you to breakfast. You do eat breakfast, right?"

Shrugging, I reply, "Sometimes."

"Well, with me you do." He takes my hand and I wiggle off the edge.

I hop to the floor and grab that fancy coffee he made me. One sip. Two sips. He's waiting, but smiling. Three sips. "What? It's really good. I could get used to waking up like this every morning."

That receives laughter packaged in lighthearted happiness, something I haven't seen on him since he walked into that party with a case of Heineken under his arm. It looks good on him.

I hang back and watch him walk into the bathroom. Damn good from all angles. He peeks back out, and says, "Come on. I'm going to wash you from head to toe, taking my time."

Rawr.

He doesn't have to tell me twice.

"WHAT?" Ethan asks, looking up at me.

With a fork in the air and piece of pancake hanging from it, I'm in awe. "Nothing."

"Then why are you staring at me?"

"I'm impressed."

"With?" He eats the dangling pancake.

Thank God, because it was about to fall, and I have no doubt after sitting across from him for the last ten minutes that he would eat it right off the table if that happened. "I don't think I've ever seen anyone eat so much food so fast before. You do realize I'm not going to steal it?" He laughs, so I add, "And this isn't a race, right?"

Another chuckle comes while he's chewing. He takes a few big gulps of orange juice then says, "I have two brothers. Back then they played year-round sports. If I didn't eat fast, they'd take it. It's only breakfast that became a competition. Our mother would kick our asses if we tried to inhale our dinner."

"Are you the youngest, middle, or oldest?"

"I'm in the middle. We're all two years apart. My oldest brother lives in LA. My younger back in Houston near my folks." He looks down, the subject clouding the happier expression he was just wearing.

"Do you see them?"

"Not often. My younger brother came to visit twice since I've been here. My older brother is busy with work."

"Are you close?"

"Decently. Closer to my brother in Houston. As I said, my older brother is busy."

"I'm an only child."

"Yeah? What's that like?"

"It's a lot of attention for one person, and lonely all the same. That's why Melanie and I are so close. She's also an only child."

"It's good you have each other."

"Yeah." I try a new topic. "How long have you lived in that apartment? Or do I call it a penthouse?"

That doesn't seem to ease the strain in the crinkles of his brow. The fork is set down and he wipes his mouth with a paper napkin he pulls from the dispenser on the table. "Whatever you want to call it is fine."

"What do you call it?"

"Both. Depends who I'm talking to."

"Why?"

"I don't know. Just seems if you're in a position of power, people respect you when you use terms that fit the image they want to see."

"Last night at dinner, Chip was trying to land a meeting with you." I pause, searching his eyes for answers to questions I don't feel comfortable asking, especially with the hard lines of his face when he's deep in thought like now. He doesn't scare me though. I'm determined to keep those quiet moments he drifts into away while he's with me, easing some of his burdens for a bit. I clear my throat and ask, "If I search your name online, what will I find?"

When his gaze shifts my way, his napkin is set on top of the empty plate and he rubs his hands over his face. "Two lawsuits and a lot of photos of me with various women, headlines about drugs, alcohol, and my ex-girlfriend."

Wow. "I wasn't expecting that."

"What were you expecting?"

The check is set on the table. "A sex tape leak or caught yachting with the royals in the South of France. Maybe that you broke an arm while trying out for the major leagues. A long trail of discarded hearts left in your wake. My mind has gone crazy with all the things I've imagined you didn't want me to see. So no, I wasn't expecting drugs or lawsuits."

"Now I feel like a disappointment," he jokes while taking my hand.

"You're anything but that."

"You give me too much credit, Ms. Davis."

"I'm starting to think most people don't give you enough, Mr. Everest."

"I think the same about you." He sets his black card on the check tray and the waitress walks by, scooping it up.

The tips of our fingers mirror together, and he says, "Especially Chip Newsom. Is he as bad as he seems?"

"Worse."

"I suspected as much." The receipt is returned and Ethan stands, tucking his card back into his wallet. "How about a walk in the park?"

"Sounds romantic."

"You know me. Mr. Romantic." He's laughing at his words like they're a joke. Contrary to what he said, I don't know him like I want to, and what he doesn't realize is that I do want to know him. I want to know everything about him.

"You are romantic."

"I think eating you for breakfast on my table might prove differently."

"That was good, so good," I sigh. "But you making me coffee, now that was romance at its finest."

"And here I thought you would say letting you eat pretzels in bed was what won you over."

I take his hand in mine and lift it to my lips. I kiss it once, twice, three times for luck, and say, "Eh, it wasn't about the pretzels, though that was a perk. It wasn't even about our activities."

"What is it about, Singer?"

We stop in front of a department store where we pretend to window-shop while I give his question more thought before answering. The dress on display is gorgeous but I know by the avenue I'm on that it's outside my budget. Catching his eyes on me in the reflection of the glass, I say, "It's always been about that almost kiss. That is what romance novels are written about or what makes a movie worth watching until the end. An almost kiss that changed the course of two lives. That moment in time was serendipitous."

"And yet, here we are." Here we are, on a crowded Manhattan sidewalk, his hands cupping my face, our eyes closed with our lips pressed together—Kissing in public.

18

Ethan

"What the fuck were you thinking?" Reegan stands with his back to me. His arms are crossed and his stare penetrates the glass. Pissed mode. I've only seen it directed at other people before. Now his anger is all on me.

"I wasn't thinking. I was feeling. For the first time since this whole fucking mess started, I was feeling again, and I'm not going to stop."

Squinted eyes are directed on me. "What do you mean by that?"

Sitting in my lawyer's office at four thirty on a Saturday afternoon is not how I planned to spend my day. But it's New York City, and gossip travels fast. "Can you shut it down?"

"I already did to an extent, but they told me they're checking with the other department to find out if the story sold from there."

"How can they sell a story they won't carry on their own site?"

"They carried it. I got it off."

"Fuck."

"That's what I said. Ethan, we've talked about this—"

I raise my hands in protest. "Just stop there. Singer Davis can only improve my image."

"Singer Davis will be a casualty in this war. The photos your ex-girlfriend sold may have been set up, but they exist, they're tangible and out there. I'm starting to think you're going to have to settle."

"I'm not settling. I refuse. I know the truth, and I'm willing to fight for it."

"Are you willing to walk away with nothing for that truth?"

I stand and walk to the door. "I'm willing to walk away from you right now."

"Ethan? You know the risk you're taking by seeing Ms. Davis."

With my hand on the door, I stop, and look back. "Remind me again."

"The press will dissect her entire life. If she has any skeletons in her closet—"

"They won't find anything. She's a good girl."

"The Bad-Boy Billionaire Preys on the Poor Girl Next Door. Or how about Ethan Everest Lures Innocent into Bedroom Drama?"

"First of all, those headlines really fucking suck. Don't give up your day job. Secondly, lures? I hardly lured her."

"Hardly?" he asks, raising his eyebrow.

"Why does talking *to you* about Singer make me feel sleazy?"

He waves me off and sits behind his desk. I come back and sit, realizing we need to work this out before I return to her.

He asks, "You seem to think you're still this regular small-town Joe."

"Houston is the fourth largest city in the U.S., so small town doesn't really apply."

"It's smaller than New York."

"Population wise only. I'll give you that."

"Whatever the fuck we're talking about, forget it. Everything that Dariya exposed, Singer Davis will be questioned about. Do you really want her walking her dog at the park and a reporter jumps out of the bushes to ask if she snorts coke or is a supplier for your drug habit?"

"See? Here's where I have the problem. You know I didn't do heroin or coke, or any other illegal drug that night—"

"What I know is the photos don't say that. Dariya may have set you up, but she did it with an end goal, and that goal is money. So you have two choices: settle when they come back with an offer or we fight and try to make over your image."

"I'm fine with my image. It weeds out the snakes."

"I think it brings out the snakes."

I laugh, but I'm not amused. "There's a lot of truth found in that statement." Wanting to leave before I'm late, I ask, "What do you suggest?"

"Give her what she wants—a payday. What's a million compared to the billions you might lose?"

"Settling is as good as admitting guilt. I'm not guilty. If I settle with Dariya, I don't just lose a million dollars , I lose Singer and my family's trust along with it."

"Is she that important? You're willing to fight this over a woman you don't know? That's what you're saying?"

"I'm saying I know her." I want to know her better. "I shouldn't have to hide her. She thinks I'm embarrassed to be seen with her. How shitty is that?"

"The case shouldn't be discussed outside of your legal team. You know that. So if you want to tell her details, she needs to sign a non-disclosure agreement first. I can have one drafted up today. Anyone you bring into your life should be signing an NDA."

"No way is she signing one. Singer is trustworthy."

"Again, I'll remind you, she better be trustworthy, or you, my friend, could be in the hole for a lot more than a million."

"She won't fuck me over. I know she won't. She's nothing like Dariya."

"Fuck her in public if you want. She's great for your image. But will you be happy when she's embroiled in this mess and her life is strewn across the gossip blogs? I'm recommending you shut Dariya down and focus on the bigger case. You settling won't play a part in fighting for your company. The drugs, maybe. But they can drug test you if they want."

"They're forcing me out." *What is he thinking?* "That could be financially disastrous for me. What are you thinking, Reegan? Are you on my side or theirs?"

A hard glare hits me. "I hope that's rhetorical. You may be paying me, but I stood by you when your friends decided to fuck you over, Ethan. You think they didn't try to keep me working for them? They did. So don't doubt my loyalty. I gave up a lot to stand by not only my friend, but what I believed was the right side of this wrong."

Our standoff simmers. He's right. He's been here. "I appreciate you standing by me. I just can't stomach the thought of paying Dariya a cent. Those photos ruined me publicly and created this nightmare. But catching her fucking my best friend . . . that was messed up. I lost a lot of faith in people after that." I blow out a deep breath. "Singer is my redemption. With her, I'm finally doing something right, putting my life back on the course I was supposed to be on."

Sitting back in his large leather chair, Reegan shakes his head. "You can't invest in a relationship right now, Ethan. Stay focused on building your business. You don't have time for the other stuff."

"The other stuff is what helps me through the days."

"I'm curious. Do you feel like she was a missed opportunity or does she help you forget about this mess for a while?"

Standing up, I walk to the window and look out over a city I once thought I could rule. I was naïve, blinded by the bright lights and attention. "Both." Honesty.

I hear the tap of papers being aligned behind me. When I turn around, he says, "We have two choices if you're going to pursue this. Make the relationship public. We'll have the world believing they're witnessing the next Camelot in the making. Or keep it behind closed doors and protect what you have until we are done with this legal mess." Looking up at me, he waits. When I don't say anything, he stands. "Tell me how to proceed."

Checking the time again, I need to get back. "Let me talk to her tonight."

"Call me tomorrow."

I head for the door again. "Do you ever take a day off?"

"No."

"Good. I want my money's worth."

"You're getting it and more. Now fuck off," he says, laughing. "I have work to do."

"Hey, Reegan?"

"You still here?"

The door is open. "Thanks."

"You're welcome. Save the mush for Singer, and go."

"Outta here. Bye."

Not five minutes later, I get a text from Reegan. The public photo of Singer and me kissing this morning has been squashed. *Thank fuck.*

Leaning forward in the car, I ask, "Aaron, what do you think of Singer?"

The smile I see in the mirror grows, but his sunglasses hide his eyes. "What do you think of Singer?"

I sit back and look out the window, pondering my feelings and everything that was said a few minutes earlier in Reegan's office. I was honest with him. I can be open with Aaron. "I like her."

"I can tell you like her." I glance his way, and even though I don't know if he's looking at me behind his Ray-Bans, I feel like he is. "Do you mind if I ask what it is you like about her?"

I'm surprised by the question. I've not had to think about it. I just feel it when I'm around her. No need to rush to a conclusion, so I think back from the first time I saw her to this morning lying on my kitchen table. "Everything."

His smile grows. "She's a remarkable woman."

"Yes, she is." I glance out the window and then confess, "She thinks she's just a challenge to me, someone I want to conquer, and nothing more."

"I imagine that's not your intention." His sunglasses are off and his eyes are questioning mine.

"She challenges me, but she's so much more."

"Maybe you should be telling her that."

He's right. "I hear ya. Loud and clear." Looking as the shops pass by, I say, "Stop at a flower shop."

The smile is back. "Smart man."

I roll my eyes, but laugh. Despite my lack of trust in most people, I trust Aaron implicitly.

Within the hour, the car is waiting curbside. Taking Reegan's advice, I stay inside the vehicle, but it irks me to see Aaron and Singer laughing when she walks out of her apartment. Irks might be too strong. I like that they get along. Aaron may be my driver, but he's also my friend, even if we keep things more centered on business. So maybe jealousy fits better than irks.

She slips in the back seat with me, and I kiss her the second the door closes. Laughter trickles through the car, music to my ears, and then she asks, "Did you miss me?"

"I did. More than you'd believe if I told you."

"Tell me anyway."

"I missed you, Singer Davis."

Wrapping her arms around me, she hugs my neck and I embrace her by the waist, sliding her onto my lap. "I missed you, too, Ethan Everest."

Smiling, I close my eyes and enjoy the feel of her in my arms. *Feeling.* It's all about feelings—instinctive and natural —when I'm with her. I could get drunk on the emotions consuming me. All for her.

Singer is the opposite of Dariya in every way.

With Singer there are no hidden agendas. No games. She's open and kind. No charades or façades. She's the same woman I met that first day and just as intriguing. I want to impress her. I want to win her heart with my secrets exposed, with honesty flowing freely between us. I want to make her feel how she makes me feel.

I don't see only a pretty woman sitting next to me. Her inner beauty is what draws me to her, making me want to be better for her.

As we drive through traffic, I notice her outfit. "You changed clothes."

"I thought I'd put on a skirt for you."

"What you're wearing isn't as important as what you're not wearing." I rub my hand over her thigh and rest it just below her hip. "Just sayin'." I'm tempted to go under that skirt, but Aaron doesn't need to see my girl.

"I don't want you to close down on me or to upset you. I'm trying to understand what's happening between us. So can I ask you something personal?"

I hold her hand, our fingers weaving together. "You can ask me anything."

"I was planning to take you out, treat you, but I think this morning seems to be an exception, not the rule you live by."

"What are you saying?"

"As soon as we got back to the apartment, you were pacing and stressed and had to leave after you made your call. I don't want to be a source of stress for you. You've said things were complicated. Did I make them worse for you?"

"You make things better for me. But we do need to talk about what's going on before this . . ." I take a breath, not wanting to freak her out. I don't want to stress her. I'm happy to carry that weight for the both of us. "We should talk tonight. Unfortunately, until we do, we shouldn't be going out in public."

"But we were out before—the pub, the baseball game, this morning . . ."

"Since things have progressed between us, and please believe me when I say, I'm glad it has, we are a media liability for my cases."

"Cases? Lawsuits?"

"Yes." My throat feels thick, not wanting to do this now in a car with Aaron listening. "Can we talk in private later?"

"Yes. That's fine." Her eyes dart to the front, and I know she understands. "I was actually thinking we could drop you off at the apartment and I could run a few errands with Aaron."

"Of course. You have the car at your disposal."

"About that."

I laugh. "Yeah?"

"I was also thinking we could give Aaron the day off tomorrow. If that's okay with you."

"Okay."

Although I readily agree, I can tell she's compelled to justify it and I'm fascinated, so I let her. "He works a lot of hours and even though I don't know what he's paid, I'm sure he's paid well. He seems happy every time I see him so I'm assuming he's fine with the conditions of the job. It just seems like he probably hasn't had a day off in a while. Sunday is the day of rest, and since I plan to be resting with you all day, he can have a day for himself."

"I have baseball tickets for tomorrow. Playoff tickets."

Her eyes are bright and my favorite shade of mischief green. "*Yeaahhh*, about that—"

I burst out laughing. "What now?"

"What if you gave the tickets to Aaron?" I shoot a glare into his gleeful eyes in the mirror. "We could watch the game at your apartment or even at mine. I make great Buffalo wings, and I'll get Heineken for you."

"And?"

"You're driving a hard bargain, aren't you?"

"I always drive hard when it comes to things I want."

She moves closer, and whispers, "What if I serve you those wings and beer naked? Will that convince you?"

It's funny how bargaining works.

She had me at the wings.

The beer was the cherry on top.

But her naked? "Deal."

Sitting back, quite pleased with herself, she asks Aaron, "I take it you heard all that?"

"Thanks, Singer."

My mouth falls open, and my arms go wide. "Really, man? What am I? Chopped liver back here?"

He shrugs. "She's got my back."

"She does in fact have that." I reach over, cup the back of her neck, and bring her close to kiss. "You have a big heart."

Her hands rub covertly over bigger parts of me. After a sweet kiss, she says, "If we have to stay in tonight, I look forward to making the most of it."

I slip my tongue past her eager lips and press in deeper, kissing her to show her how much I plan to make the most of tonight. "You're going to be my undoing in more ways than one, aren't you?"

"If I have any say in the matter."

With our foreheads pressed together, my voice is low, but my feelings are clear. And strangely enough, I don't feel an ounce of concern with that revelation.

This woman.

19

Singer

Aaron helped me find the local butcher, baker, and candle-stick maker. Okay, the last one was just a joke we had going while running our errands. Although, I did find a great-smelling candle for Ethan. I don't know if he likes candles, but I bought it anyway because although it's clear he has money to burn, and the penthouse, it seems he's missing some of the basics. He's missing the things that make a *pent*house a home.

That's an area where I can help. Not that he's asked for my help, and it's not like I'm moving in. I'm just buying a few things to make his apartment more homey for him.

When the car pulls up to the private elevator in the parking garage, Lars is standing tall, more like a guard than a doorman. He's still as intimidating as he was before. He opens my door and tells me to proceed to the elevator to go to the penthouse, and he'll bring everything upstairs after.

It's all so secret agent-y and I'm curious to hear more details from Ethan tonight, but for now, I push the button and do as I'm told. When the elevator door opens, Ethan's standing there—well-worn concert T-shirt, a little too tight around his biceps, but wow on displaying his hard body—worn-in jeans that are starting to shred at the knees and hang off that part of his body where I know that defined, muscular V is hidden. Black Adidas and day-old scruff on his square jaw, evident this morning, grown since then. Good Lord, this man sure knows how to make an impression.

With a roguish grin, he takes my hand and pulls me inside. "I've been waiting for you, Singer."

Before I can speak, he twirls me down into a dip and kisses me, stealing my breath and my heart right along with it. When I land firmly on my feet, I tap his band tee. "I love The Resistance."

The elevator door slides open to the penthouse. He starts to walk, but stops and smirks. Signaling to the hall, he says, "Come on. I have a surprise for you."

I take his hand and walk out. "Lars said he'd bring up the stuff I bought."

"Yes, don't worry. He won't disturb us. He'll set it in the hall and leave."

"Why do you have him?" I ask, truly curious.

"Because I'm worth a lot of money. When you come into that kind of money, you find you have more enemies than friends."

"With all those enemies, is the money worth it?"

"There are perks."

Looking around the place, I say, "Obviously, but what are the downfalls?"

He stops and turns to me. Rubbing my arms, Ethan replies so easily, "You don't trust many people and then discover most have an agenda, so I've been somewhat of an isolationist."

I love the feel of his steady and strong heartbeat as I rest my hands on his chest, but his words make me sad. He was the life of that party, the guy everyone wanted to talk to, including me. Just one short year later and people have tried to extinguish that life that lit up his eyes. "That's a big price to pay."

"I'm willing to pay if it means I have genuine people in my life. Quality over quantity."

I rest my head on his chest and whisper, "It's sad you have to choose one or the other."

Rubbing my back, he kisses the top of my head. "It is sad, but I'm not sad when I'm with you."

Whispering, I say, "I've chosen the same. I'd rather have one or two quality people in my life than a dozen fake friends."

"You have Melanie. She's a good friend to have in your corner."

"She's like my sister, so I'm in hers and she's in my corner. I'm also in your corner, Ethan."

"I won't take that for granted, Singer."

Glimmers of that once vivacious life reside in his eyes when he looks at me. I want to see him happy again. All the time, not just in our stolen moments together. Twirling out, I hold on to his hand and say, "Tell me about this surprise you have for me."

"How about I show you?"

"Even better."

We hurry to the bedroom, but he stops in the doorway. He says, "It's in the closet."

"Oh now you're letting me look in your closet?" I sass as I shimmy past him.

"Ignore the skeletons."

"Eh, we all have them." I open the door and my mouth falls open. It takes me a moment to compose myself. I point and start talking and then stop and catch my breath. "That's the dress, the one we saw in the window."

"It's yours." I turn back to find him leaning against the doorframe. Arms crossed. Eyes trained on me.

"You bought the dress for me? How did you know I liked it?"

"I saw the way you admired it."

I don't go to the dress. It will still be there. I go to the man instead, because his thoughtfulness is so overwhelming. He draws me into his arms, and I realize that his arms are a sanctuary, a safe haven when wrapped around me. "Thank you."

"My pleasure, but it comes with a condition."

Leaning back, I smirk, thinking I've just been set up for something sexual in return. Little does he know I'll happily oblige when it comes to being naked with him. I poke his ribs. "Lay it on me."

"I will, but that will be later." He winks and I giggle, but then his bashful side comes out, and my heart melts, watching him. "I have an event. I want you to attend with me."

"I thought I was a liability?"

"You're not to me, but I am to you."

Reaching up, I drag the tips of my fingers through the hair above his ears and ask, "Are you going to ruin me, Ethan Everest?"

His forehead finds mine before he slips to the side and whispers into my ear, "God, I hope not."

"What am I supposed to say to the offer of that pretty dress?"

"The dress is yours."

"What about you?"

"I'm yours," he replies, not as softly.

Mine? I need to see his eyes, so I lean back, finding the truth centered in the middle. "Privately or publicly?"

"Whatever you want, I'll be."

"As much as my first reaction is publicly, I don't want you to be anything other than happy. I don't want to cause more complications, and I don't want my life turned upside down. So tell me the pros and cons of us going to an event, a very public event from what it sounds like."

The apartment alarm sounds and he starts to leave. "That's Lars. I'll be right back."

I return to the closet, take the hanger from the hook, and carry the dress to the bathroom. I slip off my skirt and top and let the beautiful gown slide down over my body. Admiring myself in the mirror, the fit is keenly flattering. Then I hear, "Everything you wear looks incredible on you."

I don't have to check the mirror to know my cheeks are flaming a deep ruby. The flush is spreading because the way he looks at me is as if I'm the most beautiful woman he's ever seen. "I don't know if I'll ever get used to all the compliments you give me."

From behind, his hands slide around my waist. "This shade of purple brings out your eyes. They're vibrant."

"It's not because of the dress."

A response isn't needed. He knows how I feel about him. He asks, "Will you go to the event?"

"I'll go, but I don't understand exactly what I'm dealing with. I think we should go as friends, since you wouldn't be expected to attend alone. We'll just save the PDA for after the party."

"I'll take you however I can have you." He kisses my

neck. "But I need to warn you. I might get jealous from all the attention you're going to get."

"Don't worry. I'm sure I'll be too busy worrying about all the attention the ladies will be giving you to notice the attention paid to me."

He kisses my neck again and then licks the shell of my ear. Spinning in his arms, I ask, "Can I see your closet again?"

Surprise overtakes him. "I'm kissing you in what I thought was foreplay, and you want to spend time in my closet?"

"Yes," I reply, nodding eagerly.

"Fine, go ahead." He laughs. His laughter is hearty and rewarding. It makes me wonder if he has as many opportunities to laugh freely. "I thought you might like that. I was impressed when I bought the place."

I run from his arms and back into the closet. Spinning around, I say, "There's so much space. It's bigger than my living room and kitchen combined."

Following me, he stops in the doorway and watches, a soft, amused smile on his face. "Well, maybe you can move in." The words seem to slip out before he can stop them. Even in jest. We both look at each other. A few feet apart suddenly seem like a mile. He's too far away, and I'm not sure what to say. I can tell by how he shifts and looks away he's just as unsure as me. "You brought beer?"

"Yes. And wine, but the beer is for the game tomorrow."

"What else did you bring?" He shoves his hands in his pockets and shifts, something I've discovered he does when he's unsure of himself or how I might react. Not exactly nervous, but not completely confident. Makes me wonder if he was always this way, or whether it's something to do with his lack of trust in people. *Who hurt you?*

I want to loop back to the previous topic. I decide to not let it slide by without addressing. Not because I want him to feel uncomfortable, but because I want him to know he can say things about a future between us without ruining what we're slowly building together—a relationship.

With my hand on my hip, I address the elephant in the closet. "I know you don't approve of the location of my place, but I like the apartment itself. So even though I love your closet, it's safe for now." I walk past him. "Are you hungry? I'm starved."

"Starving."

A hard slap on the ass causes me to squeal and whip my head around. Rubbing my ass, my eyes are wide. "Wow. That kind of stung."

"I'm sorry. I didn't mean to hur—"

"Next time, do it during foreplay." I click my tongue and wink at him.

He mumbles, "Fuck, that's hot," as I head for the bathroom.

Letting the straps slide down over my shoulders, I look back just before I disappear into the en-suite. "I'd love a glass of wine."

"Your wish is my command."

From inside the bathroom, I call, "Keep that up and I might actually consider the closet offer."

Light. Sexy. Carefree laughter trails behind as he leaves the room. It's a wonderful sound. I hang the dress on the hanger and admire it once more before grabbing one of his neatly folded T-shirts and a pair of his boxer shorts and joining Ethan in the kitchen.

20

Singer

Two glasses of pinot noir are waiting on the white marble island when I enter.

"The Crowe Brothers?" he asks, eyeing my shirt.

"I liked the design."

"My brother sent me that shirt from one of their gigs in Austin. If you like The Resistance, I'll play some music by The Crowe Brothers. I think you'll like them." Ethan takes his phone, and within seconds music filters through the apartment though I don't see any speakers.

This place is so uber-fancy. I love it.

He's unloaded the bags. The contents cover the rest of the large island, and he seems to be taking inventory. "What are you making?"

"Spaghetti and meatballs." I look his way to catch his reaction.

When he smiles I do, too. "I love spaghetti and meatballs. It's been a long time since I've had it."

"I figured living in this castle in the sky all by yourself you might eat takeout a lot."

He pulls a pasta pot out from under the cabinet and sets it on a burner. "I actually eat out most nights. I have a lot of dinner meetings."

"Is that set in stone or would you like to eventually be home for meals?"

I'm not as sneaky as I thought. He uses the fancy pot filler to fill the shiny copper pot I suspect has never been used for something as basic as pasta. His eyes catch mine on him and he does a terrible job of hiding that wry grin that's forcing its way out. "I'd be home more if there were reasons to be."

I'm not one to generally hold back my thoughts, and I feel so comfortable around him, that I lean against the counter, and come right out and ask, "Do you want to get married and have kids one day?"

There's no flinching or cringing, and I love the smile that remains—genuine and sweet. "One day, I would. It's always how I saw my life."

"Is that why this place is so big?"

That makes him laugh, reminding me of the first time I saw him. Laid-back and magnetic. I hope I've contributed to this glorious side of him. "This was purchased out of ego and stubbornness." I start on the meatballs and let him continue telling his story. "My mom wanted me to buy a smaller place in SoHo. I wanted a bigger place with better resale. My more practical side. I saw this penthouse and my ego loved the exclusivity of the building and the entrance. But sure, I hope I find someone to live here with me."

"How long do you plan to stay if you're worried about resale?"

"You should always worry about resale, Singer."

"Not if it's your forever home."

"Do you want to live in an apartment for your forever home?"

"No," I reply, rolling a ball and coating it in breadcrumbs before setting it on a tray with the others. "I want to live in a home with shutters and a front porch, so I can sit out and wave to the neighbors or watch my kids play with the other kids on the street."

The water isn't boiling, but I swear I see a bead of sweat on Ethan's forehead. "I don't know if I'll ever be able to live like that." He comes to join me and sits on a barstool next to the tray.

"That's not appealing to you?"

"It is. So much about that image sounds serene. But like I said earlier, money of this magnitude excludes you from living in suburbia America on a quiet cul-de-sac of colonials. My kids will have security around them, at least at times. My wife will need protection. I can't take risks with the people close to me. The world is full of bad people, Singer. You need to know what's involved when you get involved with me."

Money didn't buy him happiness. It bought him a pretty cell to bide his time. He deserves more than a prison others have built for him. We all do. "Is that a warning?"

I want to make another meatball, but concern is etched in the lines of his brow and my stomach twists. He says, "I shouldn't have kissed you this morning on the street."

The twisting tightens. "Why?"

"There are photos. A blog picked them up. Fortunately, they were pulled before they spread to other sites."

Wait a minute. *What?* "Hold on." I set the meatball on the tray and wash my hands. When I dry them, I say, "Back up. Someone took a picture of us kissing?"

"Yes."

"Why? Why would they do that? Why would they want it?" He takes a drink of his wine and then offers me mine. I put the tray in the oven and take the glass, the hint not subtle. "It's probably best if I drink, right?"

"Probably."

I take a sip then say, "This goes back to not searching your name online. Am I correct?"

"You are."

"So the paparazzi follow you around and take photos, then sell them to online outlets?"

"Yes."

Anxiety ravages my stomach while my imagination goes wild. "Not to say you're not interesting, because I'm completely fascinated by you, but why are photographers following you around?"

"Eight months ago, maybe more, I was set up by my best friend and my girlfriend at the time. She took me to a party. Said it was a photographer friend visiting from Milan. The hotel room was a mess. Drugs everywhere. White lines across glass tables, bowls of weed, booze, the whole bit. I found a spot on the couch and started going through emails while my girlfriend proceeded to get high on everything they had to offer."

I watch as sadness comes over him and his gaze drops along with his head. "I trusted her. This was her life, her element, her friends. She always partied hard. I think she liked to show me off, to one-up her other friends—who was dating who, who snagged who, who fucked who. It was a game to them. That's fine. She could have her good time, and I could have a drink and not be bothered. This party in particular I didn't want to go to. She insisted. We even had a fight over it. I gave in to get her to calm down." The somber look in his eyes breaks my heart.

"That was a big mistake. I trusted her. We'd been to a ton of parties together. My friends. Her friends. I thought it was like any other night. But I was bored so I got up to leave and was harassed by her. She wanted to fight. I wanted to leave. She pushed a bottle of whiskey against my chest and I proceeded to get drunk. Another big mistake on my part."

"What happened?"

"I got drunk and fell asleep. Cops showed up. I was arrested. My girlfriend was nowhere to be found."

"What?" I ask in disbelief. "Where was she?"

"Fucking my best friend, Keith. I'd been friends with him since I was little."

I don't mean to gasp, but it comes anyway. "How'd you find out?"

He refills his wine glass and adds a little more to mine. "After Aaron bailed me out, I went over to her place to find out what happened. I walked in on her bent over the couch with Keith fucking her from behind. Understandably, everything fell apart, including half of his apartment by the time I left."

"That's horrible."

"The worst was still to come. Photos showed up online."

"Photos of me passed out with dusted cocaine nearby, the empty bottle of Jack." I reach over and touch his hand, wrapping it inside mine. *How could anyone be so underhanded and cruel to this incredible man?*

"Keith sent an email with the photos, my mug shot, and links to the online stories to the board of directors. Matthews received it and forwarded it to me. My ex-friend and ex-girlfriend had plotted my demise. Their plan was in motion. The cherry on top was reading about my ex-girlfriend pregnant with my baby in a story she sold for ten thousand dollars."

"Ethan," I say, my heart in my throat, aching for this man that's caught between anger and pain, "I'm so sorry." I'm not sure what to say so I offer what I can. I may not have any deep relationships in New York, but I can trust my friends. Ethan was abandoned with nowhere to turn. *Who purposely hurts someone like that?* It makes me admire him even more, because he still has a soul. That could destroy many people. "That's why you don't want pictures of us out there? They'll make you look bad?"

"They'll make *you* look bad. I'm used to it. I'll take the hit, time and time again, but I don't want them near you."

"I can take care of myself, Ethan."

"I know you can. But they're nasty. They're sharks looking for fresh meat. I can't sacrifice you like that."

"What will they do to you?"

"Every photo caught is ammo used against me. If I'm seen with multiple women then it appears I'm the same playboy they claim I am. The board of directors will find me unfit, and my ex will strengthen her case that I'm irresponsible and owe her damages."

"Damages? For what?"

"Apparently, for breaking her heart."

Taking the package of noodles, he opens them. By the slump of his normally strong shoulders, he still feels so burdened by what they did. I go to him, wanting to take away his pain, wanting to erase the betrayal he's trapped in the middle of. I hug him from behind and rest my cheek on his back. Reaching back around, his hand settles on my hip. I take the noodles and put them in the boiling water. "Doesn't sound like she has one."

He turns around. "I think that's the meanest thing I've ever heard you say."

Soft laughter wells inside me, and I wrap my arms around his neck. "I'm riled up, and it's the truth. She set you up and is now playing the victim. She can't possibly have a heart when she's out to destroy yours."

"True." Kissing my forehead, his arms tighten around my waist, and he holds me to him. "But she might be pregnant with my child."

I'm tempted to look up, wanting to see his eyes, but his hold on me won't allow me to budge. "Ethan?"

"Yeah?"

"You're not asking for my opinion on it, but I can tell you're wondering."

His breathing picks up, his chest expanding and returning. "I am. Your opinion matters to me."

"You having a child won't scare me away."

Our eyes meet with no space left to spare between our bodies. "What will, Singer Davis?"

"I'm stronger than I look."

"You look pretty damn strong to me."

"Faith will carry you a long way in life, Ethan."

"I think I've lost some along the way."

"That's okay. I have enough for the both of us," I say, reciting the text he once sent.

"I think you're amazing."

Lifting up on my toes, I pull him down and we kiss. Together we tend to the meal, as if we're having a normal night in. Nothing is normal about this man, least of all tonight, even if we are good at pretending we're a normal couple.

Garlic bread is slotted in next to the meatballs, and plates are pulled from the cabinet. A timer is set for each item, and then I ask, "If you don't mind me asking, what does your company do?"

"It's an online social media company. I developed it in high school but started the business while in college. It just kind of took off. It's publicly traded now, so I don't have a ton of say anymore, but I have rights."

"So you want the company?"

"No, I want my reputation restored. I have a dozen other companies now. I'm not going poor anytime soon."

"I know you feel alone, but you have people around you who care. I can tell how much Aaron cares about you."

"He's been good to me. He's loyal."

"He posted your bail."

"I had to call someone I could rely on, so I called the man I pay to be in my life."

Moving between his legs when he sits back down on a barstool, I rub his muscular thighs. "He would have been there for you even if you didn't pay him."

"That's why I sent him to you."

"You don't have to worry about me so much."

"I can't help it. Anyway, that's what friends do." And then he smiles at me, and it would be very easy to allow that smile to pass as genuine. But I think I know differently now.

I see the edges of pain in his eyes. I want to see his genuine smile, but I won't pretend and be lighthearted to achieve that. He just shared something very perturbing, and I want him to know he has another friend. "I'm sorry about what happened, Ethan. That must have been such a hard thing to go through."

"Still is." Rubbing my hand over his cheek, I lean in. His hands cover my ass and he brings me closer. "But I don't want to talk about them anymore."

"What do you want to talk about?"

"Us. I want to talk about us."

"Okay. Let's talk about us."

"I know it's early to be having a conversation like this, but as you now know, we have to decide what we are going to do or be. I like you. I don't want to hide that from you, but I'm not sure I'm ready to share you with the world yet."

"What are you saying?"

He kisses my cheek and leans back to look into my eyes. "If you feel the same about me, I want us to really try this relationship out."

"I care about you deeply, but are we rushing this?"

"Despite all my bad judgments the night I was set up, that wasn't my biggest regret."

"What was?"

"Walking away from you a year ago. I don't want to make that mistake twice."

This is fast and complicated, but I deserve someone who recognizes what he has, and by how his vulnerable side resides in the worry lines of his brow, he does. I would have kissed him last year, and I like being with him too much to walk away, so I say, "Then don't."

21

Singer

I like watching Ethan eat.

There is something so satisfying about it. He eats like there's no tomorrow. Looking up from his plate, he says, "This is amazing."

I finished a few minutes earlier and watch him. "You're just saying that because you're hungry."

"I'm saying that because this is delicious."

"Thanks. Can I ask you something about the press?"

"Anything."

"Why does the press want to bury you so badly?"

Setting his fork down, he wipes his mouth with a napkin, seeming to lose his appetite. "The press creates their idols, and then they want to destroy them all in the name of sales and ratings."

"You talk about wanting to be with me, but then you tell these stories like you're trying to scare me away. I'm lost when it comes to you, Ethan."

"I'm lost when it comes to you, falling faster with each passing day."

The weight of the conversation carries into the worries in his eyes. He stares at me, maybe wondering if I'm going to bolt for the door or judge him like everyone else has. "You say that, so light like a sunny day, but when I look into your eyes, I see the opposite. I don't want to burden you."

"You're anything but a burden. The trouble is I don't want to burden you."

"So here we are once again doing a dance of me trying to help you and you trying to help me. Where will that leave us? I feel like I've lost track of the ball and which court it hit."

"I'm not going to lie. It won't be easy to be with me."

"I'm with you now, and it's easier than I thought." His gaze holds mine, and a small smile plays across his mouth. I finally ask, "What happens if we aren't just friends in public? I understand the paparazzi stuff, but what else? What else is involved with us dating?"

"I give my lawyer a directive."

"That's romantic."

Chuckling, he nods. "I can't always be charming. Sometimes business takes the romance right out of the relationship."

"How does us pretending to be platonic help your case? Why would dating someone you care about hurt your image?"

"I don't have the luxury of dating freely. I'm not just a man. I'm a brand. The brand can't afford flings and one-night stands. The man can't afford to have his heart broken."

"Again?"

"I didn't love her. I thought I would, but I wasn't there yet. Despite my reservations in that relationship, I stayed. I don't know why. It was easy. Fun. It was stupid. I should have left long before the fallout. But because of the complications involved, my legal team has advised me to keep things 'light' with you. The problem is that I can't. Just looking at you . . . even Nicolina saw how I looked at you."

"She told you that?"

"She did. She also told me you're lovely and not to let you go."

I relish how he's opening up, lighting up all his truths for me to see him through the darkness that keeps him buried. "I'm drawn to you, something inside pulls me closer and keeps me here."

My chair is pulled closer, causing me to laugh, but it stops when he says, "I'm drawn to your smile, to your laugh, to the way you see the world—so open and honest—not tainted." Touching my cheek, he adds, "You're the most gorgeous woman I've ever seen, but it was deeper with you from the minute I saw you. I felt a connection, something real."

I want more. I want him. Inching even closer, I reach over and touch his chest, feeling his heavy beat just beneath. "I want in here, Ethan."

"You're already there."

My chin is lifted and our lips meet in a passionate caress. We part, and when I slowly open my eyes, he says, "I've been dying to get back in bed with you all day."

I lead him to the bedroom and make love to him. Slow for him, deep for me. We're in no hurry as I try to piece back this man kiss-by-kiss, thrust-by-thrust, caress-by-caress. Faith, hope, and love become the glue that grows stronger the more time we spend together.

It's just after midnight when I wake to the sound of his peaceful slumber. He's not snoring, but he's deep in sleep.

For someone who says he doesn't sleep well, he's doing a fine job. Maybe it's because I'm here. I hope it is.

I push a few stray stands away from his eyes, lean in, and kiss him softly.

There's so much to think about, but my attraction seems to be trumping the red flags in our way. Our way. *Our.* Ethan and I went from practically strangers to becoming a *we* in a matter of weeks. Sure, that's the normal track for dating, but his life is complicated, and the way the details are being doled out concerns me.

His life is exciting on the surface, but what lies beneath the shiny exterior?

I lie on my back, processing the information he's shared. Is the press trying to skewer him because he's young, rich, and handsome? Why would his best friend and girlfriend set him up? Lawsuits and money. What stress he must be under.

Looking around the room, there's no expense spared. I pull the covers to my neck. Even these sheets are wonderfully luxurious. So soft and sateen. Melanie would freak out if she could see this apartment. She'll flip out hearing about it.

"Can't sleep?" Ethan asks, his voice husky and completely sexy.

Rolling toward him, I rest on my side. "Happy."

"C'mere." One eye peeks open, and he stretches out an arm. "What are you happy about?"

"Being here." With you.

I expect a yawn, but I get a smile instead. "You're right. It must be awesome being here with me." He starts chuckling and says, "I'm kidding. It's nice to have you here."

I'm still laughing when I ask, "What happens tomorrow?"

"We eat wings and watch baseball." Grabbing a good handful of my backside, he adds, "And don't forget, you'll be naked."

"I'm also going to need another bath in that amazing tub. A little wine and some downtime. I wish I had my book. I still haven't finished."

"I have a copy. I can read it to you in the tub, with all the wine you can drink."

My eyelids grow heavy again. "Sounds divine."

The top of my head is kissed, and he whispers, "Sweet dreams, Singer Davis."

"Sweet dreams, Ethan Everest."

A DEAL'S A DEAL. I served the wings naked with a little apron I found in the hall closet. Ethan forgot about the game altogether, and we missed five innings while I let him round my bases. Twice.

Despite the fun of the day, my mind has been preoccupied with a weird phenomenon since I woke from a nap. I didn't bother with it early on because Ethan was in such a good mood, and I didn't want to ruin it.

But who cleaned the kitchen while we slept last night? I thought Ethan was in bed all night, but somehow it was cleaned and everything put back where it belongs, hidden away behind high-end cabinet doors.

The questions were running rampant, so I finally ask, "Who cleaned the kitchen?"

Without looking up from his laptop on the coffee table, he replies, "The housekeeper," as if I should know who he's talking about.

"She comes in the middle of the night?"

"No. She comes early in the morning. She straightens things up and makes sure I have coffee supplies and fresh food in the fridge for my breakfast."

"What happens to her?"

Angling his body in my direction, he chuckles and finally looks my way. "Nothing happens to her. She comes in, cleans, then leaves before I come out of my room, and then returns later in the day when I'm at work."

"So you never see her?"

"I always see her. I told you I don't sleep well." As if he catches himself, with a languid little smirk, he adds, "Usually."

"What's her name?"

"Pamela."

"You're telling me this like it's normal."

"It is normal. Pamela is a very common name." *I almost feel as though he's mocking me.*

I roll my eyes, but my smile gives away my lack of annoyance. "You know what I mean."

"You're overthinking this."

"I always overthink things."

"That you do, dear Singer. That you do."

"That's because I feel like everything's a mystery with you."

"Not everything. I've shown you the skeletons in my closet, but no, I haven't dragged them out. I'm quite open with you."

The scoff is a precursor to my wide eyes and open mouth. "People are walking around an apartment where I'm sleeping naked. I need to know these things, Ethan. I'm not trying to be demanding, but you said I'm in"—I can't back down now—"in your heart. That means you want me in your life. Pamela is in your life. A little heads-up on the people who surround you, who keep your life running so smoothly, would be helpful."

His eyes don't seem to settle on anything in particular, much like his thoughts seem to be rolling through his head. I'm uneasy. Again. And I hate it, but I remain quiet because I have to give him time to think through his response. I've shown him my vulnerabilities when it comes to us. I need him to decide if he's ready to reveal his own. The intensity in his focus moves from the distance to me. "I don't need you to clean or cook for me, Singer. I don't need you to grocery shop or make my bed. That's not why I'm with you. That's not why you're here now. You're here because I can't stop these feelings from growing. You're here because you make my soul lighter. You make me happy. You're here because I'm falling in love with you."

He's . . . what?

He takes a deep breath and then his eyes shift to the side and back again. He continues, "Pamela Lowenstein. She's forty-three with two kids. Oldest son starts Columbia this fall. Younger daughter will be a sophomore in high school."

"Wait." My hands fly up in front of me. "Back up."

"To Pamela? Or her kids?"

"Before Pamela."

"You asked me about the kitchen."

"After that." His devious smile gives him away. "You're going to make me work for this, aren't you?"

"No." He stands and comes around the couch. Taking me by the wrists, he places my hands around his neck. "I'm falling for you."

"Say it again. Exactly," I insist with a grin a mile wide.

With a roll of his eyes, he leans down until our noses almost touch. "I'm falling in love with you, Singer Davis."

And I'm dead from all the swoons, a mere puddle of

overflowing emotions for this man. With his hands roaming my sides, my body tilts toward his. "I'm falling for you."

"Say it. Exactly."

Giggling, I roll my eyes this time, but deep inside, I know he needs to hear it. With my fingers tickling the back of his neck, I kiss his chin. "I'm falling in love with you, Ethan Everest."

"So what you're saying is that you never clean up after yourself?"

"Ahh, we're back to cleaning." He smiles. Rubbing his forehead, he looks up at me under dark lashes, and a wry grin spreads across his mouth, making me smile. "I really don't like to clean."

Raising my chin, I nod. "I can live with that." I'm not the neatest person out there, but never cleaning again sounds like a luxury I've never contemplated. Although I find pride when I clean my apartment, I might be able to let someone else clean the toilets. I walk to the table where I set my purse. Pulling my phone out, I'm about to text Aaron, but remember we gave him the day off. Inwardly, I berate myself for already relying on him so much. I won't have him forever and the spoiled look is unattractive on anyone. "I should probably go."

"Do you have to?"

"It's already after five. I need to do laundry and get ready for the week."

His expression softens, a small need wrapped in the crinkle around his eyes. "You can stay if you want."

"I appreciate that, but I've invaded your space two nights in a row. Surely—"

"Invade it some more." I'm kissed with lips that set my soul on fire. His presence overwhelms me. His body owns mine with the gentlest of touches. He makes me want to give in, to bend for him, to be what he needs, and right now, he needs me.

It's exhilarating to be with him, but I need to be clear-headed. With my hands on his chest, I break us apart, and take a step back. "You're so sure and—"

"I want you to stay." His words are rushed, almost frantic.

"I may be falling but I don't want to crash."

Strong arms wrap around me. "I'll catch you."

I whisper, "Seems you found faith again."

"Not just faith. Trust. I have trust in you, and us."

"So we are friends in public, more in private. What happens when the cases are over? Or am I a secret forever?"

"To the people who matter, we don't hide. We're dating. It's everyone else I want to keep out. Not forever. For now."

"Okay." I exhale a deep breath. I'm not a dirty secret, but I don't want to be the cause of his downfall either. "I need to go to my place. I need to check in with Melanie and have a few hours of normalcy away from your fire-hot kisses and the weak knees I have from being around you. This place. You." *It's intoxicating, making me delirious.*

The intensity between us seems to be tapering off, his taut jaw unclenches. Understanding washes over his face, and he nods. "I'll order a car. I would take you myself, but—"

"I know. We would be seen together, and we can't be."

He nods this time for a different reason while pressing a few buttons on his phone. "We have legal meetings next week. There's potential for the cases to settle. I know Keith is bleeding financially, and if he carries on with this lawsuit, all the money will go to pay his legal bill."

As we walk to the elevator, I really love that he still drapes his arm over my shoulder. He lends his strength to me, which is comforting. "The car will be in the garage. Go to the bottom level. "

"Okay." I stop to wait, the button already pressed. "The other case, what's the worst that can happen?"

"She claims I sexually assaulted her that night and she's bearing my child, which she also claims is a future witness against me as a destructive father, so she wants full custody and twenty thousand in childcare."

"Wow," I sigh. "I don't know the cost of raising a child a year, but that is a lot of money."

"That's what she wants per month."

"Excuse me?"

"I know. I feel the same when it comes to paying her anything."

"But you said you caught her with your best friend?"

"I did, but it's my word against hers."

The pieces click into place. "The child could be his."

Shame colors his expression and his face lowers. "If the baby is mine, she'll use the arrest and photos to claim I'm unfit and have a lottery winner's landfall at my expense."

"What about the baby?"

"I'll fight for my child. I'll spend every dollar if I have to. I'll take care of my kid no matter what."

I don't want to ask about finances. I'm in no position to know how his life will or won't be affected, but I know I'd rather see him happy and poor than rich and desolate. "I'm here for you, Ethan. Your secrets are safe with me." I embrace him, my arms around his middle, and my head against him. Each of the beats of his heart are strong, but steady.

"I know you are." Kissing my head, he replies, "Thank you."

He needs me. "I'm just a phone call away. If you need to vent to someone, let it be me."

Smiling, I lift up and kiss him just as the elevator dings and the doors open. Backing into the elevator, he reaches out and grabs my hand, tugging me against him again and kissing me twice as hard with more passion than ever before.

When I'm good and breathless, I'm released. My fingertips go to my mouth, and I press them against my tingling lips. That's when I know for sure.

I'm long past falling.

I'm head over feet in *deep* with this man.

22

Singer

A bottle of champagne is popped open, followed by Mel warning me, "You need to hurry. He'll be here any minute."

"I'm almost ready," I shout from the bathroom. "Just one little"—she appears in the reflection with two glasses of bubbly, so I stop shouting—"touch up."

"You look beautiful," she says, smiling. "You're gonna knock him on his ass."

"I'm quite partial to that ass. I'd hate to see it injured." I laugh.

"You are so far gone. Good sex will do that to a girl."

I love having sex with Ethan. No one ever put my needs first . . . or even last when I think about my lame boyfriends of the past. "It's not just the sex, Mel," I reply a little too dreamily. So much so that I giggle inwardly.

"I love seeing this side of you. So happy." She hip bumps me. "And goofy."

"Goofy?"

"In the best of ways. Carefree. You look gorgeous."

"This dress is gorgeous." I smooth my hands down my waist and over my hips admiring the fine material.

"It's not the dress that makes the woman. It's the woman in love who makes the dress."

I take a glass from the counter and tap it against hers. "Now that I'll toast to."

We both sip, then she says, "Mike and I decided we're staying in."

"I thought you wanted to go out. It's Saturday night. You live for Saturday night."

Shrugging, she sits on the side of the tub and watches me finish up. "He said he wanted to stay in."

"And so it begins. Women are so adaptable. We mold ourselves to what we think men want—"

"I don't mind staying in. We're going to watch movies."

"But what do you really want to do?" I ask, eyeing her in the reflection of the mirror.

"Dance. He's not a dancer, so he doesn't like going to the clubs. But he's a nice guy and I like being treated nicely. He's different from the losers I've dated."

"You deserve nice, my friend. I just want you happy too."

"I don't *need* to dance. I just *like* to dance. There's a difference. I also don't want to be alone the rest of my life. Anyway," she says, standing and walking to the door. "What guy likes to go to a club? Not many, so *compromising* on this may mean he'll *compromise* for me on something else. That's how relationships work." She leaves on that note, whistling as she walks away.

A knock echoes into the apartment. *Ethan*. Giddiness runs through my body. I quickly finish applying my lipstick while listening to Melanie greet him. "Well, don't you look handsome?"

She sounds like my mother talking to my prom date,

which makes me laugh. I toss my lipstick in my purse, slip on a pair of very sexy four-inch sparkling Jimmy Choo heels that mysteriously appeared in the back seat of the car when Aaron picked me up after getting my hair done earlier. I was afraid to search online to see the price, but Mel happily did and warned me not to look, to just enjoy. She also made me promise she could borrow them along with the dress when she had a Cinderella event to attend.

I could stand here for days and stare at this deep purple dress and the incredible shoes, but I think it's best to hurry and let him stare instead. I'm going for jaw dropping, and he doesn't disappoint.

Jaw dropping goes both ways.

Standing in the doorway of my apartment is the most attractive man I have ever seen. Black tailored tuxedo, clearly custom-made for his trim, but athletic build. A bow tie wraps around his neck that matches the midnight sky, and a perfectly pressed white pintucked shirt spans the opening of the jacket. I've never been one to use the term debonair, but James Bond has nothing on the strikingly handsome, debonair Ethan Everest.

"Hi," I say, breathless, though I had plenty seconds before he stole them from me.

"Hello, Singer." With his eyes still on mine, he says, "You look stunning."

The blush I've started calling the Everest blush, since he's the only person who can summon it, rises from my tummy covering my chest and higher to my cheeks. "Thank you."

With a man this handsome looking at me like I make his world a better place, I almost fail to notice the flowers in his hand—gorgeous pale pink peonies wrapped with greenery in tissue paper with a deep pink bow. "These reminded me of you."

I think my cheeks must now match the ribbon instead of the beautiful blooms. "They're beautiful. Thank you."

Melanie is right there, taking them from me. "I'll put these in a vase for you."

Ethan offers, "Can we give you a ride somewhere?"

She waves us off. "No. I'm good. Low-key night for Mike and me. You guys go and have fun and scoot-a-loo."

I give her a hug. "Thank you."

"You're welcome." She whispers in my ear, "Can't wait to hear all the dirty details."

I'm very aware that she said that loud enough for Ethan to hear. He chuckles, confirming my notion, and replies, "Here's hoping I don't disappoint then."

She says, "I'm sure you have no problem when it comes to pleasing a woma—"

"Okay," I end it before this conversation gets embarrassing. Grabbing Ethan's sleeve, I tug. "Goodnight, Mel."

As soon as the door is shut, I joke, "Now you see why I can't take her anywhere."

"She's great and has a good sense of humor."

"Despite embarrassing me, she is. The best."

Outside, Aaron is waiting by the car and opens the door for us. "Good evening, Aaron."

"Good evening, Ms. Davis."

"Stop charming the ladies, Aaron. You're making me look bad."

"I'm sure you hold your own quite well, Mr. Everest."

"I've always liked you, Aaron. You're good for my ego."

"That's what I'm here for. That, and driving."

Ethan unbuttons his jacket and slides in next to me. The door is shut, and suddenly my heart leaps from being alone with this man . . . well, as alone as we can be with Aaron up in the front.

His cufflink catches the light, and I take hold of his wrist for a better look. "Baseball? I think you're obsessed."

"I used to play in high school. I wasn't good enough for the minors."

"But you tried out?"

A look of awkwardness crosses his strong features and he looks down. "Yes. Twice." When he looks up at me again, he adds, "Twice was enough. It was time I put my other skills to use."

"To create your company?"

"Yes. My peers thought I was a dumb jock. I wasn't. I made the honor roll every semester, but I kept that hidden. I knew I would be made fun of if they found out."

"Kids are cruel."

"Kids are predictable, and I like coming from the underdog position in sports and everything else. It gives me a good vantage point. Another reason is once you settle high up on that pedestal, you become lazy. That's when you're vulnerable and weak. Business, like baseball, is strategic."

I lean back, engrossed by his road to success, and ask, "Where did you go to college?"

"Princeton."

"New Jersey is a long way from Texas."

"Best decision I made. The website had grown, and by the time I started my sophomore year, I had the site running and had made millions in ads that ran along the borders of each page you clicked on. By my senior year, I owned four divisional companies under one umbrella corporation. I'd already made enough to not work the rest of my life if I chose."

"That's amazing. You made your dreams come true."

When he laughs, it's hardy, good to hear. "I can buy a baseball team, but I can't buy my way onto a team."

"I'm sure you could."

"Ha! I wouldn't want to be on a team that would want me."

"You don't seem the loner type, but you are self-deprecating."

"Underdog," he says, sending me a wink and sexy smirk. "What brought you to New York?"

The traffic is normal for Manhattan, barely flowing. "I wanted to prove to my friends and family that I was bigger than the suburbs and Pagely Whitehead."

"What's a Pagely Whitehead?"

"A Pagely Whitehead is the guy who lived next door."

"*Ahhh.* The boy next door. Let me guess. He had a crush on you?"

"Boy, did he. And he had my family convinced we were meant to be together."

"You never wanted to be Mrs. Whitehead?"

"Oh, God no. He was awful, and smelly. He's now a tax inspector for the Revenue Commission in Denver."

Ethan's face scrunches. "Tax guys aren't my favorite people. I pay a lot of taxes *and* pay the financial guys and lawyers to keep things straight and legal."

"Well, guess we have something in common because tax guys aren't my favorite either."

The car stops in front of the hotel, and a valet opens the door for us. Ethan sticks his arm out and I take it. "Goodnight, Aaron."

"Goodnight, Ms. Davis."

"So formal in front of the boss."

"Keeping up appearances," he replies with a grin.

As soon as we enter the hotel, our arms fall to our sides.

Ethan whispers, "You're listed in their media section as a family friend."

"That gives me a lot of wiggle room to flirt."

I'm hit with a playful glare. "That flirting better be directed at me, or I won't be able to keep this cover."

"Two way street, mister."

Inside the hotel, we catch an elevator just before it closes. It's crowded, but he says, "You look incredibly beautiful tonight."

No lowered voice.

No whispering just for me.

Full volume as if we're the only two in the elevator.

Tapping his hand with mine, I reply quietly, "Thank you," so only he can hear. Free from the elevator, we walk to the reception area. "You're not very good at this friend thing."

"You make it difficult to pretend I don't find you utterly breathtaking."

"We can find each other attractive. We just can't act on it."

"True."

Brushing my hand across his, I add, "We'll make up for it later though."

"Want to skip this party?"

The doors are open when we approach, and I've never seen such a glamorous party in my life. My mouth opens as I take in the gold-room lit by beautiful chandeliers and candlelight. "Can we stay for a while?"

"Ye—"

"Ethan Everest, I thought that was you . . ." A woman with a blond bob chatters on, speaking a million words a minute and holding Ethan's arms like he'll escape if she doesn't. She never introduces herself to me, and if I'm reading Ethan correctly, he doesn't know who she is.

I stand politely to the side, and from their brief conversation, she missed him in The Hamptons last summer but looks forward to catching up with him soon.

He extricates himself before she has a chance to get clingier than she already is, and leads me inside the ballroom. The gleaming crystal chandeliers are eye-catching and people are dressed to the nines.

Sneaking a peek at Ethan, I want to kiss him, to thank him, to hug him for making me feel so beautiful, for making me feel like I belong. Tonight I'm his escort, a friend of his, or a work associate. I'll go along with whatever he wants or needs me to be. "I've never been to something this fancy."

"It's not that fancy under the blinding lights."

We start walking again. Tossing his words about, I say, "I feel like I'm supposed to read between the lines."

"Maybe."

"Well, that's no help."

Our gazes catch and a twinkle resides in his, making me smile. His hand touches my lower back. "I like to keep you guessing."

"That you do, all the time."

When we arrive at our table, one of the first things I notice are assigned seats, and mine is three away from Ethan's. My gaze darts to him. His eyes lay heavy on mine already. Reaching down, he takes his place card and swaps it with the person to the right of my chair. "We're sitting next to each other."

Just as I start to sit, his fingers brush along my wrist, and he whispers, "Would you like to dance?"

"Yes," I reply, but it tends toward more of a purr against

his skin, skin I want to lick, to nip, and other things that will lead to us being naked together.

He takes my purse and sets it on the table before leading me to the dance floor. Pulling me close, we begin to sway unhurried. The song is instrumental and not particularly slow, but with Ethan's hand on my waist and holding my other in his like he owns it, it could be "When the Saints Go Marching In," and I wouldn't know the difference. Every song is a love song when our bodies are pressed together and his cheek is against mine.

We've become a slow burn on a hot night. The air in here is so combustible I worry my heart will be obliterated by it.

Our moment together is interrupted when a dark-haired man with darker eyes starts patting Ethan on the back. Ethan takes a step back from me, our hands falling to our sides—the perfect picture of platonic. A look in his eyes resembles the sadness I feel when I'm homesick. His lips move, but the words are silent, "I'm sorry."

Turning to the intruder, the man's boisterous voice overwhelms the intimacy Ethan and I were sharing. "Good to see you, Everest. How's business?"

"Stellar. Lucas McCoy, this is Singer Davis."

His eyes widen as he gives me a once-over that strips me of any respect. "The *very* lovely Singer Davis. Maybe you'll save a dance for me?"

Ethan responds before I have a chance, "Her dance card is full. Sorry, McCoy."

Lucas laughs. Ethan doesn't. Even from a foot away, I can feel the tension between them. Their *friendliness* is only surface deep, if that. I move closer to Ethan and press my arm to his. He glances at me and smiles. Lucas gets the not-so subtle hint and says, "Let's catch up sometime over drinks."

"Sure thing." Ethan shakes his hand, but that's where the courtesy ends.

Lucas looks at me and says, "If your dance card frees up, I'm happy to fill the spot."

I'm not given a chance to reply before he walks off.

Ethan shakes his head and asks, "Would you like a drink?"

"I have a feeling we could both use one."

"Sorry about that. He sued me years ago about cargo-hold rights at the shipyard in East Bay." His hand returns to my back, the heat seeping through the thin fabric of the dress as we weave our way to the bar. I feel his fingers wrap around my waist, giving me a squeeze. "He lost the lawsuit, and he's been trying to take what's mine ever since."

I'm tempted to ask if that extends to people, but by the show Lucas McCoy just displayed, I don't have to. Ethan orders a bourbon straight and champagne for me.

"What's on your mind?" Ethan asks as we step to the side where it's a little dimmer and much quieter.

"This party is so beautiful—the ballroom, the tables. Everything is dazzling."

"You're the most dazzling one here."

"You say that so easily without looking around."

"I don't have to look around. You far outshine them all."

"You're very charming."

"I'm not trying to charm you . . . well, *I am*, but I'm also telling the truth." He nudges me lightly with his elbow and lowers his voice. "Take the compliment."

With a nod of kindness, I reply, "Thank you."

"They're serving dinner. Ready to eat?"

He offers his hand then drops it. I say, "I'm afraid I don't think we're doing a good job of being just friends."

"I'm afraid you're right."

I don't want to hurt his cases or draw unwanted attention to him. "I guess we should try harder."

"Yeah," he sighs.

Once we're seated, I'm introduced to the other guests assigned to our table. Everyone seems to know Ethan already, and he flawlessly introduces each person until Lucas sits across from us. Ethan stops, and Lucas starts to rule the roost from the other side of the table. He doesn't have a date, but he's seated between two beautiful women who are more than happy to give him their attention. Anytime my eyes meet his, my stomach twists, and I look away quickly.

Intuitively, Ethan reaches his hand down to find mine under the table. Our fingers lace and our hands rest on my thigh. I like the weight of him, of us, on me. I like the warmth on my thigh where the dress has fallen to the side.

When our food is served, our hands release, and pretending he didn't just knock my world from its axis, I ask, "Do you come to many events like this?"

"No. Generally, I prefer to make my donations quieter, but if it helps to raise more money, I'll attend a few."

"Although this is a beautiful event, I don't understand how spending tens of thousands of dollars on events raises more money than using that money directly."

"People like to be seen."

"So it's part ego, part philanthropy that brings them to charity balls?"

He chuckles. "I've wondered the same thing myself. How's the food?"

"Very good."

Setting his fork down, he leans in and asks, "Would you hate me if I want to leave after dinner?"

With a smile from the possibility that lies ahead on my face, I reply, "Only if you were planning on taking me home."

His eyebrows rise as he wipes his napkin over his mouth and sets it down. "Don't worry about that. I have no intention of doing such a thing."

I find myself eating as if they're going to take my plate away before I finish. Logically I know that's not the case, but damn if I'm not ready to see where this night leads.

23

Singer

I'm twirled right off the elevator and into the hall of photography. That's what I call it, at least. Ethan's hands wrap around me from behind while the elevator door closes. My hair is swept to the side and kisses trail down my neck.

I close my eyes, savoring the feel of his lips on me.

He spins me back around and whispers, "Open your eyes."

When I do, I'm met with eyes I know well—almond-shaped eyelids, gold centers that fade into green. They're eyes I've seen cry, happy, sad, pained, remorseful, regretful, full of joy, and blissful, but today I see them on a thoughtful face with delight caught in the middle. They're eyes and a face I recognize as my own. A simple black frame, large white matte, me in the park surrounded by green grass. The photo hangs bright under the lone light along the black wall. "That's me."

"I took it the day I ran into you at the park. The photo is a gift for you."

Smiling, I turn to him. "This is for me? It's so beautiful."

"I wanted you to see how I see you."

I'm stunned to see how I look, not only to his eyes but possibly to others. I'm beautiful. I slide my arms around his neck and lift up, pressing my lips to his. "Thank you."

"You're welcome." Gentle kisses turn passionate quickly. Our tongues touch and my back hits the wall. The evening has been foreplay until now.

He licks his way to my neck, the feel of him tasting me so carnal. "God, Singer. I could fuck you right here." Cool air breezes over the trail, leading right back to the skin he nips on my neck.

"Do it. I want you to, Ethan."

With his lips to my ear, he demands, "Turn around."

I turn and my breath is whooshed from my chest when I'm pressed against the wall. The purple dress is lifted in the back. The pressure is light but sends goose bumps over my skin as fingers tap up the sides of my thighs until he's kneeling behind me. The backs of my thighs are kissed, lovingly, while his hands slide my panties down to my ankles. He lifts one, balancing me when I lift one foot and then the other. Stealing a glimpse of him, he tucks my underwear into the pocket of his tux, the purple vibrant against the stark black.

When he stands back up, he takes the straps from my shoulders and lets the dress float to the floor before lifting my arms above my head. "I want you to stay like that. Stay in that position just for me. Will you do that for me, Singer?" His voice is rough with desire and stern in his need.

"Yes."

"Good girl."

I press my cheek to the smooth wall and watch as he

drapes my dress over the back of the couch. First his jacket then his bow tie are removed.

My Adonis returns. His eyes are dark, lust wrapped in the black night centers. His large hands cover my shoulder blades and run up before dipping low again and unclasping my bra. Ethan takes my wrists and carefully brings them down and around to my back. The bra strap tightens on one wrist before being wrapped around the other, securing them together.

Lifting just a little, my back arches in response, my nipples kissing the wall and hardening. "Are we—?"

"Shh, Singer. Don't ask. Just feel." His hands come around to squeeze my breasts, pinch my nipples lightly, and move higher. The right palm holds firm over my heart, and he says, "Your heart is racing. Do I do that or is that your body responding in fear?"

"I'm not afraid of you, or this, but my heart always races around you." I swallow, closing my eyes and find relief in the coolness of the wall against my hot cheek.

"This? Say what *this* is, Singer?"

"You've got me tied up. I'm at your mercy."

"Because you trust me."

"Yes, because I trust you, Ethan."

"Do you know how much that turns me on?" I feel his cock against my fingertips. Opening my palms, I take hold of him, eliciting a deep groan that echoes around us.

Like before, his fingers tap over my hips, then his palms warm my behind. He's assertive and commanding when two fingers run between my cheeks. "Have you ever been taken from behind, Ms. Davis?"

My ankles wobble. "No."

He steadies me. "Will you wear those shoes while I'm fucking you?"

This time my knees are solid, and my back arches again to prove a point. "Do you want me to?"

"Yes."

No reason or explanation. Just yes. I don't know why it feels like the heat was turned up, but damn, I'm a wet, hot mess. "Then I will. I take it you wanted them to be seen and not just hidden under a gown."

"I want them draped over my shoulders as I thrust every ounce of my desire into that sweet, tight pussy."

Good Lord, this man. Gone is the polite, wounded guy I want to make smile. Tonight I get a predator intent on ravaging my entire body before he's done with me. His dirty-talking ways cause my thighs to rub together. He breaks character and asks, "You've never had sex with your back to your partner or you've never done anal?"

I gulp. I should be embarrassed by my lack of experience, but I'm too turned on to hide behind lies. "Neither."

"You've been with selfish boys, Singer. They treated you like a girl. I'm no boy. I'm the man that's going to treat you like the sexual woman you are." His lips find mine, and he kisses me, his tongue as masterful as his words.

Fingers slide between my legs, and he speaks into the back of my neck, "You're so ready for me. Do you like to play rough?"

"I like to play with you."

"I like that, too."

My backside is bare, exposed when he steps back. I hear the foil rip and the condom sliding down. When his hands return to my lower waist, my skin tingles in anticipation. Pulling me back by the hips, he says, "Keep your arms still. Your head back from the wall. I won't hurt you." For the first time, I'm nervous. Excited nervous, but nervous. I do as I'm told while he positions himself between my parted legs.

"I'll go slow." He eases inside, my eyes closing as I realize how empty I was before now. "Just this one time."

My eyes fly open as he pulls back, leaving the tip inside me, and slamming back up. The grip on my hips is tight as he repeats each thrust with a harsh breath hitting my back while forcing mine out each time. Closing my eyes again, I do what he asked and feel. Every thrust. Every breath. Every moan. Every part of him invades me, enters my soul and burrows deep in my heart.

This.

This.

This.

I never want this to end.

I never want him to stop.

I never want to feel empty again.

I want this.

Every day.

Every night.

I want him.

Strong fingers work their way around to the apex of my thighs, and he finds my clit. His fingers are unleashed fury as he demands my body to bow to his wants.

My body bends to his every whim. "Ethan," falls from my lips on the crescendo of an orgasm.

Grabbing hold of my hipbones he slams into me. Balancing between the real world and the stars he's sending me sailing to, I start to recover beside the large photograph. Moans that become grunts tell me he's close, so close.

My name is an uttered confession, "Sin. Sin. Sin," until he repents with his release. "Singer. Singer. Fuck. Singer."

Tired, but feeling incredible, I try to even my rampant breathing. His tongue dips to taste the sheen between us, and then he turns me around. "You're fucking beautiful."

Leaning down, he takes a nipple between his teeth and gently teases.

His touch. The pressure. It's hard to restrain myself from moaning. *He is so good. So good.* "Ah."

This time he puts his forehead to mine and whispers, "I've never felt like this. It's never been this good before."

My eyes are growing heavy, my arms beginning to ache from being held behind my back. "How?" I ask, needing his words to cover me.

"I don't know how." He cups my face and brings it up to look at him. "I only know why."

"Why?"

"Because it's you."

Like the yes he gave me earlier, things can be so simple sometimes. Not complicated, just easy honesty. He kisses me while his hand releases my wrists behind my back. "You standing naked in my apartment in those heels—I've never laid eyes on a sexier sight."

Wrapping my arms around his neck, he scoops me up into his arms. "I might want to keep them for special occasions like this."

"We can always buy more." He cuts through the living room and down the hallway that leads to his bedroom.

"I'm afraid to find out how much they cost."

"Don't be afraid. I would spend ten times that just to see you smile."

"Because you're a fool with money?"

"No. Because I'm a fool for you, and I happen to have money."

I'm totally a fool for him, too, but hearing him admit his feelings for me . . . yeah, falling for him is easy. "Best of both worlds."

Bringing me closer, he kisses me. "Stay with me."

My feet land on the ground, but my heart is still floating in the clouds.

"I'm here." *There's nowhere I'd rather be.*

And just when I think tonight can't get any better, Ethan speaks words that caress my heart.

"I want you here long after tonight."

24

Ethan

Sitting across the table from my former best friend with his smug fucking face makes me rage inside. My fingers are starting to hurt from fisting them under the table. How can he sit there and feel justified in his actions? How can he fuck over someone he called his brother without remorse? How can he fuck my whole world up in one big swoop and sleep with a clear conscience?

Fuck him.

Reegan and my legal team line my side of the table. My four lawyers against his three. We take a thirty-minute break and leave the room, filing into the conference room down the hall. I walk to the corner floor-to-ceiling windows on either side of me and stare at the city.

From behind me, Reegan asks, "How are you doing?"

"Fine." To the point. I can't let my emotions get the best of me. I must show that fuckface in the other room that he won't win. I will not let him stake claims over my money or my anger. I will show him nothing more than indifference.

Reegan sits at the table and says, "Let's all take a breath and go over the notes."

I may only want Keith to see a blank stare from me, but behind closed doors, I can't control myself. "Close him down. If I can't have that company, I don't want him to have it either."

"Things aren't always fai—"

I slam my fist on the table. "I don't want fair. I want him destroyed." Blinded by fury, when I open my eyes, the four of them are staring at me. I swallow down as much of my anger as I can and sit. "I made this company. I invented the site, developed it, put my fucking soul and every penny into it."

Reegan's voice is even, emotions aside. "You brought your friend in on it and made him a partner."

"As president, and not with equal shares."

"He may not have been CEO, but the title of president of the company gives him rights, shares, and decision-making power." He sits back. "Do you want to get something to drink and strategize? We need to review the package they're offering."

"No. I'm ready to end this. Let's mark it up and send back our final deal."

"And if he doesn't accept?"

"He's got to be running low on funds to back this legal battle. I'll use those extra shares I earned to fight it until there's nothing left of him."

Reegan sighs. "This is personal for you. I understand that. You're hurt. You're angry. I just want to make sure you understand what's at risk for you because it's still business. The fees to fight—"

"My business is personal, so I don't care how much it costs. I'm right. I'd rather die being right, than live a life that's wrong. I won't accept anything less than what I'm willing to give. This will be my final offer."

Knowing better than to argue with me, Reegan opens the two-inch-thick file before him. "Do you want to review his offer again before making a final decision?"

"No. I know what it says. Here's my counteroffer: I want one hundred million in cash. Two million shares that divest in five years based on the highest stock price during that period. My name will be removed from all deals, business properties, and contracts backdating to the first of this month." I watch as Reegan takes furious notes to keep up. The other lawyers are quiet, and the only sound is ink across their legal pads. "Neither he, nor the company, will make claims against my family, any current endeavors, or myself, including my businesses not associated with the company or my personal properties. No taxes shall come from my shares for this past year, or any other year that I will be collecting money. My share of taxes will be paid accordingly and directly from me, not through them on their tax end, so they will not receive tax breaks based on my payout or shares."

Reegan looks up when I go quiet. "You're severing all ties —future and backdating with no claims. It's a bold move, Ethan."

"If that company is run right and hits the projections financial experts expect it to, he'll make money. A lot of damn money."

"He'll make less than you and you won't be working there any longer."

"A hundred mil to get me off his payroll for now. And he gets a company. He's walking away a winner."

Reegan checks his watch then looks to one of his

associates. "You're the ultimate winner if he accepts this deal. That company could go under without you."

"Not could," I add. "It will go under without me, but I'm betting two million it lasts five years."

"You always were a risk taker. Draw up the offer. We have ten minutes."

In a flash, everyone is scattering. When Reegan and I are left alone in the conference room, he says, "I bet he won't go for it. He's such an asshole. Always was."

"How much?"

"How much of an asshole is he?"

I laugh and push back from the table. Lifting my feet onto the surface, I kick back. "No, how much do you want to bet that he'll take the deal?"

"Two K?"

"Done." We shake hands and I sit back with my hands behind my head. "I've given him plenty of opportunities to man up and make everything right. His ego is way bigger than his balls these days. He feels unbeatable, but he's about to learn that no one is invincible."

As we wait, the pleasure I thought I'd feel being in the power position isn't there. There is no satisfaction in losing your dreams *and* best friend through betrayal.

Reegan stands. "Is it wrong that I hope you're right and we close the agreement today?"

"It's been nine months of hell. Not wrong to want to end it, even if it comes at the cost of two K from you."

He laughs and reaches out to shake my hand. When I take it, I stand. "You deserve better than you got."

"Thanks. I appreciate that, and I appreciate your friendship."

"Don't thank me too soon. It's not over yet." He walks to the door. "Let's go seal our fate."

I'm so anxious to wrap this chapter of my life up. I'm done. The bastard has won . . . short-term anyway. I need to be able to focus on my other companies.

WE GET the call during dinner.

My assistant, Reegan, and the three other lawyers join me at the restaurant. We were told a response would come today, so we're waiting it out over a perfectly cooked Kobe steak and expensive wine that I'm going to charge to the company I'm about to lose.

Just as the food arrives, my mouth waters for different reasons. Dressed in a navy-blue business suit, it's not the clothes that take my breath away. She could wear a bag and look good.

It's that smile and the way her body moves so smoothly under the stiff fabric. It's the way she looks at me like I'm the only man she sees. She makes me feel invincible despite my earlier proclamation.

I stand to greet her, a polite public and platonic kiss to the cheek, and whisper to her ear, "I've been thinking about you naked all day."

She smiles, and I love her confidence as she reacts as if I only said a simple hello. With a little flirtatious swing of her hair, she whispers, "I've been thinking about how good it feels when you take me from behind and fuck me until the only comprehensible word falling from my lips is *Ethan*."

"Fuck me," I mumble on a strangled breath. My pants feel tight and I button my jacket to hide the erection I know I'm sporting.

"Gladly."

I like her smart mouth. I like kissing it. I like fucking it. I love hearing those strawberry lips say my name as if it's a swear word, or a prayer to a higher power.

Escorting her to the far end of the table, I whisper, "You've gone and done it now, Ms. Davis." I'd slap her ass but we're in public. I'll save it for later. I introduce her to everyone and just as she takes a seat at the far end of the table, Reegan's phone buzzes across the wooden tabletop.

The guests go quiet and he stands, grabs his phone, and heads for a quieter space. I'm assuming it's the enemy, but I won't let my steak go cold for them. "We should eat."

Dinner conversation picks up, and as expected, Singer charms the gentlemen flanking her.

Her gaze drifts to me each time she takes a bite or a sip of wine. I raise my glass, the minutest to not be caught, in her honor. She's gorgeous even in a suit that's not quite tailored to show off her curves. My beauty still has all eyes on her. She doesn't need expensive clothes to garner attention.

I see the looks she gets. I notice the envy of other men wishing she were theirs. I want to kiss her, to mark her as mine, but I continue to eat my steak, trying to satisfy a craving I know it never can.

Only her.

The most delicious flavor.

Now that I've gotten a taste of her, I know she's the only one I want to devour. "Fucking hell, Everest." Reegan returns, startling me.

Fucking hell is right, sneaky fucker. "Shit, you scared me."

"You did it, man. The offer is golden."

"What?"

His laughter permeates the air, drawing attention in the restaurant from surrounding guests. "They took the offer."

"They took the offer?"

He grabs me into a hug, patting me on the back. "They accepted the fucking offer, Everest!"

"Holy shit. They took the offer." Patting his back, I'm in shock. It was a shit offer for him, and a great offer for me. "We did it, man. We did it."

The team is standing and congratulations are circulating. When I reach Singer standing and smiling proudly, she says, "I'm so happy for you." I squeeze her tight, closing my eyes and dipping my head to her shoulder.

The heaviness that's plagued me this last year starts to slip away. In her arms, I feel the joy and safety of her trust and honesty. She doesn't ask me about the money, and she doesn't ask about the logistics. "I know this has been trying. Are you okay?" She just asks about me. *Me.*

What have I done right in life to deserve this woman?

I step back, restraining myself from kissing her. "I'm really okay. This is amazing news. I lose one of my businesses, but I have others. I'm more than one company, and now I can move on and prove it."

"I don't doubt that at all. You can do anything you want, Ethan."

I'm about to invite her for a quickie in the restroom when Reegan spins me around. "That's quite an increase in the net worth. Congratulations."

"And yours by ten. Thank you again."

"You're welcome."

"Oh, and since I won the bet, you can write that check for two grand to the charity of Ms. Davis's choice. I'll match it tenfold."

Reegan's eyes follow mine that lead to Singer. She sits when we do, her laughter mingling with ours when he leans over to me and says, "Fuck the press. I would have kissed her too."

A smile creases my cheeks even though I should punch the fuck out of him. "She's good. Too good for me. She's more beautiful on the inside if you can believe it."

"You deserve someone good."

"I met her at the same party I met Dariya."

"Fuck." Shaking his head, he says, "That sucks. It doesn't matter how you begin. Only matters how you finish. Eat up. We have some celebrating to do."

"Not me." I look across the long table. "I have plans."

His laugh doesn't distract me from the eyes that have captured the light and shine into my heart. A small smile appears on her sweet face, and she looks down. Even in candlelight she can't hide the pretty blush coloring her cheeks. When she takes a sip of her wine, she tips her glass for me.

I eat faster because I don't want to be away from her anymore. The sooner we eat, the sooner I get to eat *her.*

After we charge a solid amount on the company card, I cut it in half and toss it in a bin with a big fuck you very much. Aaron stands curbside, and I see the debate in Singer's eyes. "Not much longer, and then I'm showing you off all over this damn city."

"I'm going to hold you to that."

"You can hold me however you want. I'm yours, baby."

"I like this good mood. Should we continue this celebration at my place?"

"Okay. You take the car, and I'll see you there shortly." I'm feeling so good she could demand anything she wants, and I would give it to her.

Aaron pulls away, and I hit Reegan on the arm, then shake his hand. "Thanks again."

"It was a shit deal. I'm glad he took it. You were right pushing to settle. This way he can make his own billion instead of lawyer fees costing him everything."

"One down."

"One to go. She reported to the center for the paternity test two days ago. The envelope, by court order, will remain sealed until the private hearing on Thursday."

"Okay."

"What are the odds?"

"I'm feeling good enough to gamble on it."

"Good. Stay strong and I'll see you at the office tomorrow."

"See you." I step out and catch a cab. I have a hot date waiting and I refuse to be late.

25

Singer

Ethan has been weighed down in work and his trial, but three nights away from him is too long. That's what worries me. I openly admit to myself that I've completely fallen for him. I didn't expect a floodgate of romance and swoons to follow. It's like he's been freed from some invisible shackles that had been holding him back, and now he's sweeping me right off my feet. Who does that?

Ethan Everest.

That's who.

The minute Aaron drops me off in front of my building I dash inside and run up the stairs to the apartment. I want it to look as nice as it can, and considering I was like a tornado this morning before leaving for the office, I know I have some work to do. With Melanie practically living with Mike these days, I don't have to worry about us being interrupted.

I hang the jacket to my suit on a hook inside the closet door, step out of my black heels, and then work on the zipper on the back of the skirt. It seems to be stuck though.

Shoot. Running into the tiny bathroom, I turn around and try to see what the problem is. But the mirror is too high and even on my toes I'm not tall enough.

With no time to waste, I take my blouse off and pull on a tank top. I rush back into the living room and grab the mug I used this morning and an empty Little Debbie donut wrapper. I deal with those and grab the four pairs of shoes that have been left by the door, tossing them into the closet. I run back out and fluff the pillows, light a candle, and start the oven.

I'm breaking into a sweat, but time's ticking.

In a bowl, I mix half a cup of milk with a bag of blueberry muffin mix and whisk furiously. I pour the mix into the muffin pan and shove it into the oven before it's even preheated. I need it to start baking so the magic waft begins.

A knock on the door causes me to pop up and look. *Shoot.* That was fast. Bending over, I run my fingers through my hair and shake my head to fluff and give it body. I stand up and pinch my cheeks and then with my hand on the door, I take a deep breath.

When I open it, there he is. Smiling. Handsome in his suit with eyes that strip me of another item of clothing with each slow, devouring blink.

I pull him in by the lapels and land my lips right on his. Without a second to spare, our lips part and our hands are frenzied to touch. He charges forth with me guiding him inside. The door is kicked closed, the back of my knees hit the couch, and I'm on my back before we even say hello. My need for air causes me to gasp, and I look up at this gorgeous man and take a deep breath. Hovering above me, he says, "Hello, Singer."

My lips tingle. My body hums. And I feel it, his love for

me growing. Not just against my leg physically, but inside—passion blooms. "Hello."

Still staring at me, he smiles. "So this is your place?"

Although I'm in a compromising position, I laugh, then offer, "Yes, would you like a tour?"

He pushes up and takes my hands, helping me to my feet. "I would."

Leading him just four feet, I say, "This is my kitchen. I like to cook, but I don't cook all the time."

"What's that smell?"

"Oh. You just reminded me." I bend down and peek at the muffins through the oven door. Almost ready. "Muffins. Do you like muffins?"

"I love muffins, especially yours." There's a devious glint in his eyes.

"You haven't even tried my muffins."

"Oh, I've tried them." He licks his lips, and it's so seductive I'm not sure if my panties will survive. "And I can't wait to eat more of your muffins . . ."

Oh.

My.

God.

I fan myself with my hand, but his body blocks me in, cornering me. The back of his finger grazes along my jaw, his thumb toying with my bottom lip. "Is it hot from the oven? I'm feeling heated."

"It's not the oven, baby."

His other hand slides up my waist, exposing my midsection. My gaze finds that Adam's apple of his, and damn if I don't lose all train of thought. "We should, um . . . what were we doing?"

"You were giving me a tour of your . . . apartment."

"Right," I breathe out before slipping around him. "If

you keep this up, we won't make it past the kitchen counter." And I'm totally not against this idea . . .

"And the problem is?"

"The bedroom is back here." I grab his hand and drag him past the bathroom and into my bedroom. "And that's my bed," I say in an eager-beaver voice.

Ethan turns to look at me because I'm all pitchy, and my hand is now sweating. I try to shake his off, but he holds mine tighter, causing my temperature to rise even more. "I should turn on the fan."

"I'm comfortable," he replies. "Are we alone?"

"Melanie is at her boyfriend's place."

Eyeing me head to toe, he definitely notices my weird ensemble. "Nice outfit."

"It's the zipper. It's stuck. Do you mind helping me out of it?"

An eyebrow is raised in my direction. "Is that a serious question, because the answer is no, I don't mind one tiny bit. Turn around."

I do, but he doesn't start on the zipper like I expect. So I look back at him and ask, "What are you doing?"

"Enjoying the view. I might want you to wear this skirt a little longer. Have you ever played office?" Now I'm the one cocking a brow up. "Can you take dick-tation, Ms. Davis?"

"Depends on the dick-tator."

My backside is pulled against his front. "I'm very good at dick-tating my commands."

The oven timer goes off, and I jump. "Zipper?"

The damn thing is broken. I eventually have to take the muffins out and he's holding pliers to the zippy thing while in the confined space of my kitchen. We stop for a hot muffin and then go at it again. Eventually, it gives but with too much damage to the teeth to save it. "I'll take it to the dry cleaners. They can put a new zipper in."

"I want to take care of it for you." He grabs me around the waist and holds my ass. "You planning on wearing those panties all night?"

"I thought my muffins would be enough to satisfy."

"Your muffins are delicious. Go lay on the bed and let me take another bite."

"Biting?" *Rawr.* "I didn't know you were so kinky, Mr. Everest."

"You haven't seen anything yet." I'm lifted over his shoulder and carried into the bedroom, before he drops me on the bed. I bounce while laughing. Lying in the middle of the mattress, I pull off my top and bra and signal him with my best come-hither. "Don't keep me waiting, babe."

His jacket flies off, his shoes are kicked away, and while working on his shirt and tie, he says, "You called me babe."

Lifting up on my elbows, I ask, "You call me baby sometimes."

His dress shirt and undershirt come off, and while working on his belt, he smiles. "I like you calling me babe." The rest of his clothes come off and he climbs onto the mattress. "Now about those muffins . . ."

His mouth is gloriously talented. After losing myself to the ecstasy of it, twice, I return the favor.

Pinning him down, I kiss him first, my body burning with desire for this man. I rise above him and slowly slide down, his cock stretching me, igniting me in a deliciously different way. With my hands leveraged against his chest, I start to move, slowly at first and picking up speed just to watch his breathing change.

He's different tonight—direct, but conceding to my sexual pleas for more. Strong and agile, but happy to let me lead. His muscles are relaxed, but his focus intense.

His fingers dig into my hips as I rock back and forth on top of him, watching me take what I want. "God, Singer, you're so fucking beautiful." I lean down to kiss him, my nipples brushing against his chest, the feeling incredible.

Reaching above him, I grab hold of the headboard while he takes control, thrusting into me from below. His hands take my breasts and his tongue swirls around one nipple and then the other.

My head falls back, ecstasy seizing my body. His movements become erratic, my own a mess of twisted coiling, so tight I'll unravel at the hands of this man so easily once again. "Ethan. Ethan. Ethan."

"Fuck," he says, his voice riled as he bites his lip and slams me down, holding me in place. His hips press three more times before he falls under the spell that drags me under with him, an orgasm thundering through me as I squeeze around him.

Dropping on top of him, my forehead presses into the pillow under him until each quake subsides, and my breath returns. I lie still, my heart pounding against his, not able to decipher between his heartbeat and mine.

This beautiful man would do anything for me. I feel it with my eyes closed, deep inside. I know it when I open them and see it in the way he looks at me, the way he worries about me, and how he cares about me. I've never known such adoration. "I love you."

His head turns and his hands cover my back. He smiles so much the lines on the outside of his eyes crinkle. He's the kind of man who gets more handsome every day. Age will only increase this attraction. "I love you, Singer."

Our lips press together, our tongues mingling, love swirling all around. My arms wrap around his neck, and he rolls us onto our sides. The words have been felt, hanging on the tip of my tongue, but this time it's different. Not because we just had sex, but because we just made, created, grew our love.

As if he senses the shift like I do, he says, "I love you."

He loves me. The words heavy and wonderful, weighted in a gentle nature he hides from the world, to protect from getting hurt again. He now realizes I'll protect his beautiful and damaged heart as well. Saying I love you means we're a team. I take that commitment seriously and will try my damnedest to heal him with that love. My chest fills with happiness wanting to burst. "I love you, too. So much."

Maybe Mel was right. Maybe I don't see myself the way others do. He committed himself when he made his confession, vulnerable to feelings he tried so hard to bury. "Thank you."

"You have the biggest heart of anyone I've ever met."

"I think you easily rival it. Reegan asked what charity I wanted to support and told me you were going to donate twenty thousand dollars. Is this true?"

"He lost a bet and I wondered, *what would Singer do?*"

"I'm afraid you think I'm better than I am."

"You think I don't see you, but I do. Your heart shines brighter than the sun, sweet Singer." He pulls me into his embrace. "Don't ever let the world dull that shine. Okay?"

I kiss his neck. "Only if you promise to do the same."

"Together, nothing can touch us."

26

Singer

Ethan leaves in the middle of the night to avoid the chance of being seen. I'm promised this will all end soon, and we'll be free to be a couple however we want to be.

True to his word, he also made a donation to the nearest homeless shelter and enough to set Frank up for the remainder of the month. In the meantime, I have him also looking into any opportunities that Frank might be qualified for at his company. He beat me to the punch, and already has a guy looking into it.

Ethan Everest has a softer side than he lets on. I'll be careful to remember that.

I've just gotten out of the shower after a day at work when Melanie arrives home. "Hey," she says, smiling suspiciously wide.

She's up to something. Wrapping the towel around my chest a little tighter, I ask, "What's going on?"

"What do you mean?"

Swirling my finger in the air in front of her, I narrow my eyes. "That look. You look like you're up to no good."

"I'm just happy." Rolling her eyes, she says, "For you. For me. Just happy is all." She sets a bag on the kitchen counter, reaches in, and pulls out a bottle of wine. "I brought refreshments."

"Pour the wine and I'll get dressed."

As soon as I have on shorts and a tee, I join Mel in the living room, snagging a glass on my way to the couch. "I miss you. Feels like we're never here at the same time these days."

"I know. We're both caught in whirlwinds it seems. How's the love life?"

"Amazing." Sitting down, I don't hesitate to tell her everything and all that has happened. I end with my biggest confession of all, "I'm in love with Ethan Everest."

Once she picks her jaw off the floor, she says, "Wow, I have missed a lot."

"Just over one month and that's all it took."

"That time I saw him with you at happy hour, I could tell. Sparks didn't fly. They incinerated the sky."

I sip my wine and think about that kiss that he insisted was to get rid of those guys he didn't approve of. Now I wonder if it was just a way for him to kiss me. "Do you really think?"

"I know. I witnessed it. He was a smitten kitten with you. And do I need to remind you how he marked you as his the moment he leaned in and wrapped his arm around you?"

"He did not."

"He did. He positioned himself at the perfect angle. They could see his arm tucked behind you on the bar and you were none the wiser." She flops back on the couch. "It was so dreamy."

I flop back and laugh with her. "I feel like I'm living in a dream."

"There are worse places you could be."

We tap our glasses together. "I agree." After taking a too big sip, I finally tell her what I now know. "He's a millionaire."

"I think you left a few zeros off that title." She laughs lightly.

"What do you mean?"

"I've read all about him. Haven't you?"

Bending my legs under me, I confess, "I didn't search him online."

"Probably best. There's so much garbage out there." Leaning forward, she asks, "But what's it really like? Does he burn money instead of wood? Does he bathe in bills? Throw money out the window like confetti? I need to know because I really cannot compute the concept of that amount of money."

I'm too busy laughing to respond. When I collect myself, I roll my eyes and play along. "Yes, he siphons it directly into his veins through an IV drip." I can't hold back my laughter for long and let it loose before finally adding, "He keeps beer stocked in his fridge, but has this amazing coffee machine that makes magic in a mug." She's staring at me, hanging on every word. "You'll be disappointed to hear that he likes to think he's a regular guy and acts like one." I'm not though. I love him just the way he is.

When she actually does look disappointed, I say, "He has a private elevator that opens directly into his penthouse and he gave me a framed photo of me in a park. And his hallway is like an art gallery. Now mine hangs there."

With her head resting back, she rolls her neck my way, nudging me with her knee. "I'm trying not to be jealous."

"I know we used to joke about meeting someone rich—"

"It wasn't a joke to me," she says, but I can tell by the grin on her face she's teasing. She shrugs. "Mike wants us to consider a place in Tribeca."

"No," I say, shaking my head. "You're not a Tribeca girl. You're all Upper East to me."

"Aww." She grabs me by the neck and hugs me. "I knew I loved you."

"Bwahahaaha." Rubbing her arm, I embrace her. "Love you for real, but do you love Mike?"

"I think I can."

"Can or do?"

"I'm not sure, but I like him a lot, maybe love him." Her smile gives her away. Even if she's not *in love* yet, she's more than *in like* with the man. The few times I've met him he looks at her like she's a princess. She deserves someone who treats her like that.

Breaking into my thoughts, she asks, "Since we're in this lovefest, can I borrow the purple dress and the Jimmy Choos? Mike's sister is getting married at The Plaza tomorrow night and it would beat the same old worn-out black dress."

"On a Tuesday?"

"Have you seen the prices for a weekend at The Plaza? It's just an intimate ceremony at City Hall and then a reception in one of the small ballrooms. I was told it was formal though and would love to not have to wear the other. Again."

"You can wear it. Just promise me that you'll take care of both. They're special since Ethan gave them to me."

"I promise and I'll get it cleaned. I don't think we'll be too late. Maybe midnight. It is a work night, after all, and Mike likes his sleep."

"You're welcome to them. They're in the closet."

"Thanks again."

"You're welcome. Love you like a sis."

"Love you like a sis."

We kick back and watch a few episodes of one of our favorite reality shows before we head to bed. Rolling onto my stomach, I text Ethan since we're not able to spend the night together. His early morning meeting is cutting into my snuggle time with him. He promises that will change soon. I type: *Thinking about you. Missing you. I love you.*

It's the first time I've typed my love for him and seeing the words makes me feel his love. I plug in my phone on my nightstand and as I turn out the lights, I receive a message from him: *I love you. Sleep well, sweet Singer.*

Knowing I have the love of that man, I have the sweetest of dreams.

RUSHING OUT THE DOOR—LATE again—I almost don't see Frank, but when he catches my eye, I stop. Chip Newsom and his threats be damned. "Good morning, Frank. I'm surprised to see you here." I don't have any breakfast or coffee for him this morning, so I dig out some money.

"Good morning. I missed the view."

"But you slept at the hotel, right?"

"I did, but I got up to watch the sunrise. It was quite the majestic sight this morning."

Smiling, I love his appreciation for life, despite the hardships. "But it's all good where you're staying?"

"Clean. Warm. The bed has soft sheets. I almost feel guilty enjoying it as much as I do when I have so many friends on the streets."

Frank has a dirty and tough exterior, but his insides are pure gold. I hand him the few dollar bills I have. "Breakfast?"

"Too much." He tries to hand me two dollars out of the four I gave him.

"No, you hold on to it."

"Thanks." Eyeing Aaron, Frank asks, "How's your boyfriend? I take it you're an item these days?"

I look back at Aaron. "Be right there." He tips his hat, making me smile. So formal. We apparently still straddle that line between business and friends. To Frank, I reply, "We are an item, and it's going well."

"Your Prince Charming."

Laughing, I think about it. "I won't deny it."

"Good for you. You gonna move out of the neighborhood?"

"I don't have plans to do so right now."

"Let me ask ya. What's keeping *you* here?"

"My roommate. I don't want to leave my friend in a lurch."

"Miss Melanie is strong. Anyway, she has her own gentleman caller."

"How do you know all this?"

"I see and hear a lot, hanging around this street."

"I bet you do." I take a few steps back. "I have to get to work, but it was good chatting, Frank. Have a good day."

"You too, Miss Singer."

Once I'm in the car, I buckle up, my thoughts lost on all that's happened over the last few months. Ethan's life, I remind myself, is so big, important on a level I'll never relate to. What part do I play? Can I live up to what will be expected of the person standing by his side? So much pressure comes along with a man of his magnitude. I can't comprehend that side of his life, and the amount of money that plays into it.

Like this ex-girlfriend and her lawsuit. If this baby is his, and all that comes along with it, will he still want me? Our relationship has been steered off course before, but this time I worry we won't be able to steer it back on. All I know is I love him. My heart bonded with his the moment we met.

Aaron notes the silence in the car. "Got a lot on your mind, Singer?"

"Yes." My answer is on the heavier side as I stare out the window. The silence has become too much, filling my mind with the thoughts that weigh down my heart. "Ethan's on my mind."

"Do you want to talk about it?"

I catch his eyes on me in the rearview mirror. "Can you?"

"I'm very good at keeping secrets."

That makes me smile for some reason. "I worry with all that's going on with him that I'll be forgotten in the mix, or worse, asked to step aside."

"You have a big heart, and with a big heart there's more chances to get hurt. There's also more capacity to love big and wide, openly, and most of all, deeply." His eyes return to the road when the light turns green, and he adds, "But wouldn't the risk be worth it?"

Keeping my voice low, barely audible even to me, I say, "I love him."

"I know. He also knows. You know what else he knows?"

"What?"

"That you're the best thing in his life."

He knows how to make a girl feel good. Smiling, I say, "That's a lot of pressure."

"Nothing that you can't handle." Pulling up in front of

my work, he says, "Even with the delay earlier, I still managed to get you here on time."

Laughing, I slide toward the door. Before I reach the building, I turn and call, "Hey Aaron?"

"Yes," he answers, standing proudly in front of the shiny car.

"Thank you."

"You're welcome, Singer."

Acknowledging him with a singular nod, I turn and avoid making it awkward. He's got my back, and I his, but the most important part is he has my respect. He's loyal to a fault, despite how Ethan may joke in regards to him being paid. Deep down, he knows he's found a friend, someone true, someone who would do anything for him.

I'm not at my desk even five minutes before Chip pops over on the other side of my cubicle wall and leers down at me. I don't angle my body up, but my gaze flashes up. "Can I help you?"

"I need to speak with you privately." His stern voice worries me. I double-check the time. No, that's not it. "Walk with me."

"Okay."

"We'll get a coffee and talk."

Am I about to be fired? "Do I need to bring anything?"

"No." He walks away.

Dread fills my chest. Has he been stewing on that dinner with Umberto for all this time? Chip can be an ass, but he's not usually short with me. I stand slowly, worried that all the good is about to be pulled right out from under my feet.

27

Singer

Chip and I wait silently for the elevator to arrive. The doors open, and we step inside. His gaze darts to the doors and as soon as they close, he turns to me, practically breaking into song and dance. "Umberto and I are spending time together again."

My hand covers my heart. "Dang it. You scared me, Chip. I thought I was going to be fired."

"Why would you be fired?"

Rolling my eyes, I sigh exasperated. "Never mind. Back to you." I raise my voice and my hands in glee. "Oh my God. You are?" The *awwwww* in my voice takes over. I'm a sucker for romance.

He nods with a big goofy grin on his face. "He wants to get back together."

"He does? This is amazing news."

The doors open and we walk out. This time my pace is not the same dead-man-walking stride I entered the elevator with. Heading through the lobby, he says, "Yeah.

That dinner changed everything. At first he saw me with you and didn't know what to make of it. He thought I had turned straight." He laughs as if the whole world is sunshine and roses with a big basket of cute puppies on the side. "So preposterous. I could never after being with him. Coffee & Main?"

"Yes, please. So what are you going to do?"

"What do you think I'm going to do? I've been in love with that man since I met him two summers ago. The last year apart has been a tragedy by any standard in the dating world. I want to be with him."

"You should be with him then, but in the open. Don't hide your feelings. Love fully. Share with the world what sets your soul on fire." My feet stop moving. My eyes fixate on everything and nothing at all. An image of Ethan is clear as day in my mind. I repeat, mumbling, processing, "Share with the world what sets your soul on fire."

"Yeah, I heard you, and you're right."

"No."

"No?" He turns back and looks at me quizzically.

"No. I'm not talking about you."

"Huh?"

Waving my hands, I walk to where he stands, waiting to decipher my crazy. "I mean, I am talking about you, but I'm also talking about me."

"What about you?"

"I'm in love, Chip."

"You are?" His eyes go wide, a look of surprise morphing his expression. "With who? I didn't even know you were dating anyone. Well, not that you share that kind of information with me, but at dinner, it didn't appear to—Wait a minute . . . You're not in love with—"

My hand covers his mouth, keeping him from speaking his name. "No. Don't say it out loud."

I lower my hand and his words roll out in utter shock. "You can't. You've read the papers. You know he's bad news, right?"

"By how much they talk about him, I'd say they consider him good news for their advertising dollar."

"You know what I mean, Singer. He's trouble. He's embroiled in one of the biggest scandals in Manhattan. Those stories reach far beyond New York. He's not good for you. He's tainted."

"For someone so tainted, you sure wanted to work with him."

"I still do. I'm not a fool. His net worth is well over a billion dollars if not two. The man's a genius when it comes to business, but as for his personal life—"

"It's not true. They print lies."

"How do you know?"

"Because I know *him*."

With a raised eyebrow, a small grin slinks in. "How well do you know him?"

"*Very* well. And more than that, I trust him."

He wraps his arm around me and we start walking again. "Love is blind. At least when it comes to headlines. As for Ethan Everest, he's gorgeous."

"Love sees through the bullshit."

"That should be on a T-shirt."

I elbow him in the ribs playfully. "By the way, I have no money on me, so you're buying."

"I'd planned to—" A man who appears homeless by the dirt covered clothes and lengths of his matted hair approaches and tries to barge between us. Chip gripes, "Hey! Watch where you're going."

Acrid breath coats my ear as he whispers something, but the scent of him distracts me just as I'm pushed.

My world blurs as I spin, falling to my knees at the edge of the curb. I hear a horn and I flip my head back right as it whizzes by. My hair is blown wildly to the side and dirt pierces my neck and face, scaring the life from me.

"Stop that man." Chip's voice cuts through my fear, and I'm yanked back from the street. Chip is on his knees, looking in my eyes. "Are you okay? Singer, are you all right?"

The sounds of the city come blaring back all at once as I gasp deeply and tears prick my eyes. "Help me."

"It's okay, Singer. You're okay." Chip helps me to my feet, but one of my heels is broken, so my ankle wobbles.

Looking down, blood streams lightly from my knees, gravel and dirt from the street digging into my broken skin. The impact of what just happened and what could have been the end of my life if I had fallen two inches farther hits me, and my chest shakes along with my hands.

Onlookers stop to see what's going on, and I lower my gaze to the sidewalk. "Get me out here, Chip. Please."

Scanning the crowd, he says, "The man got away."

"Please. Please. Let's just go."

"Are you sure? We should call the cops. You could have been killed."

People are staring at me. "I know. I kno—I need to go."

"Come on." He helps me up and, with his arm wrapped around my waist, gets me back to the safety of our building.

Sitting in Chip's corner office, I'm lost in the view of the cityscape. It's amazing, yet right now it's also a blur of buildings. My makeup has been wiped away with my tears, but the stains of my ordeal now color my cheeks and the front of my shirt. My knees are bandaged, but the fact that the man meant to hurt me still burns. I can't seem to process what happened. "He kept walking."

From the other side of the desk, Chip sits forward, angry. "Fucking New Yorkers. City of heartless assholes."

Pivoting the chair around, I whisper, "He said something to me."

"What? When he forced his way between us like he owned the fucking sidewalk?"

"Yes." I nod.

"Are you gonna tell me or do I have to guess?"

"I don't know." My eyes meet his. "He shoved me. He pushed me and said something under his breath." My body shivers as I struggle to keep the memory alive so I can figure out this mystery. "It was all so fast."

"Are you sure? Like you said, it was fast. I'm sure you're just shaken."

"No." I spin to face the window again. "He meant to hurt me. I know it."

"What you went through today was traumatic. You should go home and get some rest. Take some Advil or even better, take a Xanax and go to bed."

I'm probably just imagining it, but I can't push down this fear. "It's probably my mind playing tricks on me. That cab could have killed me and came close. I'm just . . . yeah, shaken."

He sets two pills down. "Saint X. The only saint I pray to. Take them with water and go straight to bed." He stands and helps me up. Shoving the pills in my pocket, he helps me to the door. "Take tomorrow off. I'm sure you'll be sore."

"No, I'll be here. I can't afford the time off."

"At least call before coming in."

"Okay."

With my purse on my shoulder, I go downstairs and cut

through the lobby. Standing on the sidewalk, my hands start to tremor. I can do this. Just throw my hand and call a cab. I'll be home in no time.

I dread taking a cab, but I dread Aaron finding out about today more. If Aaron knows, Ethan will know, and I don't want him upset. As soon as the door closes, the ripped vinyl of the seat scraps the back of my knees and memories from earlier haunt me. I shake my head, refusing to let the attacker win. Pulling out my phone, I text Ethan: *I'm not feeling well. Going home to sleep. Will call tomorrow. Love you.*

I know he's in meetings all day, so I don't expect to hear from him until tonight. That gives me some room to breathe and come to terms with what really happened on that sidewalk. Was I pushed? Or did I fall?

Did he say something to me? Or was he just mumbling?

When I get home, I grab a glass of water and take one of the pills, hoping to quell the questions that plague me. Stripping my clothes off, I slip on a top and boxer shorts and climb into bed. The pill takes over fast. *Thank God.*

Right before I find comfort in the darkness of sleep, my phone buzzes. Rolling to my side, I'm too weak to reach for it and fall asleep.

I swear my soul claws its way out from my chest. I jump from my bed only to be met by a hand covering my mouth in the dark of my room. Still lost in a sleepy daze of confusion, I fight and scream for dear life. With both elbows, I swing back and punch my attacker. I'm freed and run for the front door amongst moans and a whine, "Singer!"

Landing with a thud on the floor at the end of my bed, I look back, recognizing that voice. "Ethan?"

"Yes," he groans again.

"Ethan." I wrap my arms around my body as my eyes adjust to the darkness. "What are you doing?"

"Damn, Singer. You can throw a punch."

When I flick on the overhead light, I see him holding his arms across his ribs in pain. "Fuck, that hurt."

I rush to his aide. "I'm so sorry. You scared me. What are doing sneaking around my room?"

"I'm not. I'm here to take care of you."

Oh man. "Now I feel bad. You can't sneak around a girl's apartment and not expect to get injured."

A smile grows and he shakes his head. "It's good to know you can take care of yourself if you're burglarized. Shit," he adds, "that hurt."

I think he groans a little extra to get some sympathy when I reach the bed. "I'm sorry." Normally I'd make him forget all about his ribs, but my heart is pounding in my chest, so I lie on my stomach still feeling a little woozy.

"I'm sorry for scaring you." Ethan rubs his hand over my back. His warmth is welcome. "How are you doing?"

"I've been better."

"Can I get you some tea? I have some water heated in the kettle on the stove."

My eyes find him and I giggle. "Tea? Why are you offering me tea?"

"Because that's what women are always offered in books and movies. Tea."

I begin to laugh harder. "You know, you're right." Rolling onto my back, my body aches from earlier, reminding me of what happened this morning. "Tea would be great."

When he heads toward the kitchen, I move up and fluff my pillow before sitting against it. He asks, "Sugar? Milk?"

"A little milk please."

He comes back with a mug, handing it to me, and sits down next to me. "Let me know if you need anything else."

"This is a good look on you." I take a sip while admiring him in his undershirt and boxer briefs.

Making a face, he rubs my leg gently. "I came from the office."

"In your underwear?"

Chuckling, he replies, "No. A suit, but I took it off out there. Can't crawl into bed with my girlfriend wearing a suit."

"Especially not one of your fancy-pants suits."

"Your sense of humor is still intact, but how is the rest of you?"

"I'm okay. How did you know?"

He sits next to me. "Chip called me."

Surprised, my lips part. "Really? What did he say?" I set the tea down on the nightstand.

"Not enough to keep me away." His fingers touch the bandage on my left knee. "Tell me what happened."

The memory strikes me like a lightning bolt. "Ethan."

"Yeah?"

"The man said Ethan."

His brow crumples and the dark centers of his eyes widen. "What do you mean?"

"Just before he pushed me."

"He pushed you?" Jolting back, he asks, "Who pushed you?"

"Some man."

He's off the bed, pacing beside it until he goes into the living room and returns just as quickly. With his phone in his hand, he stares at me, the intensity making me shrink down a little under the covers. "What the fuck are you talking about, Singer?" The soothing tones of his voice are gone. The distinct fury builds in his words. "Tell me what happened?"

The grip on his phone tightens by how white his knuckles become. Managing to calm my clamoring heart minutes before, it's now heavy in my chest. "What's wrong?"

"You tell me. Some guy pushes you after saying my name. Fill in the blanks for me."

Licking my lips, I try to clear the fuzziness from sleep and the pill I took. "Chip and I went for coffee down the street from the office. We were almost at the crosswalk when a man forced his way between us. He looked and smelled like he hadn't bathed in a long time."

"Homeless?"

"Most likely."

"Go on." His arms are crossed as he continues to pace the small room.

When I take too long to pick up where I left off, he stops. Harsh eyes and an expression I've never seen on him hit me. "Can you remember?"

"I'm trying, but you're scaring me."

The hard lines of his brow ease, and he sits down next to me again. Touching my arm, he says, "This is important, but you're more important. Take a minute, but I need you to try to remember the details."

Grabbing the other pillow, I pull it to my chest and hug it tightly to me. "He pushed me. He pushed me hard. I think he was trying to push me into the traffic."

"What the fuck?" He stands again as if his body can't be still. "Singer, focus and tell me all of it."

"I'm trying," I reply, tears filling my eyes. My legs curl beneath me, my knees aching from the wounds being stretched. "He breathed on me and said your name, then pushed me toward the traffic." I stop when his phone goes to his ear.

Ethan marches out of the room as if he's been given

orders to do so. I stay put, listening as best I can, but he keeps his voice low. I think he's trying to hide the conversation from me. I catch parts of it—Lars, investigate, Chip, homeless, report—then it goes quiet in the living room.

I lean forward to listen, but he appears in the doorway startling me. "Shoot," I say. "Stop doing that."

"Don't eavesdrop then."

"That conversation involves me. Were you talking to Lars?"

"I was." The bed dips when he sits at the end of the mattress. "Listen, Singer. A man saying my name and then pushing you toward the traffic . . ." He sighs. "Doesn't sound like an accident."

"It happened so fast. I could be wrong."

"But what if you're right? I don't want you staying here. Not until we get more details and know it's safe."

"Where's Melanie?" I ask, getting to my feet.

Taking me by the wrist, he says, "She had a wedding. She told me she didn't want to go, but I insisted since I was here. Anyway, what was she going to do? Stare at you?"

"Yes, one creeper staring at me is enough," I tease, moving onto his lap. I wrap my arm around his neck and kiss his head. "I'm glad you're here. Thank you for coming over."

"Funny girl. Along with your humor, your sarcasm seems to be intact." He lifts me into his arms and stands. It's a new favorite thing of his that he does. I feel protected in his arms and love the feel of his strong heartbeat. "I've been texting with her, keeping her updated. But I did promise her you'd text her if you woke before she got home."

My feet touch the ground, but I stay pressed against him. "Okay, I should do that."

"Text her and then pack a bag. You're coming with me."

His kiss is soft and lingering. *Comfort.* I find peace and comfort when his lips touch mine. Pushing my hair away from my face, he says, "I'm glad you're okay. We'll talk more in the car." Before he leaves, he adds, "I had Aaron drive Mike and Melanie to the wedding. He'll be back here in ten minutes to pick us up." He steals a kiss and returns to the living room, giving me space and time to myself. I think he knows I need a minute to sort through not just my thoughts, but to sail the rough waters of my emotions.

"So bossy." And I like it, though I don't tell him. I smile. Ethan is an impressive man as a general rule, but the way cares for me? It's hard not to want to pinch myself to make sure it's real. *How did I get so lucky?*

I text Melanie. I hope her evening hasn't been ruined. *Hope you're having fun. I'm fine. I'm going to sleep at Ethan's tonight. Are you going to Mike's or will I see you here in the morning?*

She texts back immediately: *PHEW! I'm so glad you're okay. You were passed out cold. I checked twice to make sure you were breathing. I'll be home tonight. Mike flies out for work at some ungodly hour, so I'm staying at our place. I'll see you in the morning. Tell Ethan thanks for the ride tonight. We made it just in time for the I Do's.*

A selfie of her in the bathroom pops up.

Me: *OMG! You look amazing.*

Melanie: *This dress is amazing. When Mike saw me he said he couldn't take his eyes off me and talked about marriage for the first time. I think he might propose soon.*

Me: *It's not the dress. It's my beautiful friend. The dress does look amazing on you though.*

Melanie: *Thank you. I'm glad you're fine. I didn't want to leave, but Ethan insisted he would take care of you.*

Me: *He made me tea.*

Melanie: *Whoa. That's love right there. He's a keeper. I have to run. Love you like a sis. XOX*

Me: *Love you like a sis. XOX*

I grab an overnight bag and stick with the basics. I can come back tomorrow for more. I don't think my place is unsafe, but I do want to be with Ethan tonight. As soon as I'm done, Ethan's there in a heartbeat. "I've got this. All ready to go?"

"I'm ready."

He walks out ahead of me, and I'm about to shut the door, but look inside one last time feeling like I'm forgetting something. *Am I just spooked from earlier?* Nothing immediately comes to mind, so I lock up, and follow him to the car.

28

Ethan

Aaron is quiet, understanding the severity of the situation. On the flip side, Singer doesn't seem to get it at all. She's smiling like we're on a fucking adventure to Disneyland. I'm stewing in my anger, hoping not to take it out on the innocent. But I want to break something. I want to rip someone's head off. I *need* to protect her.

I've failed her.

Watching her out of the corners of my eyes, she checks her social media then looks out the window. I might be misreading her. The light that usually shines in her eyes is dull. Maybe she's putting that smile on for me. Reaching over, I take her hand.

When she looks my way, she says, "If it's not safe for me, the apartment isn't safe for Melanie."

"She should stay with Mike tonight."

"He has an early flight so she can't. She doesn't have clothes with her."

"Tell her to get her stuff, and I'll send the car for her

tonight. Give her Aaron's number. She can text him when she's heading home so he'll be there when she's ready."

This time the smile I see is sincere. There's my kind-hearted girl. She was assaulted today, but she's more concerned about her friend's needs. *God, this girl.* Touching my cheek, she asks, "You'd do that for her?"

"For her. For you. Yes, of course. I have three other bedrooms that are never used."

"You have three other bedrooms? Why have I not been given the full tour?"

"Because the only room that matters is the one where I make love to you."

Leaning her head on my shoulder, her fingers intertwine with mine. "I love you."

With my free hand, I reach my arm over the front of her and hold her to me. "I love you, too, Singer." This is the first time we've said it when I felt something else twisting inside, something that threatens my relationship with her, my love for her.

Once we're in the penthouse, I settle her on the couch. Along with a sleeping pill she brought, I give her warm tea and ice-cold water. I want her to have everything she needs, but I don't know what that is. She's so content with the littlest of things and hates to trouble anyone. She doesn't realize she's no trouble to me.

While she's distracted by a home decorating show, I stand near the kitchen, leaning against a wall and watch her. I love her, but I'm clouding her sunny days and raining on her parade. This is unsettling on a deeper level than my well-being.

My phone vibrates in my pocket.

Lars: *I'm assigning detail to Davis until we know more.*

He's not one to make rash decisions. Snap, yes, which is

why he's the head of my security, but not rash. He would only do this if he needs more time to investigate the situation or he believed there was a threat to Singer or myself. I can take it. I can handle someone coming after me. But Singer? If someone's threatening Singer to get to me, *that* I won't accept or risk. My fingers fly across the screen: *I want her safe at any cost.*

Wanting to check on her, I join her on the couch. "Are you hungry? I have soup or fresh fruit. I can order anything you like. Craving anything?"

She points at me, a smile on her sweet face. Scrunching her lips, she narrows her eyes. "You're cute. You know that?"

I take hold of her hand and bring it to my lap, tracing her slender fingers. "Have you eaten today?"

"Have you eaten today?" she volleys back.

"I'm serious, Singer."

"So am I. You're really cute."

Although *she's* really cute right now, I'm thinking she's a bit out of it. "Did you take the sleeping pill?"

"I did," she proclaims proudly. Slinking lower on the couch, she rests her head on a pillow.

"Do you want to go to bed?"

"No. I want to stay out here with you." She glances to the TV. "How do you feel about shiplap and farmhouse sinks?"

Eyeing the TV for any kind of reference to what she's talking about, I feel lost on this conversation. "I don't know what those are."

"Have you ever been to Waco?"

"Unfortunately, yes."

She rolls onto her back and stretches her legs over my lap. The silly from seconds earlier is gone and she looks at the ceiling. "I used to tell Melanie we were going to own this city, but I'm starting to realize that maybe it will always own me. Not everyone's dreams are meant to come true. Sometimes dreams are just meant to stay what they are —dreams."

"Your dreams are goals you're still trying to achieve."

"Says the billionaire." A smile doesn't follow, but I know she doesn't mean anything by it. "An entry-level job in publishing pays less than I'm making now. You see where I live on the money I make. Where would I live if I make less? I'll tell you where. Boulder." Her eyes fill with tears and I feel the first crack in my heart. I feel powerless watching her crash from the stress of the day.

I stand and pull the blanket over her. "You've had a long day. The pill is kicking in. Just close your eyes and get some rest."

Her lids drop closed, but I leave on the TV, finding comfort in the noise. It's only eight, but this day feels like it's been going forever. When I stand, her eyes open and her fingers hold me by the watchband. "Ethan." Her voice sounds lucid, much like how her eyes appear looking at mine.

"I'm right here." For a moment I think she's awake, but she doesn't seem to register my attention, looking through me more than at me.

"I baked blueberry muffins hoping you'd fall in love."

"I did. I fell in love." Stroking her cheek, I say, "You didn't need muffins for that. Just yourself."

"Before he pushed me, he said Ethan Everest will pay." Her eyes fall closed and her mouth falls open and she passes out, instantly in a deep sleep while I'm left staring at her.

Holy fucking shit.

I run to my phone and call Lars. "Get up here. Now."

Lars is walking off the elevator within minutes. "Yes, sir?"

"Do we have the footage yet?"

"We have one, but it's not clear. We're waiting on one more from the Bank Center that has a camera aimed at that specific corner."

"Get it immediately. She's on medication, but I think it relaxed her mind enough to remember. Right before she was pushed, the man told her Ethan Everest would pay. She said he pushed her toward the oncoming traffic intentionally. He tried to fucking kill her." My hands run through my hair and over my face. "Someone is trying to get back at me by hurting her."

"Do you have any suspicions who it might be or why?"

"Not one fucking clue. *Fuck*." I pace the kitchen trying to keep our voices from traveling to her across the room. "Keith wouldn't resort to murder. Anyway, we've settled. He'll get the money he's been after for years. We need that footage to find the fucker who pushed her. She said he looked home-less so there must have been a payday for him to attack her."

"I'll get the footage. I've also sent one of my guys to talk to her boss since he witnessed it."

"This must stay on the down-low. She walked away from a crime scene. Both her and Chip Newsome could come under fire with the police. We need concrete evidence before we go to them."

"That situation was handled. We'll get the evidence we need before going to them with this."

"Tonight."

"We're working on it. I'll text you when I have new information. I emailed you the first video, and I'll send the second as soon as we get it."

"Thank you."

He goes back to the elevator and I return to Singer, who's sleeping soundly. I sit on the coffee table in front of her and stare. I've become the creeper she was joking about earlier, but I don't care.

I watch this woman in front of me, wondering how a bastard like me got so lucky. Aaron doesn't tell me much that goes on between them, so I assume their car rides must be quiet. But he has told me how she treats Frank, and that she brings them both coffee most mornings. The mornings she doesn't, she's usually running late.

Singer treats the world with a broad stroke of compassion. It makes my teeth clench thinking that someone dared to treat her with less.

I run the tips of my fingers over her delicate neck, the vein pulsing when I pass over it. With two fingers pressed to the beat, I check her heart rate. It's steady like her. A whirlwind of intrigue and beauty drew me to her so instantly. But her outlook on life, the way she sees me, the peace she brings to my life, she's my North Star. She's the one I look to when I'm struggling to find my way home.

Shiplap and a farmhouse sink.

I'm thinking those aren't common in Manhattan. The city is all about the sleek and modern, like my apartment. But I'd give those to her. I'd rip this place apart and let her have whatever her heart desires if she'll stay.

I'm careful not to wake her when I get up, though I have a feeling a train's whistle couldn't do that right now. I pick up the remote and start to close the curtains, feeling vulnerable to onlookers for the first time since I've lived here. Scanning every light I see outside this wall of windows, I realize it's not just about the view anymore. Someone out there wants to hurt me, and I'm a fish trapped in a bowl.

Other than the charity ball, we've been discrete. Even then,

*we avoided photos, and there's not been public PDA. Who knows
about her? And how?*

The curtains close, and I move to where I've set up my
laptop on the dining table to check my email for the first
video.

Lars is right. You can't see anything from that camera
angle. I click over when my box dings with a new
message. The second video is here, so I click to full screen.
My eyes narrow when I see her and Chip walking down
the street together. His arm is around her and even
though I could get caught up in that detail, that's something I'm willing to deal with later to get the other
answers I need now.

The elevator opens and Lars calls, "Sir?"

"Dining room." When I see him, I add, "Please keep your
voice down. Singer is asleep on the couch."

"Have you watched the video?"

"Watching now." I press play and watch with my hands
clasped in front of me. I know what's coming and anxiety
builds.

Lars points at a man in the upper left hand corner of the
screen. "That's him."

My gaze darts between Singer and this man. He's
disheveled with a slight limp. He appears drunk by the back
and forth swaying when he walks. A car slams on the brakes
to avoid hitting him when he crosses against the light.

Singer, in all her innocence, is laughing, not even aware
of what's about to happen. The man uses his hands to
wedge Chip and Singer apart. Grabbing hold of Singer, he
leans into her, and then shoves her.

His pace picks up, and then he runs until he's out of the
camera's view. I rewind to watch again, this time I follow
Singer. The feet of the chair skid as I stand abruptly, the

truth just as horrible as I thought. "He was definitely trying to throw her into traffic."

She stumbles, then falls to her knees catching herself on the curb. A cab drives by, and she leans back just before Chip grabs her by the arms and pulls her away from the edge. He's shouting at the man but bends down to help her.

With all those people staring, he fucking gets away.

Fuck!

I knew it was bad. I could feel it in my gut, but this is worse. I slam my fists down on the wood table. How will I ever get that image out of my head? *How?*

"Find him."

29

Ethan

"We already have a full description of the perpetrator with our co-op team. We'll find him by morning." Lars stands completely still, as if the woman I love wasn't almost killed for some vendetta against me.

"I want him tonight," I reply, leaving no room for further discussion on the matter. He's smart not to argue. After watching the video again and again, I rub the bridge of my nose and close my eyes, trying to control my rage. "I want him dead."

The statement doesn't faze Lars. He's not a henchman, and I'm not in the business of murder, but someone else is and I need to know who. I walk away. Standing behind the couch, I look at her sleeping. Even with the drugs running through her system, her sleep isn't peaceful.

I direct him to go. "Leave."

When Lars is gone, I lift Singer into my arms and carry her to the bedroom. I tuck her slumbering body under the covers and take my phone from my pocket and set it next to me when I crawl in next to her. Bringing her to me, she moves on her own, wrapping her arm around my middle and resting her head on my chest. I'm not soft, but she finds comfort in my arms, her restless muscles stilling.

Closing my eyes, I hold her, finding comfort under her body.

My arm buzzes.

Buzz.

Cloudy dreams clear for reality.

Buzz.

Buzz.

Phone.

Where's my phone?

Popping one eye open, the brightly lit screen in the dark room guides me straight to it.

Aaron.

I lift the phone to my ear. "What?" Singer shifts, so I lower my voice. "What's going on?"

"I haven't heard from Ms. Lazarus."

Pulling the phone away from my ear, I look at the time. 12:17 a.m. "Shit. I fell asleep." I sit up without thinking.

Singer mumbles and rolls to the side. "What is it?"

"Nothing," I reply, getting out of bed. "Go back to sleep."

"Ethan?" she calls, propping up on an elbow. "What is it?"

"Business." I rush into the living room, away from her so she can't hear. "Aaron?"

"Yes?"

"What's the ETA of when she was expected?"

"I called The Plaza. The Reception ended an hour ago."

"You didn't pick her up?"

"I was told to retrieve her from the apartment, so I've been waiting here."

"You're right. I'm sorry. Her boyfriend was going to see her home." My mind is not quite awake, but my thoughts are starting to connect. She probably went home with Mike. "It's just past midnight. Have you texted her or called?"

"I did. Twenty minutes ago. I haven't heard back."

"Okay, let me call Melanie, and I'll call you right ba—"

Shots ring out.

The sound of glass exploding on the other end of the phone is so loud my grip on the phone loosens, and it falls to the floor.

My breathing stops.

My body frozen to the spot.

"Oh fuck." I know what that sound was. My hands begin shaking as I reach down and pick it up.

From behind me, Singer asks, "Where's Melanie?"

I look up and see her standing there, a silhouette with the hall light behind her. "What?"

My eyes water as the sound of more shots ring and a woman's scream echoes from the phone, the speaker turned on from when it hit the floor. Singer jumps. "What was that?" Her voice shakes, terror contorting her face.

Dropping to my knees, I shout, "Aaron?" I grab the phone and shout again. "Aaron? Are you there? Aaron? Aaron! Fucking answer me." I jump to my feet and run to the security panel. We've practiced this a few times to make sure all security measures are in place, so now it's ingrained. "Code 5. Aaron. Aaron's down."

Lars's voice comes through. "Code 5. Sending Rogers to retrieve him."

"I'm coming down."

"You should stay, sir."

"Secure the penthouse behind me."

I grab my shoes and a jacket. Singer's trailing behind me,

asking a million questions, but they're background static to my thoughts. Aaron. *Fuck*.

She grabs my arm, forcing me to turn toward her. "What does 'Aaron's down' mean?"

Punching the button to call the elevator, I can't look at her, and yet, she's the only thing I want to see. She's the only one I want to be with. I want to turn the hours back—days, months even—to the time when I met her on the fire escape. Everything would be different. I cup her face, the fear prevalent in her eyes. "We don't know. It sounded like gunshots. We don't know."

"Noooo," she says, crying. Tears roll down her cheeks, her hands gripping mine as if I can save her. I'm going to do every fucking thing I can to do just that.

I try to pry her fingers off me, but she's got a viselike hold on me. "I've got to go, Singer."

"No. You're not leaving. You're not going."

"I have to be there for him."

"Is he alive? Please tell me he's okay. He's got to be okay."

Damn this fucking elevator. I look down, not able to lie to her when looking into the soul of her eyes. "He'll be okay."

"Where's Melanie?"

The elevator opens and I force her back and get in. "Stay here, Singer. Promise me you'll stay."

"Please don't go," she pleads, moving forward, "don't leave me."

Holding my hand out in front of me, I stop her from entering. "I'll be back."

"With Melanie?"

"Yes."

"I love you."

This time I look directly into her eyes. "I love you, Singer." The door closes and my back hits the wall. I don't know what I'm heading into, but I can't leave Aaron out there.

When the elevator opens, the SUV is in front of me with the door open. Lars follows me to the vehicle and slides in after I get in. "Is the penthouse covered?" I ask.

"Yes, I've got two men stationed. The alarms and perimeter have been secured."

The SUV speeds out of the parking garage, and for a brief second, I forget it's not Aaron driving.

Lars has his phone out. "The car has been tracked to Ms. Davis's residence. It's still there."

Looking down, I see the flashing dot on the screen. "That's not good." I can tell he wants to say something, but hesitates. "What? Just say it."

"It's not good." Looking up, keeping tabs on our whereabouts, he adds, "He would have checked in. He's trained. He knows to fight and then to contact us. I won't lie to you. I'm concerned for him and for your safety. This could be an ambush. We don't know what we're walking into."

"The police could be there already. Maybe it's in their hands, and they have it sorted."

"There have been calls to the police. We tracked three over a scanner. No one on duty has claimed the calls. No one's en route. They were asking for available officers to report to the scene. There's no response."

Looking at my watch. "It's been over ten minutes."

He looks down at the tracking device flashing red. "I know."

"What's going on, Lars?"

"I don't know, but we need to be careful."

"I started a private social site. We talked about girls and whose parents we could steal a few beers from without getting caught." The lights racing by outside hold my sight, but my thoughts are back in high school. I have no idea why my mind decided now was a good time to reminisce. "Twelve years later, I'm sitting here praying to God that a man who has become my friend isn't dead because of me. Is this the meaning of success? Is this the happiness that money was supposed to buy?" I turn to Lars. "I'd trade it all for the last year to disappear."

"Success comes in many forms. You aren't responsible for Ms. Davis's accident or for Aaron."

"Then who is? Because I'm feeling pretty damn responsible when the woman I love is being thrown into traffic after being told I'm going to pay the price for who knows what."

He goes quiet when a text appears on his screen. "The police are on their way, and we still haven't found the suspect from this afternoon's incident."

"It's not an incident if he intended to murder her."

"Two minutes. Remain in the vehicle until I've secured the premises."

I stare straight ahead, adrenaline pumping through my veins. The tires screech as we round the block to Singer's street. As soon as it comes to a stop, I jump out. Lars is already yelling, "Stop him."

He doesn't have to.

We all stop at the same time.

With the headlights from the car shining toward the middle of the road, we see Aaron, eclipsed by the bright lights. Blood runs down his face, his shirt soaked, his arms full—a woman's body.

Oh God.

Fuck.

I've witnessed many emotions in my life—sadness,

happiness, heartbreak, anger, deceit, and more. But I've never witnessed devastation.

Until now.

Edging closer to us is a version of this man I've never seen before. Aaron has always been so . . . unshakable, undaunted. "I . . ." he starts, but then he lowers his head without finishing.

Her body is limp. *Fuck.* An image of Singer confuses me. And then I realize why. *"Singer said I could borrow the dress. I hope you don't mind, Ethan."*

"No. It fits. It looks nice."

"We're the same size, and thank you. I've never felt more beautiful."

. . . *Oh God.* The dress. Melanie was wearing Singer's dress to the wedding.

The team moves in and I run to them, lifting her neck as Lars helps Aaron hold on to her body. "Melanie? Melanie?"

When we move her to the back of the SUV, she remains motionless, not responding. *Not breathing.*

Sirens roar in the distance, fast approaching, but there's no time to waste. I don't know if it's too late, but I will try my damnedest to save her.

I reach to take the pulse on her neck. "Melanie? Can you hear me? Mel, wake up." Struggling to find a pulse, I glance at Aaron, who's shaking his head.

"I already tried to revive her." He falters, his eyes rolling back. I catch him when he's too weak to stand, and he says, "I've been shot. Twice."

Holding him up, I shout, "Has an ambulance been called?"

Aaron clears his throat, but blood drips from the corner. Fuck.

He says, "My phone." Stopping to swallow, color draining from his face, he says, "I can't find it."

Lars responds, "We called."

Lights drown us in red and blue and we're surrounded as Lars holds on to Aaron. I shout to the police, "We need help. Our friends have been shot." I grab hold of Melanie's hand and hover over her, searching for life. Fucking hell.

Please, God, save her.

The ambulance pulls up behind the police cars, the paramedics rushing between the cops who have their guns aimed at us. The paramedics drop to help Aaron while the officers come closer, and demand, "Show us your weapons."

Lars raises his hands. "We're licensed gun carriers. We're private security for Ethan Everest."

"I'm Ethan," I say with my arms held up. "Melanie Lazarus. She's in the back of the SUV."

"She's been shot," Aaron garbles.

They approach slowly and I watch as one of the paramedics jumps up and pushes between us. "How long ago?" With a walkie-talkie, he calls for backup as he runs to the ambulance. "We've got to get her to the ambulance."

Staring at the cops, I say, "I don't have a weapon on me. I'm going to help him." I don't wait for permission. As soon as he returns, I help move her to the backboard. He's quick to secure her and then we lift. Aaron is rolled onto a gurney and maneuvered behind us.

Once we set her inside the ambulance, the paramedic jumps in and pulls the board. He's quick to check her pulse again and lower his ear to her mouth. There's a pause that extends. My movements are sluggish, realization setting in. From the other side of Melanie's body, the paramedic looks at me. It's the sadness, the distinctive look of sorrow that only comes from grief. *She's gone.* "We'll do the best we can."

A cry of anguish rips through my heart, shredding it.

Singer.

When I turn around, I see her standing with her hands over her mouth, tears streaking down her face. Boxer shorts and a T-shirt, sneakers with no socks, she's in the middle of the street next to a cab, eyes are fixed on Melanie. She runs, and I run, catching her before she can get any closer. She cries, "I need to be with her."

"Singer," I caution, my own grief hitting hard. All the money in the world . . . none of it matters if I can't protect the ones I care about. "Stay with me." I don't know if I say it for her or me, but I hold her even tighter.

Her eyes track every minute movement inside the ambulance as the paramedic tends to her best friend. Hitting my chest, she screams at me, "Let me go. I'm the only one she has."

"You can't."

"Let go of me, Ethan." Pushing off me, she punches my shoulder to make my hold loosen, but it's a losing battle. I secure my grip around her and whisper, "No. No. You can't help her." *And I'm helpless. Fuck. I can't help either of them.*

Who did this?

Who hates me this much?

She stops fighting me, her body stilling in my arms and tensing under my touch. I hate it. When she looks at me, she whispers, "I need to be there for her."

When I don't speak right away, her eyes narrow. Then her arms stretch out, pushing me away again. "What?"

Shaking my head, I hold her until the ambulance drives away, and then I release her. "Why did you do that? I need to be there when she wakes up." On a mission, she turns to go back to the cab, so I say the only thing she won't want to hear, but the only thing that will stop her from leaving. "She's gone."

"She's gone to the hospital?" she asks, almost hopeful. *Almost.* "I'm going to follow them."

"Singer." With one foot in the cab, she looks up. "She didn't make it," I say it the only way I can manage to, but it doesn't dull the truth.

She gets in the cab and closes the door, but the car doesn't move. When I see her head drop into her hands, her shoulders shaking as sobs break her apart.

I walk to the car and open the door. Tears flood her eyes, her anguish worn in the lines of her face. I reach in and help her out, bringing her into my arms. Dropping my forehead onto her shoulder, I beg, "Please forgive me."

Please don't leave me.

Please forgive me.

Even if she forgives me, I'll never be able to forgive myself for dragging her into my nightmare. For being the cause of her immense and devastating loss.

30

Singer

Ethan's back is to me. Whispers are exchanged and then he and the nurse look my way.

The phone rings *seven* times.

Three nods from the nurse.

He taps the counter *twice*.

Eleven steps to the chair next to me.

Four Mississippi seconds before he speaks. "Do you want to go for a walk?"

"No."

His hand covers mine, the blood that covered them earlier all gone. He did the best he could to clean up, but his clothes are still stained. "I think we should." His eyes are scanning the waiting room.

Twelve people. I counted. *Twelve* people who may have their lives changed forever after tonight. Maybe they have already.

I have. Mine has.

Focus on the numbers. Count. Don't stray from facts.

Forty-six black tiles. *Thirty-two* chairs. *Nine* magazines. *Five* books. Are people waiting here long enough to read books?

"Come with me, Singer."

I do as I'm told because that's easier than thinking for myself right now. *Four* overhead messages calling for Dr. Schneider.

One.

Two.

Three.

Four . . .

The air is not as I expected. It's not fresh. It's stifling. I need to be inside, closer to Melanie. "When can I see her?"

We stop near a bench a few feet from the hospital's entrance. He's staring at me with eyes I don't recognize, piercing my heart before he says the words. "Melanie is gone."

I stare at him, at his right eyebrow, never noticing that dark spot before. Reaching to touch it, I smooth it down, then pull my hand back. My breathing halts, my throat closing. He grabs my wrist when I discover the color came off, my eyes fixated on the dark red on my skin. "Singer?"

My stomach revolts. I turn and vomit into the bushes.

Melanie is gone.

Melanie is gone.

No.

I refuse to accept that.

Ethan needs to stop saying that.

He's wrong.

"You're lying," I say, my entangled emotions coming out harsher toward him.

"No." He doesn't temper his words or the intensity of his eyes. "I'm not."

Salty tears mix with dry heaves as the reality of his words sink in, my body giving out.

I'm grabbed, held tight, as I cry. "Melanie is not dead." I search his eyes, trying to find the sagey green that doesn't lie. "Right, Ethan? She's not."

He's lifting me to my feet when all I want to do is sleep. I need this nightmare to stop. "Singer? Look at me. Look at me, baby." My head is shaking, denying his tone. My eyelids are weighted as I fight against the burning that started in my stomach. When I finally look up, tears fill his eyes. "I'm sorry."

He's sorry?

I try to process his words. Sorry for—*No.* I can't. No. Not that. "No."

"Singer."

There's that tone again. "Don't say my name like that. *Please*."

The tears fall like rain down my face, the pads of his thumbs trying to soothe my pain away. But the gentlest of touches can't heal this wound. He says, "I need you to hear me. Aaron is alive, Singer. He wants to see you—"

"I need to see him." *Aaron is alive.* I swipe the back of my hands across my cheeks, and push out of his hold. "Come on."

"Singer, wait."

No, go. I must go to him. I don't make it halfway down the hall before I'm grabbed. "Let go of me, Ethan."

"He's in surgery. We have to wait."

"But—"

"He told me before he was taken in. We can be here when he wakes up, but that will be hours from now. I think we should go home and you should rest."

I yank my hands from his. "Go *home*? Home to where my

friend was hurt?" Hurt, not murdered. *Please let her be okay. Please, God.*

"I meant the penthouse."

"No." My head is shaking, the motion matching my hands. "That's *your* home." Taking a step back, I say, "Home. *Home.* Melanie. Oh God, what has happened?" I start to slip, my body too weak to carry the reality of what's real—she's gone. "She liked Mike. She thought it could be more. Tonight . . . she was excited to wear the dress. My dress. Something so pretty. *She* looked so pretty. I'm sorry I didn't ask you if you minded. I couldn't say no to her. We're sisters. Not blood, but through love. She's my family." My mind starts looping. "I couldn't say no—"

"It's okay. Of course I don't mind. Singer, breathe."

Squeezing my eyes closed, I focus on one word.

Breathe. Breathe. Breathe.

It's rough, my throat dry, but I breathe. Then I exhale slowly and open my eyes. "Strangers ask us if we're sisters. All the time. We don't look much alike, but our hair is a similar color, and we wear the same size. She's much prettier though. Her personality eclipses everyone's."

"She thought the same about you."

"Thought?"

Past tense. *Thought.*

Breathe.

We were sisters.

Breathe.

She was so much prettier.

Breathe.

Breathe.

Pressing my forehead to his chest, his arms come around me. I whisper, "She's gone, isn't she?"

"I'm sorry."

I try to push away, but he holds on tighter. "I need to talk to Melanie's family, Ethan. I need to talk to mine." Tears take over again, slipping between my lips. "Mike." Sobs wrack my body. "He needs to be called."

"I'll take care of it." Moving us off to the side, he lowers his voice. "Take a breath. Take a deep breath. You're in shock. Understandably, but I need you. Tell me how I can help you."

"I'm alive. I don't need help. I just need to know what happened."

"I can't tell you that."

"But you know."

"We shouldn't be talking here."

Looking right and then down the hall toward the exit to the left, I don't see anything but desperation in the faces of families waiting and nurses busy making rounds. "Why?"

He stares at me a good few seconds before whispering, "Someone tried to kill you. Have you forgotten?"

We're getting stares. He has blood all over him. "No, how could I?'" My arms are wide. "How could I forget?" Covering my face with my hands, I bury myself in the comfort of his arms. "I'm the one who should be dead. Not her."

Taking me by the elbow, he's not asking this time. "We have to go."

I free my arm, but follow. The tension between us is almost audible. Lars sits in the passenger seat and when I look at the driver, he's unfamiliar, upsetting my stomach again. Ethan doesn't say anything, but he hands me tissues.

I hate this—this dread, this tension, this fear, this anger, this nightmare we're living. I gasp, covering my mouth.

The dress.

The shoes.

The apartment.

We look like sisters.

Oh God.

"Her hair only varied by a few shades," I say, my thoughts barely voiced as my stomach sickens from the realization. I think I'm going to be sick.

"They thought she was me."

Lars and the driver don't react, both great at their jobs and minding their own business—eyes forward at all times. On the contrary, Ethan is staring at me like I'm already a ghost. The lights from the street reflect against the water in his eyes. Guilt forces his gaze to his lap, and then morphs into shame. "I'm sorry."

"For what?" I ask, my anger simmering. This is not the man I know. Images of that party last year come flashing back with every street lamp that lights up the car.

White smile. Full lips.

Dynamic green eyes.

Six three and impossible to ignore.

I turn away, not because he's not still so damn stunningly handsome, but because he can't look me in the eyes when he replies, "For Melanie."

Hearing her name causes my stomach to lurch and the pain is too much to contain. It leaks through tears and cries I can't hold back, not even to reassure him. The door opens and I hesitate. Looking at the steel elevator that leads to the penthouse feels more like a sentence than a safe haven.

But I get out.

I know I don't have a choice.

I also don't have anywhere else to go.

Lars rides up. His back is to us like the first time Ethan brought me here. This time there's no flirting or sneaky peeks. No sexual tension and no undressing each other. Our souls are already bared to the point of ragged. Nothing exists, but three people who went to war and two who came back injured.

Stepping out first, I catch a glimpse of the photo of me, but I don't stop. I keep walking through the penthouse and straight to the bedroom. The dim light comes on when I walk into the bathroom. Sitting on the edge of the tub, I stare ahead at the large mirror. Similar to how I didn't recognize Ethan back in the vehicle, I don't recognize myself now.

Sallow.

Dark circles.

Exhausted eyes that refuse to open wider.

I turn and start to fill the bath with water. I don't bother turning the lights any brighter. I like the nighttime setting. It's comforting in the darkness. Stripping off my clothes, I leave them in a pile at my feet before painstakingly pulling the bandages from my knees. I feel as dirty as I look, so I step in before the tub is full and sink down under the water. Holding my breath for as long as I can.

One Mississippi.

Two Mississippi.

Three Mississippi.

Four Mississippi.

Five Mississippi.

Six Mississippi.

Seven Mississippi.

Eight Mississippi.

Nine Mississippi.

Ten Mississippi.

When I come up for air, Ethan is sitting on the far edge of the tub. "Do you want to come in?" I ask, my voice sounding more normal than it should.

"Are you sure?"

Pouring body wash under the rushing waters, I reply, "I

wouldn't have asked you if I wasn't." I'm curt. Rude. When I shouldn't be. I don't like this. This version of me. *This version of us.* It's tainted like the clothes he's taking off.

When he gets in, the water rises higher before crashing over the edge into the draining reservoir. I move without him having to ask. I don't even know if he wants me on his side, but I want him on mine, so I move. His arms wrap around me when my back presses to his chest.

My best friend is dead and . . . the image of seeing her moved into the ambulance—lifeless—clenches my heart, my breath stopping in my chest. Will it away. Will it away. My hands squeeze his. *Will it away.* When I start breathing again, the moon draws my attention.

The pain becomes an unbearable ache in my chest. His silence deepens the open wounds already swallowing me. "I know what you're doing, Ethan. You're taking the blame to justify what happened. You're trying to coax reasoning into something that has none. It's murder. We can't make sense of that."

"If we wouldn't have been dat—"

"We wouldn't have found love." I lean my head back on his shoulder. "We're damaged, but not broken." Maneuvering through the silky waters, I sit sideways so I can see his face. Daring to touch him, I'm gentle when I caress his cheek, and turn him toward me. "Look at me." When he doesn't, or can't, I beg, "Look at me, Ethan. Please."

"I can't."

"Why? Why are you keeping me out?"

"Because I caused the pain that hurts you too much."

Taking his face between both hands, I plead, "You didn't. Please don't shut me out. I can't bear it. I won't survive." I move even closer, pressing my lips to his, forcing him to feel me if he won't look. "I need you, Ethan." I kiss the side of his lips. "Hold me." When his arms come around me, I push for more. "Touch me. Please."

"How?" When I kiss him this time, I receive one lighter in return. "Show me."

I lean my head against his cheek and find his hand under the water. Lifting it, I bring to the curve of my neck. "Touch me, Ethan. Touch me with the love you feel."

His fingers span the back of my neck and he brings me closer. We kiss, this time with the purpose I'm wanting, the feeling I need. With one hand on my back and the other sliding down my front, my breathing becomes jagged. His tongue is firm, but pliable, wrapping around mine and owning the rest of my mouth. The hardness beneath me tempts as I try to forget the outside world and live in his for a while. I lift up and position him, easing down and watching his face, the ecstasy that forms from our bond taking over.

Finally.

I can breathe.

His gaze lifts to mine and I feel the pounding of my heart beneath my hand.

The air leaving my chest.

The love I feel for this man.

Finally.

We exist again. My heartstring reattached to his. The gentle, but stormy-colored eyes. I'll take them. They aren't bright like the day I met him, but they're his and mine, and I'll take this over shame and guilt and pain any day.

My hands find the muscles in his thighs and I lift. He pulls. I push. He thrusts.

We love.

We love.

We love.

I wrap my arms around his neck, needing every part of my body touching his. All of my soul tangled with his. All of me, *his*.

His.

We make love until we both find the peace we used to take for granted. We make peace until we both find a place to land. We land in each other's arms a knotted mess, keeping the outside world at bay for a short time. We keep the lights low and our voices lower, but in the dark of the safest haven I know, only three words are uttered. First by me. Then by him.

"I love you."

Words that come with unspoken promises. Something we lost in the wreckage is found in each other's arms.

Hope

. . . and then I cry.

31

Singer

I awoke when the phone rang and sat up to see Ethan and Lars sitting at the table. The call came around seven in the morning. Aaron was out of surgery and was resting. With no complications they said he could have visitors mid-morning. I wanted to be his first.

I wasn't.

His daughter was.

At fourteen, I could see the resemblance to her father. They share the same eyes that seem wise beyond their years. After meeting her quickly, I watch her from down the hall, giving her time and space with her father despite feeling anxious to see him myself. "Did you know he had a daughter?" I ask Ethan quietly as we walk to the waiting area.

"Yes."

"He works all hours of the day for you and sometimes night. When does he see her?"

"She's in school, but sometimes in the evenings she rides

along with him. He closes the glass and they talk upfront. They're very close."

"I didn't even know there was a glass divider in the car."

I catch the roll of his eyes. "That's because he never used it with you. With me, he's not so polite."

I refuse to think about Melanie, and with Aaron set to recover, I focus my thoughts on him. "He was young when he had her."

"He *was* young. He's only thirty-two."

"Is he married?"

After sitting, Ethan looks around before leaning forward and resting his arms on his legs. "She died in a car accident when Caroline was seven."

My gasp is heard before I cover my mouth. "That's awful."

"He once told me that they dated all through high school and when she got pregnant he had no doubt about what they should do. They eloped and came back a married couple, living with his parents until he graduated from college. His wife was happy to stay home and raise their daughter."

"Caroline is a pretty name."

"She's a great girl. Very levelheaded."

"Like Aaron."

"Just like her father."

"Ms. Davis?" I look up when I hear my name. A nurse smiles. "Mr. Westinghouse can see you now."

Taking Ethan's hand, we walk down the hall to Aaron's room. When we push open the door, his daughter is next to her father, and Aaron turns toward us. With a smile, he says, "Good morning, Singer. Morning, Ethan."

"Good morning." I go to him and hug him gently.

Jokingly, he says, "Careful or you'll make the boss man jealous."

Ethan comes over and says, "Too late." They shake hands, keeping it professional, but I can see Ethan getting choked up. "How are you?"

"Good as can be after being shot twice."

One of his arms is in a cast and his leg is wrapped the same. "Twice?"

He nods. "Once in the arm. Once in the leg. Neither was life-threatening fortunately." The smile falls from his face when he looks at me. "I'm sorry, Singer."

The words of reassurance I want to give him get caught in my throat, the sharp edges stabbing me. Ethan is behind me, his hands on my shoulders, speaking for me when I can't. "We're glad you're okay. I don't want to think about training someone else."

Aaron laughs and when it turns into a hacking cough, Caroline pours him a glass of water. When his throat is clear, he asks his daughter to excuse them for a few minutes. She goes and as he watches her I can see the love in his eyes. As soon as the door closes, he says, "She doesn't know the details, and she doesn't need to." His eyes find mine and his voice shakes. "I'm sorry I couldn't save her."

With my hands on the railing of the bed, I hold myself up while walking around to the chair on the other side. I sit, but I don't look at him. I can't. He continues, "She held on as long as she could." My pain resurfaces like a bullet to my own heart when he adds, "You were a sister to her."

"She said that?"

He angles toward me despite his own pain. "She said she loved you like a sister. I promised I would tell you."

I bury my face in my hands unable to look at him, though he bears no responsibility for something he couldn't control. I want to make him feel better, but my own heart-break prevents me from giving away something I don't have. Finally, I ask what I know her parents are going to ask of me, "Did she suffer more than she had to?"

"She said what she wanted to say."

"Did she say more?"

"She sent love to her parents and said she was in love. Life was good because she fell in love."

The tears cloud my view and my cries make me barrel over and rock. "She was my best friend. She *was* my sister." The deep-seated guilt bubbles. "When we came to New York, I promised we would make all our dreams come true. And look what's happened. I will never forgive myself."

Ethan is there, right in front of me, kneeling. The pressure of his hands breaks through my spinning mind, and I look at him. "Don't do this, Singer. You're the one who told me it's not our fault."

Standing, I go to the door. "She was killed because they were trying to kill me. How can I live with that?" Turning to Aaron, I say, "I'm thankful you're okay, but I can't stay. I'm so sorry." I run out of the room and down the hall. As soon as I exit the hospital flashes go off and reporters start shouting my name, aiming questions and their cameras at me.

Desperately searching for the SUV, I can't find it and my body starts caving in to block them out. My body is shielded, Lars directing me to stay close as he puts himself between them and me. "Twenty feet northeast." We hurry ahead. The door is opened and I climb in. He's next to me, and says to the driver, "Drive."

I'm quiet for minutes, but with him sitting so close, I can't let this opportunity slip by. "It's true, isn't it? Someone meant to kill me, not her."

A miniscule squint of Lars's eyes reveals the break from

his usual composure, but then his expression loses emotion. "I think you should speak to Mr. Everest."

"I have. I want the whole truth now. He'll say anything to protect me. I don't need emotional protection. I need answers." I stare at him, not letting him off the hook. "Please tell me. I'm better with information. I can't move on when I don't have answers."

Mulling it over, I see him shift his gaze out the window, a debate raging between his professionalism and his humanity.

I push harder. "Please, Lars. Please."

He swallows hard enough for me to pick up on the action. Looking me over, he says, "Without the suspect in custody, this is only my opinion."

"I'll take it."

There's a coldness that he relies on, protecting himself with a clear wall that divides us. I'm starting to think it's how he protects himself from getting attached to his clients. It's sad that he seems detached from people in general. But maybe that's why he's so good at his job. "I do believe someone meant to kill you, and that Ms. Lazarus was murdered because of mistaken identity."

My unfounded conclusions are founded in an expert's confirmation. My best friend is dead because of me, because of my relationship with Ethan. That's the part that's the hardest to stomach. Could I have prevented this? Is it as simple as saying if I wouldn't have started dating him, she'd be alive?

I have a feeling it's not.

Conflicted, I say, "Thank you," and turn back to my own thoughts.

"I'm sorry about your friend."

Hearing him continue speaking so openly surprises me.

He's an observer, but right now, he feels more like a confidant, a friend. When our eyes meet, the coldness that was there is gone, the ice melted into warmer browns. "Thank you."

"How are you doing?"

"The best I can." We're having a conversation. Lars and I are talking and it's not uncomfortable or weird. It's . . . nice. "I'll see her family today. They fly in—"

"I have a car scheduled to pick them up."

"Ethan thinks of everything."

"I know in your mind, amidst the chaos of emotions you must be sorting through, on the surface it will be easy to fall into the trap of blame. I'm not trying to butt in where I shouldn't, but he's hurting inside. The attack on you was awful, but he carries that blame on his shoulders. Now the death of your friend and Aaron being shot . . . " He stops as if he's said too much.

"I worry about him. I do. I feel like I'm worrying about everyone, and I'm struggling."

"You're allowed to mourn, Singer."

I close my eyes, tired of this nightmare I can't seem to wake from. Turning back to the not-so-fascinating sidewalks of Manhattan, I say, "I hate the guilt I'm feeling for everyone."

"He's a grown man who can handle himself."

"Lars—" I don't want to talk about it anymore.

"I think people have this impression that he can handle any tackle life throws his way."

"Is that a football reference?"

"He can throw down. I've seen him stand up to assholes, but on the inside, he's this guy who created something phenomenal, this incredible brainy tech company. So Ethan has this unique balance that allows him to relate easily to a variety of people. What they don't see is his struggle to be all things for everyone."

"I think there's a life lesson in here somewhere."

"There always is when there's a sport reference involved." His own joke makes him smile.

I'm not in the mood to laugh, but seeing a man of his disposition smile, forces mine out on this overcast day. "Okay, but the point is?"

"Sometimes we don't choose the load we're meant to carry. Sometimes we do. But we have to stay in the game. Despite a bad play or fumble, we have to fight for the ball to get a touchdown or the other guys win. Don't let the bad guys win, Singer. Fight."

We're shadowed in darkness when the SUV pulls into the parking garage, stopping in front of the elevator. A man I don't recognize is stationed in front of it, and I take a deep breath, not sure if I'm ready to be locked away in the tower. Going back to my apartment is not an option though.

Lars opens the door and gets out, holding it for me. I slide across the black leather and step out. Our eyes meet, and I say, "Fight."

He nods with a small smile, but says nothing. Within seconds, his façade of indifference is back in place.

The ride in the elevator is quiet despite the man in here with me. I'm too tired to make polite conversation, so I lean my head against the stainless steel wall and wait in silence.

The door opens and I walk into the penthouse, rounding the corner to the living room and almost stumble over two suitcases.

Two suitcases.

Two suitcases I recognize, but they're not mine. Standing there, I'm baffled and my heart hurts. I grab my phone from my pocket and call Ethan.

"Hey," he answers right away. "Where are you?"

"The penthouse," I reply, kind of hating myself for calling it that more often than not lately.

"Will you be there when I get back?"

"Ethan," I say, resting against the back of the couch. "I know this is hard on you. I'm not trying to take that away, but I'm feeling suffocated in this place, by the security, by people all around me, needing me to react or respond or be one thing or the next. I'll be here. I don't mean to sound like I'm not grateful, or I don't want to see you. I do, but I need time with my thoughts."

"I'll give you whatever you need, Singer."

"I know. I know you will because you're putting yourself last when you need to be putting yourself first. Don't bury your feelings like you did over the last year. Deal with them head-on. I'm going to try my best to do the same."

"It's a dark place to go."

"You don't have to live there. You can just visit, but you need to do it for you, and for me." His breathing is the only sound shared from the other end of the line. "I need to ask you something."

"Okay."

"Why are these suitcases here?"

"I had someone pick up some of your clothes for you. You needed more than a pair of jeans and my T-shirts."

"Those are Melanie's suitcases."

"What do you mean? They weren't supposed to touch anything except clothes from your room."

"They did," I say, tearing up again when I thought I had cried them already. "My clothes are in her suitcases."

"I'm sorry. They must have misunder—"

"They were under my bed. They didn't know, but now I'm here, staring at *her* suitcases." My anguish rolls through me and I start to cry. "She got them for college graduation to take her on all the adventures she dreamed of going on. They're hers, but they're here."

"I can have them removed."

"Removed like her." *No. We can't . . .*

"Jesus, Singer." His voice is panicked. "I didn't mean. Fuck. I'll be there in less than fifteen minutes."

I hang up, drop the phone on the couch, and kick the cases as hard as I can, and they land with a thud. I don't feel better like I thought I would. I feel worse.

Melanie's dreams were stolen from her just like her life. Sinking to the floor, pain shoots through my scabbed knees, but I don't care. I rest my head on the large navy-blue suitcase; my arms extend over it, wishing it were my friend.

Why bother wiping tears away? Who's that for anyway? Me? I don't need to lie to myself by pretending this doesn't hurt.

The metaphor of my stuff in her cases isn't lost. She'd want me to eat life up, to live it fully, to celebrate the little things like romance movies at Christmas and the big things like finding love in a city of eight and a half million people.

Closing my weary eyes, I try to turn off my mind. My body gives in and relaxes, and my thoughts begin to numb.

The chime of the alarm.

The elevator door closing.

The footfall of his shoes across the floor.

I almost expect him to pick me up. I'm glad he doesn't.

Ethan sits down next to me and lays his head on the suitcase. Our gazes connect and our hands latch together.

Together.

I can't fumble us. He's on my team, and I've got to fight for the ball and for us. Moving closer, I slip onto his lap and rest my head against his chest. One kiss to his neck is followed by another. "I love you."

"I love you so much, Singer."

Finding this mini reprieve from the outside world and the bad, I stay curled in his arms, one word ever-present as I begin to fall asleep.

Fight.

32

Ethan

Chip stopped by. Working in my home office today, I came out for water and kind of hung around the kitchen. As if I didn't have enough to deal with, I'm adding jealousy into the mix. *Fuck.* He's been talking to Singer in a hushed voice, and it's driving me mad. *What are they talking about? Why is he still here? Why are they whispering?*

I've been trying to deal with the court case scheduled for tomorrow, but my mind is focused on the quiet voices and the muted words they share. A few smiles are exchanged between them as well. *Is it wrong to want to hoard all her smiles and the little happiness she has right now?*

In the meantime, I get an email that, despite everything that's happened, we weren't granted a motion for continuance. I let Reegan deal with that. Melanie's parents are due to arrive any minute, and I'm edgy.

I set my glass on the island. Too loudly. Singer and Chip turn to me. I say, "Sorry," even though I'm not.

Singer comes into the kitchen. "Can I make you something? Are you hungry?"

"I'm fine." *Stop being so good when I only have bad intentions right now.* "How are you?"

"I'm fine." Reading between my lines too well, she comes closer, and whispers, "Is something wrong?"

"Why is he here?"

"Because he's my boss, and he's worried about me. Don't forget that he was there when I was pushed. He helped me—"

"I haven't forgotten." I cross my arms over my chest. "He had his hands all over you."

Her head bobs back. "What are you talking about?"

"I saw the footage," I reply, spitting out the pungent words because I'm a total asshole when it comes to things that belong to me.

She crosses her arms and purses her lips. "And?"

"He had his arm around you."

"What?" Her eyes go wide like this is new information. She was his escort to the dinner. She said it was a deal they made, but why did he put his arm around her like he had a right to? "You're kidding me, right?"

"No, I'm not kidding." What part of my pissed-off expression would give her that idea?

"You're being ridiculous."

"Am I?" I ask to her back . . . while she walks away. I'm tough like that.

She whips around, and I'm leveled to the ground with one hard glare. "You are, Ethan. I'm finished with this conversation. We will continue it later," she grits through her teeth. She returns to him and makes some excuse for him to leave since tensions are rising. At least she tells him we're under a lot of stress. We are, so it's not a lie.

I make myself scarce, not willing to torture myself by watching them hug goodbye, but Singer appears in the doorway to my office shortly after. "I've never been back here."

My eyes stay focused on the documents in front of me. My monitor is the only streaming light in the room, highlighting the top of my desk. "You're welcome anywhere in the penthouse. Treat it as your own."

"Why do you have the curtains closed?"

"It didn't feel right to let the sunshine in."

The doorway is abandoned as she comes around behind me and slides her arms over my shoulders. "We're not enemies. We shouldn't treat each other as such."

"I don't know what's going on, and when that happens my mind gets the best of me."

"So that was jealousy? It felt like anger."

"It was both."

"Chip is gay. The only reason I'm telling you this is not to ease your jealousy, but to temper the anger directed toward us." *He's gay.*

Fuck, I'm an idiot.

I blow out the hot air of rage I was holding in, and drop my head. "I'm sorry."

"I don't need an apology. I don't want you to feel bad. I just want you to give me the benefit of the doubt next time."

"You deserve that."

The papers crumble when she moves around and leans against the desk. "Look at me, Ethan."

I do because I meant it when I said I would give her anything. My attention is the simplest request to fulfill.

"I do deserve that, but I need you to know what you see is what you get. We're new, but I thought we knew each other better than that back there."

"We do. I trust you. I don't know what that was, and I don't want to come up with excuses. In the video he had his arm around you. I wasn't expecting that. My team saw it too and I felt—" My phone lights up, and I look down. "Melanie's parents are here."

The news takes her aback. Her breath is jagged on the cusp of a sob, but she stops herself. Standing up, she kisses my head before raising her chin. I don't want her stalwart. I don't want her to keep things in. I like her delicate nature. I like her innocence, which the last few days have stolen from her. Watching her, she walks to the door but stops and says, "I need you, Ethan. I can't do this alone."

I stand. Telling me how I can help her helps me, because it means she needs me, and I *need* that. I take her hand, and we walk down the hall together. We wait outside the elevator for its arrival. The light above the door flashes on, and her grip tightens. As soon as the door slides open, I hear her suck in a breath.

Seeing them reminds me of my own parents, making me miss them. But my guilt overrides all else as I watch Melanie's mother cry from the sight of Singer.

Singer practically lunges into her arms. Whispers of apologies echo around us, soothing words from Melanie's mother given so gently as she embraces Singer just as tightly in response.

Propriety takes over and I swallow down my own feelings on the matter. "Mr. and Mrs. Lazarus, I wanted to extend my deepest condolences."

Melanie's father's eyes lock on mine, and he extends his hand. Shaking it, I add, "I'm sorry we're meeting under these circumstances." I knew this moment would be hard— *understatement of the year*—but seeing his tears, knowing I have something to do with them, it breaks me, and I look down to hide my weaknesses. *And guilt.*

Singer hugs him, and he releases my hand to embrace her. There's gentleness, one of trust and love, reflecting the sisterhood between Singer and Melanie. "Your parents," he struggles to say, "are worried about you. You should call them."

"I will," she replies. Taking a deep breath she tries to regain a composure that's more than broken, one that shows she's strong in the face of adversity. I hate that she feels she has to, because being strong for everyone else will weaken you. Like she scolds me for doing, she needs to take care of herself first. "Come in."

She leads them into the living room, leaving their bags near the elevator. I wait for them to pass and take up the tail of this unsettling and tricky situation.

It's inappropriate on every level, and I should feel guiltier for thinking it at all, but seeing her walk so comfortably around the penthouse, so naturally a part of my life, provides some sort of balm to this nightmare. *She's become my home.*

Standing between the kitchen and the dining table, she states, "I could use a drink. I know that's not something we usually do together, the roles we played in each other's lives, but I'm not going to make it much longer if I don't."

Melanie's mother says, "I could really use a vodka martini."

Maybe that's what breaks the ice, puts this child and parent relationship on an even playing field, but the heaviness sort of lifts.

There are tears, buckets of them, but I can see by the way they look at Singer, how they treat her like their own.

The media has already gotten hold of the details and so

much has come to light in the last twenty-four hours. Singer doesn't pretend she isn't the intended victim, but they don't treat her as such.

Instead, they remember their daughter and her friend, they reminisce and they hug many times. When Melanie's boyfriend, Mike, arrives an hour later, he is accepted like family. It took two transfers and an overnight flight to get back here last minute.

Through the laughter, he pulls a ring from his pocket. It's the one he's carried for the last few days looking for the right moment to pop the question. As smiles disappear and tears reappear, I step away from the table, the pain too much to watch play out.

A buzz of energy covers my shoulders when Singer's hands rub gently. Glancing behind me, she catches my eye and asks, "Are you okay?"

"No."

"I'm here for you."

How? How is she so strong? So resilient? So forgiving? How can I not be madly in love with this woman? My hand covers one of hers, and as Mike hands the engagement ring to her parents as a token of his eternal love for their daughter, we keep our eyes on the city that now haunts us.

As the hours burn away, they eventually say their goodbyes. Singer and I ride the elevator with the three of them, all bonded by a tragedy that never should have happened.

They have full access to a car, and I'm taking care of their expenses while they're here. They don't want to stay long. The police have asked to retain the body for a full autopsy. They've asked to take her home.

It's a battle no parent should ever have to fight.

When they're gone, Singer says, "Melanie was in love

with love, but I could tell she really did love Mike. I could see it in his eyes. She would have said yes to his proposal."

I nod, not sure what to say with heavier questions hanging over us.

We all know what killed Melanie. The question that lingers is *who* killed her. We're left standing there with Lars, neither of us wanting to go back up just yet. Singer says, "I want to go for a walk. I need fresh air."

I glance to Lars before saying, "It's not safe for you to take a walk."

"I can't stay cooped up there forever."

"It's not forever. It's until a killer, who wants you dead, is caught," I snap.

Her chin rises in challenge, her eyes narrowing. "You can't keep me here."

"That's obvious. How did you get out the other night anyway?" I'm in no mood to contain my temper. "I gave direct orders and was told the penthouse was on lockdown." I'm waiting for either Singer or Lars to respond and neither is anxious to engage.

He glances to her, but she's just looking aimlessly around the garage, her arms stubbornly crossed over her chest. She swings a hand out and asks, "What are these cars?"

"What do you mean?" Not interested in the change of topic.

"Whose are they? There's only one elevator on this floor. Yours. But there are six cars and a motorcycle. Who do they belong to?"

I point at a Corvette parked near the exit, hoping to throw her off the scent of the trail she's wanting to travel down. "That's his."

She's too quick. "And the others?"

"Mine," I finally fess up. I'm not ashamed. I tug at my collar, feeling the heat of her gaze.

"Why do you have so many? Who needs"—she counts the cars—"five vehicles, not counting the town car?"

"I had reasons when I bought them."

Walking forward, she looks at the exit. "It's things like this that make me wonder why I don't know these things. Why didn't I ask more questions? I just accepted everything so easily, so readily." When I see her eyes, she adds, "I let your life, your money overshadow mine. If I had been paying attention maybe this could have been prevented."

"Singer," I caution. This line of thought will only lead her to more pain, more emotional devastation.

Spinning my way, her eyes narrow and her stance is solid. With her hand out, she wiggles her fingers. "Give me the keys to the Lambo."

"No way." I cross my arms in protest.

Lars steps into the alcove of the elevator to avoid the fight we both see coming. Smart man.

Her demands are getting harsher. "Hand them over, Everest."

"No."

A finely defined eyebrow is cocked. "I'll walk then." She turns on the heel of her sneaker and heads for the exit.

Damn. She's doesn't play fair.

Making me choose between her safety and my favorite car—there's no contest, but this is going to hurt. I signal to Lars. "Get her the keys."

Lars goes inside the office, grabs the keys from the hook, and returns. She snatches the keys without so much as a thank you as she swings them around her finger and marches toward the car. I'm hot on her heels. "Where are you going? How long are you planning on being gone?"

Abruptly, she comes to a stop, and turns back to me. "You are not my keeper, but because this is your car, I'll give you the courtesy of answering your questions." Spinning the key ring around her index finger, she smirks. So sexy that I'd love to kiss that grin right off her face. "I'm not sure on either."

As if that will satisfy me, she heads to the car again. I run to the passenger side, not letting her go alone. Speaking to me over the top of the car, she says, "You can come with me on two conditions."

Over the hood of the car, I eye her. "Name them."

"First, there's no destination. You're either comfortable with that or not. If you're not, you should stay here where you're safe and hidden from the world."

Her sarcasm is duly noted and not appreciated. *Sassy fucking mouth. Damn kissable lips.* "Second?"

"Second, no more questions. Capiche?"

"Unlock the car, Singer."

Holding the key fob in the air, she asks, "Do you agree?"

"I agree," I reply, rolling my eyes.

The lock pops, and I lift the door.

As soon as she starts the car, she says, "Buckle up, Mr. Everest, I'm taking you on an adventure."

The gears grind, and I cringe. We're not off to a good start. "Do you know how to handle a machine of this magnitude?"

"Don't worry your cotton socks. If I can handle you, this car will be a piece of cake. The real question is—do you trust me?"

I set myself up for that one, so I don't bother feeding the comedic beast. It's too good to see her smile to take this little joy away from her. I take a deep breath instead, and as she gets a feel for the gears while twisting my insides with each grind, I give up control for a little while and buckle up. "I trust you."

As we roll out of the parking garage, the overhead lights reflect in her eyes, and I see a glint of the girl who first stole my heart. If it takes sacrificing a four-hundred-thousand-dollar car, so be it. That spark of life is worth more.

33

Singer

Ethan is struggling. I see it, though he's trying to remain calm. I know some of it is because I suck at driving a stick, but most of it is guilt. I refuse to let him do that. He's had a year of hardships and enough loss to last five lifetimes. He needs a break. He needs to smile. He needs to find happiness, and that's what I intend to help him do.

It's just after nine at night and the streets are way too packed to let this baby loose. I'm really not good with a manual transmission in traffic. "Sorry," I say, sneaking a peek at him.

"Don't be." I feel joyful when I see him smile for the first time today.

"It's been awhile since I've driven a stick shift."

"By the way you're torturing this innocent car, I'm surprised you know how to drive one at all."

"Dang, man," I tease, "don't go easy on me or anything." We stop at a light. I had pumped the brake when we went through the last intersection. I'm not willing to risk this car on last-minute slipups. "Maybe you should drive."

"If you wanted me to take you for a ride, all you had to do was ask." He winks, but his heart isn't in it. I start to wonder if we're putting on a front for each other.

"Will you take me for a ride, Mr. Everest?"

"Take the next right."

Several blocks down, I pull into a hotel roundabout, and we swap seats. Reaching into the back, he pulls out a baseball hat and puts it on as if he's missed it as much as the car. He's at home behind the wheel, which makes me curious how often he gets to drive it. "When was the last time you drove this car?"

"It's been a few months."

My lips part. "Really? Such a waste."

"Brace yourself." He punches the pedal when all the lanes are clear, zipping us across four and taking a right. The horsepower sends my back to the seat and my hands out to hold on to the door and dash. But his words remind me of last night, our connection a constant in this maddening world. I'm bracing, holding on for my life, not from his driving or the danger of the speed limit that's currently being broken. I'm bracing myself for the plummet that's surely circling outside my consciousness.

Once we're across the Henry Hudson Bridge, I realize where we are and break my own rules. "We're leaving the city?"

"First, there's no destination. Second, no questions. You made me promise, baby. I'm holding you to the same."

I see the smirk tempting the corners of his lush lips. I love their fullness, their pressure, the way they possess mine with each kiss. And damn do I want a kiss. "Very funny."

"Those are the rules if you want to go on an adventure, Ms. Davis."

His phone lights up, a text filling up a portion of the screen. I lean in, out of habit, to read it, which makes him laugh. "Nosy much?"

Sitting back, I laugh. "Sorry."

"It's okay. I have nothing to hide from you, Singer. Do you mind reading it to me?"

"It has a bunch of question marks. That's it." I look to him for the explanation.

"Thanks."

"Thanks? That's it? No, I need more. We're sharing here, so share."

"He's wondering where I am. It's not safe, so he's checking in."

Resting my head on the seat, I watch him behind the wheel commanding the car like he commands my body—owning every last inch of it. "When I'm with you, I forget about your money. Do you ever forget?"

"I'm reminded every damn minute of every damn day, except when I'm with you." He lifts my hand to his lips and kisses gently. "You're a nice escape, Ms. Davis."

I bring his to my lips and kiss with the same affection. Sitting back, I admire the scenery. I like the lack of skyscrapers and enjoy seeing all the trees. They're hard to see at night, but knowing they're there, reminds me of home. Home. *Melanie.*

My heart hurts, so I try to push that pain aside again for just a little while. "With all your money, I would have thought Lars would have a tracker on this baby."

"He does." Ethan laughs. "He was tailing us in the city, but I lost him a few blocks before the bridge when I turned off the tracking device. I think he got the message."

Smiling that Ethan is now the rebel, I ask, "What message was that?"

"That I wanted to be alone with you."

His hand returns to the steering wheel, but I wish I could hold it longer, Reality is always on standby ready to smack me right back into it. I say, "As much as I love the thought of us escaping the city for a while, it's not safe to do so. I don't want anyone hurting you."

"They're trying, Singer." He looks at me before his gaze shifts back to the road again. "It's you I'm worried about, not me."

"Then why did you agree to this?"

"Because you needed to get out. I could tell you were restless." Reaching forward he presses a button. "The tracker is back on. For our safety."

It feels so final to know that our little bubble has burst once again, but I'm starting to realize this is it. If I want to be with him, this is how our life will be—busted bubbles and tracking devices.

JUST OUTSIDE YONKERS is a little old-timey roadside diner. The parking lot is gravel and the lights stay on twenty-four hours a day. There aren't any other Lamborghinis in the parking lot, but there are a few Mercedes and a BMW. Also a few trucks that have seen better days, and a few cars similar to the one I had in Boulder before I sold it to move to New York.

I could spend a few hours sitting in a window booth, staring at the highway as cars pass by. It would satisfy the people-watching craving I haven't fed in a long time. Ethan's shoulders are stiff, his demeanor intimidating if I didn't know him better. He's on high alert. I understand, but it's the same feeling I wanted to escape when I took the car in the first place. Here it is swallowing us again. He won't admit he has safety concerns sitting in this restaurant, but I feel it in the way his hand on my back has added pressure as he grips the back of my shirt. I see it when he asks me to sit next to him on the same side of the booth, me tucked on the inside, both of us facing the door.

"Melanie found love. We came to New York in pursuit of our dream careers, but she found love." I look at Ethan and add, "Like us, which is better than any job could ever be."

The waitress is nice when she tips the mugs over and fills each with black coffee. I add cream and sugar and am about to take a sip but ask, "Is this our life?"

His eyes are on the door thirty feet or so ahead of us. "What do you mean?"

"Always trying to outrun the tracker." Lowering my voice, sadness refusing to hide, I add, "Or a killer? Hiding someplace, trying to find a few minutes of peace before we hop back into the fire that is meant to burn us, and eventually will? This can't be it."

The width of his hand spans my thigh, curling around between my legs. It's not sexual, but protective. Rubbing up and down a few times, his nerves transfer to me. "I don't know how to answer that, Singer."

"With the truth."

"I don't have the answers."

"We deserve the fairy tale. It took a year-long detour to get here then . . . now it's just days full of despair."

Looking at me through the corners of his eyes, he drops his head and shakes it. "I hope not, but I can't make any promises." He rubs his temples, and I miss that hand on my body. "We need to be realistic. You're in danger because someone wants to get to me. It's working. They're getting to me."

Two plates of eggs, soggy bacon, and pancakes are placed before us, abruptly interrupting us. The waitress refills our mugs. The heaviness of this conversation is bigger than this booth allows. I'm sure she felt the weight of it and quickly leaves us be. I'm not hungry, but I pick off a piece of bacon and try to stomach it while trying to swallow his words to digest them. "What are you saying, Ethan?"

The plate is pushed away and he moves, putting space between us. He spins the Astros cap around on his head, the bill at the back as he holds his forehead in his hands.

I don't take another bite.

I don't move.

I don't breathe while watching him struggle with whatever decisions he's made on his own. He can't look in my direction, much less at me.

It's that bad.

I reach out to touch him, but his body bends away. When my hand returns to my lap, he says, "You know what I'm saying, Singer."

I do.

I know. I want to cry, but instead, I force him to use the words he's hiding behind. "I want you to say it." Trying to put distance between us, the molding of the wood paneled wall digs into my shoulder blades. "Look at me and say it."

Regret comes in many forms. His comes in the murky shade of moss. The bill of the cap comes back around, and he lowers it to shadow those heartbreaking eyes. "We thought we were clever. I thought I could take you to a charity ball right under the nose of the press and get away with it. Just a night out with you. Don't you see, they saw through the act? They saw through me because I can't hide how I feel about you, and worse, I never wanted to. So the moment you walked into my life, you became a target. I don't know who wants to get to me, but it worked. He found my weakness. I am forever responsible for Melanie's death and Aaron's wounds, and I will carry that guilt with me to the grave. Don't make me carry yours."

I thought I could hold back the tears, the pain, the anger and fear that have been smothering me since yesterday. I can't. I'm foolish for thinking that was even a possibility. Sliding my plate away, I take a napkin and wipe away the tears that have fallen down my face. Soon enough, this napkin will be in shreds, just like this chance at love I thought I had. I take a sobering deep breath and say, "Move."

"No." Strong, firm, not budging.

"Move or I'll scream." My voice is controlled and low, but my crying has caught the attention of other customers. I don't want people staring at me. I just want to cry in peace, under the darkness of night.

Reluctantly, he slides out and stands, becoming an obstacle in my way. I push past and head for the door as he's reaching for his wallet. I don't make it far, just to the other side of the car, under the bright neon diner sign.

Headlights flicker from across the street and my heart stops cold in my chest as I fall to the ground. Strong arms embrace me, that deep melody of a voice I had trusted whispers in my ear, "You're okay. That's Lars."

Turning to look above me, Ethan's expression is one of strength with that defined jaw and focused eyes in control. He's not broken like Lars thinks. Helping me up from my knees, those same strong arms that didn't let me fall now hold me up. The reality that I'm ducking to a gravel lot to save myself sinks in. His strength can't save me if someone wants me dead. So he's right. I'll give him that sad credit while I stand on my own two feet again. "I can't stay."

"I'll take you back to the penthouse," he says, holding me too tight, his fear of losing me taking over.

It's too late. "I mean with you. I can't stay with you." His silence cuts through the night, louder than the cars driving by. I'm freed from his confines and add, "I'm leaving New York."

34

Singer

The hospital is quiet this time of night. Without Ethan and Lars, and some guy named Rogers, it's easy to sneak in and out undetected by the press or any other looky-loos. It's funny how they felt suffocating when I was in the middle of it, but two days after I walked away, I miss them.

I miss Ethan more, but I'm not allowed to think about him. My hands shake too much, and my heart breaks as if it's the first time all over again. There wasn't a goodbye or a final *I love you* to hold on to. We were just done. He let me walk away. My guess is he finally realized I wasn't cut out for his world.

Two nights in a hotel were mysteriously paid for, and I didn't return to argue. I just accepted his generosity of payment, space, and time.

I knock lightly, just in case he's sleeping. Knowing Aaron, he's probably wide awake.

"Come in."

Yep.

Pushing the door open, I tiptoe in. I have no idea why since he's looking right at me. "Singer. It's good to see you."

"It's good to see you." Moving bedside, I show him a Snickers and a Mars Bar. "I didn't know if you were a candy-bar man, but I figured it's hard to go wrong with chocolate."

"Thank you. I like both."

"Then both it shall be." I set them on the rolling cart next to his cup of water and rest my hands on the rail. "How are you feeling?"

"Tired."

"No surprise there. Why aren't you resting?"

"All I do is rest. I think that's what's making me tired."

I giggle, not sure if I should, but it feels good. "Can I get you anything? Food or coffee, a magazine or book?"

"Nah. I can't have much yet, and I have a stack of stuff to read." He nods toward the nightstand. A pile of magazines is tucked under a bouquet of flowers.

"Those are pretty."

Maybe it's the lack of conversation or my inability to hide my feelings, but he finally puts me out of my misery and asks, "What brings you by?"

"I've been thinking about you."

"What did I say about making Ethan jealous?"

It's good to see him smile, but I'm not in the right frame of mind. "I'm leaving New York."

I hate that I'm the one to take his smile away, but I had to tell him.

"Where are you going?"

"Home to Boulder. I need time and to save some money, so I'm moving back home. I can't afford my rent here anyway." I hate crying in front of him. He's been shot. *Twice.* Here I am crying over money, or the lack thereof. I don't believe the lie I've been telling myself, so to him, I confess, "I'm scared. There. I said it."

"It's okay to be scared, Singer." His hand covers mine, giving comfort when I need it most.

My stiff upper lip crumbles like the walls around me. "I miss her. I can't go back to that apartment."

"Understandable." His words don't come fast; I wish he were willing to fill in the quiet space between us. When he does, I look up into his tear-filled eyes. "I was on the phone with Ethan when the bullet shattered the glass and shot me in the arm."

"You don't have to tell me—"

"I think you should know."

I nod and take a tissue from the box nearby, knowing I'm probably going to go through them all. "Okay." I come around and sit in the chair beside him.

"She was later than expected. I was supposed to pick her up and take her to the penthouse. It was a simple assignment. But she was late. The window shattered, and I was dragged from the car. I kicked and knocked the guy to the ground. Grabbing a piece of glass, I cut his neck, wanting to end him." He looks away. "Ms. Lazarus's scream carried down the street. The man in the mask lifted his gun and shot her before I could take him down. The gun went off again and got my leg." His tone changes, his demeanor one he was trained to put on—to hide his real feelings. I know he's burying them to protect himself. I'm doing the same. "Wounds are strange. Whether it's from a knife or gun, where you're struck makes the difference. I was shot twice. Once in the arm. Once in the leg. I knew I wasn't going to die. But a tiny half-inch bullet to the stomach with no help in sight . . ." He swallows and stares in the direction of the door.

"I don't know what to say, Aaron."

"I don't either. I just want to know why. Why?" he asks, searching my eyes. "If she'd come home earlier, or maybe much later, would this have happened? Was the shooter waiting and decided to take me out too?"

I drop my chin to my chest. Being strong isn't all it's cracked up to be. But hearing him question if he could have saved her, beating himself up—no wonder he's not resting. Standing, I cover his hand with mine this time. "You did your best. I know you. I know you did, but you could have been killed. As it is, I'm not living and it would be worse if I had your death on my conscience too. I cry, which reminds me I'm human, but sometimes I wiggle my toes or my fingers to see if I can still feel. My heart is here in my chest because it aches. One day I'm going to get used to that feeling, and then what happens? I forget her? I move on like she never existed?"

"You move on and live for the both of you. That's how you honor her life and her memory."

How do I continue to live a life she was such a part of? That hole seems too great to fill, my mind struggling to figure how I move on without Melanie by my side.

He takes a good long hard look at me. "You didn't only come into Ethan's life; you came into mine too. You came into all of ours and brought sunshine with you. How does one repay the sun for shining?"

I look down in thought. "I don't know."

"It's not your question to answer."

My eyes flash up to meet his that shine a little brighter than when I first got here. "Don't stop feeling. Just learn to live again. It may be difficult at times. Wounded hearts take time to heal. The world can be tough, so go gentle on yourself."

Aaron has become my friend.

Not my driver.

Not Ethan's employee.

My friend.

He's the man who tried to save my best friend and was shot in the process. "I owe you so much. I may not be here, but know I'm eternally grateful for what you did for Melanie."

"She died in my arms."

"She lived longer because you held her and helped her find peace."

"She smiled." He smiles from the memory as tears roll down his cheeks. "She knew she was going to die, but she smiled. She comforted me in her last minutes."

I don't care if I'm breaking unwritten rules. I get up and hug him. Gently, but so he knows I care. "Thank you. Thank you for taking care of my friend." Standing up, I back away, our goodbye too troubling to say. "I have to go." I wipe my tears and give him the smile he deserves. "Can you do me a favor?"

"Sure. Anything."

"Check in on Ethan every now and then. Make sure he's okay."

"I promise." He lowers his bed to rest and says, "I'll be seeing you, Singer."

He knows he won't, but I appreciate that he gives me an easy out.

"I'll be seeing you." I look back before I shut the door. He reaches for the Snickers. That makes me smile. He's a man after my own heart.

I walk outside, adjusting my purse on my shoulder. Stopping under the hospital awning, I see him. It's not Ethan, but Lars is just as eye-catching. And damn intimidating with his arms crossed and sunglasses on at night. I start to wonder if maybe he's been hiding in my shadows all along. He comes to me as an SUV is pulled around. "Evening," I say as if I expected him to be here all along.

"Good evening, Ms. Davis. Can I give you a lift?"

"Thanks."

The door opens, and I climb in. When he's seated next to me, the doors lock. "Mr. Everest's orders are to take you wherever you want to go."

"Anywhere?"

"Yes. Anywhere."

I don't hesitate. It's time. "Take me to the airport."

I'VE ALWAYS BEEN one to tackle my problems head-on, but when life itself is the problem, I choose to hide in my room . . . in Boulder . . . at my parents' house . . . in my childhood bedroom where I am once again surrounded by posters of boy bands and rock stars, quotes and my treasured books.

The patchwork quilt my grandmother made me covers my head, the light shining through the small holes of the crocheted blanket. Charlotte's Web is open. The first book I fell in love with and my first heartbreak over a fictional character. It felt fitting to read it again, searching for meaning. Charlotte's life had to have meaning, after all, or there was no purpose to the story.

The last few weeks I've struggled to think of my own purpose, especially in New York. What if I would have listened to Melanie? She wanted to go home, but she stayed for me. I think of Aaron and all of his *whys.* The same questions linger in my mind, but the answers won't bring her back.

She's gone forever, a sad fact I have to constantly remind myself of.

Rolling onto my back, I close the book and stare through the holes of the blanket. The blades of the fan spin slowly, and the feathers Melanie hung on the chain when we were eleven blow gently, swirling in the air. She won that clip at the school carnival and wore them in her hair every day that school year. On the last day of school, she clipped it to the pull chain and left them there. They just became part of the room, something I never thought about or bothered to take down. Watching them now, I'm glad I left them.

I've only visited her parents once. Not after the funeral. Not that weekend at all. I attended, standing in the back near an arrangement from Ethan. That was a knife to my heart though the gesture was kind. I would have preferred to stand next to him. It's probably better he sent the flowers. Why drag it out like we have a chance? There's no surviving this for any of us. Too much tragedy to look on the bright side.

I wore a royal-blue dress Melanie would have fought me to wear on a Saturday night. The feathers were proudly clipped in my hair. I'm sure I looked crazy, but Mel would have gotten a big kick out of it. She loved when I stepped onto the wild side, always saying I dressed too conservatively, considering the body I have. My red heels dug into the earth and my knees locked while I stared behind round sunglasses as the casket was lowered into the ground. I couldn't bear to go to their house afterward, to give condolences when I owed them my life.

Instead, I visit one Wednesday afternoon. I don't plan it. What started out as a walk to the store ends with me standing on their front porch crying.

There's something different about this visit compared to

the one in New York. I think the something is me. I'm different here than I was there. In the city, I was putting on a brave face for Ethan, Melanie's parents, Mike, Aaron, his daughter, Chip, and even Lars. Here, I have no one else to comfort. Here, it's me with my guilt, facing my fears, and finally giving myself a gift that Melanie would have wanted me to have all along—the ability to grieve.

I cried rivers in New York, but I've unleashed oceans in Colorado. I step onto their porch on a random Saturday afternoon, and sit on their swing, pushing off the wooden deck with the toe of my shoe. The gummy bear bag has been ripped open, a good portion already eaten. The cap of the bottle of white wine has been twisted off.

Melanie's father finds me first. He doesn't say anything but sits in the Adirondack chair and stares at the kids riding their bikes as parents arrive home from work. Her mother finds us shortly after. I stop swinging, and she sits next to me, takes a drink from the bottle, and eats two gummy bears —red. Those were Melanie's favorite flavor, too.

That makes me smile.

In sync, we push off and start swinging. It starts with a laugh. *Mine.* Then we're all laughing. The good times we had with Melanie far outweigh her tragic ending. We're so lucky to have had so many years with her, so many good times, and so many great memories to share now. So fortunate.

In celebration of her life, we order pizza and watch the Romance Channel with a glass of wine in one hand and a handful of gummy bears in the other. It's therapeutic. It's a reprieve that gives me enough space—*and permission*—to finally grieve.

When I leave, I sleep through the night for the first time since her death. I haven't found peace, the hole still existing, acclimating to its new home in my heart. But I'm taking it step-by-step, learning to walk through this life without her and to live. Her life may not be in the present, but our past strengthens me daily. Slowly, I'm starting to put this tragedy to rest. Slowly, I'm learning to live again.

35

Ethan

I stood there and did nothing.

I let her walk away from me.

I let her get in the car with Lars that was parked across the street and leave me. Not just at a diner outside Yonkers, but out of my life. For good.

How could I do that?

Why didn't I stop her?

She would have hated me if I had made her stay.

Sitting across the table from Dariya, I'm having flashbacks of settling the case with Keith, and so many from the spring day at a party in the Bronx. I've been staring through her since we sat down. She's been staring right back at me. I don't see her though. She's nothing to me, nothing but the woman who destroyed my life.

Reegan slides a package across the table to the judge, who asks, "What is this?"

"Evidence."

"More? Explain and make it quick."

Weeks after our first settlement hearing and two more meetings, Reegan says, "Video of the plaintiff and her lover together in front of the building where my client was setup."

The judge takes the package and then glances to Dariya. "Do I need to watch this or can we save some time?"

She shifts in her seat and her lawyer clears his throat. After a silent conversation is exchanged with her, he sighs. "We'll settle the case."

Reegan interjects, "We won't."

Dariya turns to me. "Ethan?"

I have no sympathy. I've lost everything because of her. She deserves nothing more, not even my time. When I don't respond, Reegan defers to the judge. "We'd like the paternity test results."

Above the top of her reading glasses, she asks, "Are you sure, Mr. Everest?"

"I am." I am completely confident Dariya's baby is not mine. The math doesn't add up for me, but for Keith—he's about to be a dad. The thought makes me sad. A year earlier I would have been thrilled for him. Now I just pity this baby for getting stuck with Keith and Dariya as parents.

The clerk passes the envelope to the judge who is sitting at the head of the table in her private chambers downtown. Dariya's eyes sway to the end, and I turn my chair to face the judge. Reegan looks back, no nerves, no anxiety. Full confidence. Ready to fight against the remaining charges or to fight for my child. My future decided by a test.

The judge unfolds the piece of paper and reads aloud, "There is a ninety-nine point seven percent chance the child *is not* Mr. Everest's."

Dariya smiles. "So there is a chance it can be?"

Her lawyer shakes his head. Leaning closer to her, he whispers, "Due to variations in testing and genetics, history of cultures, that is considered conclusive evidence that he cannot be the father."

"But it's not one hundred percent?"

"If he was the father it would be."

She looks up as anger takes over. Holding her arm over her pregnant belly, she says, "He must be. He assaulted me."

I'm about to argue, but Reegan stops me. "Do not speak." Standing up to match her stance, he adds, "We are filing to have a lie detector test administered immediately to settle this once and for all. We will also be filing a one hundred million dollar lawsuit for slander and damaging Mr. Everest's livelihood and standing in the community."

"You can't do that," she says, slamming her hands on the table.

I sit back, letting Reegan shut this down once and for all. "We assume that your lawyer has spoken to you prior to filing against my client regarding the consequences of your lies coming to light."

Turning to her lawyer, she yells, "You promised me I would win. Now look what's happening. You're fired."

"You lied," he says, stacking his files. "I would highly recommend you settle here and now before this gets worse."

Her glare hits mine. "If I agree to drop the other charges, will you drop yours?"

Reegan leans down and whispers in my ear, "Rhubarb, banana, strawberry, curd."

For a stuffy lawyer type, he sure knows how to entertain. I reply, "Oysters," but it's damn hard to keep a straight face.

When he stands back up, he says, "We'll drop all charges if a few conditions are met."

"What?" she asks.

The public apology comes the next day, making Page Six news as well as many online sites picking up the gossip. I can't help but wonder if Singer has heard the news. We never intended to sue if everything went away and my record is clean again. Validation is reward enough.

Dariya went into early labor a week later. The father missed the birth, but she and the baby went home with him. It was the first time I'd seen Keith since we sat across the table as enemies. This time I only have to see them in the papers.

With this side of my life wrapped up in a neat bow, my reputation has been restored. I've gone from the bad-boy billionaire to most eligible bachelor in the headlines. I don't need attention of any sort, but that makes me laugh. If they only knew that my heart isn't taking applications. Even if the position has been vacated, I refuse to fill the job.

I'm free. *My heart isn't.*

I received the call I'd been waiting for. Lars and I went straight to the police station. The police are holding the man who allegedly attacked Singer. I come to find out that Singer had come to identify her attacker while I was stuck in daylong meetings with my vengeful ex. Aaron had paid for her ticket. I paid Aaron. As much as I want to meet her at the station, see her, talk to her, I give her the space she needs.

When I see the fucker who tried to kill her, he matches the man on the video and her description. He's going to prison, but we're convinced Singer's attack and Melanie's murder are related, and he can lead us to Melanie's killer.

The police captain assures us the suspect has been inter-rogated thoroughly, but I bet Lars could get the information we need out of him. Unfortunately, the bars that hold him captive now protect him. *From us.*

"How is she?" I ask Lars as soon as we get in the SUV.

"She's quiet. We've been tailing her from the hotel and

back, but she's only left once." When I look at him, he knows what I really want. "She got Indian food from the corner restaurant."

"At least she's still here. And eating."

"I'm not sure for how long, sir."

"Me either."

THIRTY-FIVE DAYS.

She's been gone for thirty-five days. A clean break. Thirty-two from the city. Thirty-five from me. It's better she left. I repeat that throughout the day like a mantra.

I've tried to leave her alone—really fucking tried—but she is still everywhere—in my heart, taking up space in my soul, my dreams, a few things around the penthouse I can't bring myself to throw away or send to her. I can't let go. I won't let her go.

I pay her rent hoping for her to return, but she took the clothes from the suitcases that had been brought over and I think that might be all she ever wants. Maybe in time, she'll return to collect the things she misses.

Maybe in time she'll return to collect me.

The two times I called her I hung up. Damn caller ID. I'm not sure if I'm more upset that I made the call or that she didn't answer or call me back.

When I walk into the living room, Aaron has his leg propped up on the coffee table and is flicking through the TV channels. I ask, "Anything good on?" I'm starting to get used to having him and Caroline around. And when I say starting to, I mean, I'm used to opening my fridge and seeing new stuff stocked in there and finding junk food in my pantry. I love a good treat like the next guy, but teenage girls love their ice cream and cookies. Aaron says it's what girls eat when they're upset over boys. I'm staying far and clear of that business.

"No. Looking for sports. How can someone have over two thousand channels and only ten are sports?"

I sit down in the chair, and ask, "Have you decided what you want to do long-term?"

The TV is clicked off, and he scoots his body upright on the couch. "Your offer is generous. I'd like to keep driving for you, but do you think I can do the job you need me to do?"

The real question he wants to know he's not asking, but I'll answer it anyway. "I think you'll be capable of doing the job, or I wouldn't have offered it."

"I might not move as fast."

"You might move faster."

Optimism is generally his forte, but I know the recovery process is going to be long. I also know he wants what's best for me. I want the same for him and for his daughter. "And Caroline's college tuition is still included?"

"Whether you take the job or not, she's covered."

"I want her to get the best."

"If she keeps her grades up, I can write a letter to Princeton on her behalf."

He swings his uninjured leg down, keeping the other on the coffee table. "Do you mean that?"

"Yes. I mean it or I wouldn't have offered. She's a smart girl. Let's get her interning this summer at Everest Enterprises and get her on the fast track to the college of her choice."

"Thank you."

"You don't owe me thanks. I'm to blame for your injuries."

"No. You're not. You take the blame, but it lies squarely on the shooter's shoulders."

I appreciate him trying to lessen the load, but I owe him so much. He says, "If you're dumb enough to hire this injured soldier, I need to be smart and say yes. So yes, I'm on board."

Our hands fly together as we shake on it. "This is good news. I needed some."

When I stand, he says, "I should have told you before, but I didn't know how you would feel about it."

There's this feeling, an instinct, or your gut guiding you, when something seems not quite right. I've been living with that feeling since the night of the shooting, but he sure knows how to twist it. I sit back down and wait.

He says, "Singer came to see me the night she left."

Singer.

Singer Davis with the red lips and the blue dress. My whole heart is wrapped in that beguiling package. I wait again, though I want to ask a million questions.

Looking straight at me, he says, "I'm not saying anything new, but she's special. Have you talked to her?"

"I haven't."

"You should."

"She hasn't talked to me either."

"Are you going to play a schoolyard game of he said, she said or she didn't, so I'm not?" I stand, wanting to get a glass of water and get back to work, but he says, "She loves you."

"I love her."

"Then what are you doing?"

"Giving her life back to her."

"What does that do to yours?"

"Aaron, come on, man. I don't want to do this."

"I told her what happened that night and guess what?"

"What?"

"She cried for her friend but comforted me. *Me?* The man who let her friend die."

"You were shot trying to save her. Singer knows you risked your life for Melanie."

Reaching for his crutches, he lifts and ambles up, balancing on them. "I'm not looking for reassurance. The guilt from losing an innocent life I could have protected will never go away. What I do know is she told me to make sure you're okay."

"I'm fine," I reply defensively.

"You're not. You're burying yourself in work, and while there's nothing wrong with working hard, it's all you do."

"I have to deal with skyrocketing rents for my cargo holds in East Bay that are stalled in negotiation. I can't sit around and shoot the shit. Sorry, no offense, so if you'll excuse me."

"No. I won't. You know why? Because you're a wealthy motherfucker, but money didn't buy the happiness you had."

"Happiness isn't tangible. It slips right on by if you're not keeping tabs on it."

"Not even thirty and already so jaded. I'd give anything to have one more day with my wife. Anything but my daughter. So when you say happiness isn't tangible, it's a lie you tell yourself. I get to look at my happiness every morning and every night. I get to hug and watch her grow up before my eyes—too fast if you ask me. So when lumping everything that hurts you or makes you feel something bigger than that inflated ego of yours, remember, they're not just words for tossing around casually."

He goes the long way around the couch. I think to avoid

passing by me. I say, "Singer was real. She's tangible, but she's not mine."

Turning back, he asks, "Who said?"

"She did."

"Did she? Or did she need time to grieve?"

"Stop giving me hope when there is none."

"Hope is a tricky emotion," he says with a smile. "Sometimes it's the only thing we have left to hold on to. And sometimes, it's just a mirage, leading us to nothing. The only way to know if something's real is by going after it. You're a smart man, Ethan. Hope didn't build your billion-dollar businesses. You did. How did you do it?"

"I went after it."

"I'm going to take a nap." The wink reinforces how clever he thinks he is. I see through him. I know what he's doing. "It was good talking to you."

And it might be working. "You too."

When I leave, his words about grieving make sense. Maybe I can move forward while grieving the loss of Singer . . . or maybe I can't. Maybe she's lost to me forever, and I won't be given a choice.

36

Singer

"I appreciate you looking out for me, but I would like to finally settle into a career. Greenberg's Grocers doesn't even have a book section."

My mom gives me the smile—the sympathetic one that says so much without saying anything at all.

I'm not trying to nag.

I care about you.

I'm worried about your future.

Do you think a job in publishing will pan out?

Stay in Boulder.

Meet a man and settle down.

Do you want to get married?

Whatever happened to what's his name from high school?

Do you want kids?

I want grandkids one day.

I heard Carrie Landers got a promotion and is pregnant with her second.

What do you think about us retiring to Boca Raton?

Will you bring your family to visit us if we move?
Did you pick up milk today while you were out?

Okay, I might be getting carried away a bit, but I see it. Her dreams for me are fading a little more each day that I stay here. The idea of being the spinster Mel and I used to joke about isn't that far-fetched when playing solitaire on a metal TV tray while watching Jeopardy in the den of your parents' home at five o'clock at night. "I need to get out of this house," I say to no one in particular since no one's around.

My mom walks in and leans against the doorway. "Want to go out for dinner? Just you and me?"

I jump at the offer, desperate to get out of the house. "Yes." When I walk toward the stairs, I tug at my cutoffs so my ass isn't hanging out more than it is already.

"Wear something pretty. Maybe a dress?"

"Okaaay." I head upstairs and flip through my closet. I don't have much—some things from college, a few things my mom's bought for me since I've been home, and the clothes that were brought to the penthouse.

It's almost like I never left. My shoes are lined up on the floor, purses stacked on the shelf, and my makeup stored neatly in my Caboodles box. If I weren't desperate to leave the house, I'd stay and mope about how sad my life has become. But there's no time for that.

I grab my blue dress with the red polka dots and get dressed. This dress always reminds me of Ethan. My soul aches in ways that are varied from the grief of Melanie's death. I've been grieving the loss of love in my life. *His love. I miss the other half of my heart.*

Thirty minutes later, I come down to find my mom looking so pretty, dressed fancy for a date with her daughter.

She smiles at me. "You always had such a nice figure. That dress looks beautiful, Singer."

"Thanks, Mom."

I SHOULD HAVE CAUGHT the warning signs. I didn't, though the tip-off should have been when she told me to wear a dress. I was so caught up in needing a change of scenery, I didn't pick up on the signs clearly there—the dress and the comment about my figure.

So when she pulls into the parking lot of the Hotel Boulderado, I might have shot daggers in her direction. "What are we doing? I was thinking Mexican food or even Ray's Home Cooking. Why are we at a hotel?"

She shifts the car into park and feigns innocence. "Why would we get all dressed up for Ray's or a cantina?"

My blinks are slow, my glare judgmental. "I don't want to socialize, Mom. Whatever this is that you're doing, I'm not in the mood."

"You need to get out, Singer. It's not healthy to sit around like you have."

"Where are we? Why are we here?"

"It's Katherine Collier's reception."

"What? We can't crash a wedding, Mom."

"We're not. We were invited. Anyway, this is the reception. The wedding was at St. Gabriel's earlier. You know I'm still good friends with her mother, and I thought you might like to see some familiar faces."

"I haven't seen her since we graduated from high school."

"Good," she says, tapping my arm. "It will be good to reconnect."

If I were at home, I'd go to my room and glower in private, but deep down, I know she's right. I'm not betraying Melanie by trying to move forward, by trying to live. She'd want that. I know this. Logically, I do, but . . . I drop my head and close my eyes. Dragging my lower lip under my teeth, I know what I should do, and even though I don't want to, I need to. "Okay," I say, opening my door.

When we walk into the hotel, I stop her before we walk any farther. "They know about Melanie?"

"Yes. They know."

"What will they think of me?"

"What do you mean?"

Struggling to hold eye contact, I look down the corridor that leads to the ballrooms. "That it was supposed to be me."

"Singer," she snaps. "Look at me." When I do, she takes my hands. "Stop that. I mean it. Stop it. What happened is horrific on every level. I miss her sweet smile. You'll miss her forever, but that doesn't mean you were supposed to replace her. I know it's complicated, and I don't fully understand why someone wanted to kill . . ." Her hand covers her mouth as her emotions get the better of her. When she's strong enough to look up again, she adds, "I don't want to think about it. I know I have to, just like you, but if you were meant to die, you would have. You're alive for a reason. You're alive. Make the most of the time you have. Live, Singer. Live the best life you can."

I throw my arms around her. I can't argue with her. Not over this. "I love you, Mom."

"I love you, too." *And this is why I'm here.* There is no better place to find solace and comfort than in my mom's arms. Her embrace is comforting. And right now? *Needed.* "Let's go celebrate life."

"Okay." We enter the reception, the celebration already

in full swing. I smile because the room is full of love, full of life, full of happiness and is infectious. "Should we say hi to Katherine?"

"Go on without me. I'm going to talk to her mother, and let her know we're here. You go mingle and enjoy."

She walks off and I look for the bar. I need liquid courage to face friends from high school. Lifting up on my toes, I see it across the room. Keeping my head down, trying to blend in with the Collier family and friends, I take the long route, walking on the outskirts of the tables and far from the dance floor.

"Well, if it isn't Singer Davis."

Turning toward my name, I see the last person I thought I'd ever see again, but my performance is Oscar worthy. "Pagely Whitehead. I did *not* expect to see you again . . . I mean here." Okay, so maybe not Oscar worthy.

"Katherine and I dated in school. It didn't last long, but we kept in touch, and our parents are friends."

"Wow, this city is smaller than I thought." I find my knuckles planted on my hips as I attempt the correct the worst smile ever. One positive, he doesn't smell anymore, or I can't smell him from here.

"I heard about Melanie. Anyway, I thought you two were going to do big things in the Big Apple." He chuckles but I hear the hostility in his tone. "She was always . . . a big talker about dreams. A lot like you. Always dreaming for a life better than ours. So yeah, sorry she's dead. Yep."

His words are cruel, and I'm defensive. So when he pops that last P, I bite the inside of my cheek to keep from going off on him. He doesn't owe her anything. They weren't friends. Melanie was popular in school. She wasn't a mean girl, but she kept her circle tight. Really, just the two of us.

But he does owe me respect when it comes to my friend.

"I get that she rejected your come-ons in high school. I get that you feel big and mighty coming all the way back from Denver to hang out with the little people. I get that you want to hurt me like maybe Melanie, or myself, hurt you because we didn't want to go out with you. I get it. You're bitter. You're looking to flaunt your peacock feathers and show us that it's our loss. *I get it.* But here's the truth, Pagely. You don't have to put on a production. My best friend was murdered, and I had to see her lifeless body carried away." I stop and debate whether I should go on. Yes, I should because he started this, but I want to finish it. "You win. I'm nothing in your eyes but a failure. I never got my dream job in New York. We could barely afford our rent. I failed in all ways, and here I am back home with nothing to show for the last three years of my life, not even my best friend. So you win, Pagely."

I lost Melanie. I lost Ethan when I walked away.

I suck in a breath while staring at his souring face then add, "I'm barely hanging on right now. I just want to forget that I failed her parents, my parents, myself, and *apparently* you. Just tonight. Because tomorrow I'll be stuck here in reality, and you will be off doing, oh, I don't know"—I shrug —"accounting or something?"

"I didn't mean—"

"You did. You did mean. You intended to put me in my place, and you have. It's all good, though. I'm glad your dreams have come true. I'm not giving up on mine, but I will mourn the death of my friend unapologetically for as long as I want. So if you'll excuse me, there's a bottle of vodka with my name on it."

I leave him standing there, yet guilt has already begun creeping in. I shouldn't feel bad, but I just add it to the tally and step up to the bar. "Vodka soda. Make it a double." I should look for Katherine and give her my best wishes, maybe apologize for crashing her reception, but after seeing my past come back to haunt me and rub my nose in my failures, this drink is badly needed.

The bartender sets it in front of me and says, "That will be twelve dollars."

"Shoot. I'm sorry. I thought it was an open bar." *Figures.* "I'll be right back."

"I'll take care of her drink. Keep the change."

A twenty is exchanged over my shoulder. I don't turn. I can't. I know that voice. That watch. That hand. The musky ocean cologne. The feel of his gaze so real that I swear his arms are wrapped around me.

I know the man.

Ethan.

Tears didn't fall today. I felt accomplished that I held them back, but knowing he's behind me, they fill my eyes. I turn and am in his arms—strong arms that feel like home. My head is tucked against his chest, my arms around him, squeezing him tight. There's no space between us, no room for words quite yet. My heart bangs against the prison of my ribs, trying to escape into his.

His hands rub my back as a kiss is placed on the top of my head. I look right into the bright greens I first fell in love with, that happy-go-lucky smile that's not New York, but all Texas—charming and laid-back. Ethan from last year seems to have returned, as though he's comfortable in his own body again. He looks good. *So good. Yet here I am . . . a mess.*

"Hey baby."

Damn my traitorous cheeks as they heat under his gaze.

Damn this smile that can't hide when I see his.

Damn my arms as they cling to the front of his shirt pulling him closer.

Damn these lips for seeking out his.

Damn me.
Damn him.
But since we're damned already . . .
Our bodies come together.
No more almosts.
Just definites.
Our lips meet in a long-lost, star-crossed-lovers embrace.
I've missed this.
I've missed him.

We begin to sway, the world fading away. It's just us. With my heart tied in knots over this man, I look into those eyes that see all of me: the happy, the sad, the weak, the strong, the lonely, the needy. *He came for me.* He let me go but has come here for me. Surely it's not to say goodbye or have that final kiss we missed. Does he still love me? I have replayed his words over and over again. *"We need to be realistic. You're in danger because someone wants to get to me. It's working. They're getting to me."* The man standing here doesn't seem to be the same as the desolate one who couldn't see a way forward for us. Who believed that we were better apart. The man in front of me seems lighter, less . . . restrained.

The man in front of me loves me. It's in his eyes. And for the first time in a nearly two months, I want to cry in joy.

"I heard what you said back there," he says.

"To the bartender?"

"No," he replies, shaking his head. "To Pagely."

"Oh. *That.*"

"Yeah, that."

"He's an ass."

"You're the bravest person I've ever known."

My mouth slacks. "How am I brave when I feel so weak?"

"You're finally putting yourself and your needs first. You're also right. You don't owe him or anyone else anything." Lifting my chin, I see his smile. "Want me to kick his ass out back?"

"As much as that might be very satisfying to watch, it won't bring Melanie back."

"No, but the suggestion was worth seeing you smile again."

He's the man who sees through me and knows I love him deeply. Our fingers entwine, and with my body pressed to his I ask, "Why are you here?"

"Because I don't want to live without you."

37

Singer

"Don't make me cry, Ethan."

His hands are on my waist, mine under his jacket, wrapped around his middle. "Even if they're happy tears?"

"I don't want to cry anymore."

"I never want to see you cry sad tears again. What can I do to make you happy?"

Leaning my head on his chest, I listen to his heart beating and savor his scent. "You're doing it."

"That was easy," he replies, cocooning me.

"I never said I was hard."

"What if I am?"

Popping back, my eyes are wide. "Wow, zero to a hundred just like that, huh?"

He shrugs. "Want to dance?"

"Thought you'd never ask."

Leading me to the dance floor, he spins me out, making me laugh. When he whips me back to him, I'm caught in how much I feel for him, how much I missed him. "You came all the way to Boulder just to dance with me?"

He stops in the middle of the dance floor and cups my face. "No, I came for so much more, Singer." Our lips meet again in want and need, in equal fervor as it deepens. When the clapping begins, we pause. Our eyes open, our lips still attached. As the applause grows, I duck my head, hiding in his arms. He eats up the attention. "Thank you. Thanks."

I roll my eyes and grab his hand. "Come on. Let's get out of here." We pass the bride and groom who are clapping and smiling along with everyone else. As we stride by, I say, "You look beautiful. Congratulations on the nuptials."

"Congrats to you." She's eyeing Ethan. Before I leave, she adds, "Melanie will be missed."

"She will be," I reply, and for the first time, I don't cry when thinking about her. Because in this moment something becomes very clear. Many will miss her vivacious and outgoing self. It makes me sad, but it also reinforces how incredibly fortunate I have been. I hold many, many wonderful memories in my heart. My best friend, my sister, my candy-loving goof. We were all lucky to know her, to have her as part of our lives.

Ethan's arm is around my waist as we walk toward the door. My mom is with Katherine's, a soft smile on her face. I pull Ethan to a stop and go to her. "Mom, this is Ethan Everest. Ethan, my mother, Nance."

My mom hugs him. "I've heard so much about you."

"It's nice to meet you."

When they step back, she pinches my chin lightly. "It's good to see that smile again." Looking to Ethan, she says, "Take care of her. She has a lot of people who love her."

This is a point where our happy bubble could burst. But

it doesn't. He says, "I will, ma'am. I promise. I'll protect her with my life."

"Let's hope it doesn't come to that." Turning to me, she asks, "Should we expect you home tonight?"

I glance to Ethan. "I could lie."

"You don't have to," she says. "You're not a little girl anymore."

Ethan's hand is on my shoulder, giving me a gentle squeeze as I say, "I'll see you in the morning."

"I love you, Sing."

Hugging her, I tell her because we should always tell the ones we love how we feel. We may not get another chance. "I love you, too."

We leave the reception we crashed, running to the parking lot. I stop outside the hotel doors and laugh. "My mom drove."

A black SUV pulls up. "I've got us covered."

He opens the door and I climb inside. Lars is behind the wheel, another wonderful surprise. "Good to see you, Ms. Davis."

Now I really start laughing. "I should have known." The door is closed and Ethan pulls the seatbelt over me and buckles me in. I have a feeling safety will always be a priority with him. "If Aaron were here, the whole gang would be back together."

Ethan says, "He wanted to come. He tried. It was almost sad leaving him behind, but I gave him free rein of the penthouse, so he wasn't too upset."

Lars asks, "Where can I take you?"

I look to Ethan who is looking at me. He asks, "Where do you want to go?"

"Anywhere I can be alone with you."

"Let's go back to the suite."

It's dark inside the vehicle, but there's enough light to see Ethan, his straight nose and full lips, the way the shadow cuts under his jaw, and the Adam's apple that sticks out just enough to tempt me into kissing it.

I do.

Unlocking my seatbelt, I maneuver onto his lap. I kiss his neck because I can, and I never thought I would get to again. His fingers run into my hair, and he tilts my head back and kisses me. He's not careful or gentle. He kisses me with all the pent-up passion from the last forty-five days apart.

Losing track of time and distance, the SUV comes to a stop and Lars gets out. Ethan doesn't rush his words. He looks at me, and says, "I've missed you, Singer Davis."

"I've missed you. So much, Ethan Everest."

Just inside the lobby, I look up. "I've always dreamed of staying at the St. Julien."

"Glad to make that dream come true. Come on. I want you naked in a bath in the next ten minutes."

A blonde, too pretty for my liking and ogling Ethan like he's naked, greets him, "Good evening, Mr. Everest. Can I send anything up to make your stay more comfortable?"

"I have everything I need," he says, lifting my hand subtly as we walk. "Thank you."

"It's always going to be like that, isn't it?"

We reach the elevators and while waiting, he asks, "Like what?"

"Women hitting on you right in front me."

"Women that want me for my money don't interest me."

Nudging him in the ribs with my elbow, I whisper, "Although the money attracts women, I have a feeling you didn't do too bad before you had it."

Smirking, he winks at me. "You might be right." The

doors open, and he grabs me from behind and lifts me into the elevator. After pushing the button, he adds, "But I only have eyes for you."

Reaching around, I playfully smack the side of his leg. "Feels like you have more than eyes for me, hot stuff."

His hands work their way up the sides of my ribs, and I hold my breath momentarily. He says, "I like this hot-stuff business."

Turning around in his arms, I reach up and rest mine around his neck. "I like you."

The elevator dings, and he glances up as the doors open. "I more than like you, Singer. Let me show how much more."

With my hand wrapped in his, we walk down the hall, and he unlocks the door. We walk into the suite, and I go straight to the glass doors that lead to a large balcony. "Wow, this is an amazing view."

"You're telling me."

When I look back, he's looking at me with that smile that gets me every damn time. I go to him, and he meets me halfway. "What are we doing, Ethan?"

"Falling in love."

"I feel like we've been here before."

"Let's do it right this time." He kisses me. And kisses me. Kisses me until I'm weak in the knees and holding his arms so I don't become a puddle of mush at his feet.

It doesn't take long before our clothes are shed, our bodies are intimately reunited, and we're flying high on each other. My thoughts blur as my body takes over, our connection carnal, our desire raw and deep. I fall to the side in a bundle of satiated fireworks, every nerve tingling as the sparks of fire flutter out.

He rolls to his side and is watching me as my eyes open. I reach over and touch his cheek. "How was it for you?"

Smiling, he replies, "You don't ever have to ask. It's incredible every time with you."

"You don't have to woo me, Mr. Everest."

"What if I want to, Ms. Davis?"

"Well then, by all means, go right ahead. Woo away."

Taking my hand in his, he kisses my fingertips. "Will you marry me?"

My neck twinges from the hard double take. "Ethan?"

"It's fast." He kisses the palm of my hand. "I know, but I don't need more time to know I don't want to be without you again."

Not able to find the words, I nod like a crazy person. Yes. Yes. *But can we?* "Ethan?" I repeat, still stunned.

"Aaron made me see. My life has no meaning without you. I settled the company case. I won against my ex-girlfriend. I can't take away the pain caused by what happened, but we can try to heal together. I don't just miss you, Singer. I need you." Stealing a kiss, he says, "I don't care about anything else unless you are there to share it. The money. The companies. The stuff. None of it matters. *People* matter. And maybe it took this tragedy to realize it, but I don't want to hide behind timelines established by society. I feel everything for you. You make me feel alive. We have one life guaranteed, and I want to spend mine with you. Marry me, Singer."

Wiping my eyes, I sniffle and then laugh. "You promised me you wouldn't make me cry."

"No," he replies, smiling and kissing one of my tears away. "I promised I would never make you cry sad tears."

"I love you too much to let you go again."

He sits up excitedly, the bed bouncing from the action. "Is that a yes?"

Dragging him down to me, I kiss him this time and whisper against his lips, "That's a yes."

ETHAN's still in the shower when room service knocks on the door with our dinner. I throw a plush white robe on and rush into the living room, but I grab my chest when I see Lars sitting on the couch. "Good Lord, you gave me a heart attack."

"Sorry," he says, getting up to answer the door. "Two-room suite. I'm in that bedroom, but I won't disturb you."

With my heart still pounding, I say, "I guess that's smart you're staying there."

"Safety measure."

"Yeah, I guess that's necessary."

The knock echoes in the room again. He says, "I think it would be safer if you wait in the bedroom."

I have a feeling I'm going to hear that a lot more from now on. He's right, so I go and shut the door behind me, making my way to the bathroom. Ethan is drying off, and I go to the counter to lean against it. "You didn't tell me Lars was staying with us."

His eyes meet mine. I'm learning when he doesn't answer right away, he's working around a way to tell me something that would be a lot easier if he was direct. I wait him out, not letting him off the hook. He finally drops the towel on the floor and walks into the bedroom. Damn, he has a great ass, all muscles rotating, that sexy indentation at the sides, leading to sculpted legs. He plays dirty. I follow him into the bedroom and sit on the bed. "Well?"

"Well, what? He's staying in the other room. We thought it best since we didn't have lead-time to secure the hotel.

"Why do you need to secure the hotel?"

"You know, Singer."

"But we're in Boulder, not Manhattan."

Eyebrows tug to the center, and his mouth goes to one side. "It would be nice if the threat was eliminated, but until it is, this seemed like a good bandage on the situation."

As fear creeps back into my veins, I ask what I'm not sure I want the answer to, "Do you think we're in danger here?"

"I think we're in danger anywhere. Everywhere."

"Then what do we do?"

"We live. We spite whoever it is and live." He comes over, and I lean toward him when the bed dips. Rubbing my arms, he says, "Let's enjoy tonight. We can worry about everything else tomorrow. We're safe here. Lars is across the hall. So if we need anything, we call out for him."

"What happens tomorrow?"

Chuckling, he asks, "You're not going to let this go tonight, are you?"

"No, I can't."

He gets up and opens the door. "Can we talk about it over dinner? I'm starving."

"Yes, I'm hungry too."

We set the food on the table and sit across from each other. He sets his beer down and says, "I need to fly back tomorrow. I'd like you to go with me."

"Why so soon?"

"I'm in the middle of renegotiations. I have a meeting I can't move tomorrow afternoon."

"What will I do there?"

"What have you've been doing here, other than the

missing me part?" He waggles his eyebrows, making me smile.

"I'm looking for a job."

"Look for one in New York. Chip told me to tell you he'd like to have you back."

Now I chuckle. "I don't want to go back to a job I hated."

"You know you don't have to work at all, right?"

He's a billionaire.

It's easy to forget because he's so easygoing *most of the time.* Maybe I've been naïve to not realize what being with him really means. It just never occurred to me. "I want to work though."

"Then work. But you can be there with me and look for a job."

"Ethan, I'm not sure what to say to that."

"We're going to be married. You can literally do anything you want to do. I'll support you . . ." He seems to catch himself and how that actually sounds. "Emotionally, as your husband, your friend, and financially. We're partners. That's what marriage is to me."

Reaching across the table, I hold my palm up. When he sets his in mine, I say, "That's what it means to me as well, but I don't want to feel like another one of your obligations."

His laughter is deep as his hand squeezes mine. "You are the furthest thing from a burden to me, Singer. Money's not fun if you can't spend it on the people you love. Let's have some fun and spend our money together." He releases me and pulls something out of his robe. Kneeling beside me, he holds a box. "I should have given this to you earlier, but sometimes when I look at you, I feel so grateful I forget to show you how much you mean to me."

My heart races, my lips part, and those pesky tears resurface. Happy tears only.

He kisses the palm of my hand and says, "Singer Davis, my biggest regret will always be not kissing you on that fire escape. If I had, we would have gotten here a lot faster. The universe sometimes has a mind of its own. But no matter what has happened, we fought our fate and found our destiny. You are *it* for me. You are everything—my heart, my love, my soul, my minutes, my everything. I want to be everything for you."

While slipping the ring on my finger, he spins it gently around my finger, admiring it. The diamond is big. Like really freaking huge. The ring is prettier than I ever allowed myself to dream about. But it's the man who holds my complete attention, who captures my whole heart and forever seals it as his to keep. He says, "Aaron once asked me how do you repay the sun for shining."

My heart clenches watching this amazing man repeating words I never understood, words according to Aaron that weren't meant for me. Ethan says, "I didn't understand what he meant at the time."

"You do now?"

"I figured it out. That's what brought me to Boulder today."

"What is it? What brought you here?"

Pulling me to my feet, he takes one hand in his and the other holds my waist as we start to slow dance. "It's never been about repaying the sun. It's about making the sun shine in the dark. Let me be your moon and light your night. Will you marry me, Singer?"

I'm nodding as the happy tears fall down my cheeks, a beautiful ache in my chest reminding me we can live. We can live the rest of our lives together, appreciating every minute of this wonderful life. "I want to be everything you deserve. I'll shine for you during the day if you shine for me at night." I lift up and kiss him.

"Sealed with a kiss?"

Untying the belt of his robe, I give him my best wink. "I have a better way to seal this deal."

I start pulling him toward the bed, but he stops me. "On one condition."

"Name it. Anything."

"I get to call you Singer Everest one day."

My heart swells. He's the most wonderful man I've ever known and is offering me his hand in return for mine. I can't refuse my soul its mate and will not make the same mistake twice. This time, I'm ready. Yanking the belt from the loops, I toss it and watch as the robe falls open. Dropping mine to the floor, I turn around, giving him full view of my backside as I wiggle it just for him. "If you insist," I tease.

"I insist, indeed." His robe falls to the floor and he stalks toward me.

I crawl onto the bed and sit in the middle. "Batter up."

"I'm going for a homerun."

"I think your odds are very good."

"God, I'm going to fucking love this union."

"The sex tonight or once we're married?"

Taking me down on the mattress, he settles between my legs and says, "Both, but let's start with tonight."

Best deal we ever sealed.

38

Singer

The sky is bluer.

The air warmer.

The sun brighter.

My steps peppier.

Life is good for the first time since . . .

I am missing Ethan already. He flew out on a private jet early this morning. He wanted to drive me home first. Well, Lars drove. Ethan and I made out in the back. He wanted me to leave right then with him, to leave my clothes behind. "Buy more," he said. "Leave it all behind. We'll get you all new stuff. Just come with me."

I kissed lower than his lips for that sweet offer, but I couldn't leave Boulder like that. The car came to a stop in my driveway, and Lars opened the door. I promptly fell onto the grass on my ass. If I hadn't been laughing so hard, I might have been embarrassed that my underwear remained in Ethan's hand . . . inside the car when I tumbled out.

After righting me, Ethan kissed me goodbye but kept my

panties. They left and I retrieved the key from under the planter and tiptoed into the house. Not wanting to wake anyone, I tried my darnedest to be quiet, but it's too hard to keep all this happiness contained.

Busted before I reach the stairs, my mom says, "Good morning."

Swinging my head to the side, I see her sitting at the breakfast table and detour to join her. "Good morning." While I pour a cup of coffee, she watches me. "What?"

"You. It's good to see you smiling." I stir in creamer, and she adds, "You're in love with him."

"I am."

"No one's ever made you smile like this."

I pick my mug up with my left hand and bend my wrist forward while I sip.

Maybe I should have done that when she wasn't trying to actually drink her coffee, considering I'm wearing said coffee now.

She jumps, dabbing my hand and the ring with napkins. "Oh my. I'm so sorry, but oh my God, Singer. Are you engaged?"

"I am," I reply, lifting in my seat with excitement. I hold out my hand. "Ethan asked me to marry him."

"And you said yes?"

"Yes, of course. You said it yourself. I love him. I don't want to imagine a life without him, but when I do, it looks a lot like the last month and a half. Sad and pathetic."

"I don't think I've ever seen a diamond that big. Did he mine for that in the mountains?"

Staring at the ring, I admire it. "It's a bit, *or a lot*, big. It's stunning."

"It sure is, and wow."

"Six carats, emerald cut. I love the setting. He said I

could take it in and get whatever I want if I prefer something else."

"Do you?" she asks, sitting in the chair next to me.

"I love it, but I'm not sure if I want to walk around with something so big on my hand. You know, for safety reasons."

"Update me on that situation. Marriage means you're going back to New York to be with him?" Her tone is eerily calm, her eyes fixed on me over the lip of her cup while she takes a drink.

"I am."

"Will you get your old job back?"

The way he referred to it as "our money" has me wanting to fall into this good life with him. "He's accomplished so much already. I haven't. I'm going to keep working, at least until we have children. I'll make the decision then if I'll go back after."

"I looked him up online."

I take a loud intake of air and blow out. "Okay."

"I assume you know how much money he's worth?"

"I do."

"When you came home last month, you said he had a lot of money and maybe that was why someone tried to kill you. I'm your mother. This worries me. All the money in the world isn't worth risking your life."

"We don't know who or why things happened, but I don't feel unsafe when I'm with him."

"Singer—"

"Mom. Please. Please let me celebrate an engagement to a man that I would give my life for."

"Don't say that. It may happen."

I stand, wanting to run from the room and pretend I never had this conversation. But I'm a woman now, so I don't have to escape uncomfortable situations. I need to handle them. "He has security. Until this psycho is caught, I'll have detail as well."

"Detail?"

"Security."

"Sit. Please."

Giving her the courtesy she deserves, I sit back down. "I don't want to live my life afraid. What kind of life will that be?"

"None." Her smile returns. "Congratulations on the engagement. He seems polite and very nice. You weren't wrong when you said he was handsome. So tell me, when are you leaving me again?"

"I'm not leaving you. I'm starting my life."

TWO DAYS LATER, I fly in a private jet for the first time. I have to admit, it's really nice. If that's a perk of this new life, I'm on board with it. *Pardon the pun.*

With Ethan in meetings at the office all afternoon, I return to the penthouse. The new driver is nice, but he's not Aaron. I'm excited to see Aaron and hope he's up when I arrive. The elevator door opens, and my mouth follows suit. I can barely squeeze the suitcase into the hallway. Vase upon vase fills the black corridor. The gallery lights shine to highlight the hundreds, maybe thousands of pink peonies.

They smell just as pretty as they look. I can only imagine how much he spent on these flowers. I leave my suitcase by the door and walk the narrow path between the vases.

"Hello," I call when I reach the open area of the apartment.

No one returns a hello though. With no one around and

Ethan working until dinner, I decide to do something I've wanted to do for weeks.

With time on my side and no one to talk me out of it, I return to my apartment.

———

EVEN IN BROAD DAYLIGHT, standing at the curb, the red-brick, pre-war building feels ominous. I don't look at the middle of the street, not wanting to see if anything remains of her death. The taxi pulls away, and I hear, "It's good to see you, Ms. Singer."

Lowering my gaze from the floor where I used to live, I see Frank. "Hi." I don't make him get up. I go to him. "How are you, Frank?"

"You know. The usual. You've been missed."

"Have I?"

With a snaggletooth smile, he says, "Yes. And Ms. Lazarus."

I try not to snap at him for bringing her death up, but it's a struggle. It's only natural for people to mention it, to mention her. That's something I have to get used to. "I miss her, too."

"She was a really nice lady."

"She was."

An awkward silence falls around us, so I reach into my purse and dig out a twenty. "It's all I've got on me, but it's yours."

He takes it, and graciously thanks me. "I didn't know if you'd ever be back, but in case you were, I've been holding on to something for you."

"For me? You didn't need to get me anything."

"I'd like to take credit, but it's something I found."

Curious, I watch as he goes back to his pallet and digs through a backpack. When he comes back, he holds out his hand. "I think this belongs to you now." A silver chain dangles between his fingers. Half a heart with the word *BEST* on it gleams in the late afternoon sun.

He lowers his hand when I gasp. "Are you all right, Ms. Davis?"

"That was Mel's." The sob jolts my chest, rising in my throat. "She never took it off."

"The clasp is broken. I found it in the street."

I reach for it, taking it into the palm of my hand. "I can't believe you found this."

"I saw it and thought you'd want it."

"I do. Thank you so much, Frank." He laughs it off, but I hug him. He'll never know how much this means to me. My words feeling inadequate, but the only gift I have to give. "Thank you."

"You're welcome. I'm really sorry."

"Thank you, Frank. This means so much to me. Thank you." My fingers close around the jewelry and I head inside. It's time to face my demons. I need to start someday, so I'll start today, feeling stronger with the bracelet.

When I unlock the door, I'm assaulted by memories. I shake my head, hoping to shake them long enough to stay. They're memories haunting the apartment, not her. Still, I wish I could call out her name and she'd come racing into the living room from her room.

Raising my chin, I go inside and shut the door behind me. I ignore her room, not even looking in that direction when I go to mine. Opening the door to the tiny closet, I take a quick inventory and then bend down and dig out a few flattened boxes I stored under the bed.

Tossing them on the bed, I'm grabbed from behind, a

hand over my mouth, taking away any option of screaming. "You should have saved me a dance, Ms. Davis."

My mind goes into overdrive. I know that voice. *"The very lovely Singer Davis. Maybe you'll save a dance for me?"*

The charity ball.

Oh my God.

His hand loosens and his mouth is at my ear, my body cringing. "Can I trust you not to scream for help?"

My thoughts are ping-ponging around my brain in rapid succession. I nod slowly, and his hand lowers. "If you scream, I'll kill you before anyone can save you. Then I'll kill your family. Do you understand?"

Nodding, I reply quietly, "Yes."

When I turn around, I come face-to-face with the man responsible for killing my best friend, and my would-be killer.

The man Ethan despises.

39

Singer

Lucas McCoy.

At first, I'm thrown off as to why Lucas McCoy is in my apartment. But all it takes is one look at his neck to know why. While he stands near the living room window looking out, I see it, and remember: "*Grabbing a piece of glass, I cut his neck, wanting to end him.*" Aaron's words.

"That's a bad scar on your neck. It's still healing?" I ask, keeping my eye on him. I stare at him from the couch with his shaking hands and nervous eye twitch. He's not the same man I met at the ball. This is a man living with demons. A man living with demons has nothing to lose, but I do.

His hand covers his neck, and he looks back at me. "Shut up." He begins pacing the floor in front of me. To the kitchen, five steps back to the couch. To the bedrooms, fifteen steps back. To the bathroom, ten steps back. Most of what he's been muttering has been incoherent, although I did pick up "I didn't mean to" several times. I also caught: "Accidents happen. One did happen."

I can argue that Melanie's death may be an accident to him, but it is everything to me. I don't because he's not stable. My biggest fear is I may be another one of his accidents if I don't get out of here quick. *Accidents.* Oh my God. "You tried to kill me by having me pushed into traffic. How much did you pay that homeless man to murder me?"

I'm pinned by the devil himself. "Thirty dollars. That's what your life is worth."

My eyes dart to every nook and cranny, searching for something that can help me. But the last time I was here, Melanie had just straightened the living room. I need to get a knife from the kitchen, but he's currently walking by it, leaving me no chance to get over there.

"What do you want, Lucas?"

"It was supposed to be a message. To end this standoff. He's ruined me, *is* ruining me."

"Who?"

His dark eyes hit me like a shark in the deep ocean, no emotion, only a killer and his prey. He begins to circle. "You know too much," he stammers.

"No, I don't."

"He wasn't here and then he was, making my life hell. My father. I've become the disappointment he said I would become. While he's off partying like he's not destroying lives."

Trying to reach him, to calm him, I keep my voice controlled and patient, soft, respectful. "Who are you talking about, Lucas?"

He snaps to reality when hearing his name. "Fuck, what am I going to do with you?"

"You don't have to do anything with me." Sickness blackens my stomach, turning it. I swallow, the bile burning my throat. I glance to my purse by the door, too far to get and dig a phone out before he can stop me. I let my guard down. I wasn't thinking it wasn't safe to be here. Looking at the TV cabinet, a photo of Mel and me during spring break our junior year in college sits in a frame she bought in Jacksonville and took to Boulder. It was our first taste of the world outside our Colorado bubble. We stayed up late for months talking about all the places we wanted to go, all the cities and countries we wanted to visit.

We didn't get that chance because we chose to move to New York. Sitting here, that feeling of wanting to conquer the world comes rushing back. I have to fight. Lars's words cross my mind. *Don't let the bad guys win, Singer. Fight.*

Looking at the photo once more, I may have lost my friend, but I realize I've found this amazing group of people who want me to live, to fight, to save myself. They all believe in me. I need to do the same. "I won't tell anyone anything. I swear."

By his harsh tone, he's losing the last bit of humanity he had left. "It's out of control. There's no coming back from this. Don't you see? I killed someone. If I'm caught, which is only a matter of time, I'll spend the rest of my life in prison. I went to the best private school in Manhattan. I attended Yale, our family tradition. I've brought shame and embarrassment to the McCoy name when all I wanted was respect, to show them I can advance the family in standing and financially."

"You can. You can earn that respect, Lucas."

"No I can't!" Walking to the kitchen bar, he reaches into his coat pocket and pulls out a gun. "I was golden. If he'd stayed in Texas, I would own full cargo holding rights in East Bay."

It's out of control. There's no coming back from this. Don't you see? I've killed someone.

Ethan. *Oh God.*

The renegotiation of rights.

Melanie died over the right to move cargo in and out of East Bay. My disgust must be obvious. Her life. Her life meant more than a ship docking with crap from who knows where.

While my mind revolts in anger, between gritted teeth he continues, "None of this would have happened. But he had to move here. He had to take over what wasn't his to take. So I'll take something of his. I'll destroy him like he destroyed me."

I plead for my life. "Please. Those rights aren't worth losing more lives than have already been lost."

"To me they are."

"He'll end the negotiations. You don't know him like I do. He will agree to end them if it means sparing lives."

"Sparing *your* life. That's what you want when my life is already ruined. So why should I be the only one who suffers?"

I stand, and he yells, "Sit."

"No." I take a deep breath, resolved that there is a good possibility I will die today. But I won't die without a fight. "I want you to see my friend in this photo. You killed her, and if I'm going to die, I want this photo with me." I take one step and then another. Four steps. The frame is in hand.

Two Mississippi seconds before he says, "It was an accident. I wanted to scare you . . . her. I thought she was you."

I nod, attempting to stay calm under his chaotic gaze.

After looking at the photo one last time, I see his hand around his neck covering the scar. "I was fighting for my life. She screamed. It scared me. I didn't know what to do, so I fired." He pauses, briefly turning his eyes downward in shame before looking me in the eyes. "That night was the first time I ever shot a gun. That guy, the driver. I thought he'd be dead. I didn't realize I'd shot her until she collapsed, but I was fighting for my life."

I have no sympathy for this man; my patience ran out before I arrived. "Guess you won."

Hate fills his gaze when it's aimed my way. "I was cementing my family's legacy."

"Your family has billions. McCoy Properties owns half the buildings in Manhattan." Raising my voice, I say, "My friend's life is worth more than another million to your family that won't even ripple the McCoy waters."

"Shut up."

"No. Because if you're going to kill me, it won't be an accident. You will be making that choice. You're already going to hell, so are you willing to risk a last-ditch effort for redemption by killing me?"

A debate wars inside his shaking head, his eyes finally landing on the gun. *Fight.* I throw the frame as hard as I can, praying to God that it lands exactly on target. This is my only chance.

The frame hits him on the side of the head and falls to the ground shattering at his feet. I dash for the door, but I'm not fast enough before he fires the gun. The world seems to slow when your life's at risk, but I force my way through the quicksand of time and reach the door.

I can taste freedom, but my ankles are pulled out from under me. My scream echoes through the apartment instead of down the hall as my back hits the hardwood floors. A fist slams across my face, and my jaw wrenches in pain as my brain is shaken.

Find the moonlight in the dark. Ethan.

My eyes fly open and I gasp for air.

I will not give up.

My arm is swinging, landing a hard jab to his ear, knocking him sideways. I scramble to my feet, but in that second I have to decide how my fate will play out—the stairs.

I will never make it out of this building alive. I know that. One shot is all he needs, and I doubt he'll miss a second time. I'm collateral damage to him now.

Plan B is put into play before I think it through. I kick his arm as hard as I can, and the gun slides across the floor. Lucas is quicker than I am and knocks me on my ass with a thud. He crawls on his hands and knees toward the gun, but I grab one of his feet and yank as hard as I can.

In one swift second, he turns and aims the gun straight at my face. There's no other out, no escape, not even enough time to move out of the way.

This is it.

One Mississippi.

Two Mississippi.

Three Mississippi.

Four . . . Bang.

I don't feel any pain.

I don't accept death with open arms while searching for peace.

Looking up, Frank has Lucas pinned. Frank. *Thank God.* Blood covers his hands and runs from Lucas's nose. I spy the handle of the gun on the kitchen floor but stop, pausing to make sure Frank's all right.

"Get the gun, Singer."

And I do. I grab it and rush back. Standing above them with the gun in my trembling hands, he adds, "Call the police."

Walking a wide berth around them, I keep the gun aimed on Lucas, who appears lifeless, while Frank gets up.

He takes the gun from my hands, aiming it on Melanie's killer while I call 9-1-1.

You LEARN a lot about people in life-or-death situations. I never knew Frank was a marine veteran who fell on hard times after suffering from post-traumatic stress syndrome. That's on me for not asking more about his story, about his incredible life. I'll make it right with him. I owe him my life after all.

I learned a lot about myself as well. Although I'm a work in progress, this year has taught me so much.

I'm strong.

Of mind. *And body*.

I'm a dreamer.

With my head in the clouds, my feet are still planted firmly on the ground.

I'm a romantic.

Give me a great romance novel over a baseball game any day. Although I can admit the sport is growing on me. The box suite seats help.

I'm a believer.

Karma exists, and destiny plays a hand in our daily lives.

I love with all my heart and make sure to show it every day.

I may have picked that lesson up from a certain someone with the biggest heart and—well, other big attributes, but that's personal.

I'm a fighter.

Period.

Sitting in the back of the ambulance, I have a blanket wrapped around me that the EMTs insisted I wear, even though it's eighty degrees out. My legs are dangling, and I've been watching Ethan "handle" the situation. Arms crossed. Intense focus. Full height with broad shoulders. Standing in a suit he wore to work that was clearly tailor-made for him. It's a sight to behold. The hottie.

I've learned a lot about Ethan Everest. For one, no one messes with the ones he loves. His love for me runs deep. My love for him is bigger than the mountain sharing his name.

When he returns to me, he's touching my knees, his eyes subtle in their vibrancy. His concern shows right through. And he can't keep his hands off me; I will never complain about that. He's been talking for a minute, but all I see are those kissable lips moving, drawing me to them. I reach up to kiss him, but he stops me and asks, "What do you think?"

"I think it sounds great."

Lifting up, I go in for the kiss, but he stops me again, moving eye level with me. "You sure?"

Rolling my eyes, I say, "Yes, I'm sure. I promise. Now kiss me." I have no idea what I just promised, but when his lips press to mine in the most searing, soul-scorching kiss, I know I'll make him a million more for another just like this.

EPILOGUE

Ethan

Damn, that's how she did it.

"She took the stairs." I look behind me at Lars and repeat, "Singer released the emergency lock and took the stairs. That's how she got out."

"It can't be that easy. The place was on a Code 5 lockdown."

I smile. "Impressive." Tired at staring at a stairwell, I walk down the corridor to the kitchen. "Obviously, we can't have that happen again. I'm not worried about her getting out. I am worried about who can get in." I add, "This is top priority. We aren't under a threat, but I need to know it's safe, that she's safe if we are threatened."

"Escape options are there for those reasons. But I'll make sure the floor is secure from intruders, sir, and will report back with full details."

He's about to leave, but I add, "She's clever."

Nodding, he agrees. "She is, sir."

"Don't let your guard down when it comes to her."

"Yes, sir."

"She's charming."

"She is, sir."

"She gives you that innocent look and just like that . . . putty in her hands."

"I wouldn't go that far, sir."

Just me then. I'm okay with that. I am also okay with buying Frank a house in New Jersey. He's been there a week and has already signed up to volunteer at a local shelter. She's insisted we also help when we can. She doesn't realize I would have done it without the sweet talk. He saved her life. I can change his. There's no decision. The choice was already made.

I open the large jar of gummy bears she keeps on the counter and dig for a clear one. I abandon the idea of being a picky gummy bear eater, which Singer accuses me of, and take a handful before offering Lars some. He declines but I pop another in my mouth before continuing my internal rant. I think she does it to see if she can get away with it.

She'll bake you muffins and then go for the hard sell, but it's the soft sell you have to be on your toes for. You don't even know you're agreeing to something until—BAM—and she's walking out of the room, shaking her ass, knowing she owns yours.

It's okay. I'll take her soft or hard sell any day to see that look of satisfaction on her face. Lars coughs, and I realize I was rambling to myself. I clear my throat and put the candy jar down. "We should get back to work."

"Right. Yes, sir."

The elevator door opens, and Singer comes bounding out. "Guess what?"

She runs into my arms and I lift her off her feet. "What?"

"I got the job. It's part-time for now, but I'm going to prove how hard I'm willing to work and win them over."

"Congratulations. I knew you would get it." I kiss her, just because I can, whenever I want.

When her feet land back on the ground, she says, "Hi, Lars. Having a good day?"

"Yes, Ms. Davis."

"Ugh. Please stop with the Ms. Davis business. Singer. Just Singer. Please."

"As you request, Singer."

"Good." Switching her attention to me, she teases, "Who's running your company while you're standing around eating gummy bears?"

"Matthews and Reegan have it under control, and they're damn good bears. Are you going to need a few minutes or are you ready to go?"

"I'm ready. My suitcases are in the bedroom. When I saw Aaron downstairs, he said he'll get them in a minute."

The elevator arrives like it's Grand Central Station around here. Caroline and Aaron pop out. Caroline runs to Singer and asks, "Will you show me the makeup trick now? I've been waiting all day."

Wrapping her arm around Caroline's shoulder, they head down the hall. "Of course. I can show you before we leave, and you can practice over the next few days, then show me."

Aaron asks, "In the bedroom?"

"Yep," I reply. "You sure you're up for it?"

"I'm up for it. I feel good. It's been six months, but how heavy is it?"

"It's a woman's suitcase, so I would say pretty damn heavy."

"I'm just kidding. I'm fine."

"Are you guys settled in?" Two months ago, an apartment on the twelfth floor came on the market. We promptly took it off the market and gave it to Aaron and Caroline. With him in recovery, it was fine having them in the penthouse, but it was time for Singer and me to have some time alone. They've become of part of our family. Singer refers to Caroline as her niece. Their close bond is good for both of them.

Lars helps with the other cases, and I grab my laptop and stow it away in my backpack. This trip to Texas may be considered personal, but I still need to work. Once we signed the contracts for the extra cargo holds in East Bay, business has been booming.

McCoy Properties lost its contract and sold their holdings to me. They're close to filing Chapter II due to bad business dealings and the sentence Lucas was handed down for three consecutive life terms in prison.

Needless to say, Singer is doing better than I am, putting everything in the past. She has her melancholy moments, she might always have those, but she's optimistic for a happy future.

She showed Lucas mercy that I wouldn't have. I would have shot him in the apartment.

Taking a deep breath, I grab my phone from the counter and head to the car. We're Texas bound. I'm looking into buying some property near Austin. I think it will be good for us to have the option from the fast-paced city life of New York. Also, it gets way too cold here in the winter.

Once we're in the SUV, Lars says, "The jet is ready and on standby."

"We're running late," I add, nudging Singer.

She laughs. "Sorry, but eyeliner is very tricky business. Luckily Caroline's a fast learner. It could have been worse."

Maneuvering under my arm, she relaxes. "Did you tell your parents when we're arriving?"

"My parents are supposed to be picking us up, so I texted them the change in time."

"Do they know you're bringing Lars?"

"I told them, but they still insisted we stay with them."

"This is good, Ethan. It's time to heal, and for all of us to move on."

Hope is something we still give a lot of credence to. It's carried us through some of our darkest times, so we hold tightly to it. Leaning forward, I tell Aaron, "Don't forget about the stop."

"I'm on it."

Singer looks surprised. "What stop? I thought we were running late already?"

"It's only a little out of the way. The plane won't leave without us, so don't worry."

Lars opens the door for us, and we slide out.

Singer smiles and it's the prettiest sight. Her tone has a lilt and her eyes reveal her inner happiness. "What are we doing here?"

I take the left hand that wears the promise to meet me at the end of the aisle and lead her inside the building. "You'll see."

The apartment is open for us, just as promised. Looking around, not much has changed. The couch is in a different place and the small dining table doesn't have a widescreen TV balanced on it. But it feels the same. It feels like a new start deep down in my heart.

Taking her by the waist, I pull her close. "I don't want to live with regrets, and this was where the biggest one of my life happened. Come with me." I walk to the window and lift up the pane. It's not a warm spring day like the last time we were here. It's cold, so I tighten her coat belt around her waist and make sure her neck is warm under her scarf before I help her through the small opening onto the fire escape. I've waited so long to right this wrong, and I don't want to squander another minute. The universe is counting on me.

"Fifth step up," I say, not needing to say more. Her grin tells me she knows what I'm doing. She even does it too when she scoots to one side, giving me room to sit down.

Sitting here with her again, I feel at peace. This is my do-over and I'm going to do it right. I pull two Heinekens from my coat pocket and open one for her then one for me. Her laughter echoes between the buildings above as she takes the can. Just like the sexy siren she is, she takes an impressive sip.

I take a drink while keeping my eyes on her. She's prettier than any sunset I've ever seen, her beauty more than skin-deep. She's changed a lot over the last year and a half, becoming more comfortable with who she is, but she was always amazing to me. I lift up.

This time our lips meet in a kiss that was always destined to be—familiar and still so damn enticing. In this kiss, I'm living my destiny. I can finally forgive the past choices I made and look forward to *our* future.

Leaning back, I push a few stray strands of hair behind her ear and caress her cheek. "Remember the promise you made me?"

"Which one is that?" Her hands begin to wander over my shoulder and down the front of my shirt. "I've made you lots of promises."

"The one about eloping."

"What?" Her body straightens, her fingers fidgeting with the top button of my shirt. "When did I promise that?"

"The night of the attack at your apartment."

"On the back of the ambulance?"

"Yep."

She stares at me for a few seconds and asks, "What did I promise exactly?"

"That we could run away, just the two of us, and get married."

Her shoulders ease and her smile reappears. Taking my face between her hands, she says, "Yes, Ethan Everest. I would run anywhere in the world with you. Marriage is a deal I'm happy to seal as long as it's sealed with you."

And we seal it with another kiss, right there on a fire escape in a small Bronx apartment.

And again later that night.

But that's another story . . .

The Resistance - the band shirt Singer wore in Everest is a hot bad boy rocker series. You can meet Johnny Outlaw, sexy lead singer, by clicking The Resistance on Amazon.

You can also get a sneak peek by flipping the page.

**Ethan wears a Crowe Brothers concert T-shirt in Everest. This is a NEW Spin-off series of The Resistance coming in 2018. I cannot wait for you to meet Jet and Dallas Crowe.

PART I

THE RESISTANCE

Copyright © S. L. Scott 2014

The right of S.L. Scott to be identified as the author of this work has been asserted by her under the *Copyright Amendment (Moral Rights) Act 2000*

This work is copyright. Apart from any use as permitted under the Copyright Act 1968, no part may be reproduced, copied, scanned, stored in a retrieval system, recorded or transmitted, in any form or by any means, without the prior written permission of the publisher.

This book is a work of fiction. Names, characters, places and incidents are either a product of the author's imagination or are used fictitiously. Any resemblance to actual people living or dead, events or locales is entirely coincidental.

ISBN: 978-1-940071-15-2

PROLOGUE

Prologue

I'm a fucking fool.

I'm not even sure how I got into this mess, but I know I need to get myself out of it. I look down at the hand on my thigh inching up higher and my stomach rolls. Squeezing out from between the tight confines of the third row in this van, a girl on each side wanting a piece of me, I fall over the seat into the cargo area and move away from their astonished stares. They're speaking German and I don't know what the fuck they're saying, but I've been in this type of situation enough to know how it will end, if I let it.

Everything has changed... or sometime around my last birthday I changed.

I didn't invite these chicks. Dex did. He'll fuck'em all before the night's through and the bad part is, they'll let him. Thinking they're special, that they'll be the one to tame him. They'll let him do what he wants just to be close to him.

Beyond this set up being predictable at this point, it's really fucking old or I am, probably both. I ignore their taps on my shoulder and them calling my name. I ignore every-thing to do with them and focus on my phone.

On the inside, I'm freaking the fuck out that I'm sitting in the cargo hold of a huge van in Germany with attractive girls willing to do anything I want them to, but I prefer to look at a photo of a little blonde with hazel eyes. Freaking the fuck out might be an understatement.

I'm a player or was, supposed to be, maybe still am. I don't keep score or anything like that, but I've slept with plenty of women, sometimes more than one at a time. I used to blame my lifestyle, but more recently, I realized I'm the common denominator in the bad relationships I've had.

The car comes to a stop and the driver rushes around to the back to let me out. I stumble while climbing out, and hurry inside away from the sound of my name being called. The girls will be upset when they realize I'm not staying to play, but Dex will be thrilled—more pussy for him.

Cory hops out from the front, and follows me. "Wait up," he says, jogging to catch up.

When we reach the elevators, we look back. Dex is helping the girls out of the vehicle one-by-one. With a cigarette hanging from the corner of his mouth, he's sloppy, already drunk. He never lacks for female companionship. By the way he acts, I don't see the appeal, but I don't think that's why they're hooking up with him anyway.

Cory looks at me and nods once. "What's up? What happened back there?"

The elevator doors open and we step in, pushing the button for our floor. "Over it. Over it all."

"The girl from Vegas?"

"She's not from Vegas, but yeah, I've kind of been thinking about her."

When the brass doors reopen, we walk down the hall to

our rooms. Cory and I don't do small talk. We've been friends for years, best friends if I think about it.

"Maybe you should call her," he suggests as we open our doors.

"Maybe I will."

"Night."

"Night," I mumble and shut the door behind me.

CHAPTER 1

Holliday Hughes

"Comfort zones are like women. You have to try a few before you find the one that feels right." ~ Johnny Outlaw

That damn lime and coconut song has been playing on a loop in my head, driving me nuts for hours. I make a mental note: Fire Tracy in the morning for subjecting me to that song twenty-thousand times yesterday. She called it inspirational. I call it torture after the first two times.

Rolling over, I look at the time. 4:36 a.m. I have four hours before I need to be on the road. This may be a business trip, but it will still be good to get away for a few days. I need a break. I've been in a bad mood lately. The spa and I have a date I'm really looking forward to. The thought alone relaxes me. I close my eyes and try to get a few more hours of sleep before I need to leave for Las Vegas.

I get two tops.

I tighten my robe at the neck. Just as I open my front door to get the paper, I hear a male voice say, "Hello?"

Peeking through the crack, I hold the door protectively in front of me just in case I need to close and lock it quickly. "Hi."

"I'm your new neighbor. I just moved in last week. I'm Danny."

Curious, I slowly stick my head out to get a better look at this Danny. Strands of my sandy blonde hair fall in front of my eyes, so I tuck it behind my ear and get an eyeful. To my surprise, he's quite handsome and has a big smile. "Oh, um," I say, dragging my hand down the back of my hair, hoping to tame the wild strands. "Hi. I'm Holli. Welcome to the neighborhood."

He nods toward the paper on the bottom of the shared Spanish tiled steps that lead to our townhomes. "I'll get your paper since you're not dressed."

"Thanks." I watch him. He looks like he just got back from a run or workout—a little sweaty, but not gross, in that sexy kind of way. Or maybe Danny's just sexy. He's well built with short, brown hair and when he bends over, I notice his strong legs and arms. Well-defined muscles lead to—*Oh my God!* Not just my face, but my entire body heats from embarrassment. Hoping he doesn't say anything about me checking him out, I turn away and start picking at a piece of peeling stucco near my house number. "Um, so are you settled in, liking your place?"

His chuckling confirms I was busted. But he's a gentleman, so he acts as if it didn't happen. "I like the neighborhood. The place is great," he says. "I like all the space, especially the patio. I'm thinking of having a party to break it in, maybe in a few weeks after I finish unpacking." He hands me the paper and takes two steps back. "You should stop by."

Nodding, I look into his eyes. I think they're brown, lighter than mine, more honey-colored. His offer is friendly, not a come on, which is good since we're neighbors now. "Thanks for the invitation."

Walking back to his door, he steals one more glimpse over his shoulder. "Have a great day. See you around, Holli."

"Yeah, see you around."

I shut the door, paper in hand, and fall against the wood with a smile on my face. One of my golden rules is not to date where I sleep, but I still appreciate that my new hottie neighbor is easy on the eyes. He might know it, but he doesn't seem arrogant.

I lock the door and get ready to leave.

Los Angeles is hot, smoggy, and grey at this hour and I have a feeling it won't be much different a few hours from now. I close the patio door and lock it, double checking for safety. After pulling the drapes closed, I take one last look around to make sure I'm not forgetting anything. I text Tracy and let her know I'm leaving. She doesn't reply, but I'm not surprised. Her boyfriend proposed last night after six years of dating. Being the kind boss and friend I am, I let her out of this trip, so she could spend the weekend with their families to celebrate the engagement.

There are selfish reasons as well for letting her off the hook. I really don't think I can handle hours of sitting in the car with her as she reads bridal magazines and plans every detail of her big day. After too many dud dates in the last couple of months, I'm not in the right frame of mind to plan her happily ever after.

With my garment bag in one hand and my suitcase in the other, I click the button, disarming my car's alarm as I walk to my parking space. I've lived here a couple of years. I wanted a place near the beach that also had space for my office, and I was fortunate enough to find both in this townhome.

A meme I created went viral three years ago this month. Who knew a snarky-mouthed fruit would be the way I make my fortune. I took it though and ran with the brand, building it into a small empire I named Limelight. The company is lean and I keep my costs under control. My fortune has grown by a few million in the last year alone.

I back out onto the street and take the scenic route, one block up to the beach. Driving slowly along with my windows down, I let the sound of the waves and the smell of the ocean center me. At the first stoplight, I take one deep salty air breath, roll the window back up, and leave for Vegas.

An hour into the trip, Tracy calls. I answer, but before I have a chance to speak, she asks, "Can I please tell you all about it again?" Happy laughter punctuates her question.

"Of course. Tell me everything." I'll indulge her wedding fantasies because that's what friends do... and because I have four hours to kill in the car. Listening to her takes my mind off the time and the miles stretching ahead of me as she relives every last detail of the proposal. Fortunately for me, she skims over the engagement sex.

Her excitement is contagious and because I've known her and her fiancé, Adam, for so many years, my happiness exudes. "Congratulations again."

"Thank you for letting me stay home this weekend. You'll be great and don't be nervous. It's just a rah-rah go get'em presentation and cocktail party. The rest of the time is all yours."

"You know how much I hate these kinds of events."

"You don't have to prove anything to anyone. Your company's success speaks for itself."

"Thanks. I'll try to remember that."

"Drive safely and squeeze in some fun."

I laugh. "You know I'll try. Bye." When we hang up, I turn on some music and let the miles drift behind me.

After a stop for gas half-way and a coffee later, I enter the glistening city in the desert. Pulling up to my hotel, I valet my car and take my own luggage to my room after checking in. I like this hotel because of the amenities, but the men aren't bad to look at either—a little edgy, a lot sexy—lucky for this single girl.

I spend a couple of hours checking emails and work on a proposal before I realize the time and need to get ready for the night. It's Vegas, so I mix business with some sexy. I pull on a black fitted skirt that hits mid-thigh, an emerald green silk camisole with spaghetti straps, and a short black jacket. I slip on my favorite new pair of stilettos and after one last check of my makeup and hair, I head out.

The meet and greet isn't long, but I slip out at one point to use the restroom. As I'm walking back toward the ballroom, I'm drawn to a man standing with a group of people nearby. His magnetism captures me. He might just be the best looking man I've ever seen—tall, dark hair, strong jaw leading me up to seductive eyes aimed at me. His head tilts and for a split second in time, everyone else disappears. I break the connection by looking away, everything feeling too intense in the moment. When he laughs, I add that to his ongoing list of great attributes.

When I pass, the feel of his gaze landing heavy on my backside warms my body. With my hand on the door, I pause, wanting to look back so badly. I resist the urge, open the door, and return to the party. The presentation portion of the evening is interesting. Despite that, my thoughts repeatedly drift back to the hot guy in the corridor—fitted jeans, black shirt, leather wristband. *Damn I'm weak to a leather wristband.*

I'm mentally brought back to the presentation when my company is recognized as one to watch. The acknowledgement is nice, and it feels good to be among my peers.

The dinner becomes more of a party as everyone wanders around instead of taking their seats. I'm not hungry and need to psych myself up to mingle. Tracy is awesome in these types of situations. Me, not so much.

The ballroom is dimly lit, I'm guessing to set the ambiance, but since this is business, I can do without the romance. I head straight for the bar just like everyone else— one big cattle call to the liquor to make the rest of the night a little more bearable.

"I usually hate these things," I hear from the guy behind me. When I look over my shoulder, he gives me a half-smile —half-friendly, half-creepy. "But they don't usually have attractive women either."

I roll my eyes while turning my back on him and his cheesy pick-up line.

"I'm sorry. That was bad. I know," he says with a weird nasally laugh.

His breath hits my neck and I jerk back. "Do you mind? Ever hear of personal space?"

"Sorry. You're just really pretty." He shrugs as if that makes everything better. "Your beauty is making me stupid."

"You think?" *Big mistake.*

He actually takes my sarcastic comment as a conversation opener. "Yes, I do. But I can't be the first to be dumbfounded by your beauty."

Standing on my tiptoes to see how many more people

are in front of me, I exhale, disappointed by the long line. One person in line would have been too many at this point. "Excuse me," I say and slip out of line. I find the table with my name tag on it, set my purse down, and take off my jacket. This hotel ballroom is crowded and too warm.

Saved by a friendly face, I see Cara, a marketing strategist I know from L.A. Weaving between the tables, I sit down in a chair next to her. With her eyes focused on the paperwork in front of her, I ask, "Working during the party?"

She looks up, smiling when she sees me. Opening her arms, she leans in and hugs me. "Holli, it's so good to see you."

I went with a different company than hers for a campaign a while back and glad she's not holding it against me. "Good to see you again."

"Congratulations on your success. Well deserved."

"I'm not sure if a smartass lime deserves the success it's gotten, but I'll take it."

She taps my leg. "You deserve it. It's funny and quite catchy. Just take the accolades."

"Thanks."

Looking over my shoulder, she leans in and whispers, "I'm skipping out of here early, but I'm meeting a few people for dinner tomorrow. If you're still in Vegas, you should join us."

"I'd love that. Thanks."

She stands up and grabs the papers in front of her. "Fantastic. I'll text you the details tomorrow. I'm so glad we ran into each other."

"Me too. See you tomorrow."

I'm left sitting alone. When I look around the room, like Cara, I'm thinking that skipping out early might be the way to go. If I do, I know Tracy will kick my ass, so I decide to suffer and give this party one last chance. But I definitely need a drink and the line for the bar in here is still way too long.

I head for the doors to buy a drink in one of the many hotel bars—any bar without a line. Guy from the bar line jumps in front of me as I try to exit, startling me. "Hey, hey, hey. You're not leaving already, are you?"

Since my glare and earlier hints didn't work, I reply, "I'll be back, no need to worry yourself."

His head starts bobbing up and down, confidently, and a big Cheshire cat grin covers his face. I start walking again as he keeps talking... again. "Cool. I'll see you later then."

I feel no need to respond to the come on, and will try to avoid him when I return. Following the wide-tiled path through the casino, which reminds me of the Yellow Brick Road, guiding me to what feels like Oz, a bar in all its gloriousness with no lines in site. Inside the darkened room, the sounds of the casino fade away as current hits play overhead. Still on a mission for a cocktail, I step up to the bar and wait.

If you would like to continuing reading The Resistance and meet Holliday and Johnny, click here: THE RESISTANCE

ON A PERSONAL NOTE

Everest was a labor of love for over one and a half years. I loved spending time with these characters as the story developed and seeing them come alive in their own world.

I owe so much to the team that took this journey with me. Each person adds so much to make this story shine. Thank you: Adriana, Amy Bosica, Andrea Johnston, Heather M., Irene, Karen L., Kristen Johnson, Lynsey Johnson, Marion, Marla, and Melissa Krehley.

My family is my everything. I'm so grateful to not only have their support, but their love <3

XOXO,

Suzie

ABOUT THE AUTHOR

To keep up to date with her writing and more, her website is www.slscottauthor.com to receive her newsletter with all of her publishing adventures and giveaways, sign up for her newsletter: http://bit.ly/1TheScoop

Join S.L.'s Facebook group here: http://bit.ly/1TheScoop

For more information:
www.slscottauthor.com

ALSO BY S.L. SCOTT

The Kingwood Duet

SAVAGE

SAVIOR

SACRED

SOLACE

Hard to Resist Series

The Resistance

The Reckoning

The Redemption

The Revolution

The Rebellion

Talk to Me Duet

Sweet Talk

Dirty Talk

Welcome to Paradise Series

Good Vibrations

Good Intentions

Good Sensations

Happy Endings

Welcome to Paradise Series Set

From the Inside Out Series

Scorned

Jealousy

Dylan

Austin

From the Inside Out Compilation

Stand Alone Books

Everest

Missing Grace

Until I Met You

Drunk on Love

Naturally, Charlie

A Prior Engagement

Lost in Translation

Sleeping with Mr. Sexy

Morning Glory

To keep up to date with her writing and more, her website is www.slscottauthor.com to receive her newsletter with all of her publishing adventures and giveaways, sign up for her newsletter: http://bit.ly/1TheScoop

Join S.L.'s Facebook group here: bit.ly/FBSLGroup